K. SEAN HARRIS

The Heart Collector

An Epic Novel

First Edition
10 9 8 7 6 5 4 3

This is a work of fiction. Names, characters, places and incidents either are the products of the author's imagination or are used fictitiously, and any resemblance to actual persons, living or dead, events or locales, is entirely coincidental.

Cover concept by: K. Sean Harris
Cover Design by: Sanya Dockery
Book Design, Layout & Typesetting by: Sanya Dockery

Published by: Book Fetish

Printed in China

ISBN: 978-976-610-827-4

Such is the way of an adulterous woman; she eateth, and wipeth her mouth, and saith, I have done no wickedness.
PROVERBS 30:20

She perceiveth that her merchandise is good: her candle goeth not out by night.
PROVERBS 31:18

Chapter 1

"Open cell D7!" The burly corrections officer bellowed to his colleague manning the control booth. The cell door slid open noisily and its occupant, a young, voluptuous caramel-complexioned vixen, got up off the cot and quickly stepped out of the small cell.

"My, my...aren't we eager to go," the officer drawled sarcastically as he undressed her with his eyes. He knew exactly what her body looked like underneath the coarse fabric of her blue jumpsuit. He had been present – illegally so – at several strip searches involving the beautiful woman. He disliked her though. She was one of the few on the cell block that had refused to do him any sexual favours. Bitch. Who did she think she was?

Corrections Officer Martin Bailey considered himself a ladies man and was very offended when the young woman had told him to go to hell when he had approached her. She had laughed in his face when he had offered her perks like the use of a cell phone, and food from the outside that wasn't sold in the commissary. She had not been impressed.

Jade ignored his leering as she took a last look at the confined space that had been her home for the past four years. Four *long* years. It was finally over. She *knew* that no matter what the future might hold, there was no way she would go back to jail. She would die first. She looked straight ahead as she walked briskly down the cell block towards an uncertain future. When she got the letter from the parole board informing her that she had been approved for early release, her joy had been tempered by the fact that she had an immigration hold. The bastards were going to deport her. That had caught her by surprise. As far as she knew, under the new immigration law, only non-citizens convicted of violent crimes would be subject to deportation. She had been convicted of possession of illegal drugs with the intent to distribute. Since when was that considered a violent crime? Jade sighed as she got to the checkout point. There were four other prisoners being released. Difference was they would be going home to their families. Jade knew one of them. Kianna. A notorious booster from Newark. She had done a year and a half for attempting to steal $10,000 worth of merchandise from Macy's.

"Hi Jade," Kianna said, grinning from ear to ear. "What's good?"

"Not a damn thing," Jade sneered. "They're gonna send me back to Jamaica."

"Oh, damn..." Kianna said as she prepared to step through the gate. She waved excitedly to two Latino men who were leaning against a black SUV parked outside the prison gates.

Jade glanced at them. They looked like hardened street thugs. Stoic expressions; lots of tattoos; bulging muscles; sagging, baggy pants and Timberland boots. The taller of the two was very handsome though; reminded Jade of Chino, the Puerto Rican gangster who was the reason for her current situation.

"That's fucked up," Kianna was saying, "you got family down there?"

"I don't even wanna talk about it girl," Jade replied. "Be safe and stay outta jail."

"I feel you, shit must be depressing," Kianna said. "I aint coming back to this motherfucker. Take care."

She waved goodbye, shot the corrections officer at the gate a dirty look and walked briskly towards her freedom.

Jade watched her knowing that this would not be her last visit to a facility such as this. Kianna was addicted to the fast life. She was only twenty years old and had been in and out of jail since she was fifteen. Jade sighed as two officers led her to a marked police van and placed her in the back. There were eight other women in there, six latinos and two blacks. Apparently the van had been to other prisons to pick up those with immigration holds before stopping here. Jade ignored the women and looked out the window, clasping her long, elegant fingers in her lap. She was handcuffed. A feeling she could never get used to. The van pulled off a few minutes later. Jade looked out at the lush countryside that was commonplace in upstate New York. A deer looked up at the van as it drove past, then deciding it wasn't worthy of attention, quickly lowered its head and resumed eating. New York was experiencing beautiful spring weather; Jade's favourite time of the year. She remembered when she first arrived in America, some fourteen years ago. That first winter had been terrible. She *hated* cold weather. She was always so happy when the snow began to melt announcing the arrival of spring. When her parents had kicked her out and she went to live with Chino, she had always insisted that they spent the winter somewhere sunny. The last Christmas they had spent together before she got arrested, they had gone to Hawaii. It had been a fabulous trip. Jade sighed. She still couldn't believe Chino had deserted her like this. It had hurt even more to hear that he was dating Juanita, her supposedly best friend. She had not heard from either of them for the past two years.

Jade felt eyes on her and looked to her right. The tall, buxom woman with the short red hair was staring at her openly. Jade knew what *that* look meant. She hoped she was placed in a different section from the woman. Not that she was afraid, but she could do without the hassle. There was no way that woman was going to touch her. Those days were long over with. She gave the woman a cold, withering look before turning away. She remembered her second night in captivity when her cell mate and four of her friends raped her.

Chapter 2

Jade had been lying on her bunk fully dressed in her state-issued jump suit, staring at the ceiling and feeling a bit sorry for herself when her cell mate had come in, accompanied by four women. Jade had immediately become wary. She recognized one of the women as the person who had poked her tongue out at her in a suggestive manner out in the exercise yard earlier that day.

"Hi cutie," the girl said to her, standing by Jade's bunk, and casually resting her calloused hand on Jade's thigh.

Jade swatted her hand away and sat up.

"Don't touch me," she told the woman disdainfully. The thought of a woman touching her filled her with disgust. She was strictly dickly.

The woman had laughed.

"Fiesty...mmmm...I like that...gonna have fun taming your wild ass," she told Jade with a wide grin, exposing teeth that, in a perfect world, would have been corrected by braces many years ago.

"Dream on bitch," Jade had retorted. She had been in the company of drug dealers and killers for the past two years. It had made her a tough little cookie who didn't take kindly to being bossed around by anyone. Even Chino, whose name caused shivers in the Soundview Projects in the Bronx where he was lord and master, usually let her have her way. Though she had been in somewhat of a daze since the sentencing and subsequent trip to prison, she was not intimidated by her surroundings. She just missed her freedom and the fabulous life she was used to living. It was proving difficult to adjust. Maybe this latest challenge would wake her out of her stupor.

The women had then ignored Jade and chatted and played cards on her roommate's bunk, which was below Jade's, until the corrections officer on duty bellowed into the PA system that everyone should report to their cells as it was time for lights out. Three hours later, Jade was awakened from her deep slumber when she was lifted unceremoniously from her top bunk and placed on her cell mate's bottom bunk. One woman clamped her hand over Jade's mouth while one held her legs and yet another held her hands. Jade struggled mightily, biting the hand covering her mouth, and twisting her legs until she got one free. She kicked out in the semi-darkness – the cell was dark but just a wee bit of light was filtering in under the thick steel door from the main recreational area where the officers always left one of the lights on – hitting the woman that had been holding her feet in the face.

"Bitch!" the woman growled and they doubled their efforts, twisting Jade's arms painfully until she cooperated. Anna-

Kay, the six foot butch that had made a pass at Jade earlier, anxiously removed Jade's jumper and underwear, grinning lustfully. She then proceeded to feast on Jade's anatomy like it was an all-you-can-eat buffet. Jade resigned herself and ceased struggling. She felt angry, violated and utterly disgusted. She knew that unless she did something drastic, this would be a regular occurrence. She pondered the best way to seek retribution as the big dyke noisily sucked her unwillingly wet pussy.

"Time's up," a corrections officer that Jade had never seen before said, as he shone a flashlight into the cell.

"Next time you'll be the one burying your face in my pussy," Anna-Kay told Jade as she straightened up.

"Fuck you," Jade responded, as she quickly pulled up her jumper. She scowled angrily at the corrections officer. Corrupt, perverted bastard.

Anna-Kay chuckled and left the cell with her gang in tow. The officer treated Jade to a lingering gaze before he turned off the flashlight and went back out to the control booth.

Jade stood up and looked at her cell mate. She had been a part of the attack. She was standing by the tiny, metallic sink watching Jade.

"Get out of my way," she said, "I'm going to bed."

Jade was incredulous. The gall of this bitch to think that she could help her friends to rape her and then act as if nothing had happened. Jade moved quickly over to her and administered a vicious slap to the woman's face. The cell mate, a thirty-five year old Panamanian, cursed in her native tongue, hurling expletives at Jade as they grappled with each other in the small cell. The alarm sounded and Jade could hear the officers rushing towards the cell. She growled and slammed her cell mate into the wall and punched her repeatedly in the face. The cell door slid open and as per prison guidelines, two officers in riot gear pulled Jade off the woman and hauled her out to the corridor. They threw her on the ground face down and cuffed her hands painfully behind her back. She was initially given seven days in solitary confinement for fighting. But after it was ascertained that she had broken the woman's jaw, she was given an additional seven days. When she told the disciplinary committee about the rape, she was coldly advised to write a report and that there was no excuse for fighting.

Jade didn't mind being in solitary. It was important for her to establish a reputation that she was not someone to be messed with. This was just the beginning. The big dyke bitch was next. No one was going to have their way with her and get away with it.

Chapter 3

Jade was jolted back to the present when she realized that the van had ceased moving for several minutes. She looked out the window. They had arrived at the immigration detention center. It was a tall, grey, unfriendly building. Just another fucking prison. Jade sighed. She hoped they wouldn't have her here too long. She had heard horror stories about people who after serving lengthy prison sentences, were housed in detention centers for years before they were sent home. She had no idea what awaited her in Jamaica, but at least she would be free.

"Ok, let's go!" a tall, potbellied corrections officer with a thick, handlebar moustache bellowed to the women. They rose and made their way out of the van and followed the officer in single file to the processing area. It was crowded and noisy. There was over a hundred women waiting to be processed. There were two women in animated conversation in the line next to the one Jade was in. They were obviously Jamaicans.

"Mi can't wait fi reach home," the short, voluptuous one was saying to the woman in front of her. "Mi baby father ah keep big dance fi mi when mi touch dung. Stone Love and one next big sound ah go play."

"Fi real, dat good man," the other woman responded. "We haffi keep in touch cause mi woulda love fi come to the dance."

"Yeah, man, we ah go keep the link strong," she agreed. She then added, chuckling, "Mi baby father say him run out de woman that him was living with de last time mi talk to him."

"Den nuh must," her new found friend replied. "De real big woman ah come home fi tek her rightful spot."

They both laughed raucously as they gave each other hi-fives.

Jade rolled her large, brown eyes and looked away as she reached the front of the line. Still handcuffed, she picked up the two see-through laundry bags that held her belongings and went to the officer. After the paperwork was concluded, the cuffs were taken off and she was led to the tier where she would be housed until she was deported.

The corrections officer buzzed the large, blue metallic door and Jade entered the tier. All eyes were on her as she made her way to cell A4. Jade ignored them all and went straight inside the cell. She was happily surprised to see that it was one person to a cell. It would make things that much more pleasant having her own personal space. She spent the next few minutes organizing her stuff as best she could. After lying on her bunk for a few minutes, she got up and went out into the recreational area to watch some T.V. There were two television sets; one was showing an episode of Judge Judy and the other, music videos on BET. Jade opted to watch the latter. She sat on one of the back benches and ignored the woman next to her. The women sitting on the front bench directly in front of the T.V. had a comment for everything. Rhianna's video, for her hit single *Take A Bow*, was on.

"Rassclaat, she feel seh she ah Beyonce," the one who the others obviously deferred to was saying. She was seated in the middle, in a sprawling position. "Mi even hear seh she ah fuck Jay-Z."

The one to her right laughed boisterously. "If Beyonce ever find out she ah go buss Rhianna's skinny ass."

Jade couldn't quite place the girl's accent. *Probably from Guyana or one of those islands*, she mused.

"I can't stand those women," the girl next to Jade said quietly.

Jade looked at her, taken aback by the softness of the woman's tone and her diction. It sounded as out of place in these surroundings as hearing secular music being played in church.

Jade didn't respond but continued to look at the young lady.

"Hi, I'm Maxine," she said, offering her hand.

Jade shook it, marveling at how tiny her hands were. She was a very petite woman. Probably barely weighed a hundred pounds in wet clothes. She was very demure and ladylike. Obviously well-bred. What the hell was she doing in a place like this? Jade's interest was piqued.

"I'm Jade."

"Pretty name. I'm bored out of my mind with the mindless chatter from these women...let's go have a chat," Maxine suggested.

"Ok," Jade agreed, rising.

They walked over to Jade's cell and went in. They sat on Jade's bunk.

"You play cards?" Jade asked, reaching for the deck.

"Yes, I'm excellent at gin rummy," she responded.

Jade grinned. "We'll see just how excellent you are."

Jade shuffled the deck.

"So...what's a nice girl like you doing in a detention center waiting to be deported?" Jade asked.

Maxine smiled. It was a sad, weary smile.

"Even after three years I'm still asking myself the same question. And the answer is another question. How could I have been so gullible and stupid?" she responded.

Jade was silent, waiting for her to elaborate.

Maxine plucked a card from the pack.

"Three years ago, while on vacation in New York for Thanksgiving weekend, a friend of mine asked me to follow her somewhere. The car had a broken taillight and we were stopped by the cops. One of the officers was very rude to us and my friend responded to him in kind. Anyways, to cut a long story short, they searched the vehicle and twenty five pounds of compressed ganja and sixteen ounces of crack cocaine were found in the trunk."

Maxine paused and sighed, as though overwhelmed by the memory.

"You can imagine my shock. I had no idea my friend was mixed up in the narcotics business. I had heard that she was dating a known drug dealer but she had denied it when I asked her. Said he was in the music business. We used to attend the same prep school together, and we had re-established contact at University and kept in touch ever since, though she had migrated to New York. So, we got arrested and my *friend* told the cops when they interviewed us separately, that the drugs belonged to *me*. Fortunately, my family is well off and I was able to obtain the services of a good lawyer. The case dragged on for some time and instead of risking losing a trial and getting the maximum, I took the lawyer's advice and copped to a plea bargain. I served 28 months at the Albion Correctional Facility. It has been the defining experience of my life. I'll never quite view the world through the same lens again."

"Damn...that's fucked up," Jade commented. "So what happened to your friend?"

"I have no idea what happened to that bitch," Maxine stated matter-of-factly.

Jade laughed. So she had some spunk to her after all.

They spoke at length and Jade told her about her own situation. Maxine was appalled that Jade's parents hadn't come to her aid after she was arrested.

"You were young and silly," Maxine commented. "Couldn't they understand that was the time you needed them most...and to think you are their only child. Wow."

"I'm an embarrassment to them," Jade told her. "They love to tell people that I ran away from home and was now an adult so if I wished to be away from the family there was nothing they could do."

"So what are you going to do when you get to Jamaica?" Maxine asked as the loud buzzer sounded indicating that it was time for lockdown.

"I have no idea," Jade replied honestly.

"Well if you need any help I'll be there for you," Maxine told her as she got up to go to her cell. "Talk to you later. We'll be on lockdown for the next three hours."

Jade nodded. She retrieved her tattered copy of Sun Tzu's *The Art of War* and picked up where she had left off. She would be at war soon when she arrived in Jamaica.

At war with life.

At war with uncertainty.

At war to survive.

And survive she would.

By any means necessary.

Chapter 4

Jade and Maxine were inseparable over the course of the next two weeks. Maxine had been on the tier for two weeks prior to Jade's arrival and had pretty much kept to herself. She had been drawn to Jade from the get-go and they became fast friends. Jade felt better about the future. She now knew someone she could count on in Jamaica. Someone who had the means to help her get her feet off the ground. Maxine's family was a relatively rich one. Her dad was the chief accountant at one of Jamaica's largest manufacturing companies and her mom was a pediatrician with a successful practice. They also operated a gift shop in a popular all-inclusive resort in Ocho Rios. Maxine had been in charge of the gift shop before her unfortunate incident. Maxine gave Jade a contact number and an address so that she could reach her when she got to Jamaica, providing she left before Jade, which was likely to be the case.

It was. Without warning, early one Monday morning, two and a half weeks after Jade had arrived on the tier, Maxine was awakened by the sound of her cell door being buzzed open. An officer brusquely told her she would be leaving now and had five minutes to get ready. Maxine quickly washed her face, brushed her teeth and combed her hair. She was not allowed to tell anyone goodbye and four hours later, she was on a flight to Jamaica.

Jade realized Maxine was gone when she didn't see her come out for breakfast that morning. When she checked her cell, it was empty. Jade was happy for her though she would miss her company. It took a little over a month for them to send home Maxine. Jade hoped they would be just as speedy with her. She occupied her time by reading anything she could find and exercising. She had utilized the equipment in the exercise yard while she was in prison so her body was well-toned and in tip top shape. All the lesbians had wanted her but after she had stabbed Anna-Kay, the big dyke that had raped her on her second night in prison, with a sharpened comb in the large shower that accommodated twelve inmates at a time, they knew better than to try and force her. She had also gained some weight. In all the right places. Her thighs were tantalizingly thicker and her heart-shaped ass had sprouted a few more inches. With her beautiful face and hour-glass figure, she was absolutely stunning. Even in her plain grey sweatsuit and all-white sneakers – this was the only approved street clothes they could wear at the detention center – she stood out from the other women. A rose amongst thorns.

Two incident free months passed before Jade was deported. Just when she was getting antsy that it was taking too long, they came and got her early one Friday morning. She hurriedly got dressed and noted with a small measure of dissatisfaction that one of the loudmouths on the tier was being sent home that day as well. Jade was introspective on the ride to the airport. She completely ignored her unwelcome companion. And continued to do so even after the woman called her a 'bitch' and a 'dutty gal' because she didn't respond to any of her comments and questions. If they weren't both handcuffed, Jade knew there would have been a fight. That bitch was way too garrulous. Someone needed to shut her up. Preferably with a hard punch to the mouth. Jade soon became lost in her thoughts: Chino's betrayal, her parents turning their backs on her, incarceration, the blessing of meeting Maxine. Everything happened for a reason; Jade firmly believed that. What the reason or purpose was for all the bad things that had happened to her over the last few years, she had no idea. If someone had told her ten years ago that her life would have been like this at this juncture, she would have thought that he or she was crazy. But that's life for you. Shit happens. They arrived at the airport and after they were handed over to the U.S. Marshall accompanying them on the flight, the handcuffs were removed and they were given their belongings. They were taken to the extreme rear of the aircraft and placed beside each other. Fifteen minutes later they were airborne and Jade was on a one way flight to meet her destiny.

Chapter 5

Miraculously, Jade's traveling companion was mostly quiet during the flight. Jade had no idea that it was possible for her to keep her mouth closed for longer than ten seconds. Jade selected a chicken sandwich and fruit punch from the lunch options and smiled inwardly at the flight attendant's attitude towards her and the other woman. She obviously thought that because they were being deported they weren't worthy to be served their meal in the same friendly and courteous manner as the rest of the other passengers. *Silly cow* Jade thought. *You're nothing but a glorified waitress.*

Jade reminisced as she ate her lunch slowly. Her life had gone into a completely different direction once Chino had become a part of it. Her parent's only child never stood a chance against the smooth-talking, tall, handsome, edgy Latino. Despite her strict upbringing, or perhaps because of it, she had been drawn like a moth to the flame to Chino's bad boy image and dangerous lifestyle. She was sixteen and getting ready to graduate from the private Catholic high school she attended when she met him. She had gone to the movies with two of her friends and Chino, driving pass the theatre, had spotted her and came over. She had been waiting for her dad to pick her up. He had come over to her and said hi and asked for her number. He had made her nervous. He was very handsome and soft spoken but he had a very dangerous aura. His presence had intoxicated her virgin soul. She had quickly given him her number, mainly because she wanted him to have it and partially because she didn't want her father to pull up and see her talking to him. Her dad was very overbearing and would have grilled her incessantly on the drive home. Pretty soon Chino was all she could think about and she started lying to her parents about where she was so she could spend time with him. She lost her virginity two weeks after meeting him at a posh hotel suite in Manhattan on a day she should have been in school. It had been a painful, yet sweet and memorable experience.

Champagne, flowers, luxury suite, Jacuzzi...not many women could say they lost their virginity in such fine style. Chino had gone all out to make it a special day. After that, she realized Chino was getting annoyed at not being able to see her when he wanted to, which was often. He loved having her around him and hid nothing. He never tried to shield her from his lifestyle. She remembered one day they were on their way to have lunch when Chino got a call from one of his lieutenants. One of their dealers had come up short with the weekly sum he was to pay to Chino. Chino made a detour and went up to the block where the dealer was located.

The guy was sitting on a stoop with some other men when they arrived. Leaving Jade in the Lincoln Navigator, Chino had hopped out and went over to the guy. The guy stood up to greet him as if everything was ok. Chino responded by whipping out his gun and relieving the guy of most of his teeth. Adding a few hearty kicks to the stomach, Chino told him he would be back to collect the rest of his money tomorrow evening at this time. Instead of turning Jade off, Chino's violent nature turned her on to him even more. It amazed her how he treated her like a delicate flower yet was capable of immeasurable acts of violence against any one who crossed him.

Not wanting Chino to get tired of not being able to see her when he pleased, Jade started rebelling openly. She began leaving the house whenever she pleased and returning when it suited her. Her parents, especially her father, were alarmed at the sudden change in their daughter, and attempted to take her to counseling. Jade refused, telling them that nothing was wrong with her; she was simply growing up and was not a little girl anymore. After two weeks of constant fighting, her dad told her she could no longer live there if she couldn't abide by their rules. Chino came to get her that very same night and she never went back home. She had called home two weeks later to wish her mom happy mother's day but her dad had answered the phone and hung up when he realized it was her. Her parents didn't come to her graduation but Chino and her new best friend, Juanita, were there, so that was good enough for her. Jade was a very bright girl and had been awarded a full scholarship to attend New York State University but she no longer wanted to attend college. At least not yet. The next twenty months were a blur of nothing but trendy designer couture, vacations at hot spots, posh cars and the good life. It all came crashing down when the DEA raided one of their apartments and Jade was the only one home with fifty-five thousand dollars in cash and half a kilo of raw cocaine. She took the fall for Chino and he obtained one of the best criminal lawyers in the city to get Jade the best deal possible, which was twelve years with the possibility of parole after serving a third.

Things were alright at first. Chino stood by her for the first year and a half. He ensured that her account was always filled with the maximum of five hundred dollars and that she got a weekly visit from him and Juanita. He sent her any book she wanted and anything else that she was allowed to have from the outside. Then gradually Jade noticed that she couldn't get him on the phone as often anymore, he was hardly coming to visit and he had stopped putting money in her account. Then she found out that he was dating Juanita, her best friend. It had almost been too much to bear. Doing time for the same man that had fucked her over. Wasting her scholarship for the same man that fucked her over. Messed up her relationship with her family for the same man that fucked her over. Lost her precious virginity to the same man that fucked her over. She had lost so much giving her heart to Chino. And what did she have to show for it? Nothing but a future filled with uncertainty and a broken heart that seemed unable to heal. What was going to happen to her in Jamaica? How could she ever trust or love another man? The answer to both would come in due time. The stewardess was now informing the passengers that they were preparing to land soon. Five minutes later the plane landed. They had arrived in Jamaica.

Chapter 6

"Yes to bloodclaat! Mi reach home!" the woman who was deported along with Jade said boisterously when everyone was collecting their things to disembark. "Fuck off Uncle Sam!"

Jade looked at her disgustedly. So did many of the other passengers. She noticed and started cursing. Wondering out loud why 'everybody ah watch har like seh she ah bumbo-claat T.V.' One of the flight attendants had to sternly tell her to stop the foul language immediately. She relented but continued to mutter under her breath. Jade's heart was pounding mightily as she descended the stairs. She couldn't believe that she was actually back in Jamaica. She walked amongst the other passengers as they made their way to customs. She waited in one of the lines for several minutes then went up to the customs officer when it was her turn.

He took her temporary passport that she had been issued and looked at it. He then looked at her with a smirk.

"What could a pretty woman such as yuhself do for Uncle Sam to send you home?" he asked, as he leaned forward in the booth to get a better view of Jade's breasts straining against the top of her sweat suit. Jade's expression was stoic as she looked at him. She didn't respond.

Undaunted, he lowered his voice conspiratorially. "Yuh have somewhere to stay? If not yuh can come home with me...mi get off work at 5. Yuh can just wait fi mi by the entrance to de parking lot. Mi drive a nice Honda Accord."

Jade burst out laughing. She couldn't help it. How this ugly moron even thought he stood a chance with her just because she was deported was beyond her. And was she supposed to be impressed that he drove a Honda Accord? *Negro please, I used to drive everything from an X5 to a Jaguar* Jade mused.

He scowled and shoved the passport back to Jade.

"Go around that corner and knock on the first door," he growled as he dismissed her. He then indicated for the person next in line to step forward. He cut his eyes at Jade as she walked off still chuckling.

Jade placed an extra sway in her hips as she made her way around the corner. She knew he was watching. She knocked on the first door. It was partially open. An obese male cop was sitting behind a cluttered desk, joking with a female officer seated in front of him. They both looked towards the door when they heard the knocking.

"Come in!" the cop thundered. Jade wondered why he felt the need to shout. She stepped in and closed the door behind her.

"Good afternoon," Jade said politely as she stood there, her skin crawling as the cop undressed her with his beady eyes.

"Have a seat," he said, leaning back in the chair which groaned in protest.

Jade sat, wondering if the man had gotten this fat while on the job. She didn't know the recruitment policy of Jamaica's police force but she couldn't imagine him passing any kind of physical test.

"So..." the cop began clasping his hands behind his meaty head, "you have been deported from which country?"

"The United States," Jade replied.

"Yuh deh home enuh," the female cop interjected. "Yuh nuh haffi ah twang like dat. Yuh nah impress no body."

Jade looked at her bemused. "For your information I migrated fourteen years ago. I'm only twenty two. I know no other way to speak."

The obese cop grinned widely. Jade wanted to puke as she noticed remnants of his recently eaten lunch on his teeth. *Couldn't the other officer have told him? My god,* Jade thought disgustedly.

"So why dem deport yuh?" he asked as he removed a form from a file on the desk.

"My extraordinarily good looks," Jade told him smiling.

"Answer the question!" the female cop shouted.

"Relax, Constable Green," he said, returning Jade's smile. "She's only playing around."

He handed the form and a pen to Jade. "Fill this out," he instructed. It was a short, simple form. Jade wrote a fictitious address and phone number for her contact information and gave an incorrect last name.

"Come!" the female officer said, openly showing her hostility to Jade. She walked over to the little table to the left of the desk. Jade sighed and followed. The woman fingerprinted her with much ceremony and then Jade sat back down.

"Ok, well, that's it," the male cop said to her, giving her what he thought was a seductive look. "I'll be calling to check up on you from time to time."

Jade rose, relieved it was over. She smiled prettily. "I'm counting on it..."

The cop felt the beginning of an erection. Whatever he wanted to say in response died in his throat as Jade exited the room without a backward glance. She was happy he had forgotten to seize the temporary passport. It had information in it that she wouldn't want them to have. She was pretty much anonymous right now as far as their records were concerned. Jade made her way outside. She needed to get access to a phone quickly so that she could call Maxine to come and pick her up.

Chapter 7

"Taxi Miss?" a short, fat man in a T-shirt that was two sizes too small for him asked when Jade got outside. Jade ignored him. The arrival area was swarming with people; passengers from the two flights that had arrived in the past hour and the people who came to pick them up. Also in the mix were security personnel, hustlers, taxi operators and airport personnel providing assistance to those who needed it.

Jade walked through the crowd very conscious of some of the knowing stares she was getting. The two see-through laundry bags she was carrying was a dead giveaway that she had been deported. She went away from the crowd and sat on one of the chairs outside the fast food joint. She looked around for a pay phone but then remembered that she didn't have any Jamaican money. She did have four hundred and fifty US dollars though. The State had given her all the money that was in her account at the time of her release when she got to the airport. Jade had to smile at her circumstances. She would have to spend that money carefully. Things could have been worse. She could have been flat broke. She needed to know the current exchange rate and she needed a phone pronto. Maxine would be able to help her with anything she needed. Jade started to perspire. The early afternoon sun was blazing in all its glory. She removed her sweat suit top and tied it around her waist. The ribbed white tank top she was wearing underneath was ideal for the hot, humid weather. She started to cool down immediately. Jade looked around in wonder. The airport looked completely different from what she remembered. It was extremely modern and well kept. Loud music interrupted her thoughts. A black Yukon Denali playing an unfamiliar reggae track with a thumping bass pulled up at the curb a few meters away and a girl stepped out. She glanced at Jade through her aviator Dior shades as she strutted by and went inside the fast food joint.

The driver of the vehicle, presumably her man, was watching Jade. She glanced at him briefly. He said something to the guy in the back and the guy exited the vehicle and came over to where Jade was sitting.

She looked at him expressionlessly.

"What's up pretty girl...my boss says that he wants your phone number yeah," the guy drawled in a fake British accent. "His baby mother was the girl who just went into the restaurant so he couldn't come himself, you get me?"

Jade thought for a second. She wasn't interested but you never know. At this point it would be good to have as many options as possible. He just might come in useful.

"I'll take his number," Jade replied.

The guy was about to argue but then he spotted the boss' girl coming back out of the restaurant. She stopped by the table just as he gave Jade the number.

"You can't do better than that Jimmy?" she sneered looking at Jade from head to toe.

"Stop trying to mess with my game Dahlia," he replied grinning.

Dahlia sucked her teeth. "Nigga you aint got no game."

"Nice suitcase," she said to Jade before walking off with a hearty laugh.

"Don't mind her," Jimmy said, smiling apologetically. "Make sure you call..."

Jade smiled to herself as she watched him hop into the truck. Dahlia cast a last look her way and the SUV joined the traffic heading out of the airport.

I most certainly will, Jade mused. Dahlia would pay for looking down on her. As soon as she got herself together she would make it a point of duty to take her man and then dismiss him when he was no longer of any use to her. Dahlia would get what's coming to her soon enough. Smug bitch. She wasn't even pretty. Thank god for designer gear and horse hair. Jade sighed. She couldn't wait to get back to normal. But first things first. Where the hell was she going to get a phone to call Maxine? She saw a well-dressed man exiting the restaurant. She decided to ask him nicely for a quick call.

"Excuse me sir," she said. "I'm sorry to bother you but may I please borrow your phone to make a quick call? I need to get in touch with the person who's to pick me up."

"Sure," he said after a moment's hesitation, handing Jade his Blackberry Curve.

"Thank you," she said as she quickly dialed the number Maxine had given her.

It rang twice then a recording came on that the number was no longer in service. Jade checked the number and tried again. Same result. She handed back the gentleman his phone.

"One more thing," she said, handing him a slip of paper. "Do you happen to know where this address is?"

He took it and thought for a moment. "I know this street...but it doesn't go up to 40. It's a dead end road and it ends at 20 or 21, can't remember which. My brother has a garage on that road."

"Thank you very much, sir," Jade said to him and sat back down. The man was going to say something else to her but when he saw the disappointed look on her face, he walked off, looking back a few times at the sad, beautiful, young lady. Maxine had deliberately given her false information. Jade couldn't understand why she would do that. She sighed in anger and disappointment. Now what?

Chapter 8

Duane Weatherburn, government minister responsible for the Ministry of Mining, Energy and Environment, exited the airport after a brief interview with reporters in the VIP lounge. He was returning from a successful three day visit to China. He was in high spirits. He had done well in the negotiations with a Chinese energy conglomerate and also had a very productive meeting with environmental specialists. And despite the long flight, he was still feeling the soothing, rejuvenating effects of the full body massage he had received prior to heading to the airport. The Chinese certainly knew their stuff. His driver was outside waiting for him in a forest green Mitsubishi Pajero, the preferred SUV for most government officials.

"How you doing Eddie?" he said by way of greeting as he climbed into the back seat, tipping the porter who placed his luggage in the trunk five hundred dollars.

"Not too bad Mr. Weatherburn," Eddie replied. His boss could be a real pain in the ass sometimes but when he was in a good mood he wasn't a bad boss to have. Very kind when he wanted to be as well. Eddie had been with him for twelve years. He stayed mainly because he knew deep down he was a good man and unlike most politicians, really tried to make a difference. His boss also trusted him and Eddie liked that. He was privy to many of the Minister's secrets. Secrets that would cause serious scandals if revealed.

"I'm going to head straight to the office Eddie," Weatherburn said as he loosened his tie a bit and relaxed on the plush leather seat. It would be better to head straight to the office now and get a few urgent things out of the way so that he could go home early and get some much needed rest. At forty-five, he was one of the youngest government ministers but between his demanding portfolio, demanding wife and the various committees that he was on, he needed his rest.

"Ok boss," Eddie responded as he headed out.

"Jesus Christ..." Duane Weatherburn muttered softly as he looked out the window at one of the most beautiful faces he had ever seen. "Pull over Eddie."

His driver did so. Weatherburn continued to stare at the young lady sitting at the table by herself. She looked at the vehicle, perhaps feeling his gaze. She couldn't see inside though, as the windows were heavily tinted.

Eddie chuckled to himself. The boss was at it again. He loved young, beautiful women, and looking at the girl that the boss was staring at, she definitely fit the bill and then some.

"Eddie, inform that young lady that I'd like to have a word with her," he said, never taking his eyes off Jade.

Eddie put the vehicle in park and approached Jade. Eddie cleared his throat as Jade waited for him to speak.

"Umm...good afternoon," Eddie began, "how yuh doing?"

"Good afternoon. Not good," Jade replied matter-of-factly.

"Sorry to hear that...umm...my boss would like to have a word with you," he went on, "he's asking you to come inside the vehicle."

Jade chuckled. It was the second time in less than half an hour that a 'boss' had sent their employee to her.

"Do I look like I'm stupid?" Jade asked Eddie. "Clearly you think I am if you expect me to go inside a tinted vehicle with a total stranger."

"No...no...it's just that my boss is an important government minister and he has to be discreet...you know," Eddie explained.

"No I don't know," Jade replied, giving him a hard time. "I'm not going inside that vehicle so if your boss wants to speak to me he has to come to me."

Eddie sighed and went back over to the SUV. Weatherburn lowered his window.

"Boss, she says that you have to come to her," Eddie told him.

Weatherburn looked beyond Eddie at Jade. She was staring at him with a look that said 'Yeah that's what I said'. Weatherburn smiled. It was a smile that had dropped quite a few panties far and wide but Jade didn't even return his smile.

"Eddie hand her your mobile," Weatherburn instructed.

Eddie went back and handed her the phone. Jade looked at the SUV questioningly. The phone then rang and Weatherburn looked at her waiting for her to answer.

Jade pressed the talk button but didn't speak.

"I'm Duane Weatherburn," he said.

"Ok," Jade replied in a tone which suggested that the name meant nothing to her.

"Minister of Mining, Energy and Environment," he expounded.

"How nice," Jade drawled sarcastically. "What is it you want?"

"You," Weatherburn said. "Are you an American?"

"No," Jade replied. "Just lived there for many years. You want me...just like that. You don't even know me. What you mean is that you want to fuck me. Correct?"

Weatherburn chuckled. This young woman was something else.

"Ok, here's the deal. I'm an important man and also a married one. However, I am absolutely captivated by your beauty and would love to have the opportunity to get to know you. I didn't get your name by the way."

Jade didn't respond immediately. Suddenly she just knew that everything was going to be ok. Someone above was definitely looking out for her. Just when she didn't know what her next move would be, this opportunity had presented itself. Meeting a rich, smitten man was just what the doctor ordered. If she played her cards right, she could turn this into something very fruitful.

"Name's Jade...I'm listening..."

"Ok...pretty name...really suits you. Can you please come inside the vehicle? Matter of fact, allow me to take you to your destination or wherever you want to go."

Jade ended the call and handed the phone back to Eddie. She sat there a few seconds longer and then got up and picked up her bags. Eddie quickly took them from her and placed them in the trunk, wondering why she had her things in laundry bags. Jade then entered the vehicle and sat on the back seat.

"I won't bite you know...at least not yet..." Weatherburn said to Jade as Eddie drove off.

Jade merely looked at him. There were acres of space between them in the large SUV as she had planted herself by the door on the other side behind Eddie.

Weatherburn was intrigued by the gorgeous young woman who nothing seemed to faze. It was obvious to him that she had been deported. There could be no other reason for the laundry bags she was toting as luggage. He would talk to her about that later. She probably needed his assistance but wasn't desperate. A woman with her face and body always had one foot in the door. Jade looked out the window as Weatherburn watched her in silence. The sea sandwiched the Palisadoes road on which they were traveling. Jade figured that during heavy rains the road was most likely impassable. There were no barriers to keep the sea off of it. She thought that was ridiculous. It was the only way to and from the airport. How could they leave it like that? She asked Weatherburn about it. He was impressed at her observation. He explained that his government had only been in power for six months after being in the political wilderness for fourteen years and that rectifying this problem was one of the main things on the agenda. Jade found it incredible that his party had lost three elections back to back since the last time she was in Jamaica. She wasn't someone who was very interested in politics but she didn't think that it was a good thing for one party to be in power so long.

Weatherburn excused himself and took and made several calls as they entered New Kingston. *The place looks so different*, Jade thought, as she looked out of the window, impressed at the bustling, modern metropolis that was New Kingston.

"Eddie, stop by Chante's Closet," Weatherburn instructed as he punched numbers on his mobile, making yet another call.

"Yes, boss," Eddie replied. *The boss really wants to impress this one*, he thought, as he turned onto Braemar Avenue where the popular boutique was located. Chante's Closet was one of the most expensive and exclusive boutiques in Kingston.

He pulled into the small parking lot. It was filled with luxury vehicles. He parked behind a silver Lexus RX350. Weatherburn gestured for Jade to accompany him as he exited the vehicle still on his phone.

"I won't get in office before another two hours," Weatherburn was saying on the phone as he held the door open for Jade to enter the store. "Ok, so I'll have my personal assistant fax you the information and we discuss it later."

He ended the call and smiled at an attractive woman dressed in a smart, pinstripe pants suit that was approaching them with a broad smile.

"Good to see you Minister," she said as she hugged him warmly.

"Hi Chante," Weatherburn responded. "I brought you a customer today." They went back a long way. Duane Weatherburn had been the last man she was with before she became a full fledged lesbian six years ago. Their parting had been amicable and they had remained good friends. He always supported her boutique by bringing his mistresses there. He never brought his wife though.

"Hello," Chante said to Jade, giving her a hug that was a bit too tight for Jade's liking. "You're so beautiful."

"Hi, and thank you," Jade replied, in a polite but reserved manner. She was convinced the woman was a lesbian. She had this intense look on her face whenever she looked at her.

"Ok, show her around so that she can select a few outfits," Weatherburn said to Chante as he sat down on one of the couches provided for customers and checked his email on his PDA. A few of the customers came over to say hi to the popular government minister.

Chante took Jade by the hand which Jade discreetly removed after a few seconds and led her over to the casual wear section. Jade was very excited but tried not to let it show. This would be her first time trying on some nice clothes in four years. She couldn't wait to get out of the plain grey sweat suit and white sneakers that she was wearing. She picked up four pairs of jeans – two pairs of True Religion boot cut jeans and two pairs of Seven for All Mankind jeans with the new high-waist look. She selected several tops to go with them and then while she went into the dressing room to fit, Chante picked out a selection of dresses for her to choose from.

"Need any help?" Chante asked from outside the dressing room door.

"No, thanks," Jade replied quickly, as she looked at her reflection in the mirror. She looked so curvy and sexy in her new jeans. The real Jade was back. Satisfied that everything fit her perfectly, she exited the dressing room and looked at the dresses Chante had picked out. She selected a lovely red Gucci dress which showed tons of cleavage and a more modest but sexy black Anna Molinari cocktail dress from the batch. Now she needed shoes and accessories. Seventy minutes and a hundred and ten thousand dollars later, Jade and Weatherburn exited the store. She was wearing one of her new outfits and her smiling face was framed by white oversized Chanel shades. She felt and looked fabulous.

"Thank you very much," Jade said to Weatherburn softly as Eddie drove out into the streaming mid-afternoon traffic. Though this was the way he would *have* to treat her if he intended to get anywhere, she hadn't expected him to do so much so soon. "This was very nice of you."

Weatherburn merely smiled and patted her hand. He hadn't planned on spending so much money on her the first time out but what the hell. She was going to be his and despite the circumstances that had befallen her, she was obviously a woman who was used to the finer things in life.

"I'm going to drop you off at a reputable salon so that you can get your hair and nails done," Weatherburn said. "I'm going to leave you there and pick you up when you're through ...then we'll have dinner."

"Ok," Jade agreed. She was feeling more comfortable with Weatherburn by the minute. He wasn't pushy and he definitely knew how to treat a lady. They had yet to have a serious conversation and really get to know each other – he knew absolutely nothing about her – but that would come later. Right now he was pushing all the right buttons. Jade's initial coldness towards him had thawed considerably.

Damn, Eddie mused, *Jade have the boss weak and him don't even get none yet.* Eddie had never seen him go to such great lengths at such an early stage. Jade definitely had the boss under her spell.

Chapter 9

When they got to the salon, Weatherburn handed Jade a credit card along with a card on which he wrote down both his and Eddie's mobile numbers. He then told her that she should ask for Theresa, the owner. She would take good care of her. He reached over to give Jade a soft peck on the lips. She didn't resist. She then murmured that she would see him later and hopped out of the vehicle, placing the credit card in her new, otherwise empty Chanel pocketbook.

Weatherburn watched her enter the salon. She was ridiculously sexy. He could still taste her succulent lips, though the kiss was brief. He didn't understand why he was so taken by her. Yes, she was beautiful, but there had to be something else. He felt bewitched. He doubted he could ever say no to her. That was a scary feeling. One he was not used to having.

"Take me to the office Eddie," he said quietly, when Jade disappeared inside the building. His phone rang as they headed out. It was his wife.

ঔৣ☬✞ঔৣ

Dunga, the guy who had sent his right-hand man to speak to Jade outside the airport, thought about her for the umpteenth time as he played pool with some of the boys at the sports bar he owned on Constant Spring Road. He was annoyed but grudgingly impressed that she had not given him her phone number. Usually women were quick to show interest in him. He was a good looking man, tall and wiry. He also had money. Lots of it. He was a talented producer who had put together an impressive string of hit productions over the past six years. Several international artists had taken notice and two tracks that he produced for Rapid Fire, a popular Atlanta based rapper, were ringtone smash hits as well as number one hits on the billboard charts.

Dahlia had teased Jimmy when they got back inside the vehicle that he needed to take his new deportee girl shopping. Dunga could not recall the last time he had seen such a naturally beautiful woman. He knew that Dahlia had noticed the woman's startling beauty as well because she kept making snide comments about the woman. *Jealousy.* He had taken Dahlia straight to the salon as she was complaining that the girl in New York had not done her hair the way she wanted it. There was a big party going on tonight and Dahlia wanted to look her best. He straightened up after sinking a shot. He really hoped the beautiful mystery woman called. He just *had* to meet her.

All eyes were on Jade when she stepped inside the swanky salon. It was called House of Beauty and clients were taken on appointment basis only, according to the small sign on the wall behind the receptionist.

"Hi, may I speak with Theresa please?" Jade said to the receptionist.

"Who may I say wants to see her?" the girl queried, "she's kind of busy with a client at the moment."

"Tell her I'm from Duane Weatherburn's office," Jade replied, wondering why women always had to give her attitude.

The girl scowled at Jade and buzzed Theresa on the intercom.

"She'll be with you momentarily," she announced and then started leafing through a magazine, ignoring Jade.

"I suppose I can have a seat while I wait," Jade commented sarcastically, and sat on one of the chairs opposite the receptionist, without waiting for a response.

But is who this yankee bitch think seh she ah feisty with, the girl thought as she glared at Jade. *Come in yah ah show-off herself.*

A few minutes later, a woman came out to the reception area and the receptionist nodded towards Jade.

"I'm Theresa," the woman said, walking over to her. "How can I help you?"

"I need to get my hair done...and also a manicure and pedicure. Duane told me to ask for you," Jade replied, as she stood up.

Theresa was silent for a moment. The salon was quite busy but she couldn't say no to Weatherburn. He was like family. Her younger brother, a counselor in the East St. Andrew Division, owed his start in politics to Weatherburn who was like a father to him.

"Ok, follow me," Theresa said.

Jade trooped behind her, amused at the look the receptionist gave her as she walked by. *Women can be so silly sometimes*, she mused as she looked around. The clientele seemed to be mostly young, professional women. Jade wondered idly how so many of them got the time off from work to visit the salon. Theresa directed Jade to sit at the lone empty sink.

"Kareen will wash your hair but I'll do the styling and cutting personally," Theresa said as she gestured for Kareen, who was just returning from her lunch break, to attend to Jade.

ଓଃଓଃଓଃ

Weatherburn arrived at the ministry thirty minutes after dropping off Jade at the salon. He was in a good mood despite his wife's phone call to bitch about him not calling when he arrived to let her know that he had gotten back safely, and bumping into that asshole Bradley Saunders in the lobby. He cursed inwardly for not using his private entrance. Bradley Saunders was a journalist who hated Weatherburn's guts. Weatherburn used to take his biased, scathing articles personally until Eddie, his driver, told him why Saunders hated him so much. Two years ago, Weatherburn had a brief affair with a young woman by the name of Naudria Sinclair. At the time she had been Saunders' fiancé. He had found out about it but married her nevertheless and had a hard-on for Weatherburn ever since. Weatherburn found the whole thing funny but he still didn't like Saunders. Petty motherfucker. Acting like he was still in high school. Carrying pussy feelings and compromising his journalistic integrity over a woman. Pathetic.

Weatherburn ignored him and responded heartily to the 'Welcome back Minister' and 'Good to have you back boss' comments as he headed to the elevator. His office was on the seventh floor. Heather, his personal assistant for the past nine months, smiled when she saw her boss. She rose from behind her desk and followed him into his office bringing a thick file with her. She locked the door behind her.

"How was the flight?" she asked as she placed the file on his desk and walked around to where he was standing by the large window.

"It wasn't too bad," Weatherburn replied as he shrugged off his jacket and handed it to her. He watched as she walked over to put it in the closet. She was wearing, as usual, a black skirt suit and a white blouse, with her hair in a tight bun. A pair of Calvin Klein reading glasses was perched on her thirty-three year old nose. She was an average-looking woman, with an average body, one of the reasons Weatherburn was positive no one suspected that they had a sexual relationship. She had been recommended to him by one of his colleagues who had left politics to migrate to Canada. Efficient, discreet, loyal and gave head better than a porn star. His colleague had been right on all counts. He loosened his tie and plopped down on his large, comfortable leather swivel chair. Heather then squatted in front of him and loosened his trousers. She pulled it along with his boxers down to his ankles as he quickly buzzed his secretary on the intercom and told her that he would be in a meeting for the next half an hour and was not to be disturbed. He then clasped his hands behind his head and closed his eyes with a soft moan as he felt her warm, knowledgeable mouth envelope his dick. Heather sucked his throbbing shaft enthusiastically and reached down with her free hand to massage her pussy through her thin black stockings. She climaxed three times before she pushed her boss over the edge and swallowed all that he had to offer.

ঙ্গঙ্গঙ্গ

Jade admired her new hair do in the large wall to wall mirror. The short, somewhat spiky cut suited her chiseled features to perfection. Her prominent model-esque cheekbones and sultry brown eyes now looked even more captivating. Theresa had done a fabulous job. Initially Jade had been reluctant to cut her hair but Theresa had convinced her and she was glad she did.

"Wow...you look so gorgeous," Theresa commented with a broad smile, pleased with her handiwork.

"Thanks...I really like the cut," Jade said. She admired herself for a few minutes before going over to the nail technician who was now ready for her.

"Hi," Jade said, smiling at the young lady who seemed to be in awe of her beauty.

"Hi, you look so pretty," the girl told her.

Jade sat and placed her hands in the container with warm water.

"I just need a simple French manicure," Jade instructed. She absolutely hated elaborate designs or bright colours on her fingers. She glanced up at the clock on the wall to her right. It was now 3:30 p.m. She should be through in another hour and a half or less. Jade sighed contentedly. Yesterday this time she was at the detention center dressed in her drab grey sweat suit sitting in her tiny cell reading a book. Today she was fully attired in designer garb, sitting in a salon, looking absolutely fabulous getting her nails done.

What a difference a day made.

ଔଓଔଓଔଓ

"I'm through babes...where you at?" Dahlia asked, smacking her gum loudly in the phone.

Dunga winced. Damn he hated when she did that.

"I'm at the sports bar," he told her.

"You coming to get me?" she asked, looking at her reflection in the mirror. *Looks a hundred percent better,* she mused. *That bitch Latisha will never get a chance to fuck up my head again.* She would find a new hairdresser as soon as she went back to New York. It was twice in a row now that Latisha had done her hair and she was not pleased.

"Yeah, I'll come and scoop you up," Dunga replied. "Are you hungry?"

"Yeah, but I just called Momma and she has prepared dinner. We could just eat there when we go to pick up Samantha."

Samantha was their five year old daughter and the apple of his eye. She used to live with her mother in New York but Dunga insisted that she attended school in Jamaica so she had been living here for the past year. Dunga arranged for Dahlia's mom to keep her as he had a really busy schedule but he ensured that she spent time with her daddy often enough. His own mother lived alone and kept her occasionally as well. His mother didn't have to work as Dunga took excellent care of her but she volunteered three times a week at the J. Richard Black Home for under-priveleged children where she worked as a counselor.

"Ok, cool," Dunga responded. He didn't have a problem with that. Dahlia's mom was a good cook but not nearly as good as *his* mother. "I'll be there in about ten minutes."

Dunga terminated the call and gestured for Jimmy to come over.

"I'm going to pick up Dahlia and swing by her mom for a bit. I'll link up with you at the studio later," Dunga told him. He rarely went anywhere without Jimmy who was like the eyes in the back of his head but sometimes Jimmy's company wasn't necessary.

"Alright, later then," Jimmy told him and went back to his pool game.

Dunga then headed downstairs and hopped into his Denali. There were only two of them in the island and though it was a gas guzzler, Dunga wouldn't trade it for the world. In his estimation the only SUV that could compare was the Range Rover but he still preferred the Denali. Besides, one of his enemies drove a black Range Rover and there was no way in hell he would drive the same model vehicle. He headed out to pick up Dahlia at the salon. She could act real diva-like more often than not, and at times he wished she would tone down the ghetto fabulousness a bit but she was the mother of his child and she had been with him before he had money so he didn't sweat it too much. The mystery woman at the airport crossed his mind. He checked his mobile to see if he had missed any calls though he knew he hadn't. He chuckled. He was behaving like a smitten schoolboy and he hadn't even met her yet. Damn.

Chapter 10

"I'm through," Jade said. She was in Theresa's tiny office at the back of the salon using Theresa's private line.

"Ok, I'm just finishing up some things with my secretary... I'll be there in about twenty minutes," Weatherburn replied.

"Alright, see you then." Jade hung up and sat at Theresa's desk, and picked up a copy of Elle magazine. It was the latest issue and had all the new trends for the summer. Theresa had taken a liking to her and was very accommodating. When Jade was through, she had ushered Jade in her office and told her to make herself comfortable. She had then closed the door behind Jade and went back out to her work station to finish up a client's hair. Ten minutes later, she returned and perched on one side of the desk. She was sipping bottled water.

"So, Jade," she began, "you're from the States?"

"Well I was born here but had migrated fourteen years ago," Jade replied.

"Ok, so you're here to visit?"

"I'm exploring the possibilities of returning home for good," Jade told her.

"I see...so where will you be staying? You know... we could keep in touch and hang out sometime," Theresa suggested.

Jade didn't detect any sexual vibes coming from Theresa and it wouldn't hurt to have a female to hang with from time to time so she agreed. She took Theresa's numbers and told her that she would call her when she got settled. Theresa's mobile then rang. It was Weatherburn.

"Hi Theresa, took care of my friend?" he asked.

"Hi Duane, shame on you...you know she's in good hands," Theresa replied with a grin.

Weatherburn chuckled. Theresa did indeed have a reputation for being one of the best hairstylists in Kingston.

"Tell her I'm outside, take care."

"Bye Duane." She got up off the desk and slipped her LG Prada phone back in its case.

"He's here," she told Jade.

Jade gave her a hug and told her thanks for everything and that she'd be in touch.

Jade then strutted through the salon, deliberately provoking the receptionist by telling her a chirpy goodbye knowing the girl didn't like her. The girl glared but didn't respond. Jade laughed and exited the building.

Weatherburn gasped when he saw Jade. His heartbeat accelerated and his dick awakened from its slumber. He didn't think it was possible for her to look any more beautiful but it was. Jade looked absolutely stunning. He would be the envy of every man – and even some women he was sure – whenever he took Jade anywhere with him.

"Oh my god," he murmured when she entered the vehicle. "Words cannot describe how gorgeous you are Jade."

Jade chuckled.

"Thank you, Duane," she replied.

Weatherburn took a deep breath.

"Let's go get something to eat...you should be hungry," he said. He was hungry as well. And not just for food.

"Yeah, I'm famished," Jade agreed.

Weatherburn instructed Eddie to drive over to Rob's Chophouse on Dominica Drive. They had the best spare ribs in Kingston. Jade went into her pocketbook and took out the credit card to give back to Weatherburn. He told her to keep it, that it was hers to use from now on. Jade smiled and placed it back in her pocketbook. Weatherburn really was going all out. Pushing all the right buttons. Jade hoped he didn't think that he was going to be able to control her because he was spending all this money on her. If so, he would be in for a rude awakening. They would have a serious conversation over dinner. Lay all the cards on the table so that they were both on the same page.

It was a new Visa Card with a two hundred and fifty thousand dollar limit. A good chunk of that was already spent today. Jade was definitely an expensive acquisition. But he was willing to bet his last dollar that she would be worth every penny. In *every* way. His erection throbbed in his trousers. He couldn't wait to make love to her. His turgid shaft seeped a bit of pre-cum at the thought.

"Daddy! Mommy!" Samantha shrieked as she bounded down the patio steps, ignoring her grandmother's pleas to stop the running.

Dunga grinned as he exited the vehicle. He loved her so much. She was the sweetest little girl on earth. She looked just like him but had her mother's caramel complexion. She screamed with delight as he scooped her up and held her high in the air. Though she had seen him yesterday, and had not seen her mother in a month, she still came to him first. She had a special bond with her daddy.

"How's my princess?" Dunga asked as he made funny faces at her.

"I'm fine daddy," she told him grinning from ear to ear, exposing her huge gap caused by the tooth fairy's last visit.

"You don't miss your mommy?" Dahlia pouted, holding her arms out to take her from Dunga. He knew she was only half-joking. It was no secret that she somewhat resented the fact that Samantha was closer to her daddy.

Samantha giggled and went into her mother's arms. They then trooped inside where Dahlia's mom was getting the table ready for dinner.

❧❧❧

"What time are you coming home Duane?" his wife, Jessica, asked. She wanted to have dinner with him this evening as she had invited two of her old college chums to dinner and wanted them to meet her powerful husband. "I have some friends coming over for dinner and I really want them to meet you."

Weatherburn sighed inwardly. He hated when she behaved like he was a trophy or something. He just couldn't understand why Jessica always felt the need to impress others.

"I won't be home until late," he replied, happy to burst her bubble. "I have some things to deal with that cannot wait."

"You never have time for me anymore," she pouted unfairly. Being his wife for fifteen years, she more than understood that the nature of his work sometimes allowed him very little time for home. Even more so now that his party was back in power. She didn't complain about the increased income and the perks that came with being the wife of an important government minister though.

"Jessica, I really don't have time for any of your tantrums," he said, "I'll see you later."

Jessica slammed the phone down in his ears. She was very disappointed. She just hated when things didn't go her way. Now she would have to tell Susan and Rebecca that her husband wouldn't be able to make it. She took out her anger on the maid and the cook, cursing that the table wasn't properly set and that the pot roast was dry.

❧❧❧

Weatherburn got more than his usual attention when he stepped inside Rob's Chophouse. The place was full as usual with the who's who of Kingston high society. Supreme Court Judge Nelson Mcleish waved to him; he nodded to Jacqueline Weir, President of The Jamaica Chamber of Business and he stopped to exchange playful barbs with Frederick Spencer, his political opponent but good friend who was also a partner in one of Jamaica's most prestigious law firms. Everyone was staring at his beautiful unknown companion. Some discreetly, others openly. Weatherburn didn't mind the gossip. He was used to it and besides, it wasn't unusual for him to be in the company of a woman other than his wife. The manager himself came over and led them to the back section where the reserved tables were located. Weatherburn didn't require a reservation. Him showing up meant that some unlucky soul lost theirs. Jade seemed unperturbed by all the attention. She took her seat nonchalantly, smiling and thanking the manager as he held her chair out.

Weatherburn ordered for the both of them. He ordered roasted prime beef sirloin served with a red wine and mushroom sauce, grilled salmon, sautéed potatoes, fresh string beans, mango sorbet and red wine. They chatted while they waited for the food to arrive.

"As you can see Jade," Weatherburn began, "I'm totally taken by you and guess what? I have absolutely no qualms in admitting it...and showing it. I want you."

Jade smiled. He couldn't read the look in her pretty brown eyes.

"I can see that...and you can have me. But on my terms," Jade replied, still smiling though her eyes were serious. "I don't want a relationship. I want an arrangement."

Weatherburn leaned forward, resting his chin on his clasped hands.

"I'm listening," he said.

"I'm not a whore. Nor am I a little young naïve woman frightened by money and power. I come from an upper middle class background and I am used to the finer things in life. My first and only real boyfriend was of the street variety but he had money and power and treated me like a queen."

She paused and waited until the waiter placed their food on the table before resuming. The dinner looked delicious. She tasted a small piece of the succulent sirloin.

"This is divine," she said.

Weatherburn smiled but was too anxious to hear the rest of what she had to say to eat.

She took a sip of the wine before continuing.

"I got caught up in a situation and to cut a long story short, here I am. Yes, meeting you has gotten things off to a good start but if I hadn't met you, I would have still been ok. I'm not interested in having what one would call a normal relationship with any man. Without going into details, my last relationship taught me a lot and all I'm focused on at this point is getting things together and looking out for number one."

Weatherburn ignored the vibration of his cell phone on his hip. He finally dug into his food and had a piece of the grilled salmon. The food here was excellent. The restaurant deserved all the various awards it had won since it opened its doors three years ago.

"So, Duane, though I will make a reasonable effort to accommodate your needs, you will treat me with the utmost respect and as such, will make no effort to rule or control me. I will do as I please, when I please. Now, I know how men are, especially Jamaican men. If they spend money on you, they think you belong to them. You have already spent a good amount of money in the few hours since we met. If you know deep down you cannot handle this sort of arrangement, cut your losses and we part ways right here."

Weatherburn chewed his food thoughtfully. Well there it was. She was willing to be his 'kept' woman but free to do as she pleased. He would be the laughing stock of his close friends if they ever found out that he had agreed to something like that. On the flip side, they wouldn't know the intricacies of the relationship and he would be the object of their envy when they met Jade. None of them had ever been with such a beautiful, captivating woman.

"Do you find me attractive Jade?" he asked. This was important to him. His ego would not allow him to go through with this – at least for an extended period as there was no way he was going to pass up the opportunity to be intimate with her - but it would be more gratifying if there was a modicum of interest on her part beyond what he could do for her financially.

Jade sipped her wine and appraised the man old enough to be her father. He was attractive, his cherubic face and absence of grey hair making him seem younger than his years. He was in relatively good shape. There was a slight roundness at the stomach but not bad for a man his age. He was also powerful and used to being in charge yet she was in total control of this situation. That was an aphrodisiac in itself and added to his overall attractiveness.

"I do," Jade replied truthfully. If she hadn't there was no way she could go through with this regardless of the benefits as she would not have been able to fuck him. "By the way, you will be only the second man to have intimate knowledge of me."

His ego soared. As did his dick. He swore it was going to topple the table with the force at which it sprang. Pure natural beauty, immeasurable sex appeal coupled with limited mileage and intelligence to boot. For the second time that evening, his juices overflowed slightly and dampened his boxers. He had never wanted anyone so badly in his life.

Chapter 11

“You good?” Dahlia asked as she and Dunga headed home. He seemed a bit more quiet than usual.

“Yeah, I’m ok,” Dunga replied, not taking his eyes off the road. “Just thinking about the project I’m about to work on at the studio.” He had a meeting at the studio with a young lady that a friend of his had begged him to meet. She was currently singing back-up for a few artists but his friend was convinced that with her voice and looks, she could be successfully marketed as a solo artist. His friend had good judgement and one never knew when you might stumble across the next big thing so he had agreed readily enough.

“Ok well don’t be there all night,” Dahlia said. “Remember that I want you to go the party with me tonight.”

One of Dahlia’s good friends was keeping a big party at Liguanea Park. Dunga had promised her that he would go.

"Most likely I'll make it," Dunga replied. If later he didn't feel like going or if he felt like working late he simply wouldn't bother to go.

Dahlia didn't push the issue. She knew how Dunga was at times. Moody motherfucker. Well she wasn't missing it for the world. She had purchased a sexy Dior dress that she was sure would upstage every woman there. They had left Samantha with her grandmother though she had wanted to come home with her parents. Dahlia would pick her up to-morrow afternoon. Take her to get ice cream or something. She was also horny. She wasn't fucking around on Dunga and hadn't gotten any sex since he came to New York two weeks ago to do a studio session with a rapper from Brooklyn who everyone thought was the second coming of the Notorious B.I.G. His manager had flown in Dunga to do a track for the rapper's upcoming debut album. Hopefully Dunga came to the party with her so that they could drink lots of cham-pagne and go home and fuck each other's brains out.

"Alright see you later," Dunga said, after he pulled up at the apartment and placed her luggage in the living room.

"Ok baby," Dahlia said and kissed him on the lips.

Dunga slipped her some tongue and she moaned in his mouth.

"I want you babes..." she murmured.

"You'll get all the dick you can handle later baby," Dunga told her smiling. Despite her being his main girl for seven years, he rarely got tired of fucking her.

Dahlia grinned and kissed him again before going inside and closing the door. Her g-string was soaked.

ଔଓଔଓଔଓ

Weatherburn and Jade exited the restaurant after their two hour meal. Having consumed a significant portion of the wine, Jade was feeling quite tipsy. It was her first time drinking alcohol in four years. Eddie, who had been sitting in the SUV listening to the radio, gunned the engine when they entered the vehicle.

"I'm going to book you into the Mayberry Hotel for a week until we get an apartment sorted out," Weatherburn told her as they sat close together in the back of the Pajero. He owned two apartments but one was in Montego Bay and the one that was in Kingston was rented out to his wife's cousin. He would have to find a nice little love nest in which to put Jade.

"Ok, Duane," Jade purred, resting her head on his shoulder. He could feel her warm breath on his neck.

His erection raged once again. *If I don't fuck this woman soon I'm going to pop a blood vessel,* he mused.

They got to the Mayberry hotel in ten minutes.

"Use the credit card I gave you to book a suite for seven days," Weatherburn said to Jade when Eddie pulled up in front of the lobby. "Once you've sorted out the room come back out to me. We'll be the parked right over there." He gestured to an empty parking spot a few meters away.

Jade nodded and exited the vehicle. A bell hop quickly came over to get her bags.

Jade strutted into the bustling lobby like she was on the runway at London fashion week. Heads turned to stare at the beautiful, stylishly attired woman.

"Hi, I need to book a suite for one week," she said to one of the six receptionists at the front desk.

"Hello," the girl responded. "Ok, let's see what we have available."

She found an available suite and told Jade the cost. One hundred and fifty US dollars or the Jamaican equivalent per night. Jade handed her the credit card. She took it and her eyebrows rose slightly when she saw the name on the card. Duane A. Weatherburn. What was she doing with the minister's card? She looked at Jade.

"Is there a problem?" Jade asked, her expression daring the woman to get into her business.

"Not at all," she replied and went ahead with the transaction.

"Thank you," Jade murmured in a sarcastic tone when the woman handed her back the card and the room key. She then beckoned to the bell hop and he trooped behind her with her bags. The suite was located in a section left of the main building so she didn't have to go through the lobby going and coming from her room. That was good as she was certain Weatherburn would need to exercise a bit of discretion whenever he came to visit her. After putting her things in the room, she told the bell hop she didn't have any change at the moment but she would take care of him the next time she saw him. He told her no problem and that if she needed anything she should ask for Ross. Jade thanked him and went out to the parking lot where Weatherburn was waiting.

"All is well?" he asked when she went inside the vehicle.

"Yeah, I'm in suite 69, "she told him deadpan. They both burst out laughing.

"Take a walk Eddie," Weatherburn told him. He wanted a few moments to speak with Jade privately.

"Sure, boss," Eddie replied, and exited the vehicle and stood a few meters away by the palm trees in the middle of the circular parking lot. He lit up a cancer stick.

"I'm not going to come in tonight," Weatherburn said to Jade. He had thought about it while she was getting the room and decided he would wait until tomorrow. He was too anxious and he didn't want to embarrass himself by climaxing too quickly.

Jade was a bit surprised. She knew how badly he wanted her. She didn't mind though. Maybe he was tired from his long day and didn't want to risk not performing up to scratch.

"Ok, that's fine," she told him. Not that it really mattered but it would be nice to avoid fucking him on the first day.

"I know you'll need to get some toiletries and stuff like that but you can survive on the hotel kit until tomorrow," he told her. "Tomorrow I'll send Eddie to pick you up at midday and you can go get whatever you need."

"Ok," Jade agreed. She definitely would be getting a cell phone tomorrow as well. Maybe an iPhone or something.

He pulled her to him and kissed her long and hard. She could feel his bottled up lust as she opened her mouth to accommodate his probing tongue. He was a good kisser. That meant most likely he was good in bed. She hoped he was just as adept as using his nimble tongue elsewhere. His breathing was ragged when he finally broke the kiss.

"Goodnight Jade, I'll see you tomorrow."

She smiled at the lust in his eyes. She knew if she reached down and rubbed his dick through his trousers it would be like touching granite.

"Goodnight, D." She pinched his cheek and exited the vehicle.

She waved bye to Eddie and made her way to the suite. She was looking forward to taking a nice long shower.

ꟷꟷꟷ

The young lady finished singing and looked at Dunga nervously. He was kind of reserved when they met but she knew it wasn't shyness. Artistic people tended to be like that at times. Locked in; rarely allowing anyone in except through their art. She could relate. She wasn't sure if he liked what he heard. His stoic expression wasn't giving away anything. There were five of them in the studio: Dunga, the engineer, her friend who had hooked up the meeting and two of Dunga's associates. Everyone was waiting for Dunga's reaction. He looked at her for several moments before suddenly grinning.

"Get in the booth," he said. "I have the perfect track for you to voice on."

She didn't know whether to laugh or cry. She did both.

"Oh my god," she gushed. "You like my singing!"

Everyone laughed. Dunga and the engineer then went behind the controls and the young lady, who went by the stage name of Secret, excitedly went into the booth. Dunga dropped the beat and she listened to it in its entirety before starting to lay down her vocals. Dunga loved this part of his job. There was nothing like working with a budding artist that was hungry for success; eager to learn and to work hard. Many of them changed when they experienced a certain level of success. Became prima donnas who thought they were bigger than the music. He loved Secret's sound and he loved her look. He could definitely make her into a star.

ଓଃଓଃଓଃ

"Oh shit...Duane...fuck..." Jessica moaned as her husband pounded her mercilessly. She had been in bed half asleep when he got home. He had taken a shower and immediately reached for her when he got into the bed. She had put up a slight resistance as she was still seething that he had not come home to meet her friends for dinner. But he was not to be denied. It had been some time since she had seen him this horny.

"Mmmm....fuck me baby...yes...yes...yes right there baby..." she groaned as her pussy got wetter and wetter with each hard, deep stroke. After fifteen years of marriage her husband still knew how to fuck her just right. She clenched her teeth and started making that weird raspy sound she always made whenever her climax was approaching.

"I'm almost there baby...oh god...don't stop..." she urged just before she wrapped her legs tightly around his back and her pussy convulsed with pleasure. She climaxed not a moment too soon, as Duane, with visions of fucking Jade flashing through his mind, ejaculated mere seconds later with a primal roar as he clutched his wife tightly.

Jade finally emerged from the shower around the same time Weatherburn finished getting his groove on with his wife. She padded over to the bed, her head and luscious body wrapped in plush white towels. She lubricated her legs and arms with the lotion from the hotel kit, which surprisingly, had a very nice smell. She then got into bed and turned on the T.V. She surfed for a few minutes until she settled on an action movie showing on HBO. Slightly horny but very contented, Jade was thoroughly enjoying her new-found freedom. After the initial uncertainty and disappointment when things didn't go as planned when she landed, since

Weatherburn entered the picture it had been smooth sailing. She briefly thought of Chino. She wondered if she would ever see him again. If she did, he would be a dead man. Robbed her of her innocence and freedom, then turned his back on her and started dating her best friend. Fucking bastard. He would get his one day. There was a serious car chase taking place on screen. Best one she had seen since that amazing scene in the Deniro flick *Ronin*. She then thought of her parents; wondered if they regretted turning their backs on her. Maxine also crossed her mind. She remembered the name of the hotel that Maxine said her family owned in Ocho Rios. Jade would definitely go there one of these days. She couldn't wait to see the fake-ass trifling bitch again. Jade sighed away the unpleasant thoughts and focused on the movie. The bad guy had gotten away from the dozen or so cop cars that had been chasing him and was now chilling at his hideout spot. He took off his shirt and fixed himself a strong drink. Jade admired his chiseled torso. No sense dwelling on the past. Today was the first day of the rest of her life.

Chapter 12

Dunga closed the studio at 2 a.m. He was very pleased with the night's work. The session had been fun. He had sent Jimmy and one of the other guys to buy Chinese for everybody and Secret had done two recordings that now only needed to be harmonized, balanced and mixed. She was very talented and took direction well. She would be back in two days for them to discuss the business side of things and get the necessary paperwork signed.

"You going to the party?" Jimmy asked him as they all ventured out to the parking lot.

Dunga was checking his voicemail. Dahlia had called him at 1 a.m. and left a message when he hadn't picked up. She had said that she was heading out to the party and that he should text or call to let her know if he was coming. Dunga was in a good mood. He wouldn't mind hanging out for a bit and polishing off a bottle of champagne or two.

"Yeah, I'm kinda feeling it," Dunga told him. He then turned his attention to Secret who was waiting to tell him goodbye.

"Thanks so much for giving me a chance Dunga," she said for the third time that night, her pretty face sporting a warm and excited smile. "You won't be sorry."

Dunga laughed.

"I certainly hope so," he said as he deactivated the alarm on his SUV. "You ok getting home?"

"Yeah, thanks," she replied. "Orane will give me a ride home."

Orane was the mutual friend who had told Dunga about Secret.

"Alright. Take care and I'll see you on Tuesday," Dunga told her, and held out his hand. She ignored it and hugged him. Tightly. It was not lost on anyone present that Secret was feeling more than gratitude towards Dunga. She released him with an embarrassed smile and went over to Orane's car. The men bade each other bye and the three vehicles exited the premises. Jimmy was riding with Dunga.

"The singer want yuh bad!" Jimmy teased as they headed up Half-Way-Tree road. Dunga was going to drop Jimmy home so that he could get ready for the party. There was a black CRV at Jimmy's house that Dunga had given him to drive when he needed to. They would meet up at the 24 hour gas station on Dunrobin Avenue in an hour and then head out to the party together. Dunga and Jimmy had known each other for over fifteen years. Jimmy was his best and oldest friend. Though they had taken different paths – Dunga went into music and Jimmy had stayed in the streets hustling – they had remained good friends. When Dunga struck it big he told Jimmy to leave the streets alone and come work with him. Jimmy's job had no description. He did whatever Dunga needed him to do. Dunga liked the idea of having someone around him that he could trust and he knew that Jimmy would always have his back no matter what.

Dunga chuckled in response. Secret definitely had a crush on him. Nineteen years old; pretty, innocent face; firm mouthwatering breasts; curvy yet petite frame; long, curly Indian hair –she was obviously mixed – pleasant personality; there was plenty to like but he did not believe in mixing business with pleasure. He wasn't one of those producers who believed that if a female artist wanted them to work with her she had to sleep with them in return. Talent and marketability. Those were his two basic requirements. Dunga changed the subject and they chatted about the NBA playoffs for the rest of the journey.

ଓଃଓଃଓଃ

Dahlia was laughing and chatting with two of her friends over the din of the music when she heard the disc jockey say 'big up Dunga in the building!' He had arrived. And he hadn't even notified her that he was coming. She looked around and saw him heading towards the area where she was standing between the bar designated for the high rollers and the sound system. It took him several minutes to reach her as he was stopped at every juncture by someone who wanted to speak with him. He lingered for awhile where members of the Black Talon Crew were standing. They were a tightly knit crew that was feared and respected in the underworld. Dunga and the leader of the crew had been very good friends since childhood. Only Jimmy was closer to him.

"What's up babes," he said in her ear as he hugged her. Though she was a little annoyed with him she was pleased that he had showed up. He looked and smelled good. As usual. She held on to him possessively as she introduced him to the two women she was hanging with. Dunga knew most of her friends but these two were new friends that Dahlia had met through a mutual acquaintance a few weeks ago. When they told her that they were going to be in Jamaica soon, she had invited them to her friend's party. Dunga greeted them and sent Jimmy to get four bottles of the most expensive champagne available.

It was now 3:30 a.m. and the party was in full swing. Dunga rarely smoked marijuana but tonight he was in the mood to get high. Jimmy, who was already puffing away, rolled Dunga a fat joint. Dahlia smiled when she saw her man smoking the potent-smelling weed and guzzling the champagne like it was water. She knew the sex was going to be off the chain when they got home. God she was horny. Her pussy started to rival the champagne she was drinking. She was scared her juices would start running down her legs.

Secret was awake staring at the ceiling. She was too excited to sleep. Her dreams were on the verge of coming through. Yes, it was early days, but Dunga was arguably the most talented producer in Jamaica and with her drive and voice, she would undoubtedly make it to the top. Turn her mother's disappointment in her career choice into joy. Her mom, who had raised her on her own after her father had passed away when she was only two years old, had wanted her to become an accountant. Secret had always been good at math and her mom felt that becoming an accountant would be a wise career choice as it paid well and a good accountant was always in demand. But music was her calling. The going had been rough for the past three years. She never lasted long singing back-up for anyone despite her powerful voice as the artists whom she sang for always pressured her for sex. It usually came down to fuck me or lose the gig. She always chose the latter. She was a bit surprised at how she was reacting to Dunga. She had a major crush on the ace producer. He was the cliché tall, dark and handsome personified. Broody as well. She liked that. Turned her on. He most likely had a woman. Probably lots of women. She didn't care. She wanted him to take her virginity. Eventually.

"Rassclaat baby...if I come again I'm going to faint..." Dahlia gasped, reeling from the two intense back to back orgasms that had just rocked her frame to the core. Dunga had been fucking her for over an hour and was showing no signs of slowing down. At the party he had been mixing Moet with Hypnotiq and it seemed to have gone straight to his dick. Dunga's response was to turn her around and enter her doggystyle. He was impossibly deep.

"Jesus Christ baby!" she blasphemed. "I feel it in my fucking throat!"

Dunga slapped her ass with each stroke. He increased his tempo as he felt a familiar tingling in his scrotum. His orgasm was finally on its way.

Dahlia sensed it too.

"You coming for me baby? Hmmm...come for me baby...oh yes...I'm coming again...fuck!"

Dunga's testicles throbbed as they slammed against Dahlia's slender thighs with each urgent thrust. Dahlia climaxed the second she felt Dunga's hot semen flooding her insides.

"Mmmmm...oh my god baby...you're the best....mmmm," Dahlia cooed softly as she caught her breath. Dunga tusseled her hair playfully and went into the bathroom to pee. He sighed contentedly. That had been good. Really good. He shook his flaccid dick and flushed the toilet. He was mildly surprised to find his thoughts reverting to the beautiful mystery woman outside the airport. She was his last conscious thought before he fell into a deep and restful sleep.

Chapter 13

Jade woke up at 10:45 a.m. Saturday morning. She couldn't tell the last time she had slept so much. Her first morning as a free woman. She smiled at the thought and turned on the T.V. She turned to CNN. Gas prices were once again on the rise. A housewife in Iowa was missing and her husband was the main suspect. Fifty people were killed in a suicide bomb attack in Iraq. The United Nations was calling an emergency meeting to discuss the worldwide shortage of food and rising food prices. Researchers have discovered a substance in watermelon that produced a Viagra-like effect in men. Jade chuckled at that. She got out of bed, stretched and did some push-ups. When she really settled in she planned to start going to the gym. There was no way she was going to allow her splendid physique to look anything other than its best. She then went into the bathroom to take a shower. It was now 11:15 and Weatherburn was supposed to be sending Eddie to pick her up at 12.

Eddie was right on time. Jade was in the bathroom applying the finishing touches to her make-up when one of the receptionists buzzed her room phone to let her know that her ride was here. Jade grabbed her Coach pocket book and her oversized Burberry shades and exited the suite.

She turned several heads on the short trek to the parking lot where Eddie was waiting. Her ultra-tight, distressed True Religion jeans fitted her toned, curvy body to perfection and her breasts jutted provocatively from the confines of the black, ribbed Prada tank top that she was wearing. Suede Christian Louboutin sandals completed her attire. Jade loved designer gear. Always did. Always would. Only the best was good enough and after four years of being deprived, she had a lot of catching up to do. The shopping excursion that Weatherburn had taken her on was just an appetizer.

"Good afternoon, Eddie," she said as she climbed into the back of the SUV.

"Hello, Jade," Eddie responded pleasantly. He liked Jade. For someone so beautiful she could have easily been a snobbish bitch but she was very cool and down to earth. "Ok, so what's the first stop?"

"Food!" Jade replied laughing. "I'm so hungry."

Eddie laughed and drove out onto Trafalgar Road. There were several restaurants and fast food joints on the hip strip that she could choose from. Jade took Eddie's recommendation and they stopped at Jumbo's On the Deck. Jade insisted that he parked the vehicle and had lunch with her. She didn't have to tell him twice. They went inside the semi-crowded restaurant and of course, all eyes were on Jade. They took a corner table and Jade ordered a sloppy BBQ chicken sandwich with fries while Eddie ordered a double cheeseburger with ginger beer.

They were in the middle of their meal when they were interrupted by the sound of someone clearing their throat.

They both looked up. A short, stockily-built man, sporting a large beer belly in a close-fitting Versace T-shirt was standing there with a smirk on his face.

"Excuse me," he began, "when I looked over here and saw how beautiful and stylish you were, I said to myself, Richie, a woman that hot could never be with a regular Joe so I figured that this man was simply a friend and decided to come over."

Jade was incredulous, amused and annoyed all at once. She looked him up and down.

"How the hell did you get in those jeans?" she asked with a quizzical look on her face. The man was wearing a pair of black Versace jeans that were ridiculously tight. His black face somehow turned purple in embarrassment.

He emitted a fake laugh.

"You have any idea how much these jeans cost?" he bragged in his equally fake British accent. "It's Versace. My entire outfit is Versace. Even my boxers..."

He gave Jade what she was sure he considered to be a seductive smile.

"Well you need to give those nice Versace jeans back to your sister. I would have said girlfriend but it's hard to imagine you having one," Jade told him sweetly. "You look absolutely ridiculous."

The group of four teenagers sitting at a table close by erupted in a chorus of laughter.

"Mind how yuh ah disrespect mi enuh yankee gal," he retorted, completely forgetting his accent in his anger. "Yuh check seh ah foreign yuh deh? Mi wi box yuh inna yuh face!"

Eddie, who had yet to say anything, had heard enough. He rose and slightly lifted his shirt, showing his licensed firearm.

"Leave before you get yourself in trouble," Eddie told him in a quiet voice. "Today would be the last day you box anybody."

"Is alright man," the man said, backing away. "Hey gal if mi eva see yuh pon de road watch mi an' yuh."

Jade laughed as she watched him go through the door. She wasn't scared of his threats. She knew how to take care of herself. Fucking idiot. She picked back up her sandwich and took a bite. She grinned at Eddie.

"My knight in shining armour," she teased.

Eddie blushed.

Jade laughed so hard she almost choked on her food.

❧❧❧

Dunga woke up at 12:30. He looked over at Dahlia. She was still fast asleep. She looked peaceful and erotic. Her left breast was peeking out from under the sheet and her creamy right thigh was also on display. Dunga yawned and got up. He had a busy day ahead of him. He headed to the kitchen to see what was there to eat. He was famished. He made himself an egg, bacon and cheese sandwich and poured a tall glass of orange juice. He turned on the small flat screen T.V. on the kitchen wall. It was on one of the local cable music channels. Dunga was pleased to see the video playing for a song he had produced. The artist was a young man from the innercity community of Kencot. He was talented but difficult to work with. Dunga planned to stop working with him as soon as he had made back the money he invested. At this stage in his career he wasn't going to work with anyone whom he didn't enjoy working with. Dahlia was still fast asleep when he left the house an hour later to go to the studio. He had a session with a white, dreadlocked reggae singer from France. Should be interesting.

Weatherburn called Eddie's mobile to speak to Jade just as they left the restaurant.

"What's up sugar?" he said, as he leafed through some paperwork. "Everything ok?"

"Hi Duane," Jade replied. "Yeah, I just got something to eat... gonna hit up the mall now and pick up a few necessities."

"Ok, baby," he said. "See you later."

"What time are you planning to come by?" Jade queried.

"About 7...that's ok?"

"That's fine hun. See you later."

Jade hung up and handed back Eddie his phone. She hadn't gotten any dick in four years. The drought would be ended this evening. She was looking forward to putting it on Weatherburn. Though she had only been with one man intimately, she was very experienced sexually. Chino loved sex and they used to have it often with plenty of variety thrown into the mix. Jade was adventurous at heart and used to love to experiment and try new things with Chino. They arrived in Half-Way-Tree which was home to several malls, all in the same vicinity. They parked and Eddie followed as Jade made stop after stop. She purchased lingerie; perfume; more clothing, shoes and accessories; and some toiletries. The final stop was at a mobile phone dealer. A chirpy young sales representative came over to assist them as soon as they entered the store.

"But ah wah dis!" a woman said loudly. Her double chin bobbed as she spoke. "Look how long mi stand up here so an' nuh baddy nuh come assist mi."

"Someone will be with you shortly Miss," another sales representative said to the woman quickly. The branch manager was a real pain in the ass who gave the staff a hard time any chance he got. The last thing they needed half an hour before closing time was him embarrassing them in front of the customers. He was around the back in his office. She hoped he didn't hear the belligerent woman. The woman was right though. She was next to being assisted but stupid Alvin had bypassed her and rushed to assist the gorgeous woman who had just come in.

"Shortly mi rass! Mi want service now!" she bellowed indignantly. "Yuh mussi t'ink seh mi frighten fi people. Likkle eediat bwoy mussi ah look smaddy."

She looked at Jade pointedly.

"Go and attend to the lady," Jade said to the guy. "I'll look around until I see something I want."

"What seems to be the problem?" a deep voice asked authoritatively.

The branch manager had heard the commotion.

The obese woman was happy to let him know. He listened to her patiently, apologized profusely and chastised Alvin, who meekly led the woman over to where the lower end phones were located. She smugly waddled behind him.

"Hello, I'm Orlando Williams, the manager of the store," he said to Jade, with his hand extended. Jade had been trying to decide which phone to purchase – the LG Prada or the iPhone.

"Nice to meet you," she replied, giving him a quick, firm handshake. She didn't offer her name. "I can't decide which of these phones I like more."

"Get them both!" he said laughing.

Jade smiled politely at his weak joke. The Prada was sleeker but she loved the design of the iPhone more.

The manager proceeded to tell Jade about the features of both phones. She didn't give a shit really. She just wanted a hot phone that had reliable internet service and a good camera.

"I'll just take the iPhone," Jade informed him. He was boring her to death and she was ready to go.

"Ok, good choice. So how long are you staying?" he asked as they walked over to the cashier.

"Excuse me?" Jade said, arching her elegant eyebrows.

He chuckled stupidly.

"You're obviously an American," he said. "So I was just wondering how long you would be in Jamaica."

"I see," Jade replied. She handed him the credit card wondering idly how much money was left on it. This purchase would push her total for the afternoon to over a hundred thousand.

He handed it to the cashier and instructed one of the sales representatives to fetch an iPhone from the storage area.

"You didn't answer me..." he continued, looking deeply into Jade's eyes. Jade's patience was wearing thin. Couldn't he take a hint?

"I know," Jade replied tartly. She then proceeded to ignore him by reading a promotional flyer that was on the counter. $1000 worth of free minutes with the purchase of a phone valued over $6000. The iPhone cost over 8 times that amount. The manager was saying something but Jade tuned him out. She was thinking that on Monday she needed to open a bank account. A US Currency savings account. The $450 that she had come to Jamaica with was and would remain untouched. She would use it to open the account.

The cashier cashed the item when it was brought to her and tried hard to suppress a grin. The manager thought he was god's gift to women and it pleased her to no end that the pretty woman wasn't giving him the time of day. Matter of fact she seemed positively annoyed.

"Thank you," Jade said chirpily to the cashier and collected her package and the card. She then signed up for the post-paid plan, paid a $5000 deposit and the phone was immediately activated. When she was through, she nodded curtly at the manager who was still standing there and exited the store. Eddie had been standing in front of the store smoking while he waited.

They went into the vehicle and headed out.

"You should charge it all night tonight before you use it," he advised.

Jade nodded.

"Ok, take me back to the hotel," she said. It was now close to 5 p.m. She wanted to go to the hotel and unwind for a bit before Weatherburn got there at 7.

ઉ৪ઉ৪ઉ৪

Dahlia gave the woman who was exiting the SUV next to her with several shopping bags a double take. She had just pulled up in the parking lot of the Mayberry hotel. She was taking her daughter, Samantha, to meet her two friends that she had been hanging with at the party. They were staying at the Mayberry for the duration of their eight day visit. It looked like the deported woman she had seen at the airport. But could it really be her looking that fly? Dahlia watched in disbelief as the woman shook her head at the driver of the vehicle, apparently telling him that she could manage with the bags. Dahlia climbed out of the vehicle, a red double cab Toyota Tundra that Dunga had bought for her. She was unable to take her eyes off Jade. It was definitely her. That kind of beauty was not commonplace. She opened the back door and Samantha hopped out.

ꙮꙮꙮ

Jade felt eyes on her and glanced over in the direction of the Toyota Tundra. It was the woman from the airport that had disrespected her. Jade could read the surprise, envy and jealousy in her eyes. Jade smiled. *Yeah, it's me bitch.*

"Hi," Jade said, stopping by her vehicle.

Dahlia was taken off guard. She hadn't expected Jade to stop and speak to her. She didn't respond.

"Prefer *these* bags?" Jade asked sweetly.

Dahlia sucked her teeth.

"Bitch I don't care about your fucking bags," Dahlia responded. She was getting pissed. Jade was getting under her skin.

Jade treated her to a disapproving look.

"Such language in front of the child," she commented.

Dahlia glowered at her. If it was back in the day she would've treated Jade to a nice beatdown and still would. But this was neither the time nor place.

"Was that your man in the Denali...cute," Jade said, pushing her buttons. She hadn't even seen him properly.

"Listen bitch, you're barking up the wrong fucking tree," Dahlia growled. This cunt was really trying to fuck with her. "You're messing with the wrong one. *Trust* me on that!"

Jade grinned. This was too easy.

"Don't worry," she said nonchalantly. "I'm not sure if I want him...yet."

She then walked away laughing.

Dahlia was so angry that her face was beet red. Her nostrils flared and her lips quivered. She was in war mode. She took several deep breaths to calm herself down. She was going to hurt that bitch. And hurt her badly. Fuck up that pretty face of hers. So she had made a nasty comment about her laundry bags at the airport. That didn't give her the right to see her on the street and provoke her to wrath. Implying that she could take her man if she felt like it. The gall of that bitch. She needed to find out which room she was staying in. Teach her a fucking lesson. She then made her way to the lobby. She didn't even notice that Samantha, who hated being around her mother when she was angry, was crying.

Chapter 14

The phone in Jade's suite rang just as she was about to go take a shower. She had been lying in bed naked, leafing through the latest issue of Cosmopolitan. It was Weatherburn.

"Hi Jade," he said.

"What's up Duane?" she replied.

"Getting ready to leave a meeting I had up by Stony Hill. Want to go out for dinner or eat in?"

Jade glanced at the time. It was 6:15. She hadn't realized so much time had elapsed since she got back to the hotel. She wasn't really hungry yet but would be in another hour or so.

"I'd rather stay in," she told him. "Bring Indian food."

"Ok, no problem," Weatherburn replied. "See you in a little while."

Jade hung up and did some sit-ups for fifteen minutes before taking a shower. She then lathered herself with Victoria

Secret body crème and selected a white, lace teddy to put on. White fishnet stockings which stopped at mid-thigh completed the sexy ensemble. Jade applied some make-up to her gorgeous face. Not much. A thin coat of foundation and a hint of blush. Some black around the eyes to give it that smoky effect. Nude Mac lip colour. She looked at herself in the mirror and smiled. *The stuff wet dreams are made of*. Weatherburn would probably go into cardiac arrest when he saw her.

"Hi, Dahlia," Katrina said, giving her a hug. Of the two women, she was the one Dahlia liked more. The other, Mabel, gave her a hug as well.

"Oh she's so cute!" Katrina exclaimed as she knelt down and gently pinched Samantha's cheeks. She had stopped crying.

"You look pissed," Mabel remarked. "Everything ok?"

Dahlia sighed.

"Nah, some bitch outside almost made me fuck her up," Dahlia replied.

Mabel grimaced. She hated when people used foul language in front of their kids. She put the television on the cartoon network and told Samantha to watch T.V. The three women then went out on the balcony to talk.

"So what happened?" Katrina asked.

Dahlia told them the story. Going back to when she initially saw Jade outside of the airport.

"Fucking bitch!" Katrina commiserated. "Who the hell does she think she is?"

Mabel nodded in agreement though she was wondering what all the fuss was about. Dahlia was wrong to have disrespected the woman in the first place. Actually, she kind of loved the way the woman got back at Dahlia. It was quite funny. But Dahlia was obviously pissed and Katrina was in ass-kissing mode so she kept her thoughts to herself.

"Look how many years Dunga and I have been together? This bitch really thinks she could be a threat? It takes more than a pretty face to take my man. I'm my own fucking competition...she better know that!" Dahlia bragged.

"That's right girl!" Katrina concurred, giving her a hi-five.

"She's out of order though...deserves a good ass whipping. I'm gonna try and find out which room she's staying in but if I don't, when I see her on the street its going to be on and poppin'."

Dahlia got up off of the chair and leaned against the rails. She looked down on Trafalgar road. The Saturday evening traffic was heavy. When she left here she was going to take Samantha to Devon House for ice cream. She wasn't sure what she was up to for the rest of the night though.

"I'm taking Samantha to get ice cream," Dahlia told them. "You guys wanna roll?"

"Sure," Katrina readily agreed. She loved hanging out with Dahlia. She was popular and fly and didn't take shit from anyone. Mabel agreed as well and they went back into the room. Samantha didn't want to leave the show she was watching on Nickelodeon but she didn't protest too much. She loved ice cream.

ଓଃଓଃଓଃ

"Oh my fucking god..." Weatherburn murmured quietly when he laid eyes on Jade. She was standing by the door waiting for him to come in. The bag with the containers of food almost fell from his hands. She merely smiled and waited for him to compose himself.

"You look absolutely ravishing," he croaked, as he entered the room.

"Thank you," Jade replied. She locked the door and took the bag from him.

His breathing was uneven as he watched her go over to the small refrigerator and placed the bag on top of it.

She looked at him steadily as she walked back over to where he was sitting on the edge of the bed.

"I'm not very hungry now...I think I'll eat later," she said to him.

Weatherburn loosened two more buttons on his pink polo shirt. The plan was to have eaten and relaxed for awhile before he made his move. Talk and watch some T.V. Let the momentum build up gradually. He didn't think his heart could take it any other way. But the look in Jade's pretty brown eyes told him that his nirvana was now. The damn near painful pent up lust and desire would be released now. His heart beat galloped. His seven inch erection throbbed. Jade stopped directly in front of him. She placed a solitary finger under his chin and moved it upwards. Weatherburn stood up unsteadily.

"Take off your clothes," Jade instructed softly.

Weatherburn wasn't used to women telling him what to do but to his amazement it turned him on. His dick had gotten even harder. It was as though all the blood in his body had flowed directly to his genitals. He looked at Jade as he stripped. She had her hands on her curvy hips. She had a stern yet sensual expression on her face. He undressed quickly and left his clothes in a pile on the floor. Jade's expression was stoic as she looked his naked body up and down. Inwardly she was pleased. He certainly wasn't repulsive. Dick was a decent size and it was as hard as a rock. Body was ok for a man his age.

"Undress me," Jade purred.

A bit of pre-cum seeped out of his dick. He cursed inwardly. He hoped Jade hadn't noticed.

He inched closer and slowly removed her teddy. He gasped audibly when it slid to her feet. She stepped out of it and stood there in all her glory. Her toned legs were slightly agape. Heaven beckoned between her curvy thighs. Weatherburn groaned as their lips met. Their tongues danced and his erection bore into Jade's flat stomach as he held her tightly, running his hands all over her back and buttocks. He squeezed her ass cheeks, marveling at their shape and firmness.

"Oh Jade...I envisioned this very moment from the first time I laid eyes on you," Weatherburn breathed as Jade nibbled on his bottom lip tantalizingly. "Lips are so soft...mmmm."

Jade broke the kiss slowly. She smiled and walked around him to lie on the bed.

She propped her head up on two fluffy pillows and raised her knees. Weatherburn moaned when she slowly spread her legs. The sight of her plump, clean- shaven, almost virginal pussy on wanton display made him feel like he was floating when he climbed onto the bed.

Moaning continuously, he hovered over Jade and took her right nipple in his mouth. He felt it harden as he sucked it gently. He moved to the next, caressing, licking and sucking them alternately. He heard her gasp when he created a wet trail from her breasts to her stomach. He took his time, as he kissed and nibbled his way to the promise land.

He elicited the first audible groan from Jade when his lips caressed the inside of her thighs. His breath was hot on her throbbing pussy as he teased and licked around it languidly.

"Fuck...damn..." Jade groaned as she thrust her pelvis upwards. She was surprised at his patience. She knew he wanted to fuck her in the worst way. Yet here he was treating her to some scintillating foreplay. He was showing his class. She could dig it.

Weatherburn placed his hands under her ass and finally tasted her essence.

"Oh god!" Jade exclaimed when his lips finally claimed her labia. He ran his lips and tongue all over her folds and she jerked involuntarily when he slid his tongue deep inside her wetness. "Jesus H. Christ. That. Feels. So. Fucking. Good."

She got wetter and wetter as he tongued her as though his life depended on it. She writhed and squirmed under his oral attention, holding his head in place as she fucked his face.

"I'm going to come all over your face Duane...don't stop...I feel it coming..."

Weatherburn doubled his efforts and the loud slurping noises he was making pushed Jade over the edge. She came hard. She squealed through gritted teeth as she wrapped her legs tightly around his back and squirted her pent up juices all over his face and into his mouth. In the midst of her orgasm he latched on to her engorged clit and he swore Jade was going to choke him to death. She was holding his head so tightly against her pussy that he could hardly breathe. One orgasm morphed into the next and Jade screamed at the top of her lungs as her body shook uncontrollably.

Weatherburn took a deep breath when Jade finally allowed him to raise his head. He then got up and fished a condom from out of his pants pocket. Jade watched him roll the condom on as she tried to catch her breath. That was fucking amazing. And it was only the appetizer. He climbed back onto the bed. It was time for the main course. She watched as he positioned himself between her legs. Four years. That was a long time not to be penetrated. He placed his dick at the entrance of her still dripping orifice and slid it in gently. He was met with some resistance despite her wetness.

"Ohh....ohh...go easy...oh shit..." Jade moaned, her face contorted in an intricate blend of pain and ecstasy. "It hurts so good...oh fuck..."

Weatherburn groaned loudly as he continued to gently slide his dick inside Jade. He pushed it all the way in and then was motionless for several seconds. It was the tightest, most succulent pussy he had ever been inside of. And he was a very experienced man. He looked in her pretty eyes as he started to move. He pulled out all the way to the edge and slowly pushed it back in to the hilt.

Her pussy grabbed and tugged his dick with each movement.

"So fucking tight...and fleshy...mmmm...." Weatherburn moaned as he tried valiantly to delay his climax. He could feel his orgasm building up.

"Oh yeah...fuck me!" Jade urged as he increased his tempo. It was no longer painful. Pleasure had taken center stage. She was ready to be fucked royally. It had been too long. "Give it to me Duane! Fuck this pussy like you want it!"

"Oh god Jade... you're going to make me come Jade...bloodclaat Jade...I can't hold it back Jade...Jade...Jade...ahhhhh."

Weatherburn's movements were a blur as he thrust in and out of Jade rapidly, filling the latex condom with his hot seed. He shivered inside out like he had rheumatic fever.

He looked in Jade's eyes. It was like looking in a mirror. All he could see was a reflection of his own admiration, lust and desire. He was hooked. And he knew that he was in trouble.

Chapter 15

Dunga was sitting in the lounge area of the studio smoking weed and drinking Hennessy mixed with cranberry when his cell phone rang. It was Dahlia. Jimmy, the French Rastafarian singer, his girlfriend - a waif thin model who consumed copious amounts of weed and alcohol at an alarming rate, and the singer's manager, were also present. Dunga excused himself and took the call in his private office.

"What's up baby?" he asked as he perched on the edge of his desk. He was feeling mellow. Jimmy had sourced them some good weed and the meeting with the singer had gone well. After listening to some of Dunga's as yet unreleased beats and looking at his catalogue showcasing his past work, the singer wanted him to produce six tracks on his forth-coming album. It was a good coup for Dunga as the singer was one of Europe's rising musical stars. He would make a lot of money from this project and he was also confident that they would make really good music together. That was as important to him as any financial benefit.

"Nothing much...I'm at Devon House chilling with Sam. Got her some ice cream. We're out on the lawn relaxing. Two of my friends you met last night are here as well."

"Ok, cool. I'm here at the studio kicking it with an overseas client," Dunga told her. He took a sip from his drink.

"I saw that girl today," Dahlia said, suddenly getting annoyed. Anytime that bitch crossed her mind she got angry all over again.

"What girl?" Dunga asked.

"The bitch at the airport that Jimmy was hitting on," she replied. She went on to tell him what had transpired in the parking lot at the hotel.

"Dunga? Are you hearing me?" Dahlia asked after a pregnant pause and Dunga hadn't commented on what she just told him.

"Huh? Yeah...yeah I'm listening," he said, snapping out of the trance that hearing about the mystery woman had put him in. He hadn't thought of her all day but now she was back to take up residence in his head with full force. He couldn't believe that she and Dahlia almost had an altercation. Beautiful, sexy and feisty. He didn't know what to make of her comment to Dahlia about him. He didn't even recall her looking over at him when he had sent Jimmy to approach her. "Just be cool and don't be out there getting into fights and shit like that. You know I'm yours baby."

Dahlia smiled at that but she still felt the bitch needed to be taught a lesson.

"I know honey but I can't have these females out here disrespecting me...you know."

Dunga chuckled.

"Ok babe...just be cool."

They chatted for a while longer and then Dunga ended the call and returned to the lounge. The men were in a heated conversation about who was the best soccer player in the world. The singer's model girlfriend wasn't taking part in the discussion. She was as high as a kite. Her blue eyes were low and vacant. She was cool and all but if she was his woman there was no way he would allow her to get that high. He refilled his glass with ice, poured some more Hennessy and cranberry, and joined the conversation.

ଓଃଓଃଓଃ

Jade was enjoying Weatherburn's company. He was witty, smart and had a great sense of humour. Also the sex had been great, though she wished he had lasted a little longer in the saddle. It would have been nice to have climaxed from penetration as well. Nonetheless, he had given a good account of himself. Her four year drought had been ended in fine style. They were now eating the Indian food he had bought: tandoori chicken, shrimp pakora and lamb pasanda. The food was exquisite. Jade had buzzed Ross, the bell hop, to get them a bottle of white wine. It went well with their dinner. She told him of her plans to open a bank account. He told her that she needed to get her identification straightened out first. She needed a TRN which was similar to the social security number she had in the U.S. and she needed a driver's license and a new passport. He told her that he would get all of that sorted out for her in short order. More and more Jade was realizing how fortunate she was to have met a man of

Weatherburn's caliber right off the bat. He was proving useful in a variety of ways. She was a little concerned at the rate at which he seemed to be falling for her though. He was absolutely smitten. He was like putty in her hands. When the time came for her to move on - and that was inevitable - he would be devastated. But that would be his problem. The last time she had put somebody else's well-being before hers it cost her four years of her life.

Chapter 16

Weatherburn retired to the study after having breakfast with his wife. He had gotten up a couple hours later than he usually did on a Sunday morning. The second round with Jade had worn him out. After polishing off dinner and the bottle of wine, he had fucked Jade doggystyle on one of the chairs in the suite. This time he had lasted long enough for her to climax from penetration. Her orgasm had been so intense that he had climaxed immediately. Weatherburn sighed as he sat behind his cluttered but organized desk. If there was a woman out there with a pussy sweeter than Jade's, he hoped to God he never got to meet her. It was difficult to articulate the sensations that coursed through every inch of his body when he was inside that beautiful woman. It had been one of the most enjoyable evenings of his life. He hadn't felt this virile and sexy in at least twenty years. He was positive that fate had brought Jade into his life and he would do whatever it takes to keep her there.

He looked at the receipts for all the purchases made using the credit card he had given to Jade. He had collected all of them from her last night. The card was five thousand dollars away from being maxed out. Two hundred and forty-five thousand dollars had been spent on Jade in two days. He wrote a cheque for that amount. His personal bearer would pay it at the bank tomorrow morning. A tidy sum but Jade was worth every penny. And he could afford it. The economy was tight of late but he would be ok. His net worth could more than withstand the global recession and a high maintenance mistress. He retrieved his large, worn leather encased phone book and looked up the home number of one of his associates. He needed to find Jade an apartment.

Jade buzzed Ross after she had gotten up and taken a shower. She sent him to get her some breakfast. Weatherburn had left her ten thousand dollars cash so that she wouldn't have to rely solely on the credit card whenever she needed something. The ackee and saltfish with fried dumplings was delicious. Jade thoroughly enjoyed her meal. After breakfast, she retrieved her iPhone from off the dresser where it had been charging all night. She spent the next hour setting up an email address, putting in the few contacts she had in the address book, and familiarizing herself with all the features. When she was through, she turned the T.V. on and browsed through the channels. An advertisement for *Wanted*, the new action flick with Angelina Jolie, caught her eye.

Damn! That looks good, she mused inwardly. And she hadn't been to the movies in ages. She decided to give Theresa a call to see if she would like for them to go together. Theresa was pleasantly surprised to hear from Jade.

"Sure, I'd love to!" Theresa said enthusiastically. Though the salon was closed on Sundays, she had popped in for a couple hours to deal with one of her loyal customers who had to go Canada urgently because of a family emergency. "Do we meet there or you'd like for me to pick you up?"

"You can pick me up," Jade replied. "I'm staying at the Mayberry Hotel in New Kingston. Suite 69."

"I'll call ahead to reserve the tickets," Theresa told her. The movies were always packed on a Sunday night and sometimes, depending on the movie, tickets got sold out very quickly. "Pick you up at eight?"

"Ok, see you later."

Jade was pleased that Theresa would be able to go with her. She just felt like having a girls' night out and Theresa was the only female she knew in Jamaica so far. She suddenly thought of Maxine. She definitely was going to swing by that hotel in the near future. She could just imagine the shock on Maxine's face when she sauntered into her gift shop looking like she just stepped out of the pages of Vogue magazine. Jade chuckled as she got up and stretched. It was time for her exercise routine.

❧❧❧

Dunga was at home lounging. Sunday was his chill day to relax with his daughter and laze around the house. And he was doing just that. Samantha was lying on the carpet by his feet reading a children's book he had bought for her recently while he was sitting in his favourite chair reading the newspaper. Dahlia was in the kitchen preparing dinner. Sunday was the only day she didn't mind cooking; any other day she would have ordered take-out. Dunga got to the entertainment section and noticed that *Wanted* was opening. He was a huge Angelina Jolie fan and an action movie buff. He was usually very busy on week days so if he didn't go today he would most likely end up seeing it on DVD and he didn't want that.

"Want to go check out a movie later babes?" he asked.

"Which one?" Dahlia responded as she placed the chicken in the oven. She was preparing baked chicken, fried plantain, yam salad and rice and peas.

"It's a good action flick...you'll enjoy it," Dunga told her as he reached for the phone to order tickets for two box seats. He couldn't sit anywhere else. He wouldn't feel comfortable.

"Ok babe," Dahlia said agreeably. It didn't really matter to her one way or another. She knew she would have a good time as long as she was with him.

"We're leaving at eight," Dunga advised her when he got off the phone.

Dahlia didn't respond. She was a trying to figure out what was wrong with the gravy. She tasted it again. Something was missing.

❦❦❦

"How much longer yuh expect fi live like this?" Joyce Sewell asked her daughter between mouthfuls of white rice and curried chicken. They were seated at the small dinner table having Sunday dinner. "Yuh nuh tired fi see yuh mother ah suffer? Eh?"

Secret sighed as she looked out of the dining room window at the soccer game the young men in the community were playing on the open lot adjacent to their modest two bedroom house. Her mother was being especially bitchy because she had been unable to contribute to the purchasing of groceries and other household necessities for the past three weeks. She really hated when she was flat broke. It pained her to not be able to contribute to the household expenses and to make it worse, her mother always used the opportunity to make her feel bad for following her heart and choosing a career in music. Secret couldn't wait until the money started pouring in. Her mother would be singing a different tune then. It saddened her that her mother didn't support her dream. She had been a good daughter. Her mother never had any problems with her staying out late or bringing boys to the house. She had been a good student in high school; her report card always sported mostly As. She had passed all seven of her O' levels with four distinctions. Was it so terrible that she didn't want to waste the talent that God had blessed her with? Yes, the early going was tough and the male-dominated music business was no picnic for a young, attractive woman, but nothing good in life came easy and she was positive that at the end of the day, it would be all worth it. Still not answering her mother, Secret took a sip of her fruit punch. She hoped a gig manifested itself soon though, she badly needed some cash. She didn't even have taxi fare to get to the studio to meet with Dunga on Tuesday. If Orane was busy and couldn't take her she didn't know how she was going to get there. A loud noise erupted on the soccer field. The team playing without shirts had apparently scored a goal that was being disputed by the other team.

“Everything will be ok soon, mom,” Secret finally said. “I just met with a very influential producer and he’s going to take me on. Just be a little patient, ok?”

Her mother sucked her teeth in disgust and launched into another tirade.

Secret tuned her out. Arguing with her mom was useless. She hurriedly ate the remainder of her dinner so that she could retire to her room and do some writing.

Chapter 17

"Wow! You look so hot!" Theresa exclaimed when Jade came to meet her in the lobby.

"Thanks," Jade said smiling as they gave each other a light hug. Theresa was so cool. Not a hint of jealousy or any underlying sexual connotation in her compliment.

People stared at the two attractive women as they exited the lobby. They went out to the parking lot and hopped into Theresa's fire-engine red convertible BMW.

"I love your car, it's sexy," Jade said. She was a SUV girl herself. When she really settled in and accumulated some real money, she planned to purchase either a BMW X5 or a Mercedes ML350.

"Thanks," Theresa replied as she joined the traffic streaming down Knutsford Boulevard. "I bought it two years ago. My dream car."

"Well that's always a good thing...being able to fulfill your dreams," Jade told her.

"Yeah, the first major one was owning my own business and that became a reality ten years ago. The only one left is to find a nice sperm donor and have a pretty little daughter," Theresa said.

Jade laughed heartily at that, ignoring the two guys drooling in a black Ford F150 in the adjacent lane.

"A sperm donor huh?"

"Yeah girl...good men are hard to find these days. I turned thirty two months ago. My biological clock is ticking and I do want a child."

"Well don't give up...who knows...you might find one when you least expect it," Jade opined. She had no such notions herself. At least not right now. She couldn't see herself giving what's left of her heart to another man and though she loved other people's kids, she wasn't sure if she wanted any of her own.

"Hmmm...I won't hold my breath," Theresa responded.

Sounds like you've had your fair share of bastards, Jade thought.

They had arrived at the cinema. They joined the long line of traffic heading into the larger of the two parking lots. The other one was already filled. After ten minutes they finally got a parking spot. The two women exited the car and quickly made their way to the entrance. Theresa had been right. Based on the crowd the movie would be definitely sold out. They went in the reserved tickets line and Theresa paid for their tickets.

"Popcorn and juice?" Jade asked as they approached the concession stands.

"Nah, I want a hot dog," Theresa replied. They joined a line and chatted like old friends until they got through. They entered the auditorium just as the movie was about to start. A tall, rail-thin usher with her hair in a tight bun escorted them to the box area and showed them their seats. They had gotten the two seats closest to the right aisle. Everyone else in that section was already seated.

ૡૡૡ

Dunga glanced at the two women that were coming to sit next to him. His heart skipped from left to right when he really looked at the taller of the two. It was the mystery woman. Though the lights had been dimmed, he recognized her gorgeous face as she was practically next to him. She had taken the end seat and her companion was seated right beside him. *How the hell was he supposed to concentrate on the movie now?* At least Dahlia hadn't seen her. Yet.

Chapter 18

Weatherburn frowned as he hung up the phone. That was his third call to the hotel trying to reach Jade. Apparently she wasn't there. Or was she there with someone and didn't want to pick up? He chided himself for that thought. He doubted that was the case, and even if it was, he couldn't really say anything about it now could he? After all, he had agreed to her terms. He had to admit though that the thought of Jade being with somebody else made him sick. He had it bad. Jade had engulfed his senses and permeated his soul. He knew he had to keep his emotions in check. Anything less would drive Jade away and he couldn't have that. He exited the bathroom and made his way back out to the hall. He was at a fundraising banquet for the Jamaica Diabetes Society. He rejoined his wife at their table. Also present at the table was his good friend and colleague, Gavin Lawrence, Minister of Health, and his wife. Jessica Weatherburn looked at her husband. He seemed preoccupied. Anxious even. She wondered what was on his mind. He gave her a tight smile then turned his attention to the stage where the Diablo Dance Troupe was putting on an impressive performance.

ᏋᏋᏋ

Secret was excited as she read over the lyrics to the song she just wrote. After dinner, she did the dishes and locked herself inside her room. She had immediately put pen to paper, and without giving it any thought, had penned what she was convinced would be her first hit. It was a love song which told the story of a young, inexperienced woman falling for an older man. Though the topic wasn't breaking any new ground, the lyrics were fresh, deep and passionate. She didn't want a typical 'one drop' rhythm for the song. She envisioned a jazzy kind of neo-soul beat for the track. Dunga would have to create a tailor-made beat. She was positive he would share her vision. After all, he was the inspiration. She would name it *Lust.*

ᏋᏋᏋ

Jade was enjoying the movie immensely. Amazing and unbelievable stunts elicited constant 'oohs' and 'aahs' from the captivated audience. Dunga was enjoying it too, but Jade's nearness was intoxicating. And frustrating. He knew nothing about this woman except that she was the most arrestingly beautiful woman he had ever seen. And given the fact that when he saw her she most likely was far from looking her best; that was saying a lot. She was laughing at something. She had a sexy laugh. He even liked the way she ate her popcorn. He had been stealing glances at her ever since she sat down. He was sure her friend had noticed. Dahlia hadn't. She was all snuggled up with her head resting on his chest. Dunga sighed. He knew it was ridiculous the effect this woman was having on him. He was Jamaica's top producer for Christ's sakes. He was tall and handsome. He had been with many beautiful women. Even had a couple celebrities. So why was he bugging out over this woman? He didn't like it. He didn't understand it. But apparently there was nothing he could do about it.

Chapter 19

"Shit!" Jade muttered. It was time for intermission. For as long as she could remember it always annoyed her. She thought it was so unnecessary. On cue, many people got up and quickly made their way out of the auditorium to get food or to make a quick trip to the restroom. The lights came on and the soothing sounds of a roots reggae track Jade didn't know filtered softly through the speakers.

"I'm going to the bathroom babes," Dahlia said. The large soda she had polished off was clamouring to exit her body. She took up her cute Louis Vuitton pocketbook and walked off.

Here we go, Dunga mused. He hoped Dahlia didn't create a scene when she saw the woman.

"Excuse me," Dahlia said to Theresa, who was in the middle of a conversation with Jade. She was telling her about a funny incident that occurred at the salon recently. They both looked up. Dahlia froze when her eyes met Jade's. A look of pure hatred immediately spread across her oval face. Jade looked at her coolly.

"Are you going to pass?" Theresa asked in an annoyed tone. She had adjusted her legs to enable the woman to pass.

Dahlia treated her to a withering glance before passing by the two of them as aggressively as she could.

"What the fuck is her problem?" Theresa asked. "You know her?"

Jade smiled devilishly.

"It's a long story," she replied, as she wondered if the girl was here with her man. Jade bent forward slightly and looked down the row of seats. She didn't have far to look. *He had been sitting beside Theresa all this time*! He was looking at her with an indescribable expression on his face. Jade couldn't help but to crack a smile. What were the odds? He couldn't help but to smile back. Jade leaned back in her seat without speaking to him. Theresa had noticed the byplay.

"I want to hear that 'long story' at your earliest convenience," she whispered to Jade.

Jade merely chuckled. The guy was hot. He had beautiful skin. Dark and smooth. White, even teeth. He was actually quite handsome. She would get around to giving him a call one of these days. However long she took, she knew he'd be interested.

Dahlia fumed as she touched up her make-up in the bathroom. Seeing that fucking bitch had totally ruined the night for her. She just couldn't wait for the opportunity to slap that smug, I-think-I'm-the-shit look off the bitch's face. She sucked her teeth in annoyance and made her way back to the auditorium. The movie would be back on any minute now.

ଔ

"That was really great," Jade commented an hour later when the movie ended. She and Theresa were gathering their things to leave. Jade stole a glance at the guy and his girlfriend. She scowled at Jade before turning away to leave through the other side. Exiting through that side was a longer walk but anything to avoid Jade.

"Yeah," Theresa agreed as they joined the throng of people streaming out toward the exits.

"So what are we up to now?" Jade asked, ignoring the many looks most of the men and even some of the women were throwing her way. The night was young and she wasn't ready to go back to the hotel.

Theresa was about to respond when a short Caucasian man walking with a group of people stopped Jade.

"Hello, how are you? I'm Phillip Hassan," he said, extending his chubby hand. Jade shook it as she looked at him quizzically. What the hell did this short Jewish man want with her?

"I recently brought my business to Jamaica and I'm searching for the right face to promote my product. I have a few meetings tomorrow with the top two modeling agencies in Jamaica to look at their girls but when I saw you I figured my search was over before it even started," he said with a wide grin.

"I'm flattered but what is your product?" Jade asked.

"It's called La Roseda, the world's first pink cognac. A drink geared towards sophisticated, beautiful women. It is doing very well in Europe and because of other Jamaican interests that I have here, I decided to introduce it in Jamaica," he explained proudly.

Jade had never heard of it but she would check it out online later.

"Sounds interesting," Jade replied. "Give me your contact info and I'll get in touch with you by Tuesday."

"Ok, please ensure you call me. This is a serious proposition that you will benefit from greatly in many ways if we come to an agreement."

Jade nodded nonchalantly as she accepted his business card.

"Have a good night," he said with a little bow before departing with his friends.

"Wow, just like that huh?" Theresa said, impressed.

Jade shrugged as she placed the card in her pocketbook.

"It could be nothing," she said as they resumed the trek to the parking lot. "I'll check out his company online later."

They got to the car and Theresa deactivated the alarm and they hopped in. She then pressed a button and the top disappeared in exactly thirty seconds.

"We can go to The Patio for drinks," Theresa suggested as they joined the long line of vehicles exiting the parking lot. The Patio was one of Kingston's popular hang-out spots among the money crowd. The drinks and food there were notoriously expensive.

"Sure," Jade replied. She was fine with wherever Theresa suggested as she wasn't yet familiar with the hot spots in and around Kingston. Theresa toyed with the remote control for the CD player and the sounds of Lil' Wayne's new album assaulted their eardrums. Theresa loved to play her music loud. Jade was the same way. She was happy that she and Theresa had hit it off. It was cool to have a girlfriend that she could vibe with from time to time.

ଓଡ଼ଓଡ଼ଓଡ଼

Dunga sucked his teeth in annoyance. Dahlia kept talking about how much she hated the woman and it was grating on his nerves. She was the last person he wanted to think of or hear about.

"Alright Dahlia," Dunga said. "Enough about that shit."

Dahlia shot him a dirty look but stopped talking. She had been with Dunga long enough to know that when he used that tone it was not wise to push it. She seethed in silence for the rest of the way home. He pulled up outside of the apartment and waited for her to get out. Realizing that he was going back on the road, she exited the vehicle and slammed the door shut much to Dunga's annoyance. He held his temper in check and drove off, resisting the urge to go in after her. He knew she was spoiling for a fight. That was Dahlia's style. Pick a fight and then have crazy make-up sex after her anger had been quelled. Dunga wasn't in the mood for that shit. Feeling unsettled and irritated, he called Jimmy and told him to meet him at the studio.

ଓଡ଼ଓଡ଼ଓଡ଼

The Patio was jam-packed when they got there. There was a good mixture of young adults and the older, mature set. Jade liked the set-up. There were three large bars, lots of waiters and waitresses milling around taking orders and there were adequate tables and chairs in the large, courtyard-style venue. Two large screens silently showed music videos while a disc jockey played different genres of music at a moderate level.

"This used to be a parking lot," Theresa told Jade as they waited for the waitress to return with the drinks they had ordered. "A businessman who owns a popular night club on Knutsford Boulevard bought the property a year ago and transformed it into this: Kingston's trendiest outdoor bar and lounge."

Jade nodded as she looked around. They were standing in a corner by a large palm tree – there were several of them dotting the venue. She noticed a tall, rough-looking young man staring at her intently. He was standing at a table a few meters away, flanked by several equally rough-looking men. There were two scantily clad women in the group as well. There were several buckets of champagne on the table as well as two bottles of Hennessy.

"Who is that guy?" Jade asked Theresa. "The one wearing the white blazer who keeps staring over here."

"Oh, that's Timex," Theresa snorted. "One of the most popular dancehall artists...I can't stand him. He's talented but all he sings about is guns and violence."

The waitress had returned with their drinks. Theresa told her they would keep a tab and pay when they were leaving. Jade sipped her apple martini and watched as Timex whispered something to one of the guys standing next to him.

"He's scary looking," Jade commented. His eyes were his best facial feature. They were large and framed by long, almost feminine lashes. There was a scar on his right jaw and his huge mouth was housing platinum fronts which glistened every time he opened his mouth. His hair, which was in large, untidy plaits, added to his menacing look.

"Timex seh him ah call yuh," the guy said to Jade without preamble. Jade frowned as his breath assaulted her nostrils. The smell of marijuana was so strong and overpowering she felt as though she could get high just by him standing there.

"What?" she snapped.

His eyes narrowed at her response. He pointed over to where Timex was standing.

"The man in the full white want to 'ave a word wid yuh," he growled, adding, "him ah de biggest artist inna Jamaica right now."

Jade was amused.

"Is that so? And why do you think that would matter to me? Do I look like a fucking groupie?"

The guy was taken aback by her response. *Dah yankee gal yah feisty nuh bloodclaat!* He thought inwardly.

"So yuh nah go ova deh?" the guy persisted.

"Are you daft?" Jade queried.

She then proceeded to ignore him until he walked off scowling.

ଔଓଔଓଔଓ

Timex was not amused that the woman had not come over to him. Based on what Breeda had told him she was an American. And feisty as hell. She was also the prettiest woman he had seen in a very long time. He wanted her. A woman like that would look good on his resume. He popped in a stick of gum, gestured for one of his friends to refill his glass with champagne, and sauntered over towards her.

ↂↂↂ

Jade groaned when she saw him approaching. ***Jesus*** *Christ! Why can't these assholes just leave me alone?*

ↂↂↂ

"Yes! Yes! Woi!" Secret heard her mother screaming from the bedroom. Apparently Jeffery, her mother's new boyfriend had come by to visit. She had been penned up in her room working on her music and hadn't heard him come in. He was a truck driver for a beverage company and Secret had hated him on sight. She hadn't liked the way his beady eyes had roamed all over her body when her mother had introduced them a month ago. Her mother had finally ditched Rohan, a tall, surly construction worker who used to beat her. Secret didn't like her mother's choice in men or how often she changed them but it was none of her business. Her mother wouldn't take too kindly to her daughter giving her advice on her love life. Her mother, a raving beauty in her younger days, was still an attractive and shapely woman at forty-eight. And she loved her sex, giving credence to the popular Jamaican saying that women of Indian heritage had white liver. The bed groaned loudly from their exertions. Embarrassed and disgusted, Secret put on her headphones and listened to a mix CD that Orane had given her a few weeks ago. She turned up the volume until the only thing she could hear were the soothing sounds of new R&B sensation Jasmine Sullivan.

ଔ଼ଔ଼ଔ଼

Weatherburn glanced at his watch irritably. It was now 11:30 p.m. and he still couldn't reach Jade at the hotel. Where the fuck had she gone? He was now at home in his study. His wife had retired to bed and based on the red, sheer night-gown she was wearing, she wanted some tonight. He wasn't up for it. He was extremely annoyed that he couldn't get through to Jade. All kind of thoughts were swirling around in his head. He poured himself a strong shot of Brandy. He downed it one gulp and dialed the hotel number yet again.

ଔ଼ଔ଼ଔ଼

"Goodnight," Timex said to both Jade and Theresa when he came over.

"Hi," Jade responded, trying not to cringe. He was even more fearsome looking up close.

"Mi like yuh yeah...yuh ah definitely my kind ah girl...pretty and sexy," he drawled, taking a toke of the huge marijuana joint he was smoking.

Jade emitted a mirthless chuckle.

"Thanks but no thanks...you're not my type," Jade told him matter-of-factly.

He looked at her for a few moments before responding. *Dis likkle yankee uptown bitch t'ink seh dat she better than mi.*

"I hear yuh," he finally said. "T'ink it over...mi wi see yuh again and nex' time yuh better ready fi give mi a different argument."

"That's not going to happen," Jade responded firmly. "Have a nice night and all the best with your career."

He scowled at Jade for a few seconds before shaking his head and walking off abruptly.

Theresa started laughing.

"Poor Jade," she teased.

Jade smiled.

"I'm going to have to hire a bodyguard it seems," she quipped.

The DJ switched to nineties R&B and Jade really started to groove; rocking to the infectious beat of Toni Braxton's *You're Making Me High*. She spotted the Jewish guy who had approached her outside of the cinema and raised her glass to him in greeting. He waved enthusiastically but did not come over, much to Jade's delight. An hour and a half and three martinis later, Jade and Theresa made their way to the parking lot. They never noticed the man trailing them until it was too late.

Chapter 20

"Hey gal!" a voice growled menacingly behind Jade. They had just reached the car and she was standing by the passenger door while Theresa fished for her keys in her pocketbook.

Startled, Jade turned around. It was the man that had threatened her at the restaurant yesterday while she was having lunch with Eddie. He was brandishing a knife and he reeked of alcohol.

"So what yuh have to say now, eh gal?" he taunted. "Run off yuh mouth now nuh an' see if mi nuh cut yuh inna yuh bloodclaat pretty face."

Jade kept her eyes on the knife but didn't respond. Theresa was frozen in fright.

Three powerful motor bikes and a large tinted SUV came to a stop right in front of Theresa's car. The doors to the luxury vehicle, a black Range Rover, flew open and three men came over and grabbed the would-be assailant.

"Yo, just relax," he said, his eyes bulging in fear when he saw Timex alight from the vehicle slowly. "Is a personal argument mi an' mi woman ah 'ave."

The men held him while Timex paused to relight his spliff. He took a hard toke before walking over to the man.

He administered three vicious back-handed slaps to the man's face and placed the burning tip of the marijuana joint on the man's right cheek.

The man screamed in terror.

"Him never get fi hurt yuh?" Timex asked Jade.

"No," she responded. "Thank you."

He brushed aside her thanks.

"Mi just wah fi know seh yuh alright," he said. "Gwaan home...we will tek care ah dis."

Theresa didn't need to be told twice. She jumped in and started the engine. Jade opened her door and nodded her thanks to Timex once more. She then hopped in and closed the door. The tires squealed as Theresa quickly exited the parking lot. Her heart was pounding so loudly she didn't even hear when Jade told her to slow down.

❧❧❧

Timex looked at the trembling man. He relit his spliff.

"Mi never know seh ah your girl Timex...jah know star...yuh know seh mi woulda never violate like that," the man pleaded. Everyone knew that Timex was not a man to get entangled with. He hailed from Rockfort and used to be a shotta before he made it big in music. He never left his roots behind and always travelled with known gunmen wherever he went. He had gotten in trouble with the law on numerous occasions and was even refused visas by several countries. He had his detractors but for the most part he was adored by his ever growing legions of fans.

"Yuh lucky enuh bwoy...cause if yuh did ever lay a finger pon har..." he trailed off leaving the man to imagine the worst.

Timex then turned and went back inside his Range Rover. One of his men treated the man to a departing punch to the stomach and they left the scene. Timex thought about the woman as they headed towards one of his favourite hangout spots in the Rockfort community. He really liked her. She was feisty and gorgeous. And she wasn't in the least impressed by who he was. That was a first for him. He had been with women from uptown before – most notably the daughter of a prominent businessman – and they had always been impressed by his celebrity and gangster image. He wondered if she would soften her stance now that he had been her knight in shining armour.

Theresa finally calmed down after a few minutes. She had been really shaken up by the incident. She would have freaked out if the man had actually stabbed or cut Jade.

"It's ok Theresa," Jade told her as they waited for the light to turn green at the intersection of Trafalgar Road and Knutsford Boulevard. "I have a black belt in karate. I would have disarmed him before he could have done either of us any harm."

"Really?" Theresa said, impressed. "That's good to know...I was so scared."

"Yeah so next time you're not to panic," Jade told her with a grin.

Theresa laughed and by the time she dropped Jade off at the hotel she was fine. Jade hugged her bye and promised to call soon. She smiled to herself as she made her way to the suite. She hadn't been scared when she saw the man, it wasn't the first time someone had pulled a weapon on her and though she had exaggerated about her karate skills - she only had a brown belt - she was confident she would have been able to fuck him up. She wondered if Timex was now hoping that she would view him in a different light because he had helped her. That wasn't going to happen. Not by a long shot. The only thing he had gained was her respect. She would always be cordial to him whenever she ran into him but that was it. She retrieved her key from her pocketbook and went inside the suite. She immediately stripped off her clothes and climbed into bed naked. She fell asleep almost as soon her head hit the fluffy pillow.

***

Dunga was pleased that he had decided to go to the studio. The past four hours had been very productive. He had finished up the mixing for the two tracks that had been laid last week and he had started to build a rhythm from scratch that was sounding exquisite. It was far from a typical dancehall beat, it had a very soulful, jazzy sound. It was now 3 a.m. and he was far from tired. Jimmy was there with him as well as the handyman who stayed in a small back room on the premises.

Tupac, Dunga's pitbull, was also there. Dunga kept him at the studio instead of at home.

"I'm really feeling this track," Dunga commented to Jimmy as they listened to his latest creation.

"Yeah man, it wicked...different...sound like something you would hear Jill Scott singing on," Jimmy responded knowledgeably.

"Exactly!" Dunga said excitedly. "I'm going to play it for Secret when she comes in on Tuesday and tell her to write something to it. Trust me...I just know this one is going to be something special."

Jimmy nodded in agreement as he answered a text message on his mobile. His on and off girlfriend, Sonia, wanted to know if he was going to come by. He told her yes but not right now. It had been a couple weeks since he last visited her. They had a huge argument over the fact that Jimmy rarely came by except when he wanted sex. So he had stayed away and given her some time to cool off.

They didn't leave the studio until 5 a.m. that morning.

Weatherburn called the hotel immediately after his 10 a.m. meeting. He tapped his feet on the carpeted floor in his office as he waited impatiently for the receptionist to put the call through to Jade's suite. A groggy Jade answered after several rings.

"Good morning Jade," he said tersely. "I've been trying to reach you since last night without success. Where have you been?"

"Excuse me?" Jade replied coldly, throwing off the covers and sitting up. "Who the fuck do you think you are talking to like that? Do you think I'm your child or that you own me?"

"No...no...I was just concerned Jade," Weatherburn replied quickly. "I mean you didn't have to but you could have let me know that you were going out."

"Yes, I could have," she conceded. "But I didn't. And that doesn't give you the right to question me about my whereabouts."

"You're right," Weatherburn conceded. "I'm sorry."

"Apology accepted. Just don't let it happen again." She yawned as she looked at the time. She was famished and slightly hungover. Those martinis had really crept up on her.

"I have good news," Weatherburn said, switching gears. "I found you an apartment."

"Really?" Jade said excitedly. "That's great!"

"Yeah, we'll go and take a look at it later. It's owned by an associate of mine." It had taken him several calls but he had found what seemed to be the perfect apartment. It was located in an upscale section of Manor Park in a small enclave that housed six apartments. They chatted for awhile longer before Weatherburn reluctantly ended the call. Today was an extremely busy one for him. Jade got out of bed and took a long shower before buzzing Ross to get her some breakfast. She was really excited about the apartment. She wanted it unfurnished so that she could handpick the furniture. She couldn't wait to decorate it.

After breakfast, which was a scrambled egg platter with orange juice and coffee from the hotel café, she relaxed in bed and browsed the internet on her iPhone. She googled the Jewish man's company. Hassan & Cohen LLC was located in the UK and produced various products through their different divisions. They produced cognac, beer, industrial fans and soap. *Very diverse*, Jade thought. She then focused on the cognac. It was called La Roseda and had been released in Europe eight months ago. It became popular when a super model was spotted in the VIP lounge at a trendy nightclub in London drinking the strange pink cognac all night. A few days later she mentioned in an interview that La Roseda was her new favourite drink. It instantly became the drink of choice for many club hopping women across Europe. The company had sent the super model several cases of the expensive cognac to show their appreciation for her endorsement. Now they were ready to introduce it to Jamaica and the rest of the Caribbean. And they wanted her to be the face of the marketing campaign. She was definitely interested. She dialed Mr. Hassan's number.

Chapter 21

Dunga got up at 1 p.m. After seven hours sleep, he was ready for the day. One of the artists he was producing had a video shoot at 2 p.m. and he needed to be there to ensure that things went as planned. He figured to be tied up with that until at least 8 p.m. then it was back to the studio for a late session with Ras Che, the French Rastafarian singer, to begin working on the tracks for his upcoming album. Dahlia wasn't there when he woke up. She had ignored him when he got in at 5:30 earlier that morning, pretending to be asleep when he climbed into the bed. That had been fine with him as he had needed to get his rest. Dunga yawned and went into the kitchen to get something to eat. Forty minutes later, he was on his way to Stony Hill where the video shoot was scheduled to take place.

"Hi there, great to see you again!" Mr. Hassan enthused as he kissed Jade on both cheeks in greeting. They were at the poolside of the hotel. Once Jade had called him and told him that she was interested, he had immediately set up a 2 p.m. meeting. He had brought along his lawyer, photographer and personal assistant.

Smiling brightly, Jade greeted the others and they all sat down. Hassan waved over a waiter and ordered a bottle of champagne.

"This is a celebration!" he said smiling broadly. Jade liked him already. The affable CEO was a very energetic and personable individual.

The waiter popped the bottle and filled the four glasses. Hassan toasted to success and then they got down to business. The lawyer slid a copy of the contract over to Jade. It wasn't a long or complex document; Jade merely took a few minutes to peruse it. The contract was for one year, with the option to renew if both parties were in agreement. Jade would be expected to attend all the marketing functions and promotional events for the product; she would have to be available for photo shoots and the contract was exclusive - she could not represent any other company or any other product for the duration of the contract without the permission of the company. Her remuneration for the year would be twelve thousand pounds. She would receive one thousand pounds monthly. Perks included a company vehicle and a driver, and bonuses if the sales target for each month was exceeded. Jade looked up at Mr. Hassan when she was through reading. He was looking at her expectantly.

"May I borrow your pen sir?" she asked with a smile.

Hassan laughed and handed her a solid gold parker pen. He was pleased that she had agreed to the terms of the contract. He thought it was a relatively lucrative one.

Jade signed on the dotted line - she had to sign three copies and they then ordered peppered shrimp and jerk chicken wings to go along with the champagne while Mr. Hassan outlined the upcoming activities they had planned to launch La Roseda. An aggressive print campaign along with T.V. and radio advertisements would create public awareness leading up to the launch party in a month's time. They were going to get the ball rolling right away. Jade would have two shoots tomorrow; a photo shoot early in the morning at a beach in Port Royal and a video shoot for a commercial in the evening at a night club. She listened as Francis, the photographer, outlined the concepts for the shoots. Jade sipped her champagne as she listened attentively. She couldn't wait to get started.

❧❧❧

The video shoot was not going well. Things had gotten off to a very late start and just when they had finally gotten underway, the rain had come pouring down. Dunga was sitting in his SUV fuming. He hated when his time and money got wasted. The director, who was the go to guy for videos ever since two of his videos had made it onto BET and MTV, was acting like he was Steven Speilberg. His five minutes of fame had gotten to his head in a major way. Dunga looked at the time. It was now 5 p.m. Three hours wasted. He decided he wouldn't waste another second. He called Jimmy on his mobile. Jimmy was sheltering from the rain in a bar across the street. He was with Ricochet, the artist for whose song the video was being shot.

"I'm leaving," Dunga said. "Tell the idiot director boy that the shoot is cancelled and I'll be using someone else. See you at the studio later."

"Ok, no problem," Jimmy responded. He hung up and went over to where the director was holding court with the girls that were hired to be in the video. He was telling them about the time he shot a video for a rapper in Queens, New York. Jimmy rudely interrupted him and gave him the good news.

He was pissed. He jumped up from off of the chair on which he was sitting and began cursing that he had to get paid for today.

Jimmy smirked and told him that his faggot ass wasn't getting a dime as he had showed up late and wasted important people's time. He bristled at being called a homosexual but he didn't prolong the argument as he was very much aware of Jimmy's violent reputation. He would tell his cousin, who had recently become the don of Wicker Lane, a violent inner-city community, about Dunga's disrespect. He would be eager to flex his newly acquired muscle and roughing up someone of Dunga's stature would look very good on his resume. He scowled as he watched Jimmy saunter off with the artist and two other men in tow. He would definitely go and see his cousin tonight.

ଔଓଔଓଔଓ

Weatherburn called Jade a few minutes after her new business associates had left. He told her that he would pick her up around 7:30 so they could go and check out the apartment. The call was brief as he had some urgent matters to deal with. Jade retired to her suite to relax for a bit. She had two hours to chill before Weatherburn picked her up.

ଔଔଔ

"The fool actually said we should pay him for today," Jimmy said, as he updated Dunga on his conversation with the video director.

Dunga laughed heartily. The arrogant bastard. He obviously didn't know who he was dealing with. They were at the studio preparing for the session with the French singer. It was going to be a long one.

"Anyways, enough about that clown. Get in touch with that chick who directed the video for Cyclone. She's good. We can use her," Dunga instructed. He rubbed Tupac's head who was sitting by his feet as usual. Tupac was a very dangerous dog but he was well-trained and would only attack if Dunga was attacked or if Dunga gave him the signal.

"Alright, I'll make some calls and get her number," Jimmy said. He then got up and went inside the office.

ଔଔଔ

"Hi sweetheart," Weatherburn said to Jade as he hugged her in greeting. He had arrived to pick her up at 7:45.

"You're late," Jade pouted prettily. "A gentleman never keeps a lady waiting."

Weatherburn laughed.

"I'm sorry darling. Blame the traffic."

Jade pinched his cheek playfully.

"Hi Eddie, how are you?" Jade said as they exited the hotel premises.

"I'm good, thanks," Eddie replied, looking at her through the rear view mirror.

The traffic was indeed terrible. It took them forty-five minutes to get from New Kingston to Manor Park.

Eddie opened the gate using the remote and they drove up to Townhouse C. Jade looked around. Luxury vehicles were parked in front of the other five apartments. A little boy and an older girl played with assorted toys on the small lawn in front of Townhouse A. The children were very cute. Jade waved at the little boy. He grinned and shyly turned away his head.

Eddie opened the door and stood aside allowing Jade and Weatherburn to enter.

"Wow," Jade murmured. Though she had wanted the place to be unfurnished, this was truly magnificent. Simplicity and subtle sophistication were effortlessly achieved by the bare, smooth marble tiling; pristine, white leather sofas; an exquisite black marble coffee-table; thought-provoking art adorned the pastel walls; two sculptures by one of Jamaica's most prominent artists were at opposite ends of the room and a 36 inch Plasma T.V. sat comfortably on the wall opposite the sofas. She was also happy to see an unusually designed book-shelf housing six rows of books. The place didn't look lived-in; looked more like a show-piece for an interior decorating magazine but neither did it look uncomfortable.

"This place belongs to a friend of mine who is the managing director for one of Jamaica's largest commercial banks. He only agreed to rent it because of the close business relationship that we have," Weatherburn explained as they checked out the remaining rooms. "The lease is for one year."

Jade was immensely pleased. The townhouse had exceeded her expectations. She could only imagine the monthly rental fee. It had to be really high. She was curious but declined to ask. That wasn't her business. He knew what he was getting himself into. She had been upfront from the very start. He knew that she would be high maintenance. Anytime the situation became too much for him to handle he knew what to do.

Weatherburn hugged her from behind as she stood on the back patio.

"When do I move in?" she asked. There was nothing much to see from the patio. It faced a large mansion that, in Jade's opinion, looked more like a hotel or guest house with its bright orange and green colours. Who in their right mind would paint their home in such hideously bright colours?

"You could move in now, as you can see its ready but the hotel suite is already paid for and you have four more days there so it's best to wait. They won't refund us if you vacate the suite early," he responded, as he brushed his lips against the nape of her neck.

Jade could feel his erection in the small of her back. She reached a hand around and squeezed it. Gently. Weatherburn moaned. He pulled her inside and lifted her onto the kitchen counter. He bunched her short, frayed Juicy Couture denim skirt around her waist and threw her legs on his shoulders. Jade leaned back against the wall and gasped when he exposed her fleshy folds by pulling her tiny black g-string panties to the side and started to eat her out like he hadn't had a meal in days.

ଓଃ୨୦ଓଃ୨୦ଓଃ୨୦

"Ah so de bwoy Dunga ah move?" Ratty, the newly christened don of Wicker Lane commented as he rubbed his bearded jaw. He was sitting on a stool in front of a bar he owned deep in the heart of the volatile community. Members of his inner circle were close by. He didn't like what his cousin was telling him. There was no way he would stand by idly and let a family member be disrespected, threatened and cheated. He had taken his equipment to the venue and had actually started production. How could he be blamed for the rain? And so what if he had started a few minutes late? This was Jamaica. Nothing started on time.

"Yeah man, him send over his right hand man to threaten me wid gun and tell mi seh mi nah get no money and him ah cancel the shoot," Ray Porter, the video director, said, reiterating his exaggeration of what had taken place. He had decided to spice it up with a few lies so that there would be no doubt that his cousin would take action.

"How much money de bwoy did suppose fi pay yuh?" Ratty asked.

"Eighty five thousand," his cousin replied. "Is just a little low budget video fi one ah him new artist."

"Well now him ah go have to pay one hundred and fifty thousand...interest fi di disrespect," Ratty proclaimed matter-of-factly. "Mi know which part him studio deh...mi ah go page him tonight."

Ray nodded and smiled. Good. This would give him a lot of respect on the streets when word got around.

ଔଷଔଷଔଷ

Jade called Theresa after Weatherburn had dropped her off at the hotel. Her body was still tingling from his oral assault at the townhouse. He had wanted to penetrate her but Jade wouldn't budge. No condom, no ride. He was left aching for release but she was fine. The two orgasms had left her feeling mellow.

Theresa's phone rang out to voicemail but she returned the call a few minutes later.

"Hey girl," Jade said. "What are you up to?"

"Nothing much, I was in the shower when you called," Theresa replied.

Jade asked her if she wanted to swing by the hotel so they could have drinks by the poolside. Theresa readily agreed and told her that she would be in less than an hour. Jade then went into the bathroom to take a shower. It was feeling a tad bit sticky between her legs.

ଔଷଔଷଔଷ

Dunga was getting frustrated. One of the three back-up singers doing the harmony for the first song that Ras Che had recorded was not getting it right. She sounded flat and off-key.

"Shantol! What the hell is your problem?" Dunga asked. This was the fourth time they had had to stop.

"I don't have a problem," Shantol responded defensively, feeling embarrassed. "I sound okay to me."

Dunga was incredulous.

"I didn't ask you for your opinion!" he thundered. "I'm the expert here and if I say you are off-key then you are fucking off-key!"

"Everybody take a break!" He glared at Shantol as he whipped out his mobile. This was the last time he would be giving her fat ass any work. He dialed Secret's number. Though she was now a solo artist, it would be good for her to sing back-up for Ras Che as he was a big international artist. She answered on the second ring.

"Hi, it's Dunga," he intoned.

"Hi! What's up?" she responded, unable to hide the fact that she was excited to hear his voice.

"I'm having a problem at the studio. I need a good back-up singer on short notice. I'm here working with Ras Che," he explained.

"Sure, no problem," she readily agreed. She knew that Ras Che was a big deal in Europe and besides, she would be getting paid for it and she badly needed some money. She gave him her home address.

"Ok. Jimmy will come by and pick you up shortly," Dunga told her and terminated the call.

He called over Jimmy and instructed him to go and pick up Secret at her home.

He then told Shantol to go home as her services were no longer needed.

ཅ

"Duane! Stop!" Jessica protested as she resisted her husband's advance. She had a slight headache and she was a bit pissed that he had ignored her last night after they had gotten home from the banquet. She had put on one of her sexy lingerie pieces and he had pretended not to notice; locking himself away in his study until she had fallen asleep.

"Where am I supposed to go for sex if not to my wife? Have you forgotten your marital vows? You need to perform your wifely duties," he replied, undeterred as he climbed on top of her.

"*You* didn't perform your duties as a husband last night, now did you?" Jessica retorted as she tried to prevent his hand from snaking down between her legs.

"Jessica you are really pissing me off now. I was in the study doing some work so that I can provide for my family. Last time I checked that was the primary function of a husband," he replied.

He then kissed her roughly, drowning out any further protest. He overpowered her and entered her with a firm thrust. She had been wearing only her baby blue terrycloth robe, sitting on the bed moisturizing her legs when he had come home in an uncontrollable heat. She was arid. She winced. She pounded his back and implored him to stop. He didn't. As far as he was concerned, a man could not rape his wife. All he could think of was his impending release. He had been in real physical pain from the moment he had been unable to climax at the townhouse. Jade's staunch refusal to have sex without a condom had left him aching with an intensity he hadn't felt since his early teenage years. His rhythm was fast and furious. He uttered a guttural roar as his climax rushed to the fore.

"Wow, that's great!" Theresa exclaimed. They were seated at the far end of the pool having dinner. The plan had been to knock back a few drinks but when Theresa arrived at the hotel, they both realized they were hungry. Jade was having baked chicken stuffed with calalloo while Theresa was having pan roasted chicken breast that was glazed with wine. Jade had just told her about the contract she had signed to be the face of La Roseda.

"Yeah," Jade said smiling. "It's a pretty good contract and it seems like it will be a pleasure working with them."

She then told Theresa about the townhouse and made plans for Theresa to swing by with a bottle of wine and a couple of movies to have a house warming over the weekend.

Ø3ℵ⊃Ø3ℵ⊃Ø3ℵ⊃

"It's a wrap," Dunga said smiling. Secret had nailed it in one go. Now the song would be perfect. Ras Che liked what he heard too, he was grinning from ear to ear. Everyone present in the studio knew that a hit single had just been produced.

Dunga sent and got food for everyone present. The session was not over but he wouldn't need the back-up singers for the rest of the night. Dunga decided to break for an hour before putting in some work on the next track. He was digging into his mallah chicken and shrimp fried rice when the handyman came and whispered to him that a man by the name of Ratty was at the gate and wanted to see him. Dunga frowned. He didn't know anyone by that name and he only dealt with people by appointment. He got up and went to the intercom.

"This is Dunga," he said. "How can I help you?"

"Yo, buss the gate," a voice said rudely. "Ah Ratty dis...ah me run Wicker Lane."

"Ok, good for you," Dunga replied. "What is it you want?"

"Mi need fi talk to yuh 'bout the money weh yuh owe de video director. Ah mi cousin yeah."

Dunga chuckled. So the little pussy had decided to play hard ball. This was trouble but it was best to deal with matters of this nature firmly and quickly. Dunga instructed the handyman to open the main gate.

Chapter 22

"Everyone stay inside," Dunga announced. "Do not come outside under any circumstances."

Secret looked at Dunga wide-eyed. She wondered what was going on. The air had suddenly become thick with tension. Without a word, Jimmy got up quickly and went inside the office. He returned a few seconds later with a Mac 10 submachine gun and followed Dunga outside. He was speaking in hushed tones on his cell phone. Everyone looked around at each other in stunned silence. Even Ras Che's girlfriend, who was usually spaced out and in her own world, became alert. No one was eating anymore.

Dunga went back outside with Tupac beside him. Jimmy stood in front of the main entrance where he could see everything. He made no attempt to conceal his weapon.

The men had arrived in two tinted vehicles, a green Toyota Harrier and a white Toyota Corolla. A heavy set, bearded man with a scar running across his large nose flanked by two men, was standing in front of the Corolla. Both vehicles still had their engines running. Dunga walked down the steps and approached the men.

"Yes Ratty," he said, addressing the man with the scar. It was obvious that he was the leader.

He stepped forward and stood very closely to Dunga. Tupac growled threateningly. Ratty looked at him warily.

"Mind yuh dog bite me enuh," he said.

"He only attacks on command," Dunga told him. "Anyway, I'm a busy man so get to the point. What's up?"

Ratty smirked and related all that his cousin had told him. Dunga listened without interrupting until he stopped talking.

"Finished?" Dunga asked.

"Yeah, now ah yuh fi tell mi when mi can collect de money. Yuh 'ave until weekend fi pay up," he replied, looking Dunga dead in the face.

Dunga burst out laughing.

"Get the fuck off my property pussy-hole," he said, still laughing. "You're an even bigger clown than your cousin. You know who the fuck I am?"

As if on cue, the electronic gate opened up and a black Dodge Durango and two black F1 50 trucks drove in. Nine men hopped out of the two trucks and five more exited the Durango. They opened up the doors of the two vehicles that Ratty and his men had arrived in and unceremoniously removed the occupants. Six of them had been sitting in the two vehicles armed with handguns. They were all disarmed, including the two that were standing behind Ratty. Those that dared to speak received gun butts to the face and head, and were made to lie facedown on the cold concrete.

Ratty was stunned. Everything had happened so fast.

He opened his mouth to speak but no words came out.

"You're in way over your head faggot," Dunga told him. "Be careful who fuck with next time."

With that he turned and made his way back towards the studio just as he gave Tupac the signal to attack. Ratty screamed as the powerful dog leaped on top of him and bit out a chunk of his jaw. Dunga stood on the steps and turned around to watch. He allowed Tupac to bite him again before calling him off. Ratty was on the ground screaming and writhing in pain. His face was a bloody mess. Dunga nodded at the men – his friends the Black Talon Crew - that Jimmy had called to come and deal with the situation and went inside. Jimmy followed in tow while the handyman, who had been watching the proceedings in a dark corner, took Tupac to get him cleaned up.

The men then proceeded to beat their victims severely for a few minutes before allowing them to leave.

"Everything is fine now," Dunga said with a smile when he went back inside. Everyone breathed easier as Dunga opened a bottle of Hennessy and invited everyone to help themselves to a drink. He looked over at Secret who was watching him with an indescribable look on her face. He knew she had seen everything. When he had turned around and was walking towards the studio, he had seen her peeking through a window. He wondered what she was thinking. He smiled at her.

She smiled back nervously. Her new boss was no joke. She had never seen anything in her young life like what she had just witnessed. Only a scene from an urban drug flick she had seen recently came even close. She was scared shitless and immensely turned on at the same time. Dunga was a very powerful and vicious man. He was also very sweet, talented and hardworking. Not to mention handsome. A fucking enigma. Her panties were drenched.

ઉઌઉઌઉઌ

Theresa and Jade called it a night at 11:00 p.m. Theresa had an early morning client and had to be at the salon at 7:30 a.m. while Jade had to be ready at 4:30 a.m. for her first photo shoot. Jade went to bed as soon as she got back to the suite. She didn't fall asleep right away. She was not a religious person but she considered herself to be in touch with her spirituality. She said a quick prayer thanking God for all the blessings she had received since her arrival in Jamaica. Things could have easily gone the opposite way. She had a wealthy, influential benefactor, a good paying job that wasn't a boring 9-5 gig and she had a found a good friend in Theresa. Life was good and was promising to get even better.

ઉઌઉઌઉઌ

Weatherburn was introspective as he lay in bed looking up at the decorative fan as it spun slowly around. His wife was next to him, curled up in the fetal position with her back to him. She had threatened to sleep in one of the guest bedrooms but he had told her to go ahead as there would be more room for him. She had been taken aback by his attitude. He was unrepentant about having sex with her against her will.

Her tears and declarations of feeling violated and disrespected had not moved him an iota. He had provided for and catered to this woman's whim for twenty years. She had not worked a day in her life since he had become a part of it. The least he was entitled to was some sex whenever he wanted it. She would get over it eventually. He thought of the situation with Jade. The rules were going to have to be changed eventually. The more he invested in her as time went on, the more she would have to give of herself. There was no way she could continue to act like she was independent and not obligated to him when he was spending a small fortune on her. He noticed that she had purchased an iPhone and did not even have the courtesy to give him the number. He was going to start asserting himself more and more. And when he did, he was not going to entertain any argument from her with any references to what he had agreed to in the beginning, or any notions of her leaving him. She was going to be his whether she liked it or not. He had started out too docile, too eager to impress and please. Too blinded by her sex appeal and beauty. It was time to put on back his pants and be a man.

ઉઇઉઇઉઇ

It was now 2 a.m. and Dunga, Secret and Jimmy were the only ones left at the studio. They had done one more recording with Ras Che and Secret had also provided back-up vocals for that track. Ras Che had left the studio a very satisfied client. He was due back in another two days for another session.

"Thanks so much for the opportunity to work with Ras Che," Secret told him between sips of Bailey's Irish Cream.

Dunga had a fully stocked bar at the studio and she had felt for something smooth after they had finished working.

Dunga merely smiled.

"You're very talented," he told her. "And a pleasure to work with."

Secret beamed.

"Listen to this," Dunga said as he got up and went behind the controls. She followed him. "I built it from scratch yesterday."

Secret listened in awe as the sultry beat filtered through the speakers.

"This sounds amazing," she whispered.

Dunga grinned broadly; surprised at himself for feeling relieved that she totally loved it.

"I want you to write a song to it," Dunga told her.

"I already did," she replied.

Dunga frowned.

"What do you mean?"

Secret started to sing.

Dunga had to sit down. The chemistry they had in the studio was unlike anything he had ever experienced. She had written the perfect song for a beat she hadn't heard before today. He had created the perfect beat for a song he hadn't heard before today. He couldn't take his eyes off her. She was singing with so much passion and longing that it stirred his soul. And his loins.

Chapter 23

"Have you given the song a title yet?" he asked softly when she was through.

She looked at him steadily.

"It's called *Lust.*"

They gazed in each other's eyes for what seemed like an eternity. Dunga got the message loud and clear.

"Get in the booth," Dunga instructed, knifing into the thick sexual tension.

She did his bidding and they started the recording process.

She never once took her eyes off of him. She nailed it one go.

Dunga played it over and over. It was perfect. All it now needed was the background harmony and he was going to let her do her own harmonization. He didn't want anyone else even breathing on this song. They worked until it was almost sunrise.

Secret was exhausted but exhilarated. She had just recorded her first solo joint and the intensity of the process, compounded by the feelings she had developed for Dunga, had made for one unforgettable experience.

Dunga plopped down on the sofa in front of her. He didn't want to chance sitting next to her. God knows what would happen if they even accidently brushed against each other right now.

"Later this evening when you come back we'll sort out the paperwork," he told her, trying valiantly to keep it on a business level. At least for now. God knows how much longer he would be able to hold out. She was a very pretty and talented young woman. There was an innocence about her that made her obvious wanton desire for him all the more intriguing.

"Ok," she said, sporting a tired smile.

"I need to get you home," Dunga told her, after a few moments of silence.

What you need to do is come over here and show me what I've been missing…take this virginity like it had your name on it.

Aloud, she said, "Yeah, I'm so tired."

She was dying to take a shower. Her juices had flowed continuously throughout the night. It's a wonder she wasn't dehydrated. She chuckled at the thought.

Dunga looked at her curiously but said nothing.

He got up and went into the office where Jimmy was watching T.V.

"Take Secret home," Dunga told him.

Jimmy raised his eyebrows as if to ask if he was sure.

"Yeah, take her home," he reiterated. He would fight it for as long as he could. It was one of his codes not to mix business with pleasure and he was a man who lived by the codes he had set for himself. That kind of discipline had served him well over the years. He opened the safe behind the painting he had of Quincy Jones, who was, in his estimation, the greatest producer ever. He removed thirty crisp one thousand dollar bills and placed it in an envelope.

"Give this to her," he said.

Jimmy nodded.

"You're leaving now too?" he asked.

"Yeah," Dunga replied. "In a few minutes."

"Alright later then."

He then went out to chill room where Secret was waiting.

"What's up? You look tired man," Jimmy joked.

"Yeah, been working all night," Secret said, stating the obvious.

Jimmy handed her the envelope.

"Your pay for the back-up work," he explained. "Come on...I'm taking you home now."

Secret was ecstatic to receive the money. She had not expected to be paid so soon. In the past, she had rarely gotten her money before two weeks had elapsed and even then, she had to call continuously to find out when she was getting paid. The music industry was filled with corrupt, unprofessional people. She was so thankful that Dunga wasn't one of them. Yet another admirable quality.

She glanced in the direction of his office before heading out with Jimmy.

She didn't count the money until she got home and was safely in her room. Thirty thousand dollars. It was about ten thousand more than what she had expected to be paid. Secret smiled as she undressed. It was great to have money again. As soon as she got some rest she would go to the supermarket and get some groceries. She would also give her mom five thousand dollars. That would get her off her case for a little while. She padded to the bathroom to take a quick shower. She was way too wet to fall asleep despite the fatigue.

ଔଔଔ

Dahlia stirred when Dunga got home and climbed into the bed.

She turned and slid into his arms. She opened her eyes when she felt his turgid erection. *Damn! My baby missed me*, she mused sleepily. She reached down and stroked him gently. They hadn't spoken since he dropped her off from the movies on Sunday night.

"Hi baby," she murmured as she climbed on top of him.

He moaned as she kissed his neck and ran her tongue along his shoulder blade.

"I missed you," she breathed as she positioned his dick and sat on it slowly.

Dunga uttered an unintelligible response.

"I know you're tired so I'm gonna do all the work baby," she breathed in his ear as she moved in a slow, circular motion. "Just relax my king..."

She was good to her word. Dahlia squatted on her haunches and rode his dick like a woman possessed.

"Oh yes! Spank me baby! Harder!" Dahlia shouted as Dunga spanked her ass. Her movements were a blur as she rapidly bounced up and down his throbbing shaft.

Dunga didn't last much longer. Unable to remain passive, he held her in place and began to thrust upwards like his life depended on it. The tension caused by spending those long hours at the studio with Secret demanded release. He climaxed with a strong torrent.

He fell asleep almost immediately, but not before the image of Secret's soulful, longing expression when she was singing flashed before his eyes.

Chapter 24

"That was perfect!" Francis Symes, the photographer, exclaimed. He found it difficult to believe that Jade had never modeled before. She took direction perfectly and was a natural in front of the camera. She could easily become a successful model. He didn't know if she could walk, but even if she couldn't be a runway model, she would excel at being a commercial one. "Wow, you're a natural Jade. These shots are amazing."

Jade beamed. She was wearing a fabulous white Dolce & Gabbana one piece swimsuit with gold accessories. She looked over his shoulder as he uploaded the photos to his ultra thin Mac notebook. The sunrise shots were indeed incredible. Her favourite set were the shots that were taken from behind as she relaxed on a towel facing the sunrise with the parrot beside her. She was holding a glass of La Roseda, with a half empty bottle on the sand next to her. The shoot had been short due to the chemistry between Jade and Symes. Almost every shot was a keeper. The longest part had been Jade's styling, which had taken forty-five minutes.

They had gotten to Port Royal at 5 a.m. and were taken over to Lime Cay, a small island beach two miles away, on a small company yacht. After loading the equipment back onto the yacht, the crew, consisting of eight people, then settled down for breakfast on the picturesque beach. Symes sat next to Jade and Mishka, the stylist, a petite British girl with Jamaican roots, who Jade suspected was a lesbian.

"When the billboards, advertisements and posters hit the streets and airwaves you're going to be an instant celebrity," he commented between mouthfuls of ackee and saltfish and boiled green bananas. "Are you ready to be famous?"

Jade laughed and took a sip of her orange juice. She was having liver, fried plantain and Johnny cakes.

"There are worst things a woman could be," she quipped.

Symes laughed heartily, clapping his small, manicured hands.

Jade liked him. He was an excellent photographer and the fact that he was gay made her feel comfortable around him. It was good that she didn't have to worry about any unwanted advances. He was just like one of the girls.

❧❧❧

Jade got back to the hotel at 9 a.m. She immediately took a shower and went back to bed. She wanted to be fresh for her video shoot later that evening. They would be picking her up at 4 p.m. to shoot the commercial. The phone startled her out of her dream half an hour later. It was Weatherburn.

"Good morning Jade," he said.

"Hi Duane," she murmured sleepily. "Can you call me back later? I'm trying to catch up on some sleep."

Weatherburn was silent for a moment. Then he continued as if he hadn't heard her.

"My contact at the tax department is ready to deal with the TRN number for you. Once you have that, then you can get your driver's license and whatever else you need. What's your surname? "

Jade tried to control her annoyance. Didn't she just tell this man that she needed to sleep?

"Ok, that's great," she replied. And it was. She needed to get some identification and obtaining that number was the first step. "It's Jones."

"I'm taking you to dinner tonight. We need to talk," Weatherburn told her.

"Not tonight," Jade replied. "I have to be somewhere."

"Cancel it. I'll be there to pick you up at six." He hung up without waiting for a response. Feeling very pleased, he buzzed his secretary and told her to send in the European Union representative who had come to meet with him.

What the fuck? Jade mused as she put the phone down. She had noticed his tone from the moment he had come on the line. Very aggressive. What the hell was up with him? Well, whatever it was he needed to get a grip. She went back to sleep wondering if he really expected her to be here when he showed up later.

Secret got up at 1:30 p.m. She had gotten seven hours of blissful sleep. She hummed as she wrapped herself in a towel and made her way to the bathroom. She was in very high spirits. All the sacrifice and unwavering belief in accomplishing her dream of making it in the music business was finally beginning to pay off. She took her cell phone with her. She was startled by someone's presence as she reached for the bathroom door. Her mother's new boyfriend. He was standing in the doorway of her mother's bedroom wearing only a lustful expression and a pair of cotton briefs that at one time may have been white. She had thought that she was home alone. She thanked heavens she hadn't come out of her room naked. Her mother usually left at 8:00 in the morning for work. She was a receptionist at a dental office in Cross Roads. Apparently her boyfriend was off from work today and decided to stay after spending the night. Secret's heart thumped loudly as they looked at each other. It was obvious what he was thinking. She hurriedly went inside the bathroom and locked the door. She turned on the shower but sat down on the closed toilet to calm down. She was upset that her mother had allowed him to stay knowing that she would be home unawares. She gasped when she saw the door handle turning. He was trying to come in.

❧❧❧

Dunga was in the kitchen having stew chicken with dumplings and bananas when he received the call. Dahlia had cooked before she left for the shoe store that she owned in Half-Way-Tree. The one she operated in Brooklyn was a success so she had decided to open a branch in Jamaica a year ago. It had been going well and her favourite cousin, Tisha, was the manager.

He looked at the caller ID. It was Secret.

"Hi Secret," he said pleasantly.

"Dunga, I need your help!" she whispered urgently.

Dunga turned down the volume on the T.V.

"What happened?" he asked, very concerned.

Secret explained the situation.

"I'll be there in ten minutes," Dunga promised and hung up. He rushed to pull on some clothes and grabbed his keys.

❧❧❧

The door rattled on its hinges as the man shook it hard. Secret shook even harder with fear from where she stood by the shower. He probably thought she was in the shower and couldn't hear him trying to open the door. She jumped when he kicked it. She turned off the shower.

There was silence for a few moments then he spoke.

"Open de door, mi need fi use de bathroom urgently," he said gruffly.

Secret wondered if he thought she was an idiot.

She didn't respond.

"If yuh finish shower jus' hurry up an' come out so mi can use de bathroom!" he shouted.

Secret prayed for Dunga to arrive quickly. She had told him when he got to the house to bang on the door and pretend to be the police.

It was quiet for a few moments but she could hear him breathing hard by the door.

He was still standing there.

A loud bang broke the silence.

ଓଃଓଃଓଃ

"Police! Open up!" Dunga shouted authoritatively as he banged on the front door.

There were two guys sitting on a wall across the street watching the popular producer in shock. What the hell was he doing pretending to be the police? Word on the street was that Dunga had handled an extortion attempt by a don from Wicker Lane in vicious fashion just last night. The don had apparently lost his left eye, a good chunk of flesh from his jaw and lots of blood. He was in the hospital in serious but stable condition. The doctors were planning to use flesh from his buttocks to fill the hole on the left side of his broken jaw.

Inside, Secret's tormentor froze in shock. Had she called the police? But police in Jamaica wasn't normally so quick on the scene and that is if they came at all. He ran inside the bedroom to quickly pull on his pants and shirt. He then hurried to quell the incessant banging; it wouldn't do to make them angry. He rubbed his eyes and pretended to be just waking up as he opened the door.

Dunga pushed the door and stepped inside the house quickly. He slammed it shut and pulled his licensed firearm.

"Duh nuh kill mi sar...mi ah beg yuh...just tek wah yuh want but spare mi life," he pleaded, falling to his knees. He realized that the man was not a cop so he automatically assumed he was a robber.

Dunga felt insulted. True he had not gotten a chance to dress properly or put on his jewellery but he had on a grey ribbed tank top and a pair of $450 Red Monkey jeans. The nerve of this would be rapist. Dunga kicked him in his face hard with his timberland boots.

The man hollered in pain.

Secret stayed locked inside the bathroom.

"You're a fucking animal," Dunga stated with disgust. "You see a woman and think that you should be able to fuck her just like that huh?"

He shook his head rapidly.

"No sar," he croaked through his bloody mouth. Apparently Dunga had loosened a few of his teeth with that well-placed kick. "Mi never woulda do something like dat...mi did jus' want fi use de bathroom."

Dunga looked at him coldly.

"If I ever hear that you even look at the young lady again you're a dead man," Dunga told him solemnly.

"Secret?" Dunga called out, putting the gun back into the waist band of his jeans.

Secret opened the bathroom door and came out. She rushed into Dunga's arms.

"Thank you so much," she said between sobs. "I was so scared."

"It's ok now," Dunga said soothingly, very aware that only a towel separated him from her supple body.

She broke the hug and led him by hand to the bathroom.

"Please stay with me while I take a shower. I won't be long," Secret promised, smiling through her tears.

Dunga could only manage a nod.

He watched transfixed as she removed the towel and placed it on the shower curtain rod. Secret was even sexier than he had envisioned. A 5'5" vision of creamy caramel skin; succulent, curvy thighs; pert, mouthwatering breasts and a heart-shaped ass whose size caught you by surprise. He got a rear view of her plump, hairless mound through the sexy gap between her thighs when she climbed into the shower. He sat down on the toilet seat with a heavy sigh. The next five minutes were pure torture.

Secret's legs felt weak as she lathered her body. Dunga had just rescued her from a sexual assault. He was sitting on her toilet while she took a shower. He had seen her naked body. It was surreal. She sighed. Her pussy was rivaling the water from the shower. She wished Dunga would just rip the shower curtain to shreds and violate her body.

She was wetter than she had ever been in her nineteen years.

❧❧❧

Roy Porter was so shaken up by the news of what had happened to his cousin that he had fallen ill. He had a video to shoot at 2 p.m. but was unable to function. He had been shell-shocked since he received the call from Worm, a friend of his who lived in Wicker Lane. His cousin and some of his men were at the hospital in serious condition. He had heard that Dunga's pit bull had ripped a hole in his cousin's face. The news had chilled him like he was standing in an industrial freezer. He stayed in bed all day, refusing to take anymore calls. He knew what they were calling about. Besides he thought it prudent to lay low for awhile. Suppose Dunga wanted to harm him knowing that he had to have been the one to tell his cousin about the incident? He decided he would go to the country and cool out for a little while until things blew over. His grandfather lived in a small district called Locust Tree in Westmoreland. He would pay him a three week visit. He would leave tomorrow. Lord knows he didn't have the strength to go today.

❦❦❦

Secret turned the water off and pushed the shower curtain aside.

"Hand me my towel please?" she asked Dunga.

He passed it to her with a strained look on his face.

Secret took it and dried her body.

Dunga sat there and watched her. He knew that there was no way he would be able to leave this house without succumbing to her will.

Secret saw the look of resignation in his eyes. It was going to happen. She climbed out of the shower unsteadily and wrapped the towel around her body.

Dunga rose slowly. They were standing very close to each other. Secret's lips were trembling. Dunga's phone rang. Secret opened the door and exited to give him some privacy. She looked in the living room and cautiously peeked through her mother's half open bedroom door. The disgusting man was nowhere to be seen. She then went into her bedroom.

"Yeah, I'm good...on the road dealing with some business," Dunga was saying. Dahlia had called as she hadn't gotten a chance to speak with him before he left the house.

"Ok, baby, just saying hi real quick," she said, adding, "Did you enjoy the food?"

"Of course babes...you know you're my personal chef," Dunga replied.

Dahlia laughed.

"Ok, later babe," she told him and hung up. The store was busy so she was giving a helping hand.

Dunga walked out of the bathroom. He glanced into the open room and could see Secret's reflection in the mirror on the dresser. She was sitting on the bed and applying lotion to her legs. The towel was a bit loose and one of her breasts was showing. He could tell that the nipple was hard and erect.

Secret felt his eyes and caught his gaze in the mirror.

Dunga sighed and walked into the room. He closed the door the behind him.

Chapter 25

Jade got up at 2:30 p.m. She felt refreshed. She picked out an outfit to wear to the commercial shoot. Nothing too fussy as she would be styled when she got there. She selected an army green tank top, khaki capris and Gucci trainers. She placed them on the bed and went into the bathroom to take a shower. She thought about Weatherburn as she put on her shower cap. The more she thought about it the more she didn't like what had transpired earlier. She surmised that he had convinced himself that with the amount of money he was spending on her, he should be the one in control. That could be the only explanation for his sudden aggressive, downright disrespectful behaviour; and she was positive that it was the terms of their arrangement that he wanted to discuss. Well, nothing was going to change. Matter of fact, it might be best to cut ties with him now. Everyone enters someone's life for a reason. Maybe he had served his purpose and it was time to move on. She turned on the shower and dismissed those thoughts. She would deal with Weatherburn after the shoot.

ଓଃଛଓଃଛଓଃଛ

Secret's heart did an impressive somersault when Dunga came over to her and pulled her up off the bed. He held her in his arms and gazed deep into her soulful brown eyes before he captured her trembling lips in a searing kiss. Secret clung to him tightly, fearing her knees would give way. He explored her mouth passionately, his nimble tongue seeking out the depths of her desire. Dunga broke the kiss and swiftly removed his clothing. Secret's eyes widened when she saw his manhood. It was long, thick and extremely hard. She was feeling anxious and a bit afraid but she was ready. Her virginity was beginning to feel like a burden. She was ready to shed it. Ready to find out what it felt like to have a man inside her. Many had called but Dunga was the chosen one.

"Touch it," Dunga commanded. She looked up at him and tentatively reached down and held him. She ran her soft hand along its length, marveling at its size and firmness. Dunga groaned and gently pushed her onto the bed. He climbed on top of her and kissed her neck and her breasts, sucking and nibbling on her nipples until she cried out his name. He then reclaimed her lips and kissed her hungrily as he massaged her protruding clit. She writhed and gasped loudly when he slid a finger inside her.

"Oh Dunga...oh god...Dunga...mmmm..." Secret moaned loudly with her eyes tightly shut.

Dunga fingered her gently, marveling at her tightness. Was it possible? He paused and looked at her questioningly.

She smiled shyly. Looking for the first time like the innocent young woman that she was.

"I'm a virgin," she confessed softly.

Dunga was surprised. And pleased. He didn't know they still existed.

That drove him over the edge. He kissed her passionately as he spread her legs and reached down to position his dick at the entrance of her unsoiled essence. He was not going to use a condom. He knew he was clean and she definitely was too; besides, he didn't have any with him.

Secret tensed in his arms and screamed in his mouth when after some resistance, he entered her with a firm but gentle thrust.

She tore her mouth away from his and cried out when he tore her hymen. Dunga remained still, kissing her soothingly all over her face.

"You ok?" he asked. He was halfway inside her.

She nodded tearfully.

"It hurts Dunga...but don't stop..." she told him.

Dunga gently proceeded, moving in and out of her slowly, giving her more of him with each stroke until she was able to take it all.

"Jesus Christ Dunga...ohhh...fuck..." Secret moaned. The intense burst of pain had given way to a violent wave of pleasure that made her feel as though she had to pee urgently. She was about to experience her first orgasm. Ever.

"Dunga! Dunga!" she shouted as her body convulsed and shook like a tsunami.

Dunga remained still, savouring the feel of her juices drowning his dick.

"Ohhh...ohhh," she whimpered, her body limp from the intensity of her orgasm. She felt dizzy and had no feeling in her legs. Dunga, realizing that he could really fuck her now that she was soaking wet, began to give her some deep, hard, long strokes.

"Fuck...Secret...you feel so fucking good..." Dunga said through gritted teeth as he increased his tempo. "You like it baby? Tell me how my dick feels."

"Oh Dunga...I love it...your big wood feels perfect...I was saving it for you baby...I'm yours..." Secret told him, her eyes wide as she watched his dick, glistening mightily with her secretions, move in and out of her with wild abandon.

Her words and the sinfully pleasurable feel of her incredibly wet and tight orifice drove Dunga over the edge. He knew he should withdraw but was unable to. He uttered a primal roar as he spilled his seed inside her, still plunging deeply until he was spent.

Secret cried as she hugged his shuddering, wiry frame. They were tears of joy. She was positive that she had made the right decision. They shared a deep connection. It was evident in the music they made with each other and now, in the love they made to each other. Dunga finally stopped shaking and they rose.

"You ok?" he asked for the second time in the past fifteen minutes.

Secret wiped her eyes and smiled.

"Never been better," she replied.

She walked gingerly as they went inside the bathroom to clean up. Her pussy was on fire. And so was her heart. She had fallen for Dunga big time.

Jade was picked up by the driver assigned to her at exactly 4 p.m. It was her first time meeting him. His name was Leroy and the vehicle was a lovely grey Audi Q7. Jade loved the SUV but didn't like the driver. After telling him hi, and treating him to a frosty look when he suggested that she sat in the front, she settled in the backseat and ignored him for the duration of the drive. She couldn't pinpoint exactly why she didn't like him. She just knew that she wasn't comfortable around him. She would have Mr. Hassan change him as soon as possible. The club was pretty close to the hotel, they got there in ten minutes. Mishka, the stylist, was at the entrance of the club waiting on Jade.

They hugged and Mishka hurried her upstairs to get her styled. An hour later, they were ready to begin shooting. Jade, looking ravishing in a black and white Elie Tahari halter dress and trendy black Jimmy Choo stilettos did her entrance shot where she entered the packed club and strut sexily through the crowd, making her way to the VIP section where her girlfriends were sitting bored waiting on her. As soon as she arrived, she ordered a bottle of La Roseda and then the party really got started. It was a grueling shoot and Jade was shocked at how technical the process was. After doing the entrance shot twenty times so they could shoot it from different angles, she began to wonder what the hell she had gotten herself into. It was nothing like doing a photo shoot.

ଔଓଔଓଔଓ

"Take me to the Mayberry Hotel," Weatherburn instructed Eddie as they left the House of Parliament. It had been an unusually lively session due to the presentation by the finance minister, who had given a detailed report on the ongoing investigations by his ministry in the inappropriate acceptance of a large sum of money from a foreign investor during the general elections last year by the party that had been in power at the time. It was shaping up to be a huge and embarrassing scandal.

"Yes boss," Eddie replied.

He was silent for the journey as he could see that his boss wasn't in the mood for small talk.

They got to the hotel in thirty minutes. It was now 5:55 p.m.

"Go and tell the receptionist to alert the occupant of Suite 69 that her ride is here," Weatherburn told him.

Eddie left the vehicle idling by the curb almost in front of the lobby and went inside. He returned two minutes later.

"She's not picking up boss. Doesn't seem like she's there," Eddie told him.

"What the fuck you mean she's not picking up? Go up to her fucking room and knock then!" Weatherburn spat angrily.

Eddie meekly stepped off and went around to where Jade's suite was located.

He knocked on the door several times but there was no response. Sighing, he went back to the vehicle. It was times like these he disliked working for Weatherburn. Obviously he and Jade were having issues. Why take it out on him?

Weatherburn was so upset that he didn't respond when Eddie told him that she definitely was not there. He sat there fuming in silence for several minutes, while Eddie waited patiently for further instructions. Weatherburn was really surprised that Jade had dared to disobey him like that. Had she forgotten that he held the handle? Was she so confident that she had him wrapped around her little finger that she would embarrass him like this? He would show her not to take his kindness for weakness. Before it was all said and done she would be on bended knees begging for things to go back to the way it was. Ungrateful bitch.

"Take me home!" he barked.

Eddie drove off without a word.

Jade looked at the director coldly. She just told him that she needed to pee and he was trying to tell her that they couldn't break now.

"Not only am I going to use the bathroom," she told him. "But I'm going to take a fifteen minute break as well."

She didn't wait for a response.

"Bitch!" he muttered under his breath. He could do nothing. She wasn't the usual talent where he could complain that she was being un-cooperative and get her replaced. He had been briefed by management that the company's 'star' should be catered to.

Jade called Theresa after she had finished using the bathroom. She was sitting backstage enjoying an ice cold bottle of water and ignoring Mishka who was hovering to ensure that she did not mess up her make-up.

"What's up girl?" Theresa said when she came on the line. She was on her way home.

"I'm doing the shoot for the commercial and believe you me, this shit is a hell of a lot harder than it looks," Jade told her. "I have a new found respect for any commercial I see on T.V. regardless of how shitty it is."

Theresa laughed.

They chatted for a few more minutes then Jade hung up. She relaxed for ten more minutes before going back out to resume the shoot.

ଔଔଔ

"Ok, I'll see you later," Dunga said to Secret. He was sitting in his SUV in front of her home. She was standing outside, leaning against the vehicle. After taking a shower together earlier, which had led to another lovemaking session, Dunga had given her a ride to the supermarket. He had offered to pay for the groceries but Secret had sweetly declined, whispering to him that all he had to do was ensure that she had steady work until she made it big. Dunga had laughed. He had liked that. He loved hardworking, independent women.

"Ok babe," she replied, smiling that smile that he could never get tired of seeing.

"I'll send Jimmy to pick you up around 7."

She leaned in and kissed him then went inside.

Dunga glanced across the street before driving off. Earlier when they were leaving the house, a bunch of guys had been sitting out there on the wall. They were still there. One of them waved to get his attention and got up to approach him.

"My respect, Dunga," the youth said in greeting. "Mi is ah up an' coming singer an' mi would ah like yuh fi listen to mi CD."

Dunga looked at him and took the CD from his outstretched hand.

"Sing something accapella," Dunga responded, putting him on the spot.

"Now?" the youth asked stupidly.

"No, next year," Dunga replied sarcastically. "Sing now or forever hold your peace."

The youth looked around nervously at his friends.

Then he started to sing.

Dunga was stoic as he listened to the youth's rendition of Usher's monster hit single *You Got It Bad*.

After a few lines, Dunga raised his hand, indicating for him to stop.

He handed the CD back to the youth.

"I'm going to give you some free advice," he told him. "Get a job."

With that Dunga turned the vehicle around and headed home. He needed to take a shower and get dressed and head to the studio. There was a song he wanted to finish mixing before starting the session with Secret. He thought about her as he headed onto Eastwood Park road. Life was full of curve balls. He never saw this one coming. The connection he felt with Secret on every level was nothing short of amazing. It's like she was designed for him: talented, beautiful, independent, ambitious, easygoing and pure. She was a very sweet girl. He liked her. A lot. He thought about the sex. It had been one of, if not the most intense, sexual experiences he had ever had. The second round had been just as intense. His dick felt sore but not unpleasantly so. He had ejaculated in her both times but they had stopped at the pharmacy to get a morning after pill. She would have to go on some form of birth control. The worst thing would be for her to get pregnant just when her career was about to take off. He had no idea where this was going to go, especially with a jealous baby mother in the picture but Secret was definitely going to be a big part of his life; personally and professionally.

ଔଷଔଷଔଷ

Secret was lying in bed reminiscing about her wonderful day when her mother came home. She threw her bag down on the sofa and stormed into Secret's bedroom.

"You little dutty gal!" her mother snarled. "How dare you walk around my house naked in front of my man and tempt him eh? Then cry rape when 'im can't take it nuh more?"

"What! Mommy?" Secret exclaimed as she jumped up in shock.

Her mother looked around the room and sniffed.

"Yuh fuck inna mi house?" she screamed. "Get out! Whore!"

Her mother then attacked her in a blind rage before she could even respond.

Chapter 26

Weatherburn muttered a terse howdy to his wife and Francine, her best friend, when he got home. They were sitting on the patio having drinks. His wife barely responded and the icy hello he received from Francine, who would have normally greeted him with a hug, meant that Jessica had told her what had transpired.

He sucked his teeth and went into the study. Why did Jessica have to discuss their personal business with her friends? He removed his jacket, loosened his tie and poured a shot of brandy. He downed it one gulp and poured another. He sat at his desk and looked for the 24 hour toll free number for the bank's credit card division. He found it and sipped his drink while he waited for the customer service agent to pick up. She did and he gave instructions for the credit card he had given to Jade to be cancelled. His next call was to his friend from whom he had rented the apartment. He told him that something had come up and he would no longer need the apartment. His friend didn't mind as he had only agreed to rent it to Weatherburn because of their close business relationship.

Weatherburn's mood improved significantly after he made the two calls. He chuckled as he finished off his drink. Jade would soon realize that one should never bite the hand the hand that feeds you. He then went into the bathroom to take a shower. He hadn't been to his favourite watering hole in over two weeks. Tonight was as good a night as any to round up a couple of the boys and knock back a few rounds. Good thing he hadn't dismissed Eddie for the night. He could just relax and drink to his heart's delight knowing that his driver would be there to take him home.

"So...would you say that the marriage is on the rocks?" Francine asked as she lit up a cigarette.

"Not really...I mean I still love him but I'm extremely upset about what happened. How dare he treat me like that? His wife and the mother of his children?"

Jessica sighed and took a sip of her wine.

"If he had been repentant and remorseful for his savage behaviour I would have probably forgiven him and we would have moved on but instead he's being a selfish, uncaring bastard," she continued.

Francine nodded sympathetically. She had always liked Weatherburn though. He was witty, attractive, and a hardworking, powerful man. She had always been a bit envious of her best friend's successful marriage. She had been married twice. The first marriage, to a white businessman from New Jersey, had lasted six years. She had moved back to Jamaica after the divorce and her second marriage, to the owner of a successful modeling agency, had lasted only eighteen months. It was one thing for him to cheat on her constantly with his models, but it was a whole different ballgame when she caught him with one of the male models. He had agreed to a quick settlement giving her whatever she wanted to keep it quiet.

She had mixed feelings about what had transpired between Jessica and her husband. If she had been in Jessica's shoes, she would have been immensely turned on by him forcing himself onto her. However, they were two different people and she had to support her best friend.

She patted Jessica's hand.

"I'm sure he'll come around eventually once he realizes how badly it has affected you," she offered.

Jessica grunted. She wouldn't hold her breath. Her husband was a very obstinate man.

"Mommy! Stop!" Secret cried, trying to fend her mother off without hitting her. She couldn't believe that her mother was taking her boyfriend's side.

They rolled off the bed and crashed into the dresser. A perfume bottle of DKNY Delicious Night, the last expensive item that she treated herself to several months ago, fell and smashed to pieces on the floor, filling the small room with its seductive scent. Secret desperately tried to get up but her mother, with her strength fueled by anger, held her down and slapped her repeatedly in the face.

"Yuh disgrace mi!" she shouted. "Mi neva raise yuh fi turn inna nuh whore!"

"I didn't do anything wrong!" Secret retorted, finally managing to restrain her mother's hand. Her face stung mightily and her eyes watered from the force of the slaps as well as from her disappointment of her mother's handling of the situation. "If it wasn't for my friend I would have been raped!"

Secret pushed her away and they both scrambled to their feet, chests heaving mightily from their emotional exertions.

"Mommy you don't care about me?" Secret asked, crying. "How can you believe the lies he told you?"

Her mother glared at her defiantly.

"Pack up yuh t'ings and come outta mi house now!" she responded coldly.

Secret looked at her for several moments. No matter what happened in the future, things would never be the same between them.

ଓଃଓଃଓଃ

Dunga was at the studio working when Secret called him. He shook his head in disbelief when she told him about what had transpired. How could her mother be so heartless and stupid?

"You've finished packing?" he asked.

"Yeah," Secret responded through her tears. She had already packed a suitcase and a small bag with her best stuff. The rest she would leave. Her mother could dispose of them as she saw fit.

"Ok, I'm going to send Jimmy to pick you up," he told her. "Don't worry about anything baby...you'll be alright."

Secret felt better after talking to Dunga. She didn't know what she would do without him.

ଓଃ଼ଓଃ଼ଓଃ଼

"Don't worry yourself," Jimmy said to Secret as they made their way to studio. She was crying quietly as she stared out the window. Dunga hadn't told him anything but it was obvious that things had changed between Dunga and Secret since the last time she had been at the studio. "The boss will take care of everything. You just focus on making music and don't let anything or anyone distract you."

Secret nodded. She had all the faith in the world that everything would indeed be okay. She just *knew* that Dunga would ensure that she was fine. It had been a very eventful day. It's not everyday that a girl avoids being raped, then loses her virginity to the man she is crazy over, and subsequently gets kicked out of the house by her own mother all in one go. Very emotional, heady stuff. Secret dried her eyes as they waited for the light to turn green at the Oaklands stoplight. She was still in shock and extremely hurt at her mother's behaviour but her conscience was clear. She hadn't done anything wrong and even though her mother had kicked her out, she had left the house filled with the groceries she had purchased and she had still left some money on the coffee table for her mother. Secret sighed. Everything happened for a reason and change was good as long as it was for the better. They arrived at the studio and went in, leaving her stuff inside the vehicle.

ଓଃ଼ଓଃ଼ଓଃ଼

"Ah who ah fuck yuh?" Timex growled as he plunged into the young woman from behind. His two long platinum necklaces swung with his movements. She was bent over on the edge of the bed; face down with her ass high in the air. Her pale ass cheeks sported the imprint of his rough hands.

"You Timex!" she shouted, her milky white face flushed and sweaty.

They were at his new apartment in Beverly Hills. He had purchased it a few months after his debut album had sold half a million copies in Japan and another three hundred thousand worldwide. Not bad for a hardcore dancehall album, especially with CD sales down globally.

"Say it louder!" Timex instructed as he fucked her mercilessly. He enjoyed treating her like this. He took immense pleasure from the fact that he, a product of the ghetto, who this rich, uptown-bred, half-Syrian girl wouldn't have given a first much less a second glance had he not been the most popular hardcore entertainer in Jamaica, had her wrapped around his little finger. She would do anything he wanted. *Anything.* Ironically, she was the youngest daughter of a prominent politician who was the Member of Parliament for the ghetto community which spawned him. The only time the citizens saw him was election time. The community was in a deplorable state and had been so for a very long time.

"Timex! Timex!" she shouted at the top of her lungs as she climaxed and drenched his unsheathed tool with her juices.

"Yes Leah...wet up de bloodclaat cocky!" Timex said as he gripped her long, silky hair even tighter. He was getting ready to explode.

He pulled out and turned her around quickly. He then gave his dick two quick strokes and hot semen flooded her pretty face.

"Mmmm...mmmm..." Leah moaned with her eyes tightly shut.

Timex had turned her into a freak. Ever since she had met him backstage at a stageshow in Negril three months ago where he had performed alongside two popular hip hop artists from the United States, her life had not been the same. Timex had her doing things she had never thought possible. And the way he fucked her: rough, primal and hard. Having him fuck her like that while his hit songs provided the soundtrack to their animalistic couplings was an indescribable experience. It was a thrill for her to be seeing the uncouth entertainer. Her friends found it fascinating and one of them was now seeing Timex's road manager. If her dad found out he would kill her. Her official boyfriend was the son of one of her dad's friends, a hotel tycoon who owned a chain of all-inclusive hotels across the Caribbean. The son, heir to his father's vast fortune, was currently studying economics and international relations at Princeton. He was seven years her senior. She loved the idea of being with him and knew that he would be the perfect husband in her world but right now she was young and wanted to have fun. Experience new things. Live dangerously. And Timex facilitated that. Whenever she was around him there was always that air of danger and excitement. He took her inside of some of the most dangerous inner-city communities in Kingston. She had been in the company of dons and known gunmen. Rumours abounded plenty about their relationship but the printed media merely referred to her as his 'uptown browning' and never dared mention her name.

Walking gingerly, she went inside the bathroom to clean up. She had to go home now. Her dad was having a dinner party at 10 and expected his little princess to be there. The organizer for the Miss Jamaica Universe beauty pageant was going to attend and her dad wanted her to meet him as the plan was for her to enter the next staging of the competition.

Timex slipped on his boxers and went out to the living room where four members of his entourage were smoking weed and watching *City of God*.

ଔଓଔଓଔଓ

"Ready to get some work done?" Dunga asked Secret softly. They were in his office with the door closed. He had spent the last fifteen minutes giving her a light massage and talking to her in an effort to get her to relax. It had worked.

"Yeah," Secret replied, nodding. "I'm ready. Thank you so much baby...for everything."

Dunga kissed her on the forehead and they went back out to the work area.

The unexpected turn of events had made things a bit complicated but Dunga was confident that he could handle it. The main thing now was getting Secret situated somewhere comfortable until he found her an apartment and even more importantly, keep Dahlia from discovering that he was having an intimate relationship with her. He got behind the controls and the rhythm that he intended to use for Secret's next recording filtered through the speakers. Secret sat with her notebook and pen, and closed her eyes, allowing herself to become one with the music. She was feeling very inspired. She opened her eyes and began to write. The words flowed effortlessly.

ଔଓଔଓଔଓ

After having four boisterous rounds with three of his close friends, Weatherburn reluctantly called it a night at 10:30. The vibe was great and he was having a good time but he needed to get some rest. He had to be at the airport at 8:30 in the morning as he had to fly down to Montego Bay for an important 11:00 meeting with the mayor and the board of the parish council. He had gotten disturbing news that a group of Dutch investors, who had received the go ahead to construct a new hotel close to the airport in Montego Bay, were building the hotel two stories higher than what had been agreed to. This breach was dangerous as it would interfere with the flight path of the planes flying to and from the airport. It had to be dealt with firmly and quickly before the media got wind of it. His wife was in the living room watching a movie when he got home. After instructing Eddie to pick him up promptly at 7:30 in the morning, he went straight to bed and immediately fell asleep.

ઉଷଉଷଉଷ

"Ok it's a wrap folks," the director said wearily. It was 12 a.m. and they had begun working at 5 p.m. It had been a good shoot despite the fact he didn't get along with Jade. He thought she was too opinionated and diva-like in her behaviour. But the commercial would be a very effective one. It was sexy and flashy; just like the drink it was supposed to be advertising. And he had to admit that Jade was a natural in front of the camera.

Jade was happy to hear those words. She immediately hurried backstage to change.

"You did really well," Mishka, the stylist, said as she collected the clothes and accessories from Jade.

"Thanks," Jade said, suppressing a yawn. She was drop dead tired but pleased with how things had turned out. It had felt good being in front of the camera and everyone said the commercial was going to be great so she was looking forward to seeing it. It would be aired in five days.

Jade hurriedly dressed and told everyone goodbye. Even the director with whom she had been beefing all night.

The driver was outside waiting. She hopped in and they got to the hotel quickly as there was hardly any traffic on the road. He pulled up in front of the lobby and Jade muttered a weary goodnight and made her way to her suite. She peeled off her clothes and took a very quick shower. Despite her fatigue, she found it impossible to go to bed without showering after such a long day. She then climbed into bed and promptly fell into a dreamless sleep.

Chapter 27

Dunga and the team worked tirelessly at the studio until 5:30 a.m. They had successfully recorded the song that Secret had written that night. A funky, up-tempo joint called *Sunshine* which dealt with overcoming life's hurdles. Dunga was pleased with the night's work. Secret had done her part. The rest was up to him. It was now time to get the marketing in gear. Everyone left the studio at the same time: Dunga, Secret, the engineer and Jimmy. Dunga removed Secret's stuff from Jimmy's vehicle and placed them in his and they all headed to their homes.

Dunga looked over at Secret as he cruised down Constant Spring Road. A few people already heading out to work along with several school children were on the road. She never even asked him where he was taking her. Complete trust. He liked that. He was taking her to the only place that he could think of that she would be comfortable on such short notice. He slipped in a CD containing the two tracks that they had recorded thus far and they listened to Secret's melodic voice in comfortable silence.

They arrived at the quaint three-bedroom dwelling that Dunga had purchased for his mom five years ago in twenty minutes. It was located in a quiet, residential neighbourhood in the Liguanea area. Dunga pulled up and retrieved Secret's stuff from the backseat.

"Let's go," he said and Secret exited the vehicle. He smiled at her reassuringly and they went inside the yard. Dunga rummaged through some keys and opened the lock on the patio grill. He then unlocked the front door and Secret followed him inside. He led her to the bedroom on the right side of the house as it had its own entrance via the empty carport.

He placed her things on the carpeted floor right in front of the closet.

"This is where you'll be staying for awhile," he said. "My mom lives here."

"Ok," Secret said. "When do I meet her?"

"She's in her room now praying," Dunga said with a chuckle as he looked at his watch. His mother always had devotion for around ten minutes whenever she got up at six in the morning. "I'm going to speak to her alone for a few minutes and then introduce you guys."

Secret nodded and looked around the room. It was very cozy and comfortable. Carpeted floor, nice drapes, a firm queen size bed, a twenty-seven inch T.V. and a spacious closet. It also had its own bathroom and entrance. Perfect.

Dunga checked his watch again.

"I'll soon be back."

He then left the room and closed the door behind him.

Dunga crossed the living room and knocked on his mother's bedroom door.

"Come in son," his mother said as she got up from off her knees. She had heard when he pulled up and entered the house but she wasn't one to disturb her devotion if she could help it. She also knew that he hadn't come in alone. Maybe Dahlia was with him.

Dunga entered and closed the door.

"How's my baby?" he said with a smile as he sat beside her on the bed and gave her a hug.

"Good morning son...I'm ok, thank God," she replied. "Just finishing up at the studio?"

Dunga nodded.

"I have someone I want you to meet," he said.

His mother raised her thick eyebrows. So it wasn't Dahlia that he had brought here.

"Who is it?" she asked.

"A new artist that I'm working with," he replied. "Her name is Secret. Very nice girl. She's in a spot though and I need somewhere for her to stay for a little while."

"Are you sleeping with her son?"

Dunga smiled inwardly. That was his mom. Most straightforward person he knew.

He nodded.

"Son!" his mother exclaimed, showing her displeasure. "You know I don't mind helping out but how can you put me in the middle like this? What happens when Dahlia sees her here? Huh? You cannot expect me to tell lies for you!"

"You don't need to lie mum," Dunga said soothingly. "You just tell her the truth. The girl is my new artist and she's staying here for a little while. That's all. Anyways she won't find out."

Dunga's mother sighed. She loved her only son dearly but sometimes she felt like smacking him upside his head.

"I'm sorry for asking you to do this but everything happened very quickly and I have to put her somewhere comfortable mum. I need her mind to be settled so that she can give me her best in the studio," Dunga continued. "It will only be for a little while until I find an apartment for her. You won't even know she's here."

He kissed her on the cheek.

"Come and meet her," he said as he stood up.

His mother released a huge sigh and shook her head in resignation.

"Give me a minute," she told him and went into her bathroom and closed the door.

"Ok, we'll be out in the living room."

ଔଷ ଔଷ ଔଷ

Secret was sitting on the bed when he returned to the room. She looked at him with a nervous smile. Dunga bent and gave her a kiss.

"Come and meet my mother," he said and they went out into the living room. Secret was extremely nervous as she desperately hoped the woman liked her. They sat on the couch and two minutes later, his mom, wearing a floral housedress and bed slippers, entered the room. Dunga and Secret stood.

"Mum, this is Secret, Secret meet my lovely mother, Gloria King," Dunga said. He knew despite his mother's protestations that she wouldn't let him down and he knew that she would like Secret.

"Hi," his mother said, shaking Secret's outstretched hand. "Welcome to my humble home."

"It's a pleasure to meet you Ms. King," Secret said. "Thank you so much for allowing me to stay here."

"Please, just call me Miss G," she said waving aside Secret's thanks.

"You guys must be hungry," she said marching off to the kitchen. "I'll whip up a quick breakfast."

Dunga grinned at Secret and they sat back down on the couch. He turned on the T.V. and they tuned into a local morning time program. Fifteen minutes later, they were fed scrambled eggs with fried plantain, sausages, wheat bread, mint tea and orange juice. Dunga didn't linger after breakfast. He kissed both women bye and headed home to get some sleep. Gloria declined Secret's offer to assist in doing the dishes and told her that she should go and get some rest. Secret hugged her, told her thanks again and went into her new room. She closed the door and took a nice hot shower before tumbling into the comfortable bed. Dunga was the last thing on her mind before she fell asleep.

Jade woke up just few minutes after twelve. She was famished. She buzzed Ross, the bellhop, and asked him to bring her a bacon cheeseburger with fries and a coke. He returned just as she got out of the shower. Jade, wearing just a towel around her still slightly wet frame, allowed him to enter the room and place the food on the table. She then retrieved the credit card from her pocketbook and gave him to go and pay for the food. She smiled at his nervousness as she immediately dug into the food. Poor kid. Ross returned a few minutes later.

"Umm...the card isn't working," he stammered, struggling not to stare at the swell of her breasts wrapped in the plush red towel. "They swiped it a few times but it kept declining."

Jade frowned thoughtfully as she rummaged through her pocketbook for some of the cash that Weatherburn had given to her and handed Ross a thousand dollar bill.

"Keep the change," she told him.

"Umm...thank you so much," Ross said. The change was three hundred and fifty dollars. That could buy him a good lunch at the little restaurant a few blocks from the hotel. He gave her the card and left the suite.

Jade threw the card down and took another bite of her burger. It was very odd that all of a sudden the card was no longer working. She wondered if Weatherburn had really cancelled the card because he didn't get his way yesterday. She picked up her phone and scrolled to Eddie's number. He answered on the second ring.

"Hello," Eddie said.

"Hi Eddie, it's Jade. Are you with your boss?"

"Hi Jade! No, he's in Montego Bay. I'm supposed to be picking him up at the airport later today," Eddie replied. He was in the parking lot at the Ministry shooting the breeze with two security guards. "What's up?"

"Eddie...did he go to the hotel to pick me up yesterday evening?"

"Yeah, he did," Eddie replied as he walked a few meters away for some privacy. "He was really upset that you weren't there."

"I see...tell me what happened."

Eddie did and Jade realized that Weatherburn had been embarrassed and upset and most likely had cancelled the card after that. What else had he done? Well the hotel was already paid for and she had four more days there. The only other thing he could do was not allow her to move into the apartment. He was probably waiting for her to call him and apologize and grovel. Fat chance of that happening. Then Jade remembered something. The TRN number. Weatherburn had said it would have been ready by now.

"Eddie...my TRN is supposed to be ready...do you know where it should be picked up?"

"Yeah man," Eddie replied. "The tax department is downtown."

"Do you know anyone there? Can you pick it up for me?" Jade asked hopefully.

"Umm...I do know someone there that the boss sends me to directly from time to time...but I don't know Jade..."

"Eddie just go and tell him that Weatherburn sent you to pick up the TRN for Jade Jones...please? I'd really appreciate it."

Eddie was hesitant for good reason. It was entirely possible that Weatherburn would fire him if he found out. He really liked Jade though and she always treated him with respect. And now she needed his help. How could he say no? Eddie sighed.

"Ok Jade, I'll go down there and get it for you."

"Thank you Eddie. I'm at the hotel...just call me back on this number ok?"

"Alright...later then."

Eddie hung up and walked over to the vehicle.

"Eddie yuh gone?" one of the security guards that he had been speaking with prior to Jade's call asked.

"Soon be back," Eddie replied without breaking his stride. He hopped into the vehicle and exited the premises. The tax department was about fifteen minutes away.

ଓଃଓଃଓଃ

"The dead has risen," Dahlia commented when Dunga finally stirred at 1 p.m.

"Whatever," Dunga replied with a yawn as he hopped out of bed naked and went into the bathroom to pee. "You good babes?"

She admired his chiseled physique from her perch on the edge of the bed as he urinated. She wondered how he maintained such a sexy physique seeing as he rarely made use of the home gym he had in the spare bedroom. Dahlia had just taken a shower and was getting ready to go by the store.

"Yeah, I'm ok," she replied as she slipped on her bra.

"How are things at the studio?" Dahlia asked when Dunga came back into the bedroom. She had only been to the studio a few times over the years as Dunga didn't like her going there.

"Great...working on some wicked new music," he replied. "Putting out a new artist."

"Really...what's his name?" Dahlia queried. She went into the closet to find something to wear. She selected a pair of Dolce & Gabbana skinny jeans and a Vim & Virtue graphic short sleeve tee.

"It's a she," Dunga replied as he slipped on a pair of boxers and headed out to the kitchen. He was starving.

He was putting the finishing touches on his double-deck ham and cheese sandwich when she stopped in the kitchen before heading out.

"So...a female huh...what's her name?" Dahlia asked. She was standing in the doorway twirling her car keys.

"Her name is Secret," Dunga replied as he poured some orange juice. "Why you sound surprised like I've never produced female artists before?"

"I dunno...just assumed it was male...that's all."

"Well you know what they say about assumptions," Dunga commented before taking a big bite of his sandwich.

"Whatever, will I be seeing you later?" she asked.

"I don't know what time I'll be home...I have a session tonight."

"Ok, bye," Dahlia said and exited the apartment.

Dunga could hear her driving out a few seconds later.

Dahlia felt uneasy. It wasn't the first time that she knew of Dunga producing a female artist but this was different. This was someone that he would be putting out, not an established artist that he was just producing one or two tracks for. She wondered what Secret looked like. She had this sudden urge to find out more about this girl. After all, work or not, she would be spending a lot of time with her man. Late nights at the studio and all that jazz. She would do a discreet investigation. One could never be too careful these days. Women broke up happy homes all the time. And she wasn't about to sit by idly while another woman took her man. Hell fucking no.

The meeting had been very tense and explosive. Weatherburn acted quickly and decisively. The parish council official who had signed the papers giving the Dutch investors the go ahead to build the two extra floors was ordered to resign with immediate effect. He then gave the investors notice to demolish the two extra floors within seven days. Jamaica welcomed foreign investors but they had to abide by the country's laws and this was not the first time this particular group of investors had acted as though they were above the laws of Jamaica. They had breached several environmental laws when they constructed their first hotel in Ocho Rios ten months ago but this latest transgression was much more serious. The meeting ended at 1:30 and Weatherburn, along with the mayor, went to Pot Roast on the Pier, one of Montego Bay's premier restaurants, to have lunch.

Jade had just gotten off the phone with Mr. Hassan when Eddie called.

"Hi Eddie," Jade said, answering on the first ring.

"Hi, Jade, I'm outside," Eddie told her.

"Ok, I'll be right down."

Jade, already wearing shorts and a tank top; slipped on a pair of flip flops and quickly went downstairs. Eddie was standing beside the vehicle smoking a cigarette.

He smiled and handed her the small envelope.

Jade grinned and hugged him.

Eddie was surprised and embarrassed at the gesture.

"Thank you so much Eddie," Jade said as she released him. "I really appreciate this."

"You're welcome Jade," Eddie replied. He was happy that he had helped her out. It hadn't been difficult. It was customary for him to pick up documents there from time to time. He just didn't want Weatherburn to find out that he had gone there behind his back.

Jade opened the envelope. It was a simple white card with the tax department logo, her name and the tax registration number on it. But just like her social security number in the United States, it was essential that she had it.

"Your boss is being an asshole," Jade confided. "So you probably won't be seeing much of me but do keep in touch. And thanks again."

"Ok Jade, take good care," Eddie told her. So Weatherburn had fucked up. After all his effort he had lost Jade. No wonder he had been in a bad mood since yesterday. "And don't hesitate to call if you need me for anything."

Jade smiled her thanks and made her way back to the suite. She had a dinner date with Mr. Hassan at 4 p.m. He was going to give her the itinerary for the upcoming marketing campaign and she had told him that she needed to discuss something important and personal with him. She needed somewhere to live. If he couldn't provide accommodation for her she planned to ask him for an advance so that she could find somewhere to rent. As far as she was concerned, Weatherburn had showed his true colours. He had agreed to an arrangement that he couldn't handle and instead of being a real man and bowing out gracefully, he had tried to control her by flexing his financial muscle. He had played his trump card and lost. He was waiting for a call that he would never receive. He had served his purpose. Now it was time to move on. She rummaged through her things and selected the cute black Gucci cocktail dress that she had been dying to wear.

ଔଓଔଓଔଓ

"I was about to come and check your pulse," Miss G said jokingly to Secret when she finally emerged from her room at 2:30 p.m.

Secret laughed. She had been so tired. Physically and emotionally drained. Yesterday had been a hell of a day.

"I had a really good rest," Secret told her. "The room is so comfortable."

"Well that's good," Miss G said, turning her attention back to the steaming pots on the stove. "Have a seat, lunch is pretty much ready."

Miss G hummed as she dished out a huge plate of white rice, boiled green bananas and curried chicken.

"Miss G I can't possibly eat off all of this!" Secret protested.

"Hush up and eat the food," Miss G said good-naturedly. "You could use a bit more meat on those bones."

Secret laughed. Miss G was something else.

They had a very enjoyable meal. Secret laughed heartily at Miss G's stories, especially the ones involving Dunga when he was a little boy. Secret was so full when they were through that she could hardly move.

Chapter 28

Weatherburn was back in Kingston at 4:25 p.m. Eddie was outside waiting when he exited the airport.

"How you doing boss," Eddie greeted as Weatherburn hopped into the vehicle.

"I'm ok," Weatherburn replied. "I'm going by the office."

"Ok boss."

Weatherburn had instructed both his personal assistant and his secretary not to leave the office until he got there. There were a few urgent matters he needed to tie up before tomorrow. It had been a good day. The problem had been rectified so even if the media got a hold of the story before he released an official statement, the public relations damage would be minimal. The only thing missing was that he had yet to hear from Jade. Well at the very least he would hear from her by Friday. That was her final day at the hotel. He lit a cigar and lowered the window slightly. The sky was the colour of his suit. It was going to rain soon.

ঔঌঔঌঔঌ

Jade flipped through the folder Mr. Hassan had given to her. She was surprised to see copies of the three pictures that would be used to jump start the print advertisement campaign. The team had worked very fast to produce the ads within a day of the photo shoot. She was pleased with the end result. The pictures were stunning and the tag lines effective. Her favourite was the one used on the picture with her and the parrot lounging on the beach watching the sunrise: *Sophistication knows no boundary, time or place. La Roseda…for the diva in you.*

"That one is going to be on billboards in all the major towns and cities across Jamaica by tomorrow evening. The commercial will be aired on Saturday and our official launch will be in two weeks," Mr. Hassan related between mouthfuls of honey roasted chicken and rice and peas. They were at Mr. Supper, a popular eatery located on Old Hope road.

Jade nodded and continued to look through the folder. She had a promotional visit on Friday morning at one of Jamaica's two major television stations as well as an appearance on a popular entertainment program later on that day. She was to go shopping with Mishka tomorrow for outfits to wear to all the upcoming engagements.

"What's the shopping budget?" Jade asked cheekily.

Mr. Hassan laughed.

"Don't worry...you'll be able to purchase your heart's desire. Image, after all, is everything."

Jade smiled at that. She took a bite of her oxtail and beans.

"So what was that personal matter you wanted to discuss?" Mr. Hassan asked.

"Oh, I need somewhere to live," she said matter-of-factly. "I'll only be at the hotel for three more days."

"I see," Mr. Hassan responded, chewing his food thoughtfully. "The company owns an apartment here and rented two others but they are all filled."

"Well may I be advanced my first paycheck? Then I could find somewhere to rent."

"No problem," Mr. Hassan said nodding his head vigorously. "I'll send over the cheque to you at the hotel tomorrow around midday as well as your expense credit card."

"Ok, great. Thank you."

"No problem Jade. Besides, I have to make sure my star is happy."

They both laughed and Jade raised her glass of white wine in a toast to the best boss anyone could ever have.

cscscs

Dunga got to the studio at 5 p.m. He joked around with Jimmy and the engineer as they prepared for the session with Ras Che. The singer arrived an hour later with his model girlfriend and road manager in tow. After facilitating Ras Che's pre-recording ritual of a round of Hennessey with cranberry and a marijuana joint, Dunga then got down to business. The plan was to completely finish two songs tonight. His mind briefly ran on Secret. He would call her after the first song was finished.

cscscs

Jade called Theresa when she was leaving the restaurant. She was still at work so Jade told her driver to take her over there. Theresa and the customer that she was finishing up were the only ones there. The salon was closed so everyone else had gone home. Theresa buzzed her in and told her to give her a few minutes. Jade busied herself with this month's issue of Vanity Fair while she waited. Theresa was through in ten minutes.

"So what's up girl?" she said as she plopped down on the chair beside Jade. "How was the commercial shoot?"

"I just had dinner with my boss," Jade replied as she put down the magazine. "The commercial shoot was a pain in the ass but everyone thinks it came off really well. I haven't seen the final thing yet though."

"Ok cool...when is it going to air?"

"Friday night during this popular entertainment program that I'll be making a promotional visit on as well," Jade told her.

"That's nice. That must be *Entertainment Round-up*. It's one of the most popular programs on local T.V. Your boss must have a lot of clout to get you on there in such a short space of time."

"Well money talks and he's certainly got a lot of that," Jade replied.

Theresa then locked up the salon and they hopped in her ride and headed over to the hotel. She wanted to hang out with Jade for a bit before heading home. They went up to Jade's suite and Jade poured two glasses of La Roseda. She had taken a bottle from the photo shoot back to the hotel.

"This is the drink that I'll be promoting," Jade said. "Tell me what you think."

Theresa took a sip. Then another.

"It's really good, Jade. Smooth with a slightly fruity taste," Theresa proclaimed. "I love it."

"You better," Jade said grinning, "because that's all we'll be drinking when we hang out in public from now on. Once the marketing campaign gets going and La Roseda is on the shelves, it wouldn't be a good look for me to be seen partying and drinking something else."

They went out on the balcony to sit and look at the view. They could see several people jogging in Emancipation Park.

"I need to find somewhere to live," Jade told her. "I'm checking out of the hotel on Friday."

"You shouldn't have a problem finding a nice apartment," Theresa responded. "Duane can find you one quite easily I'm sure."

"Duane is no longer in the picture," Jade said.

Theresa looked over at her in surprise. She waited for Jade to elaborate but she didn't.

"Okay, well I'll check with a few people and see if they know of anything available but ensure you get the newspaper in the morning and check the classifieds," Theresa said, wondering what Weatherburn had done to blow it with Jade.

"Thanks, I'll buzz the bell boy to bring one up in the morning."

An hour and another glass of La Roseda later, Theresa left to go home, promising to call Jade tomorrow. She thought about Jade as she headed up Trafalgar Road. Though she liked Jade a lot and considered her a good friend, she realized that she didn't know anything about her. Jade was very cool and down to earth but was also a very private person. Theresa hoped that as they got closer Jade would eventually open up and she would learn more about her. She hadn't had a close female friend since her best friend migrated to the United States almost two years ago. They were still close but had only seen each other once since the migration. It surprised her that she was so drawn to Jade, who though very intelligent and sophisticated, was obviously much younger than her.

A white Toyota Rav4 passed her in the adjacent lane and Theresa's thoughts switched from Jade to Gerald, her ex-boyfriend, who drove one as well. Though they had broken up over three months ago, she still called him up occasionally when she needed some sex, which he always willingly provided. She hadn't met anyone since the break-up that tickled her fancy and though she loved to have sex, she wasn't one to sleep around indiscriminately. Gerald had turned out to be a non-ambitious lout so she had dumped him. But he knew how to use his sizeable dick and tongue so he was now her emergency dick-in-a-glass. It had been three weeks since the last time they fucked. It was time to break the glass again. The La Roseda had given her a nice buzz. She was horny. She dialed his number as she waited for the light to turn green. He answered on the third ring. She got straight to the point and hung up. He was available and would swing by her home in half an hour. Great sex without the emotional baggage. It had its benefits.

ঔঔঔ

Jade took a shower and snuggled up in bed after Theresa left. She was in an introspective mood. It had been quite a ride since she arrived in Jamaica. So much had happened.

And it was just the beginning. She was positive that the La Roseda gig would open up a lot of doors for her. Someone once said that luck was when preparation met opportunity. Someone else opined that one created their own luck. Jade thought there was a bit of truth in both statements. She thought of her parents. She wondered if they ever regretted turning their backs on her. Or had they closed that chapter in their lives and moved on as if they didn't give birth to a daughter who had been the center of their world for sixteen years. She found it incredible that people who considered themselves Christians could be so unforgiving and cold to their own child. She then thought of Chino; wondered if he was still staying one step ahead of the law. Wondered if he was still with Juanita. Their betrayal had taught her that she should never fully put her trust in anyone. They would get theirs soon enough. Karma was a bitch.

"What's up babes?" Dunga asked. He was in his office with the door closed. They had completed the first recording and were taking a break. The others were out in the chill room eating fried chicken and fries that Dunga had ordered.

"Hi baby," Secret replied, happy to hear his voice. She was hoping he would have called.

"Everything is great. I'm in bed watching a movie," Secret told him.

"What are you wearing?"

Secret giggled.

"Just a baby tee and boy shorts."

"Mmmm...sounds good," Dunga said throatily. He couldn't wait to be inside her again.

Secret laughed.

"Babes tomorrow Jimmy is going to take you shopping. You'll have to do some photo shoots soon. I know this really good stylist that I use from time to time; she'll be going with you to pick out some outfits. Be ready at 12:30," Dunga told her, all business now.

"Okay baby," Secret replied. She was excited about that. Doing a photo shoot meant that Dunga was ready to kick start the promotional side of things. She couldn't wait to jump start what she was sure would be a successful career. With her talent and look, and with Dunga behind her, the sky was the limit. It had also been awhile since she went shopping. Which woman on earth wouldn't be excited about that?

"I have some good news but I'll keep you in suspense for now," Dunga teased.

"Baby! What is it? Tell me please!" Secret begged.

Dunga laughed loudly.

"I gotta get back to work, sleep tight sugar."

"No baby, you're so cruel!" Secret replied but she was talking to herself. Dunga had already hung up.

Secret smiled and placed the phone back on the bedside table. She was so curious and excited that she wondered how she would ever fall asleep tonight.

Chapter 29

CORRUPTION! screamed the front page headline of one of the nation's major newspapers. Weatherburn had been up since 5 a.m. dealing with reporters on the phone. Bradley Saunders had struck again. He had somehow gotten the scoop on what transpired with the Dutch investors in Montego Bay and had written a scathing article accusing the new government and Weatherburn in his capacity as Minister for Mining, Energy and Environment, of accepting kickbacks to turn a blind eye to the danger of building a hotel directly in the flight path of the Sangster International Airport. After speaking with a few reporters that he could trust to report the facts, and assuaging the Prime Minister that he had everything under control, he had a quick breakfast and shower, and made his way to the office. Eddie, having seen the article, did not even risk telling his boss good morning. Though he had indeed dealt with the situation, Weatherburn was on the hot seat as the article really placed the government in a bad light and embarrassed the Prime Minister who, when campaigning, had promised that corruption would be a thing of the past when his government took office. He was also livid that he hadn't been advised of the situation immediately. Weatherburn had invited the media to a press conference in the conference room at the ministry at 8 a.m. He needed to do something about Bradley Saunders. He was really getting under his skin.

Jade woke up at 7:30 and buzzed Ross to bring her a copy of the newspaper. He brought it up and she gave him some cash to get her an omelet and orange juice for breakfast. She counted the money she had left. Four thousand dollars. She still had the four hundred and fifty American dollars that she had taken with her to Jamaica but that was to be used to jump-start a savings account. Fortunately, Mr. Hassan would be sending over her cheque by midday. She wasn't sure exactly what the exchange rate was but the thousand pounds was over a hundred thousand Jamaican dollars. She sat at the small table and browsed through the classifieds. She was not familiar with some of the areas but she figured that the higher the rental cost, the more upscale the area. So she circled every available one and two bedroom apartment that was for over thirty-five thousand dollars monthly, as well as the two that were in New Kingston. She would discuss it with Theresa later in the evening.

Ross returned with her breakfast and she tipped him generously as usual. She then turned on the TV and put the channel on CNN so that she could catch up on news around the world.

ଔଓଔଓଔଓ

Secret was ready to go when Jimmy arrived to pick her up promptly at 12. The stylist was supposed to meet them at a store in Half-Way-Tree. Something caught Jimmy's eye when they got to Seventh Avenue Plaza. There was a huge billboard with a shot of a very pretty, voluptuous woman coming out of the sea. There was a uniquely designed bottle of pink liquor standing upright on the sand next to a towel with a parrot sitting on it. He knew that face anywhere. It was the woman that Dunga had sent him to outside the airport a few days ago. He was sure of it. The stylist was there when they entered the store. Jimmy introduced Secret to Mishka and left them to browse the store for outfits. He then went outside to call Dunga.

"You look very sweet and innocent so I'm thinking your image should be soft punk," Mishka was saying as she led Secret over to where they had some punk rock looking outfits. "Sexy but with an edge."

Secret nodded agreeably.

Mishka took up a close-fitting graphic baby tee, a fitted True Religion denim jacket and a pair of ripped Prada skinny Jeans.

"Try these on," she instructed as she handed them to Secret.

Secret went into the changing room while Mishka went over to the shoe section to see if she could find anything to complement what she had picked out so far.

ଔଓଔଓଔଓ

"Really?" Dunga said in surprise. He hadn't thought about the mystery woman since the night he had seen her at the movies. Secret and the exceptional music that he was working on with her and Ras Che, had pushed thoughts of the woman to the recesses of his mind. Now Jimmy was saying she was on a billboard advertisement for a liqueur that he had never seen before.

"Yeah man, the picture look wicked," Jimmy responded. "Alright later...I'm going back inside the store now to see what the girls are doing."

"Yeah later."

Dunga was thoughtful when he got off the phone. His life was already getting complicated as it is. Last thing he needed was to be sweating this woman. She had his number and had never called him. Obviously she wasn't interested. He had seen something in the way she had looked at him that night at the movies though. It was useless to ponder who this woman was and if he would eventually get to really meet her. He had his hands full with Secret, Dahlia and his work. It would be foolhardy to waste time dwelling on this woman. He picked up his keys and left the apartment. His daughter Samantha was participating in a school play in the afternoon and he had to go see it. Dahlia was at the store but would meet him there.

❧❧❧

Mr. Hassan sent the driver over to the hotel at 1:35 p.m. Jade quickly got dressed and hopped in the back of the SUV as usual. Leroy handed her the envelope. Jade opened it and looked which bank the cheque was drawn on. The expense credit card was in it as well.

"Take me to the Jamaica Commercial Bank," she instructed, looking away from his piercing gaze in the rear view mirror. She had forgotten to ask Mr. Hassan to change him. The guy just gave her the creeps. Jade gasped when they got to the stoplight just below the Police Post on Knutsford Boulevard. A billboard bearing her likeness was right there. She smiled excitedly. It was the shot of her lying on the beach with the parrot and watching the sunrise. It was a very striking shot. They got to the bank in fifteen minutes and something hit Jade just as she was about to exit the vehicle. She didn't have an identification card that had a photo. She had to have an ID to cash the cheque. She quickly called Mr. Hassan and told him that she couldn't find her passport and had no other form of ID. He told her to sit tight and he would call her right back.

"So everything good sexy?" Leroy asked, turning around to look at her.

Jade shot him a dirty look and ignored him. Mr. Hassan called back in five minutes and told her that she should ask for Marvin Chang. He handled the company account for the bank and would facilitate the transaction for her. Jade thanked him heartily and exited the vehicle. She went inside the bank with just five minutes to spare before closing time.

She received a lot of stares as she made her way to the information desk. She was wearing a fitted black pinstripe blazer with a pair of DKNY dress slacks. Her pair of oversized Chanel shades, matching pocketbook and a Chanel scarf completed the get-up.

"Good afternoon," she said to the young lady at the desk, who was staring at her with her mouth slightly agape. "I'm here to see Marvin Chang. The name's Jade. He's expecting me."

"One moment," she said, never taking her eyes off of Jade as she spoke into the phone quietly.

"He'll be with you shortly."

Jade thanked her and as the few seats were taken, she continued to stand by the desk. She then saw a short, compact man of Chinese descent coming towards her from the personal banking section.

"Jade?" he asked with his hand outstretched.

Jade smiled yes and accepted his clammy handshake. Chang then happily led her around to his office. Ten minutes later, Jade exited the bank with a hundred and twenty-five thousand dollars. Leroy was in front of the bank waiting. Jade hopped in and instructed him to take her to the street where Theresa's salon was located.

❧❧❧

"Ok let's go get something to eat," Jimmy said after they exited the third store that they had been to. They had managed to get Secret eight outfits along with various accessories and six pairs of shoes. A lot of money had been spent as these were some of the top stores in Kingston that carried nothing but designer gear. Mishka was pleased with the purchases. Secret was going to look really hot and glamourous yet innocent and approachable. She was going to do it all over again tomorrow with Jade, to get her outfits for her up-coming appearances and engagements. Jimmy took them to a Chinese restaurant on the second floor of the mall. He whipped out his mobile to see if he could reach the photographer that Dunga wanted to shoot Secret. Jimmy got through to him and set up a meeting at the studio so that he could meet Secret and discuss the shoot with Dunga.

ঔঌঔঌঔঌ

Weatherburn was feeling a bit better by late afternoon. The press conference hadn't been pleasant but at least he had managed to set the record straight that the government absolutely had not granted the Dutch investors permission to build the extra two stories and that the official who had illegally signed a paper giving them the go ahead had resigned with immediate effect. The lunch meeting with the Prime Minister had been intense as well but it was all over now. He buzzed Heather, his personal assistant to come in. He could use a good blow job right now. Heather had been expecting the call after she had seen the kind of day her boss was having. She knew just want he needed. She went into his office and locked the door behind her. She then went over to the small refrigerator and retrieved a small container of whip cream. Weatherburn groaned in anticipation. She was going to give him what she referred to as 'the special'. She completely removed his trousers and underwear and knelt in front of him. Weatherburn reclined and placed one leg on his desk. He closed his eyes and the stress of the past eight hours evaporated the moment he felt the combination of the cold cream and her warm tongue.

ঔঌঔঌঔঌ

"Hi girl!" Theresa said, greeting Jade enthusiastically when she came in. The shop was full of customers and they all stared at Jade openly. "I saw the billboard! You look fabulous!"

"Thanks," Jade said smiling. "Which one did you see? It's supposed to be three different ones."

"The one with you coming out of the water," Theresa replied as she continued to style her client's hair.

"Ok, I haven't seen that one yet." Jade glanced behind her. The receptionist was looking at her with an indescribable look on her face. Jade imagined she was thinking that maybe she shouldn't have been so rude the first time she had come to the salon. She was probably shocked to see that Jade and her boss had become good friends.

"I'm gonna chill in your office and make some calls," Jade told her. She figured she would call the numbers for the two available apartments in New Kingston. Maybe Theresa could take her there to check them out after she was through with work.

"Ok Jade," Theresa told her.

Jade went in the small room and closed the door.

☙❧☙❧☙❧

"Daddy!" Samantha giggled as she jumped into Dunga's arms. The play was now over and all the kids and their parents and teachers were milling about in the auditorium. The play was an original number put together by the art department as part of the school's 20th anniversary celebration.

"You were great Sam," Dunga beamed. She had done well. She had a natural talent for the stage. It was evident even at her young age. He would definitely encourage her to take it seriously as she got older.

"Thank you daddy," Samantha said, proud that her father was impressed by her performance.

Dunga put her down and she said hello to her mother who was standing there feeling a pang of jealousy. Samantha never greeted her first as long as Dunga was present. Samantha's class teacher came over to say hello and to congratulate them on the fine job that they were doing raising Samantha. She was a very well rounded and well-behaved child. They then walked out to the parking lot and of course Samantha opted to drive with her father when she realized that her parents had arrived in separate vehicles. They were going to Pizza Heaven to have Samantha's favourite: a medium pizza with extra cheese, pepperoni, pineapple and chicken strips.

⁂

Jade got through to the two numbers she called. One of the apartments, over on Haining Road in New Kingston, was no longer available but the other, located in a complex at the bottom of Holborn Road, was still available. Theresa came into the office and closed the door. Jade showed her the places she had circled in the classifieds and told her about the two that she had called.

"Call this one as well," she advised, pointing to the one on Larfur Avenue off Old Hope Road. "That's a decent area."

Jade called and a woman answered the phone. The place was still available and Jade told her that she would be coming by sometime this evening to have a look.

"I'm through here so I'll leave Charmaine to lock up and we go and check out these places," Theresa told her.

"Okay, great."

Jade rose and waited for Theresa by the main entrance while she gave Charmaine, whom she was leaving in charge, instructions.

Jade did not like the one bedroom apartment on Holborn Road. The complex was too big – at least sixty apartments were there and the place was a bit rundown.

"How can they charge thirty thousand dollars a month for this dump?" Jade asked Theresa as she turned her nose up at the peeling walls and small space. "And it's not even furnished."

Theresa chuckled.

"The location...it's in the heart of New Kingston," she replied.

Jade told the person renting the apartment that she wasn't interested and they left and went over to the one on Larfur Avenue. It was a big house that had been divided into three self-contained units. The landlady resided in one of the units. She came out and scrutinized the two well-dressed women.

"Hi, I'm Jade," she said to the woman. "We spoke earlier on the phone."

"I see, well I spoke to a lot of people today so forgive me if I can't remember," the woman replied. "I'm Mrs. Allen-Whyte. I didn't get your last name."

"Jones," Jade replied shortly, not liking the snobby old lady on sight.

"You're very beautiful. You seem quite young though. What is it you do?" she asked.

Jade was exasperated. She saw no reason why she had to be interrogated before she was allowed to view the apartment.

"I'm in marketing," Jade told her.

"Hmmm," Mrs. Allen-Whyte responded, looking at Jade over the bridge of her glasses. "Which company do you work for?"

Jade took a deep breath. This woman was really trying her patience.

"Hassan & Cohen LLC. It's an international company that has its headquarters in the UK."

Jade was gearing up to tell the woman some choice words and leave if she asked her any more questions.

Fortunately, she just looked at Jade for a moment longer and then told her that she would now show her the apartment. Jade and Theresa exchanged looks and followed the woman to the unit. It was the third one from the entrance and had a nice mango tree right by the bedroom window. Jade loved it. The place was spotless, fully furnished and had a nice ambience. She was sold.

"I'll take it," Jade announced.

"Ok, well its forty thousand a month including utilities and I'll require a month's rent as a security deposit. I'll also need two references from professional people," Mrs. Allen-Whyte responded as she looked at the time. "I would have preferred to rent the place to an older person but you seem to be a professional woman so I guess I have no problem in allowing you to reside here."

Jade swallowed a retort.

"If you have the contract ready, I can pay you now and bring the references tomorrow when I come to collect the keys."

"Yes, that is fine," she replied. "I'll go and get the contract. You may have a seat on my patio."

"What a character!" Jade exclaimed to Theresa when the woman had gone inside. "I was two seconds away from telling off the old biddy. Acting like I'm on a damn job interview. I really like the place though."

"Yeah it's very nice," Theresa agreed. "You won't be seeing much of her anyway so you should be ok."

Jade chuckled. She wasn't sure about that. Mrs. Allen-Whyte looked like the kind of woman who was inquisitive and nosy. Theresa stayed outside under the mango tree while Jade went on the landlady's patio to seal the deal. Mrs. Allen-Whyte accepted the money after expressing surprise that a young woman would be walking around with so much cash as opposed to a cheque-book. Jade simply paid her, signed the contract and collected her receipt. She and Theresa then left and went to The Pork Pit, one of Kingston's most popular places for pork dishes, to have dinner.

"Will you be staying home tonight?" Dahlia asked. They were sitting at a table in the pizza joint. Dunga looked at Samantha and smiled. She was already reaching for her third slice. He had no idea where her food went as she was a very skinny little girl. Maybe straight to her brain. She was very smart.

"I am going by the studio but I won't be there for long. Tonight is Black Wednesday. I'll be home after that," he replied.

Dahlia nodded. Black Wednesday was a party that Dunga's friends, the Black Talon Crew, held every last Wednesday of the month deep inside their community. Dunga rarely missed it as long as he was in Jamaica.

"Are you taking me?" she asked. "I want to go."

Dunga looked over at her. He wondered what her problem was. She had been edgy since earlier today. She had never asked to go there before. Matter of fact, she didn't like those guys and didn't like the fact that Dunga was so tight with them.

"No," Dunga said firmly, turning his attention back to Samantha.

Dahlia didn't push it. She should have known he wouldn't have taken her. And that place was not somewhere that she could just show up with her girls. She didn't know why she was feeling so insecure. That was not her style. Yet it was happening. She was supposed to go back to New York next week Tuesday but she was thinking of cancelling her flight and staying a bit longer. She had asked a few people today if they knew who Secret was and one of the guys, a drummer who played for a couple of the roots reggae artists from time to time said that Secret used to sing back-up for two of the artists that he played for. The guy had gone on to comment how pretty and sexy she was and how everyone had wanted a piece of her. She didn't want to discuss the way she was feeling with Dunga as she knew that he would just curse her out and say that she was being silly as it was the nature of the business that he had to work with women from time to time; some attractive, some not. She sighed and pushed her slice of pizza to the side. She didn't have much of an appetite.

❧❧❧

Jimmy dropped off Mishka and was going to take Secret home when she told him that she wanted to go by the studio instead. Jimmy knew that Dunga wasn't there but he wouldn't mind if Secret went to the studio in his absence. They got there in fifteen minutes and Secret left her many shopping bags in Jimmy's ride and they went inside. Only the caretaker and Tupac, Dunga's dog, were on the premises. Jimmy turned on the air conditioning and the lights and went into the office to make some calls. Secret got some pen and paper and curled up on one of the sofas in the chill room. She had an idea for a hook in her head and she wanted to jot it down before it disappeared.

ઉઊઉઊઉઊ

"You want to go clubbing tonight?" Theresa asked. They had finished dinner and were getting ready to leave the restaurant. "Tonight is retro night at the Quad where they play hits from the 80s and 90s. It's really good."

Jade wasn't too keen on hearing oldies all night long but Theresa seemed eager to go.

"Okay, sure," Jade replied.

They left the restaurant and Theresa dropped Jade off at the hotel. She would be back at 11 to pick her up. Jade went up to her suite to relax for a bit and to find something to wear. Her phone rang as she entered the room. It was Mishka asking her what time they would be going shopping. Jade told her 1 p.m. That should give her enough time to get some rest after partying with Theresa. Jade then decided to exercise for an hour. She hadn't done anything yesterday so she planned to make up for that with an intense hour long routine.

Chapter 30

"Rassclaat!" Breeda exclaimed as he slowed the Range Rover to a crawl. He and Timex, along with ten other people, who were travelling on two motorbikes and in a Cadillac Escalade, were on their way to the Quad nightclub when he noticed the billboard featuring Jade.

"Ah wah?" Timex asked, sitting up a bit. He was riding shotgun, allowing his good friend to drive his treasured SUV.

"Look deh! Yuh nuh remember da gal deh?" he said, pointing to the billboard.

Timex looked and rubbed his goatee. The pretty woman he had met at The Patio. She looked even hotter than he remembered. What a body.

"How mi coulda forget...bloodclaat gal hot eh man," Timex commented wistfully.

She stayed on his mind all the way to the club and like something out of a wet dream; there she was walking towards the entrance of the club with her friend. She looked gorgeous.

"Hurry up and park," Timex said as Breeda tooted the horn and one of the security guys, recognizing Timex's vehicle, removed one of the barriers and allowed them to park directly in front of the club.

"De Escalade a fi we people," Breeda said to the guy and he removed another barrier so that the Cadillac truck could park in front of the club as well.

Timex exited the vehicle and waved to a few fans who shouted out his name from the long line of people waiting to get in. He stopped and posed for pictures with a couple of excited fans before making his way to the VIP entrance.

ଔଌଔଌଔଌ

Jade was standing behind a few people lingering at the VIP entrance. Apparently one of the guys was also an artist and having seen Timex arrive, was waiting to greet him and was blocking the entrance in the process. Theresa had intended to join the regular line but Jade was having none of that. She told Theresa that there was no way she would be joining that line and if the security guard refused her entry through the VIP entrance, she would go back home. Timex stepped up and the guy greeted him with much fanfare but Timex barely paid him any mind. Jade felt his eyes on her and looked over at him.

"Pretty girl we meet again," Timex said, giving her his most charming smile.

"Hi, how are you doing?" Jade responded politely.

"Mi deh yah...feel like listen some oldies tonight yeah," Timex told her. "Yuh and yuh friend come hang out wid we."

He allowed them to step in front of him and then he and his entourage followed. The club was already packed though it wasn't even midnight yet and the crowd was dancing up a storm to the hits of yesteryear. Timex led everyone to the VIP section and he and Jade and Theresa sat down at a table while the others stood behind them in a semi-circle. A waitress quickly appeared to take his order. Timex ordered two bottles of champagne and three bottles of Hennessy along with a couple bottles of cranberry juice. The waitress, who was obviously a huge Timex fan based on her wide grin and eagerness to please, returned with the order very quickly. Timex poured champagne for Jade and Theresa.

"Thank you," Jade told him.

"So yuh a big model...mi see yuh picture pon a billboard. Looking good..." he commented. "Beautiful I should seh..."

"Thanks...it's just part of an ad campaign for the company I work for," Jade said modestly.

Timex bopped his head to the Super Cat joint that was playing. When he was growing up in the ghetto harbouring dreams of becoming an entertainer, Super Cat had been his idol. He wanted to do a collaboration with the elusive dance-hall legend one day. The streets would love that.

"Tell me about yuhself," Timex suggested, moving a little bit closer to her.

Jade took a sip of her champagne. She hoped Timex didn't think that she was going to sit here all night and chat with him. She decided to humour him for now.

She told him that she was a returning resident after living in the States for fourteen years and a few other details. They talked for awhile and surprisingly, he was able to hold a decent enough conversation. She listened attentively while he told her a condensed version of his rise to stardom. After chatting with Timex for about fifteen minutes, Jade, now feeling mellow after two glasses of champagne, stood up and started to dance. Theresa followed suit and they danced up a storm, ignoring the many stares they were receiving. No one approached though when they saw that they were there with Timex and his crew. Jade was happy that she had agreed to accompany Theresa to the club. She was having a great time.

ঙ্গঙ্গঙ্গ

"I'm going to go to a party for a few hours...would you like to come?" Dunga asked Secret. He had gone to the studio after dropping off his daughter at Dahlia's mom. Secret had been doing some writing when he arrived. Seeing as Jimmy was the only other person there, Secret had greeted him with a passionate kiss, showing him just how much she had missed him. They then had a long discussion about his plans for her career and he had finally told her the good news. Secret would be going to Europe soon to perform with Ras Che on three shows: one in his homeland of France; one in Hamburg, Germany and another in Amsterdam. Secret had screamed loudly while she jumped on Dunga and hugged him tightly.

"Oh my god! I can't believe this...oh baby," Secret had said through tears of joy. "Will you be coming?"

"I'm not sure yet," Dunga had replied.

Then Secret had showed him the hook she wrote and Dunga immediately thought of a collaboration that would take everyone by surprise. He didn't say anything to Secret about his idea but he made her sing it on a hardcore dancehall rhythm that he had built a month ago.

"I'd love to," Secret replied, happy that she didn't have to leave his presence just yet.

"It's a real hardcore ghetto party," Dunga warned.

"No problem, I'll be with you so I know I'll be safe."

Dunga chuckled.

"Ok, let's go."

They locked up the studio and transferred Secret's shopping bags to Dunga's vehicle. Dunga and Secret then drove out with Jimmy right behind them in the CRV.

They arrived at the community of Rose Grove in twenty minutes. It was a deceptive name for one of the most dangerous communities in Jamaica. Ironically, it was also one of the most disciplined. Dunga's good friend, Bowler, and his Black Talon Crew, ran the inner-city community with a tight, but fair fist. It was rumoured that there was an arsenal of guns and ammunition in the community of which the Jamaican Army would have been proud. It was also said that the community was filled with hidden tunnels as despite numerous raids by joint police and military personnel, nothing substantial was ever found. Though the police hated the power the Black Talon Crew wielded, they have pretty much left them alone in recent times as the community had the lowest crime rate of all the ghettoes in Kingston.

The streets were empty but Dunga knew that they were being watched. It wasn't until they got deep into the heart of the community that they saw people on the road. Dunga and Jimmy parked over by the empty lot next to the car wash and mechanic shop that Bowler owned. He nodded a greeting to the two men who were at the entrance to ensure that only authorized vehicles parked there. Only members of the Black Talon Crew and their close friends could use that lot. They parked and made their way over to the roof top venue where the party was being held. They could hear one of Timex's street anthems blaring from the speakers. Secret was frightened as the sound of several guns barked in appreciation of the song being played. She held Dunga's hand tightly. She looked at Dunga wide-eyed. He was watching her with an amused expression. Secret took a deep breath but didn't comment as they climbed the stairs. This was going to be quite an experience.

Bowler and the crew greeted Dunga warmly. They were standing at their usual spot behind the bar in a little area by themselves. Dunga purchased five bottles of Hennessy for the crew and a bottle of champagne for himself, Jimmy and Secret. Only the high rollers spent money at the bar, Bowler allowed the regular patrons from the community to drink beer freely all night.

The party was in high gear and a group of girls, apparently putting on a show for the Black Talon Crew were trying to outdo each other in front of the video-light. One girl was balancing on her head with her thick legs spread wide. The black thong she was wearing was not doing a good job of covering up her vagina. The prominent lips were on full display for all and sundry. The video man had his hands full trying to catch all the action as once he pointed the video light on one particular girl, another would do something even more outrageous to get his attention. This went on for another half an hour before the selector, a short, fat man with a raspy voice, turned the beat around and began to play some lovers rock. Secret sipped her champagne and leaned back gently against Dunga. He placed one of his arms around her and they grooved to the seductive sounds of Maxi Priest's *Wide World.*

"Enjoying yourself?" Dunga asked. He knew that this was nothing like she was used to and that this kind of setting wasn't for the faint of heart but she seemed to be ok.

"I'm fine baby," she said turning her head slightly for a kiss.

Dunga gave her a soft peck on the lips.

Bowler watched them, amused. *Seems as if Dunga really likes this one*, he mused. He wasn't used to seeing him being so affectionate with a woman in a public setting. He refilled his cup with Hennessy. He could dig it though. She was a very sweet little thing.

ଔଷଔଷଔଷ

"I'm leaving now," Jade said to Timex. "My friend has an appointment in the morning and needs to get some rest."

Timex looked at his watch. It was 3:30 a.m. He had a flight to catch at 7:00 a.m. His luggage was in the SUV so that he could head straight to the airport after leaving the club and getting some food at the twenty four hour fast food joint on the hip strip.

"Yeah, mi ah go leave now too," he agreed. "Mi 'ave a flight fi catch in a couple hours. Mi 'ave a show in Toronto."

"Ok, cool," Jade replied.

Timex beckoned to the crew and they all left the club together.

"So yuh enjoy yuself?" Timex asked Jade as he walked with her and Theresa to the parking lot.

"Yeah, I had a wonderful time," Jade said.

They arrived at the car and Theresa deactivated the alarm and got in after waving bye to Timex.

"Mi really like yuh enuh Jade," Timex was saying. "Mi wah yuh deh wid me. Be my girl. Think 'bout it an' when mi come back from Canada in a few days we talk some more yeah?"

Jade was going to reiterate that it wasn't going to happen but she simply nodded. It had been a good night for everyone so she decided to end it on a good note. She took his number but wouldn't give him hers.

Timex held out his arms for a hug and Jade rolled her eyes with a wry grin and gave him a quick hug.

"Bye and have a good trip," she said and got into the car.

Theresa then drove off and headed over to the hotel to drop Jade off.

Jade was thoughtful as she curled up in bed. Could she really date someone like Timex? He was far from cute but if he shaved and cut his hair he would look a lot less fearsome. He did have a nice lean body and the bulge in his fitted jeans showed great promise. Besides, looks wasn't all now was it? And she had more than enough beauty for both of them. Another plus was that he had loads of street credibility. She liked a man that had a lot of thug in him, admittedly it turned her on, but she didn't know about Timex. He was a little bit too much on the uncouth side of the tracks. He was also making good money though it was doubtful as to whether he could afford an extremely high maintenance woman such as her herself. There was also the control factor. A man like Timex wouldn't be as docile as a man like Weatherburn and even he had proven that he couldn't handle the situation. There was a lot to consider but she wouldn't completely write him off. There was also that handsome guy that she hadn't called. She wasn't sure she wanted to go there though. She would probably have to slap the shit out of his silly horse-hair wearing babymother and she didn't have time for that kind of drama. Anyways, she needed a man. And soon. She was a free woman now and after four years of being deprived, she now wanted her regular dose of good loving and someone's money to spend so that she could save hers.

ଔଓଔଓଔଓ

"Mmmm," Secret moaned as she bit into the pillow to muffle her screams.

Dunga, fueled by the champagne and his growing affection for her, was so deep inside her that she felt it in her soul. They were in her room at his mother's house and they were trying their very best to keep the sounds of their passion to a minimum. They had left the party at 4:30 a.m.

Dunga was grinding his way deep inside her with slow, circular movements as she wrapped her legs tightly around him.

"Oh Dunga...you fuck me so good baby," Secret whispered. "I feel like I'm floating...pain...pleasure...it's all a blur...you have a magic stick baby..."

Her words were threatening to push Dunga over the edge. He wasn't ready yet though. Her pussy was feeling too good. Ridiculously good. He devoured her mouth in a rough, passionate kiss. She kissed him back just as passionately, sucking his tongue ardently and writhing beneath him as they rolled all over the bed. Secret ended up astride him and she rode him slowly and forcefully. Going up high until she was on the edge; then going back down to the hilt. Her tight, succulent pussy choked his throbbing shaft with every move.

It was a struggle for Dunga to lie still and endure the sweet torture. He moaned like he was in pain as he reached up and played with her erect nipples. He felt the waves of her essence drown his dick for the second time that morning. She shuddered and slumped on his chest as she cried softly.

"I love you Dunga," Secret whispered.

Dunga was still processing her proclamation when she claimed his mouth with a kiss. Secret then scrambled on to her hands and knees.

"Fuck me hard baby," she whispered.

Dunga got up with a low, primal growl and rammed his dick inside her wetness.

"Yes! Yes! Give it to me baby!" Secret urged, backing up to meet his violent thrusts.

Dunga was unable to hold back any longer. He felt like crying his damn self as he pulled out at the last moment and decorated her back with his children.

Chapter 31

Jade woke up at 11 a.m. and after buzzing Ross to get her some breakfast she called Mr. Hassan and asked him to get two references prepared for her as she needed them in order to move into her new apartment. Mr. Hassan joked that she was the boss as she had been giving him a lot of work to do lately, and then promised to send them over with the driver when he came by to take her on the road. That reminded Jade about something. She told Mr. Hassan that Leroy made her uncomfortable and she wanted him changed. Ross returned with her breakfast and Jade ate and showered, and decided to read the company's general information and the specific information about the product she was promoting until it was time to go on the road. A dossier with the information had been in the file that Mr. Hassan had given to her.

"Dunga are you ok?" Dahlia asked when she finally got him on the phone. She had been calling him since she woke up and realized he hadn't come home. "You didn't see my missed calls? I've been calling you all morning!"

"You don't need to be blowing up my phone like that," Dunga replied. "I've told you a million times that if you call and don't get me, I will call you back as soon as I can."

He had just gotten up and was using the bathroom when she called.

"I was worried about you Dunga!" Dahlia shouted. "You said you were going to come home after Black Wednesday so I was worried when I woke up and didn't see you!"

"Stop the fucking shouting," Dunga responded coldly. "You know I can't deal with all the drama and the unnecessary worrying and panicking so just relax. Calling me continuously like a deranged person is not cool."

Dahlia was so angry she thought she was going to explode. She hated that he was making her feel like an obsessed, mad woman.

"Fuck you Dunga!" she screamed, unable to contain her anger.

Dunga hung up on her which made her even more furious. She called back four times but he didn't pick up. Dahlia was so upset that she threw her LG Prada phone into the wall, smashing it to bits.

⁂

Dunga jumped into the shower after hanging up the phone on Dahlia. He could hear it ringing as he lathered his body, humming an old Ray Charles classic. Dunga shook his head disgustedly. Dahlia was such a fucking drama queen. So what if he hadn't gone home? She knew that sometimes he slept at the studio or at his mom. The shower curtain shifted and Secret stepped into the shower with a sleepy smile. She had just woken up.

"Good morning baby," she cooed as she reached for his dick.

Dunga smiled. It was really true what they said about women of Indian descent. Secret was insatiable.

ઉଷଉଷଉଷ

The receptionist buzzed Jade to let her know that her ride was here. Jade, already dressed, grabbed her Mui Mui tote bag and went downstairs. The vehicle was idling in front of the lobby. Jade hopped into the back seat.

"Hello," she said, pleased to see that Mr. Hassan had acted swiftly in replacing Leroy. "I'm Jade."

"Yes I know, a pleasure to meet you Jade," the man said pleasantly. "My name is Nathan."

He handed her the envelope that Mr. Hassan had sent for her and headed out into the heavy lunch-time traffic streaming up Knutsford Boulevard.

"I'm going to the Village Mall in Half-Way-Tree," Jade told him as she opened the envelope.

"Yes, Ma'am," Nathan replied.

Jade looked up at him.

"Nathan, I'm twenty-two years old. Please don't ever call me Ma'am. Jade will do just fine."

"I'm terribly sorry, Jade," Nathan said quickly. "It won't happen again."

Jade looked at the references: one from an attorney and another from a doctor. Good enough to impress the old biddy. She placed them back inside the envelope.

She then asked Nathan to tell her a bit about himself. She made an extra effort to converse with him as she knew that he had been embarrassed when she had chastised him. Nathan was happy to share. He was thirty-five years old and lived with his common-law wife Shandy and their two daughters. He had been unemployed for the past six months until someone had told him about a new company that needed a few experienced drivers.

He had been designated to drive one of the company's delivery trucks but Mr. Hassan had reassigned him today.

They got to the mall and Jade called Mishka to let her know that she was in the parking lot. Mishka told her which store to meet her and Jade exited the vehicle and made her way to Lorna's Boutique.

Dahlia was having a shitty day and it was getting progressively worse. Her two friends from New York were going home tonight and though she wasn't in the mood, she had taken them, as promised, to Half-Way-Tree so that they could purchase some souvenir items and a few bottles of rum for family and friends back home. As soon as she parked and they were exiting her SUV, she spotted the billboard featuring Jade. The other women saw it too.

"Wow!" Mabel exclaimed. "Isn't that the girl you had the little verbal altercation with? She looks stunning. Damn!"

"Yes it's the bitch," Dahlia snarled, adding "and stop drooling over her. Yuh mussi fuck woman!"

Mabel shot her a dirty look and Katrina, who didn't want to mess up her friendship with Dahlia on account of Mabel, sided with Dahlia and told Mabel to chill.

"Whatever," Mabel said dismissively as they went into Arts & Craft, a popular gift shop. "The girl is hot and that's all there is to it. I aint no hater."

Dahlia contemplated hitting Mabel over the head with a heavy carving of a man with a guitar that she had picked up to look at but thought better of it. She simply ignored her from that point on, speaking only to Katrina. Mabel didn't seem to mind and that pissed off Dahlia even more. She couldn't wait to drop them off back at the hotel.

Dunga was feeling very relaxed. He had spent the entire day in bed with Secret. They had only left the room twice to indulge in Miss G's cooking. The three of them were now having dinner. Miss G had cooked oxtail and beans with white rice and yam salad. Miss G's upcoming 53rd birthday was the topic of discussion.

"So what do want for your birthday mum?" Dunga was asking.

Miss G looked at her only child as she sipped her carrot juice. He had always doted on her even before he had money. She could have never asked for a better son. He had his ways but she wouldn't trade him for the world.

"I'm fine son, you have given me everything to my comfort," she replied. "I'll just thank god for sparing my life to see another birthday. I don't need anything."

"When is your birthday Miss G?" Secret asked.

"Next week Monday dear," Miss G replied.

"C'mon mum...there must be something that you would like as a gift," Dunga insisted. "You will be getting a gift regardless of what you say so you might as well think of something."

Miss G laughed.

"Ok sir, I'll think about it."

After dinner, Secret and Dunga took a walk around the quiet neighbourhood, then they went back to her room and Secret, feeling inspired by the porno flick she had watched in bed with Dunga before dinner, found the courage to try something she could have never imagined herself doing.

"Mmmm...baby..." Dunga moaned as Secret trailed soft, fiery kisses from his chest down to his lower stomach. He squirmed as she went lower and lower until he could feel her breath on his dick. It lurched in anticipation of her hot mouth.

"Baby...what yuh doing...fuck..." Dunga groaned. He couldn't believe that it was little inexperienced Secret who had lost her virginity a few days ago who was making him behave like this. His body was a mass of quivering flesh.

She licked his shaft like a lollipop in response.

"Baby...it tastes so good...mmmm...." she moaned as she took him in her mouth gently, trying to avoid scraping him with her teeth. She concentrated on the head for now, pursing her lips and sucking insistently.

Dunga felt like screaming. He had gotten a million blow jobs from experienced women all over the world but none had made him feel this way. His toes literally curled as she confidently took more of him in, playing with his scrotum as she did so. She released it with a plop and took his testicles in her mouth, twirling them around with her tongue as she stroked his dick gently.

"I like sucking you baby...feels good in my mouth..." Secret murmured softly.

Dunga couldn't take it anymore.

"Oh shit! I'm coming baby!" Dunga shouted.

Secret stroked him rapidly and held his dick against her breasts as he spilled his seed. The hot fluid felt good on her skin. She would swallow his essence one day but she wasn't ready for that yet. Baby steps.

Dunga looked at Secret in wonder as he caught his breath. He felt as if he had been fucking the stuffing out of her instead of getting a blow job.

She smiled her innocent, pretty smile that always drove him wild.

"You're turning me into a freak Mr. Producer," she declared.

ઌ୧ઌ୧ઌ୧

"Ok, I think this will do for now," Jade said. They had only purchased seven outfits despite going to four stores. Jade was not feeling most of the stuff that they had looked at. Then she remembered the boutique that Weatherburn had taken her to when she had just arrived in Jamaica. She couldn't remember the name but when she described it to Mishka, she knew where Jade was talking about. They decided that they would go there next week Monday. Mishka had to leave shortly as she was due on the set of a video shoot.

They exited the store with their bags and Mishka waved bye saying she would catch a cab as they were going in opposite directions. Jade then headed up to her new place so that she could collect the keys and give the landlady the references.

"So what you bought for me?" Nathan joked as the red light caught them right by Devon House, one of Kingston's landmarks. Nathan waved away the dirty, disheveled fellow who was attempting to clean the windshield.

Jade laughed.

"Mr. Hassan only approved the purchasing of clothes for me...so unless you're into cross-dressing I have nothing for you," Jade teased.

Nathan laughed heartily. Jade was such a cool, down to earth person. He wondered what the previous driver had done to get on her nerves. He had heard that the guy had only lasted a few days. They arrived at her new home and Jade hopped out and rang the buzzer at Mrs. Allen-Whyte's door. She came out almost immediately.

"Good evening," Jade said pleasantly. "How are you?"

"I'm very well young lady," she responded tartly. "Did you bring the references?"

Jade handed the envelope to her in response.

She took it and read the two letters carefully. When she was finally through, she went inside to get the keys for Jade's quarters. A grey Volvo sedan entered the yard just as she was coming back out. It parked, and a man and woman exited the vehicle with a little boy in tow. The woman was looking at Jade with open hostility while the man stubbed his toe on a piece of stone because he couldn't take his eyes off Jade.

"Hello Matthew and Doreen," Mrs. Allen-Whyte chirped. "Come and meet this young lady, she's our new neighbour."

"Hi, a pleasure to meet you," Matthew said, with a broad, nervous smile. "I'm Matthew and this is my wife Doreen."

Jade accepted his limp handshake and smiled at both of

them. The wife murmured hi but it was obvious that she didn't like Jade on sight.

"You're pretty like a dolly!" the little boy chirped, eliciting laughter from everyone except his mother.

"This is Carey, my son," Matthew explained. "He's five going on fifty."

Jade stooped down and pinched Carey's cheek.

"Why thank you," Jade said sweetly. "You're such a sweet little boy."

Carey blushed as he giggled uncontrollably.

"Nice meeting you all," Jade said. "But I have to run. Bye Mrs. Allen-Whyte. Bye Carey."

With that she hopped into the vehicle and Nathan drove off. They watched until the vehicle was out of sight.

"Who is she?" Doreen asked Mrs. Allen-Whyte. "Is she a model or something?"

"Ask her when you see her again Doreen," Mrs. Allen-Whyte responded. There was no love lost between her and her stepdaughter. She figured her only son could have done much better. She looked over at him. "Matthew, I need you to lift up something for me if you don't mind."

"Sure mother," he replied quickly, knowing he couldn't very well say no. He trooped behind her inside the house while Doreen, seething from her mother-in-law's caustic reply to her query, roughly pulled Carey by his arm and went inside their home. She sighed as she went to put the container of ice cream she had bought into the refrigerator. *Just what I need,* she mused. *Some dumb model bitch who thinks she is better than everybody else as a neighbour.*

After dropping off her friends at the hotel, and declining Katrina's offer for them to have a drink seeing as they would be leaving tomorrow, Dahlia went back home. She looked around and saw no sign that Dunga had been there. She picked up the land line and called his mother. Miss G had been in her garden when she heard the phone ringing. It had stopped and then started ringing again by the time she got to it.

"Hi Miss G, its Dahlia," she said.

Miss G hadn't heard from Dahlia in a while. She figured it was because Dunga had not gone home last night why she was calling. She was not going to get involved in her son's business so if Dahlia was seeking information she was looking in the wrong direction.

"How are you Dahlia?" Miss G responded. "Haven't heard from you for awhile."

"Yeah, I've been busy, you know how it goes sometimes Miss G," Dahlia said. "So is everything ok with you?"

"Yes, thank the Lord. I have good health and strength. I was just doing some work in my garden when you called."

"Ok, that's nice."

There was a strained silence for several seconds as Miss G waited for her to bring up Dunga.

"Umm, Miss G," she began. "I can't seem to reach Dunga on his mobile. Is he there?"

"No, he's not here," Miss G responded.

"Did he sleep there last night?" Dahlia continued.

"Dahlia," Miss G replied. "Do not call me and question me about Dunga's movements. It is your responsibility to know where he sleeps at night. Not mine. You enjoy the rest of the evening. I have to get back to the garden before it gets dark."

"Ok, Miss G," Dahlia replied sullenly. "Sorry to bother you."

Dahlia sighed when she got off the phone. She should have known it wouldn't have been a good idea to call Miss G and ask her about Dunga. She had been with Dunga for over seven years and was the mother of his child, yet Miss G never really took to her. She was always cordial and never made her feel uncomfortable but Dahlia could tell that she didn't really like her for her son. Dahlia rummaged through her suitcase and took out her old phone, a blackberry pearl, and put it to charge. She would have to get a new phone to replace the one she broke earlier when she got back to New York. For now she would just put the chip in the blackberry and use that. She felt extremely edgy and irritable. She couldn't stay like this. She decided as soon as the phone was sufficiently charged, she would go down to the studio. She was not going to allow Dunga to ignore her like this. He would be extremely angry to see her turn up at the studio but so be it. Let him join the club.

Chapter 32

Jade got back to the hotel at 6 p.m. Nathan helped her bring the two large suitcases she had bought along with her shopping bags, up to her suite. She thanked him and told him that if she didn't call him to take her somewhere later, he should have a good night and she would see him in the morning at 7. She placed the Chinese food she had bought on the table and started to pack her stuff. She had accumulated quite a bit of clothing and accessories in the short time that she had been back in Jamaica. Her collection was looking quite impressive. She selected her outfit to wear to the promotional television appearance in the morning and finished packing the rest. Tonight would be her final night at the hotel. She wondered what Weatherburn was going to do when he realized that she had checked out of the hotel and still hadn't called him. He would probably try to track her down which wouldn't be too hard seeing as she was going to be in the public eye. She couldn't wait until he managed to make contact with her. It should be interesting. There was nothing he could say or do that would make her even consider giving him another chance. What he had done was petty, vindictive and spiteful. Fuck him.

ঙ৪ঙ৪ঙ৪

Dunga was in the middle of a meeting with Secret, Jimmy and the photographer that was going to shoot Secret for her promotional CD cover and posters, when the handyman came to tell him that Dahlia was outside the gate. Dunga curtly told him that she was not to be allowed on the premises, and turned his attention back to the matter at hand. How dare Dahlia come here to his place of business with her foolishness? She was really pushing it now. He could still hear the buzzer ringing repeatedly. Crazy bitch. They wrapped up the meeting and Jimmy, Secret and the photographer left to go to a photo studio on Lady Musgrave Road to do the first set of shots. They hopped in the CRV and Dahlia seeing the gate being open, reversed slightly so as to allow Jimmy to pass. Jimmy didn't acknowledge her when he drove by. He watched in his rearview as she hurriedly drove in before the gate closed. He shook his head. That was a stupid move. Dunga did not play when it came to his work. No matter *who* the fuck it was.

Secret wondered who the angry looking woman was. She wondered if she was Dunga's girlfriend. He had told her he had a beautiful little girl named Samantha but he hadn't said anything about the mother. And she had never asked. She didn't care. Dunga was a major part of her life now and no one was going to change that. Not even his baby's mother.

ଔ৯ଔ৯ଔ৯

"Jessica," Weatherburn said, holding onto his wife's hand as she passed him in the hallway leading to the bedroom. He had just gotten home after making an appearance at a function put on by one of his associates. "Are you really still upset at me...you don't miss talking to your husband?"

Jessica looked at him in disbelief. He really wasn't going to apologize. He thought she would just forget how he violated and humiliated her and just sweep it under the rug and pretend nothing had happened. When had her husband turned into such a prick?

"Unhand me," she told him coldly. "You think this is a game? You fucking bastard. I'm going to the States for an extended vacation. I can't stand being around you right now."

Weatherburn got angry. What the fuck was wrong with this woman? Five years his junior, she had gotten extremely miserable and cranky since her fortieth birthday two months ago. She had become quite adept at turning simple things into mammoth issues. He didn't know what the hell her problem was. She had a rich, powerful husband who treated her well, she was still an attractive woman, the two kids were doing well at University yet she wasn't satisfied. She needed to count her blessings instead of bugging out over one minor incident. He had a right to fuck his wife whenever he wanted to and there was no way in hell he was going to apologize for that. She hadn't worked a day since they got married and wanted to ration sex? She must be out of her goddamn mind.

"Vacation mi rass," Weatherburn retorted. "You have been on a fucking vacation for the past twenty years. You're not going anywhere."

He released her hand and strode quickly to the bedroom. He unlocked the drawer where they kept their important documents. He looked for her passport to seize it. It wasn't there. She had already removed it. He locked the draw angrily and went in search of his wife. He was just in time to see her driving out. His chest heaved mightily as he tried to clam down. His life had suddenly become a conduit for stress. His wife was acting like a deranged woman and work had been problem after problem, after problem. And then there was Jade. She still hadn't called yet though tonight was her last night at the hotel. Nothing was going right. He went into the study to pour himself a drink.

ઉજઉજઉજ

Dahlia, though inside the complex, was unable to come out of the vehicle. Tupac, Dunga's powerful pit bull, was sitting on the steps leading up to the studio. He was growling and looking at the vehicle contemptuously, daring its occupant to come out. The handyman was leaning against the wall. He refused to come over to her. She knew both he and the dog were acting on Dunga's instructions. She blew the horn loudly and repeatedly in frustration. The handyman simply relit his marijuana joint and sat on a chair that was under the small East Indian mango tree close to the wall. He inhaled deeply and crossed his legs. Dahlia realized that she was wasting her time and making a fool of herself. She gave the handyman the middle finger and turned to go out the gate. The handyman opened the gate using the remote and she drove out angrily, nearly causing a collision with an oncoming vehicle on the main road. She heard sirens immediately. It was a police car. Cursing her luck, she pulled over and waited.

ଔଓଔଓଔଓ

"That's good...pout a little more," the photographer instructed as he snapped away. "Ahhh...wonderful...that's it..."

Secret was enjoying herself. It didn't feel like work. She knew she was too short to be a fashion model but she always loved fashion and being in front of the camera. Her shyness disappeared whenever someone pointed a camera at her, whenever she had a microphone in her hand, and lately, as being with Dunga had proven; whenever she was having sex.

Jimmy looked on in approval. The pictures would be great. Secret was looking really sexy and seductive. He was very excited for Dunga. Secret was going to be a big smash, he was sure of it. She was the complete package. And this would dispel the notion that Dunga only worked with established female artists and had never built the career of one from scratch, as he had done with several male acts. It was the only thing negative that the naysayers could find to say about the ace producer. He wondered what was happening at the studio with Dunga and Dahlia.

ଔଓଔଓଔଓ

"So you're leaving tomorrow," Francine was saying to Jessica. She was a bit surprised that Jessica was taking it this far. She had just gotten home when Jessica had pulled in her driveway, with luggage in the trunk of her car.

"Yep," Jessica replied. "I'm going to stay with my cousin in Baltimore for awhile. I'll pretty much have the place to myself as he spends most of his time at his girlfriend's apartment anyway. I need to get away for awhile Francine. This thing has affected me even more deeply than I had initially thought."

They were sitting on Francine's patio drinking Bailey's Irish Cream. Francine was puffing away as usual.

"Well, if you think that's the best thing to do at this juncture then by all means go for it girl," Francine opined. "So what did he say?"

Jessica told her what her husband had said and Francine struggled not to laugh. She found his vacation retort extremely funny. They chatted for awhile longer then went inside to watch a movie from Francine's impressive DVD collection. Jessica would spend the night there and Francine would take her to the airport in the morning to catch her 8:30 flight. She would leave her car parked at Francine's place until she returned.

Dahlia rolled the window down when one of the two cops approached her SUV and stood by the driver's side.

"Good evening ma'am," the officer said, standing with his legs slightly apart and his hands on his hips. "What kind of dangerous stunt did you just pull? Yuh filming a movie?"

Dahlia was in no mood for any sarcasm from a stupid constable.

"Just give me the damn ticket," she said in her best Brooklyn accent.

The officer frowned. Feisty bitch. She didn't think she should respect the law because she apparently had a few shillings.

"That is not the attitude Miss!" the officer scolded. "We could have just had a serious accident! I'm going to charge you with dangerous and reckless driving! That will be a ten thousand dollar fine and six points off your driver's license!"

"Why the hell are you shouting?" Dahlia shouted in response as she retrieved her documents from the glove compartment and handed them to him. "I'm not deaf nor are you talking to your woman!"

She then rummaged through her pocketbook and handed him her American driver's license.

He scowled as he snatched the documents and her license out of her hand. He scrutinized her State of New York driver's license.

"So you are an American fi true," he commented. He had thought her accent was just a ploy to perhaps get out of the ticket. He stroked his chin as he pondered the situation. If he wrote her the ticket, most likely she would be leaving the island before the deadline for payment and consequent court appearance if payment was not made by the due date. Better to see if he could extract some money from her.

Dahlia smirked at him. She had a Jamaican license as well seeing as she had dual citizenship but she knew that it would have been better to give him the American one.

"I don't really want to have to give a pretty browning like you a ticket yuh know," he said, turning on the charm. "But is a serious offence this...so mi can't just mek it slide just so..."

Dahlia knew where this was going. Wordlessly, she extracted a crisp US hundred dollar bill from her pocketbook and placed it on the dashboard. No way was she going to actually hand it to him. She had heard that the police force had been cracking down heavily on the corrupt cops who accepted bribes from motorists. He could be setting her up. She waited while he eyed the money greedily. He then handed her back the documents and took up the money in one smooth motion.

"Have a good night ma'am and be more careful on the road."

Dahlia gave him a cold smile and drove off. She was still furious as she headed down Constant Spring Road. She pondered what she could do to take off a little of the edge and get back at Dunga for treating her so disrespectfully. She smiled wickedly as she picked up the blackberry and scrolled through the phonebook. She would do something she hadn't done since the early stages of their relationship many years ago.

Weatherburn called his wife's mobile a couple times but she didn't pick up. He couldn't believe she was taking things this far. Going away without his consent and not telling him when she was leaving or even where she would be staying. She had already packed too, as he had noticed that her Louis Vuitton luggage set was missing. He wondered if she had gone over to Francine's house. Or maybe she was cheating on him and using what happened as a guise to spend time with her lover. The more he thought about it the more it made sense to him. He picked up the phone and dialed his son's mobile. Peter was a freshman at Seton Hall University in New Jersey.

The gangly eighteen year old had received a basketball scholarship. His son answered on the fourth ring and Weatherburn told him that his dear mother had run off with her young lover.

ଔଓଔଓଔଓ

After packing up her stuff, Jade felt a bit bored and ventured out to the hotel poolside to have a drink. It was singers' night at the hotel poolside on Thursdays between the hours of 7 and 12. There was a fairly decent crowd out there enjoying the live performances by some of Jamaica's talented but unknown singers. Jade ordered a martini at the bar and then sat on one of the few empty chairs available. The girl on stage was not attractive but she had a fantastic shape which the outfit she was wearing did nothing to conceal. She could sing too. Her creative rendition of Roberta Flack's *Killing Me Softly* was pleasing to the ear. Jade looked around the crowd casually. There were several people, male and female looking at her. A tall bald-headed guy, who resembled a young Michael Jordon, was eyeing her from the corner where he was standing with two other guys. After a few minutes of watching Jade, he made his way over.

"Hello, beautiful," he boomed confidently as he stooped down beside her chair. "I'm Chester."

Jade coughed. His cologne was overpowering. She guessed Chester was not cognizant of the fact that sometimes less is more. The cologne was expensive but it was strong and apparently Chester had doused himself with the entire bottle.

Jade continued to cough and cover her nostrils as she gestured with her hand for him to get away from her. He rose and tried to use a smile to mask his embarrassment but the corners of his wide mouth were tight with anger. He glanced over at his friends. They were doubled over with laughter. *Fucking bitch*, he fumed inwardly. Instead of going back over to his friends, he made his way to the rest room. He would take a leak and then head for the exit. There was no way he could stay there a moment longer. He had never been so embarrassed in his life.

ଓଃଓଃଓଃ

"Hi Zingo," Dahalia purred. "It's Dahlia..."

Zingo was at home smoking a joint and watching a DVD of a recent performance he did in England with a couple of his close friends. He was a deejay whom Dunga had produced early in his career. Dunga had produced his first three big hits but they had a huge falling out over the direction of his career and his work ethic; and Dunga no longer worked with him. He had been trying to get with Dahlia for some time now, ever since he had met her backstage at Irie Jamboree, the biggest reggae show held in North America, last year. Their paths crossed from time to time and the fact that she was Dunga's girl made the prospect of bedding her even more alluring.

"What's up girl...this is a pleasant surprise," he said, as he got up from off the sofa and went into the bedroom for some privacy.

"Nothing much, I'm in the vicinity and you crossed my mind," she replied. "Are you busy?"

"No man!" Zingo responded quickly. Was this really happening? If she came over to his house it was a done deal.

What else could she possibly want? A cup of tea and a chat? He didn't think so. "Come and hang out wid me...look how long I've been begging you to give me some of your time."

Dahlia chuckled. Zingo was a very good looking man. He was also stupid and stubborn, which was the reason he and Dunga had parted ways. He had gotten too big for his britches after his initial success and started behaving in a very hype and self-destructive manner. Several high profile run-ins with the law and unnecessary beefs with other artists had made Dunga release him from his contract. The girls loved him though, and though the hits had dried up in the past three years since Dunga dropped him, he had recently launched a come-back of sorts. A remix with a reggaeton artist out of Puerto Rico had unexpectedly made it onto the billboard charts and was very popular in several markets. He had followed that up with a decent single which was getting a lot of airplay locally in Jamaica and in England, and the six shows that he had done on a recent four week mini-tour in England had been well-attended. Zingo was on the rise once again.

"True...but nothing happens before its time aint it?" Dahlia responded.

Zingo was not about to let this opportunity to fuck Dunga's woman slip by. He had really been attracted to her when they had met initially but when he had found out that she was Dunga's girl, his interest had really intensified.

"So you coming over?" he asked. "Its easy to find...once you enter Constant Spring Gardens, you just take the first right turn and I'm at number 2."

"Maybe I will...listen out for me," she teased and hung up.

Zingo lived less than ten minutes away. She felt a pang of nervousness and guilt but it was soon shoved aside by the seething anger and frustration that she was feeling towards Dunga. Resolute, she made her way to Zingo's home.

ઉઋઉઋઉઋ

"Did he stink that bad?" a man asked as he stood next to Jade at the bar. After the cologne episode with Chester, two other brave souls had approached her: a Caucasian man who looked like he would be able to lift up Kingston with one hand and a business executive who moonlighted as a jazz singer at night. The conversion with the body builder had lasted exactly five seconds while the businessman had managed to stick around for two minutes before his date had found him and given him an earful while looking at Jade in a hostile and threatening manner.

Jade looked over at the source of the voice. He was attractive in a nerdy sort of way. Intelligent-looking Ralph Lauren test frames complimented his chiseled, clean-cut features. It seemed as though he had stopped by on his way home from work. He was wearing a dark brown suit with well-worn expensive wing tips. He had a pleasant smile.

"Perhaps he did...which is why he used so much cologne to mask his odour," Jade replied.

"I'm Zachary," he said, extending a large, manicured hand.

"I'm Jade," she replied.

"You probably hear this so many times a day that it makes you sick but I'll tell you anyway...you are *the* most beautiful woman I've ever seen in person," he said. "That billboard is going to be the cause of more than a few fender benders."

Jade chuckled.

"Thank you."

"I used to do a bit of modeling myself," he shared, as he beckoned to the bartender to give him another scotch on the rocks. "But it wasn't something that my parents would allow to interfere with my studies so I didn't do it for long."

They eventually found two chairs and they talked as they watched the show.

He wasn't the type of guy that Jade usually went for but he was good company. And truth be told, he was sexy as hell. A good looking, well-built man in an exquisitely cut suit was definitely an aphrodisiac. Even Chino, as thugged out as they come, used to dress his ass off in slick Armani suits when the occasion called for it. The memory of Chino momentarily put a frown on her gorgeous face. She dismissed it immediately. Zachary was telling her about the pressure and expectations that came with being the only son of one of Jamaica's most prominent businessmen and noted politicians. She was only half-listening. His even, white teeth gleamed as he spoke and he, albeit unconsciously, licked his lips ever so often. The horniness Jade had been enduring for the past few days was now present in full force. She toyed with the idea of fucking him as she sipped her third martini of the night.

Jimmy took Secret back to the studio after the photo shoot. Dunga was there entertaining Ras Che when they arrived. Ras Che had come by to officially tell Secret about the shows that she would be doing with him in Europe and what would be expected of her. Secret listened excitedly and assured Ras Che that though this would be her first time being on a stage in front of so many people, and performing for a foreign audience, she was more than ready and could handle the pressure. Ras Che would be leaving for France in two days and he would be taking Secret's debut single to give to the radio stations in France. Dunga would be giving him five thousand euros to give to various disc jockeys to break the song in France. Dunga hated payola but it was the nature of the business. If you wanted your music to be heard and heard now, you had to pay, even if you knew the DJ personally. Dunga was confident that the song would be a hit though, so it would be money well spent. Once the song became a hit, everyone else would be requesting the song and playing it on their own accord. Secret's debut single would be officially released in Jamaica in four days and Dunga planned to shoot the video for the single before Secret left for Europe in three weeks. After discussing and agreeing to the terms of the contract for the three shows in Europe, Ras Che and Dunga worked on another recording. They had already successfully recorded three of the six tracks that Ras Che wanted him to produce for his album. The chemistry with Dunga was right, and they shared the same genuine love for the music, and had the same work ethic. It had turned out to be a very productive trip for him to Jamaica. Ras Che placed his marijuana joint in the ashtray and went inside the booth. He had a strong feeling that this album was going to be even better than his first. So much for the sophomore jinx.

Zingo stood on the verandah and watched with bated breath as Dahlia exited her SUV and opened his gate. She was really here. Dunga's woman. It didn't get much better than this. He hated Dunga with a passion. And he was sure Dahlia knew that. Then why was she here? He brushed aside the questions and smiled as she came onto the verandah.

"Hi sexy," Zingo said giving her a hug. He was shirtless and wearing a puma shorts with socks and flip flops. Two large gold chains, one with a medallion the size of a midget, adorned his neck.

"Hey you," Dahlia responded.

"Come on in," Zingo said as he held her hand and led her inside the house. His two friends appraised Dahlia in shock when she entered the living room. Wasn't that Dunga's woman? What the hell was she doing here with his enemy? Everyone knew there was no love lost between Dunga and Zingo. Dunga had slapped Zingo in his face at a party about five days after they had parted ways. Zingo, while giving a sponataneous performance at the party at the request of the promoter, had made a disrespectful comment about a 'certain producer bwoy'. Everyone had known that he was talking about Dunga. Half an hour later, Dunga and his entourage had arrived at the party and having heard about the comment on his way to the venue, Dunga had walked up to him and administer a vicious back-handed slap to Zingo's face, embarrassing him in front of everyone. No one from his crew had retaliated. They all knew that to fight back would lead to certain death. Everyone knew that Dunga was backed by the Black Talon Crew. It was best to chill. Dunga would get his one day.

Dahlia ignored their knowing stares as she followed Zingo to his bedroom. She was a bit annoyed as she had thought he was home alone. She hadn't particularly wanted anyone to actually *see* her here. Dahlia, now feeling a bit apprehensive, sat on the edge of Zingo's bed. Smiling smugly, Zingo closed the door and went over to the small refrigerator beside the bed. He extracted a half-full bottle of Moet and poured two glasses. After all, this was a special occasion.

ೋ❀ೋ❀ೋ❀

Weatherburn felt better after speaking with his son. He had put on quite a performance. He felt like taking a bow. Peter had been shocked and appalled at the news that his mother had done such a terrible thing. A weeping Weatherburn had told him not to hate his mother, as she was obviously going through a mid-life crisis. Hopefully they would be able to work things out and keep the family together though he was very distraught and embarrassed. Peter had told him to be strong and that he would try and call his mother. Weatherburn knew that Peter would call Penelope, his sister, as well. She was two years older than Peter and was in her third year at North Carolina State University where she was an accounting major. Weatherburn poured himself another drink and went into the bedroom where he sat up in bed and turned on the television. Jessica should have never taken things this far. Who knew how things would pan out now that the kids were involved? He felt no remorse about his actions. Vindictive? Sure. Childish? Perhaps. But maybe it would turn out to be true anyway and besides, Jessica should never have pushed him like this. Now they would all have to deal with the consequences.

ೋ❀ೋ❀ೋ❀

"Cheers," Zingo said, as he raised his glass for a toast.

Dahlia smiled nervously and took a big sip of the champagne. She had not been with another man in six years. She had cheated on Dunga during the first year of their relationship. Their union had been a tumultuous one in the beginning and during one of their frequent separations she had slept with another man. She had felt very guilty because, deep down, she knew that they would have gotten back together. They always did. He never knew about it and she had sworn that she would never do anything like that again. Yet here she was. Sitting on another man's bed. And not just any other man; but one of Dunga's enemies. A wave of shame washed over her as Zingo drew closer and started kissing on her neck. He placed his hand underneath her blouse and massaged her right breast. She felt repulsed. She got up abruptly, spilling some of the champagne on the floor.

"Stop...I can't do this," Dahlia said softly but firmly. "I'm sorry for leading you on but I have to go."

Zingo's expression went from surprise to incredulity to anger. He moved past her and locked the door with the key which he slipped inside the pocket of his shorts.

"Yuh mussi bloodclaat mad," he said angrily. "Mi nuh play these kinda games. Who yuh t'ink seh yuh ah go give blue balls?"

"Zingo," Dahlia began, trying to stay calm. "A woman has the right to change her mind. Call one of your many groupies and don't do anything that you'll regret. Open the door. Now."

Zingo smirked at her as he weighed the situation. She had called him and come over on her own free will. He had two witnesses that could verify that they saw her come here a few minutes after he had received a phone call, and willingly head straight to the bedroom. She knew that he was Dunga's enemy so the fact that she was here meant that she had planned to fuck him to get back at Dunga for something. That meant if anything happened there was no way she could tell Dunga. How the fuck would she explain being in his bedroom in the first place? He had waited for this moment for a long time. There was no way he was going to allow her to leave without giving her what she came for.

"Tek off yuh fucking clothes," Zingo commanded.

❧❧❧

"I have a younger sister," Zachary was saying. "She's secretly dating this guy from the ghetto...he's an entertainer...calls himself Timex. My father would kill her if he found out."

That bit of information woke Jade from her reverie. She was just picturing Zachary's strong hands roaming all over her body.

"Really?" Jade prompted.

"Yeah...the irony of the situation is that my dad is the Member of Parliament for the area where Timex comes from. Before he made it big in music he was part of a notorious criminal gang. I have warned her to stop seeing him but she told me to mind my own business."

"Wow," Jade responded. "So how do you know all of this?"

Zachary downed the last of his scotch.

"I have my sources," he said with a smile.

"What's your sister's name?" Jade queried casually.

"Her name is Leah," Zachary replied. "She's supposed to be entering the Miss Jamaica Universe beauty pageant this year."

Jade understood the allure of the streets. She had been there. Nice, well-bred catholic girl who had been unable to resist the charms of a thug from the streets. It had changed her life. She supposed this situation was a tad bit different but similar nonetheless. She doubted Zachary's sister would rebel to the point where she gave up her rich, comfortable upper-class life to be with Timex. She was probably just enjoying the thrill of it and, knowing Timex, Jade doubted he was serious about this girl anyway. She would ask Timex about her when he returned from Canada just to see his reaction.

❦❦❦

Dahlia couldn't believe that this was happening. How the fuck had she allowed herself to get into such a predicament? She could not allow Zingo to rape her. She had to get out of here.

"Zingo...think about this...if you rape me you're a dead man," Dahlia warned. "Are you willing to die for some pussy? You have your whole life and career in front of you. Are you willing to throw it all away just to prove a point? Let me go, Zingo. Or you won't live to see tomorrow."

Zingo glared at her. His erection was obvious and his chest was heaving with anxiety. He was almost at the point of no return. Almost. Her words had chilled him. If he did it and she actually told Dunga, he would probably kill her but he would kill him too. And he was positive it wouldn't be a quick death. Zingo sucked his teeth in frustration. He was so close before the bitch got cold feet.

"Just come out ah mi bloodclaat place before mi change mi mind!" he shouted angrily as he unlocked the door.

Dahlia quickly put the glass down and gripped her pocketbook tightly as she shot pass him and ran out of the house. Zingo's two friends watched in amusement as the drama unfolded. Zingo, still cursing, went on the verandah and watched as Dahlia quickly got into her SUV and gun the engine. She pulled off at a high speed and Zingo prayed that she had an accident.

"Fucking bitch!" he spat as he took out his mobile and scrolled through his phonebook. He called a young girl named Munchie from Cassava Piece to come over. She had a huge ass and a pair of large, juicy breasts. She would help him to get over the disappointment of not getting to fuck Dahlia. He told her to catch a cab to his home and then went back inside to tell his friends what had transpired.

Dahlia pulled over at a gas station when she was far enough from Zingo's house. She locked the doors and cried like a baby. It had been a really close call. Zingo could have called her bluff and raped her anyway. Only God knows what would have happened after that. She had been so stupid. Acting like a reckless fool with nothing to lose. When the truth was she had so much. A seven year relationship with someone you love was nothing to scoff at. They had a child together and were both successful people in their own right. She couldn't allow jealousy and insecurity to make her lose her man. Dunga was wrong for not calling to say that he wasn't coming home but it didn't have to go this far and she really shouldn't have gone by the studio. She sighed and thanked God over and over again for allowing her to get out of that situation. She had learnt her lesson. She dried her face and composed herself before driving off. She couldn't wait to get home and take a shower.

ଔଷ୦ଔଷ୦ଔଷ

Jade had learnt a lot from her chat with Zachary. He apparently talked a lot when he was tipsy and after having five scotches on the rocks, he was two sips away from being drunk.

"I think you've had enough," Jade said when Zachary looked around for a waitress to order another drink.

The poolside was even more packed now, as more people streamed in to enjoy the live entertainment package. There was a saxophonist performing on stage and he electrified the crowd by playing the tunes of some current R&B hits. Jade checked the time. It was now 10:45 p.m. She was pleased that she had decided to hang out by the poolside. It had been fun. She was still horny but the feeling had subsided to a manageable level. The impulsive fuck that the almost lucky Zachary would have received would not be happening. She was ready to call it a night as she had to be up early in the morning and she wanted to look her best for her television appearance.

Zachary nodded in agreement. She was right. Anything more would push him over the edge and he had to drive home. He smiled at her. She was so fucking beautiful. He mentally compared her to Roberta, his girlfriend. She was in Cuba studying medicine. Would be a doctor in two years. She was twenty seven, a year younger than he was. Roberta was a very attractive woman but comparing her to Jade was like comparing Gabrielle Union to Halle Berry. He had been trying to discover a flaw on Jade all night but to no avail. Maybe when he got lucky enough to see her naked there would be something. No woman could look this perfect.

"I'm leaving now Zach," she told him. "I gotta be up early in the morning."

"Ok my American princess," he replied. "May I have your number please...I would hate to think that I have to wait until I ran into you again to see you..."

Jade smiled.

"Give me yours...I'll call you," she promised.

Zachary gave her his number and walked her to the bottom of the stairs where her suite was located. They hugged goodnight and he parted after kissing her on the cheek. He then walked slowly but steadily out to the parking lot where his 2007 Audi TT sports car was nestled between two SUVs. He thought of Jade almost all the way home. He really liked her. He hoped she called him soon. Roberta wasn't due to come to Jamaica until June and that was a month away. There was lots of time for him to *really* get to know Jade.

Jade decided to watch some T.V. until she fell asleep. She flipped through the channels and stopped on CNN when she saw a picture of Barack Obama. Apparently he had a slight lead on Hilary Clinton in the race for the Democratic Party's nomination to represent the party in its bid to retake the White House. Jade was amazed that a black man actually had a real chance to become the President of the United States of America. She knew that racism was still a big part of everyday life in America. It would be tough for him to beat Hilary

Clinton though. She was seasoned where Obama was a bit inexperienced and she also had her husband's clout behind her. Jade hoped he pulled through though. If he won the Democratic nomination she was sure he would beat the Republican candidate in the national election. Obama looked like he was on a road to destiny. She eventually fell asleep with the T.V. watching her.

ઉઔઉઔઉઔ

Dunga went home that night. After completing the recording with Ras Che around midnight, they all left the studio at 1 a.m. He kissed Secret goodbye and told Jimmy to take her home. Dahlia had sent him a long text message apologizing profusely for her behaviour while he had been working. Dunga had replied with an apology of his own. He admitted that he should have called when he realized that he wasn't going to make it home. He could see that Secret was disappointed that he would not be staying with her tonight. He wanted to but it was best to go home. Dahlia was trying to make amends; the least he could do was meet her halfway. He got home in twenty minutes and immediately removed his clothing and climbed into the bed naked. His presence woke Dahlia up from her restless sleep. She murmured something unintelligible as she turned and hugged him. She threw one leg over him and he could feel that she was wet. He slipped his index finger inside her. She moaned and hugged him tightly and he slipped in another. He slid them inside and out in a circular motion until she shuddered and whispered her love for him over and over again. She then placed his sticky fingers in her mouth and tasted herself.

Then the real fun began.

Chapter 33

"That was splendid!" Mr. Hassan enthused. "You represented the company beautifully."

"Thank you," Jade replied.

She was on her way back to the hotel after her five minute appearance on a popular morning time program on JTL, one of Jamaica's two major television stations. She had showcased La Roseda and had eloquently conveyed the company's mission to make La Roseda the premier drink of choice for the discerning and sophisticated Jamaican woman. Richie Simpson, the usually caustic host of the show, had been very impressed by the beautiful and articulate spokesperson. He would later be teased mercilessly by members of the production crew for behaving like a smitten schoolboy.

Jade chatted with Mr. Hassan for a few more minutes then she hung up. The traffic heading to New Kingston from Lyndhurst Road where the television studio was located was terrible. Between the transportation for the school kids and the people trying to get to work, things were moving at a snail's pace. Jade was hungry. She hadn't gotten a chance to eat before Mishka had arrived at the hotel to do her make-up. She chatted with Nathan and listened to the radio until they mercifully got to the hotel after a forty-five minute drive.

ഢ൏ഢ൏ഢ൏

"Thanks, Francine," Jessica said as she gave her long-time best friend a hug. Francine had just given her a ride to the airport.

"No problem, girl. Call me later," Francine replied.

A porter came over and placed her luggage on a trolley and she made her way inside to check-in. She hadn't told Francine but when she had retrieved her phone from her pocketbook where she had left it all of last night and checked her voicemail, she had been very disturbed to hear the message. What had her bastard of a husband done? Her two children had called her twice saying that they couldn't believe she was treating their father like this and embarrassing herself and the family. And they were worried about her and she should get in touch with them as soon as possible. What had he told them? She sighed as she went up to the counter and handed over her ticket. Well she would call them after she got to Baltimore and settled in. God help her husband if he was trying to turn their kids against her.

ഢ൏ഢ൏ഢ൏

Weatherburn was in deep thought as Eddie drove him to the office. He had been having breakfast and watching the

T.V. when he had seen Jade on the morning program, looking absolutely stunning. He had almost choked on his scrambled eggs and toast. What the fuck? How the hell did she get this job? He had never heard of the drink but he knew the company quite well. The government had purchased industrial soap from them in bulk on more than one occasion since taking over office. He had immediately lost his appetite. Jade had been making moves since they last spoke, or perhaps even before. He now knew that he had been waiting in vain like Bob Marley. She obviously was not going to call him. And just like that, this woman, whom he had treated like a queen and spent a shitload of money on, was out of his life. Or so she thought. He was one of the most powerful men in Jamaica. Jade could not dismiss him like he was a little nobody. Something to be discarded with after it had outlived its usefulness. She was in for a rude awakening. He thought about her all the way to the office.

After having breakfast with Jade at the hotel restaurant, Nathan retrieved Jade's stuff from her suite and packed them into the SUV, while she checked out. Nathan had been very surprised, and pleased, when Jade had offered to treat him to breakfast. She didn't act like she was better than people and he really admired that. After Jade had completed the check-out process, they then headed to Jade's new home. Neither of them noticed the white, heavily tinted Toyota Corolla that was following.

Dunga woke up to a lovely, filling breakfast of liver, fried plantain, boiled dumplings and boiled green bananas. He smiled as he sat up in bed and took the steaming tray from Dahlia. It had been awhile since he had received breakfast in bed. Dahlia was going all out to make amends. Last night she had even sucked his dick. She had done a decent job too, especially in light of the fact that she didn't like to do it. Dunga didn't need to go on the road until late afternoon so after he ate, he took a shower and they relaxed in bed and watched *Kill Bill Vol. 1*, one of Dunga's favourite movies, on DVD.

☙❧☙❧☙❧

Miss G was not home when Secret woke up but she had left a note for Secret on the counter letting her know that she had gone to the supermarket and that Secret should ensure that she ate off her breakfast. Secret smiled. Miss G was something else. She had grown very fond of her. She was a very sweet woman. Secret looked in the microwave. There was a plate filled with calalloo and saltfish and Johnny cakes. She warmed it up and poured some orange juice. She would eat and then call Jimmy to take her to the studio. She had a melody in her head that she wanted to record. Sleep had not come easy last night. She had been very horny. Now that her flood gates had been bust wide open, she wanted Dunga all the time. Secret sighed. She would have to learn how to control her urges. Dunga would not always be available to her and there was nothing she could do about that. At least for now.

☙❧☙❧☙❧

"Thanks Nathan," Jade said after he had taken her things inside the house. "See you at 7."

"You're welcome Jade," he replied. "Nice place...looks very comfortable."

"Thanks."

Nathan waved bye and Jade locked the grill and closed the front door. She had not seen any of her neighbours when she had gotten home but she had felt eyes on her and knew that someone had been watching. Most likely the old biddy. She decided to unpack and start organizing her stuff in the closet. It was a relatively large closet but she knew it wouldn't be enough before very long. A few more trips to the mall and she would probably have to look into getting someone to redesign the closet to create more space. She could move the T.V. stand and turn the entire stretch of that wall into a lovely walk-in closet. She first picked out her outfit to wear to the taping of *Entertainment Round-Up* then she began hanging up her stuff, starting with the dresses.

ઉ૪ઊઉ૪ઊઉ૪ઊ

The man sitting in the white, tinted Toyota Corolla parked a few houses down the street from where Jade lived, stroked his goatee thoughtfully. So this was where she lived. The Audi Q7 in which she had been travelling had been parked in front of the third apartment in the yard when he had driven by slowly. After not receiving a call from Weatherburn since the last job he had done for him during the national election eight months ago, he had gotten a call this morning for not one, but two assignments. This was the more urgent of the two. He had gotten to the hotel just in the nick of time to see the woman Weatherburn had described approaching the parking lot with a man carrying luggage in tow. She had then gone into the lobby, leaving the man to make another trip to her suite for the rest of her things. He had parked face out so that he could exit quickly when they were leaving.

The jobs were lightweight, just intimidation tactics, at least for now. Nothing like the three murders he had committed during the election on Weatherburn's bequest. He put on his cap and dark glasses and drove into the yard. He stopped in front of Jade's apartment and got out, moving casually. He slipped a small envelope underneath her door then got back into his vehicle and reversed and exited the premises. That was just the first step. How she reacted would determine the second.

Chapter 34

Dunga got to the studio at 4 p.m. He checked his email to see if the photographer had already sent copies of the pictures from the shoot he did with Secret yesterday. He had. And they looked fabulous. He had also sent the design for the poster and promotional CD cover for approval. The photographer was also a good graphic artist which enabled him to provide clients with a one-stop option for them to get whatever they needed in short order. He had been working with Dunga for over four years now. Dunga was one of his favourite clients as he always paid promptly and in full. Dunga printed the material and checked to see if there was anything he wanted to change. There were. He emailed them to the photographer. Secret and Jimmy arrived just as he went out to the chill room. She hugged him tightly like she wanted to disappear inside of him. He could tell she had missed him. Badly. He then took her inside the office to show her the shots. Secret closed the door. She had other ideas.

ℭℭℭ

Jessica woke up at 4:30 p.m. and went into the bathroom to take a shower. She had arrived in Baltimore close to midday. The flight had been a pleasant one though she had been unable to take a nap because of the situation with her husband. Things had deteriorated between them so rapidly that it was threatening to drive her crazy. Her stable, ordered life had, in the course of a few days, transformed into a dramatic play where the outcome was yet to be determined. She had flown first class and as the holder of a diplomatic passport courtesy of being the wife of a government minister, going through customs had been quick and hassle-free. Her cousin had picked her up and dropped her off at the apartment. She wouldn't see him again until tomorrow. After showering, and rummaging through the refrigerator to find something to eat, she made a turkey and cheese sandwich and had it with grape juice. She then settled down in front of the T.V. and surfed through the channels as she picked up her mobile to call Francine to let her know that she had arrived safely. She was currently roaming but depending on how long she decided to stay, she might get another phone as it would work out to be much cheaper. She would call her kids next.

ℭℭℭ

"Jesus Christ!" Dunga blasphemed as he felt his scrotum tighten. Secret had been pleasuring him with her hot mouth and soft hands for the past twenty-five minutes. He was now at the point of no return. "Fuck! Ahhh!"

Secret kept him in her mouth and stroked him over the threshold. She swallowed gamely as he released his hot seed in a torrent down her willing throat. Dunga's body shook uncontrollably. Secret looked up at him with a wry smile. She had done it. And it wasn't half as bad as she thought it would have been. She could easily see herself doing this on a regular basis. And Dunga absolutely loved it. He was in seventh heaven right now. He was still shaking.

"Damn baby...that was so fucking good," he said finally, taking a deep breath as he pulled up his khaki cargo pants. He went over to the small refrigerator and extracted a small bottle of water which he drank thirstily.

Secret laughed. She got up and went into his tiny office bathroom. She washed her face and gargled with mouthwash.

"What am I going to do with you?" Dunga asked when she came out of the bathroom and perched sexily on his desk. She was wearing a brown corduroy blazer and distressed Rock and Republic jeans.

Secret gave him her pretty, innocent smile.

"I'm sure you'll figure something out baby," she purred. "Now let me see the promotional stuff and the pictures."

Jessica got through to Penelope first as Peter's mobile had rang without an answer. Perhaps he was at basketball training.

"Hi mom!" Penelope exclaimed. After speaking with her dad, she had been very disturbed once the shock of his statement had worn off and she really thought about it, it was difficult to believe that it was true but why would her dad tell such a serious lie? She was happy to hear from her mom. Now she could get both sides of the story. "Are you ok?"

"I'm fine Penny," Jessica replied. "I'm in Baltimore. I'm staying with Jeffery for a little while."

"Cool, so you're coming to look for me right?" Penny asked.

"Of course darling," her mother told her. She planned for Jeffery to drive her down there on Sunday.

"Mom..." Penelope began hesitantly, "I spoke to dad last night...and what he had to say was really crazy."

Jessica listened in disgust as Penelope told her what her husband had said. Jessica was amazed at him. In over twenty years of being with this man, and being married for twelve, she had never seen this side of him. It was like she didn't know him anymore. What kind of man would tell his kids such a lie about their mother?

"Penny, you're old enough to hear this so I'll tell you exactly what happened," Jessica said.

Penelope was shocked that her father would treat her mother like that. She now saw him in an entirely different light. Her father was behaving like a monster. They chatted for awhile longer then Penelope had to go. She was a member of the cheerleading team and the school had a big football game against their main rival that evening. Jessica then tried calling Peter again. She got him this time but their conversation did not go as well as the one with his sister. Peter actually believed his father. Jessica was incredulous. And disappointed. Granted, Peter and his father shared a special bond but this was ridiculous. He had been defiant and more than a bit rude. She got off the phone with Peter feeling very angry. She dialed her husband's mobile number.

It took her three hours but Jade finally finished organizing her clothes to her satisfaction. She then took a long bath in the large blue tub. She loved her new home. When the money really started pouring in, there were a few items she needed to purchase. She loved her music so a nice stereo would be in order and she wanted a flat screen T.V. to place on her bedroom wall. She also needed a laptop, a Mac to be exact. They were so thin and cute. She only had forty-five thousand Jamaican dollars to last her for the month until her next pay check. She was not worried though, things would work out. Too many men with deep pockets were out there for a woman such as herself to worry about money. She just had to select the lucky one and all would be well. Then she would bank her money every month and spend his. Too bad Weatherburn had started tripping. She hadn't planned to get rid of him so soon. But everything would be fine. God didn't bless her with all of this beauty and brains for nothing.

ઉଚઉଚઉଚ

Dunga, Secret and Jimmy were in the chill room having dinner. Dunga had sent Jimmy to purchase food at one of his favourite restaurants that was also a tenant on the building he owned on Constant Spring Road. He had bought pumpkin rice, barbecue chicken with cole slaw and fried plantain on the side. Secret was thoughtful as she ate. Her period was due today which was partly why she had wanted Dunga so badly last night. Usually she would wake up to it on the day it was due. It had always been like that for as long as she could remember. She hoped that it came later today. Dunga had not ejaculated inside her again since that first time but that was all it took and the morning after pill doesn't always work. She really needed to get on some form of contraceptive. With her career just getting ready to take-off, the last thing she needed or wanted was to get pregnant. As soon as her period came she would visit Dr. Watson and let him advise her on the best contraceptive to take. He had been her doctor ever since she was ten years old. He would know what's best for her. Secret's thoughts shifted to her mother. Neither of them had attempted to call the other since she kicked her out of the house. She wondered if she was ok. She would call her one day but not just yet. The emotional wounds were still very raw.

"Duane!" Jessica pounced when she her husband answered the phone. "What the hell is wrong with you? Have you lost your goddamn mind?"

"Where are you Jessica?" he demanded, ignoring her questions. "You better bring her ass home by tomorrow!"

"How dare you disrespect me like that? How could you tell our children such a vicious lie? That was very low Duane. Even for you."

"Low mi rass! I'm certain it's true...that would explain your strange behaviour...not wanting to have sex with me and then after I took what's rightfully mine you want to carry on like I've done you this great wrong. It's all a cover for what is really going on!" Weatherburn exploded. "The kids have a right to know!"

Jessica shook her head in disbelief. She was now convinced that her husband, esteemed Minister of Mining, Energy and

Environment, father of her two children and companion for the past twenty years, had lost his fucking mind. He was crazy. She hung up without responding. It didn't make any sense to continue the conversation. She plopped down on the sofa suddenly feeling exhausted. Would things ever get back to normal or had her life as she knew it changed forever?

Chapter 35

Jade noticed the envelope on the floor when she was leaving to go to the television station. Frowning, she picked it up and exited the apartment. She climbed into the back of the SUV, told Nathan hi and turned on the overhead light. She extracted the note and read it:

Stop disrespecting the big man. You have until Saturday evening to get in touch with him. Comply and all will be well. Continue to ignore him and there will be dire consequences.

Jade smiled to herself. Weatherburn wanted to play rough. She wondered how he had found out where she lived. He must have sent someone to the hotel earlier as he hadn't heard from her and knew that she had to check out today. The person had obviously followed her home. She knew it wasn't Eddie. She was positive he didn't even know about this. He would have called to let her know what was happening. She would call Eddie tomorrow and talk to him about it. In the meantime she wouldn't let it faze her. Weatherburn could threaten her all he wanted. It wasn't going to change a damn thing. And as powerful as he thought he was, he wasn't the only one who could play rough if it came down to it. After all, he was a public figure with a lot to lose. They got to the studio in fifteen minutes and Mishka, the stylist, was in the reception area waiting. They were then led to a waiting room by the show's producer and Mishka did Jade's make-up there. Half an hour later, it was time for her to go on set.

Dunga and Secret were in his office on the computer when *Entertainment Round-Up* came on. They were working on the design for Secret's Myspace music page. Dunga had one for his production company and label, House of Beats, but he wanted Secret to have her own page. It would be good promotion for her. He had been uploading two of the songs she had recorded on the playlist for her page when he looked up at the T.V. and saw that it was time for the popular entertainment program. He turned up the volume. He watched as the host, a skinny light-skinned girl who never seemed to look good no matter what she wore week-in week-out, gave a rundown of what was to come. He registered surprise when he saw Jade wearing a sexy black cocktail dress and holding a bottle of the pink cognac that he had seen on the billboard. She was popping up everywhere now. Teasing him. Reminding him that she had never even given him a call. He knew it wasn't humanly possible but somehow she looked even more beautiful every time he saw her image.

First up was a new dancehall artist who had two hot singles on the charts. That was followed by highlights from a stage show that had been held in Negril a few days ago. They went to a commercial break and when the program returned, it was Jade's turn.

"She is gorgeous," Secret commented.

Dunga nodded in agreement but didn't comment. They watched as Jade eloquently spoke about the new drink and the company behind it. The interview was short but effective. She had done a great job and was so visually appealing that women would definitely be gravitating to the drink when it became available on the market. After that it was time for the countdown of the top ten songs in the country and the music video premier of the week. Dunga was a bit annoyed at himself as he turned his attention back to the computer. No matter how long it was that Jade hadn't cross his mind, as soon as he saw her he started to have that crazy feeling she had invoked in him from the very first time he had laid eyes on her. Secret noticed that his mood had changed. She didn't say anything though. She just sat beside him quietly and watched him work on her page. It was looking good. Eye-catching and sexy. The songs had finished uploading. Dunga played each of them to ensure that all was well. They then filled in the text together regarding her professional and personal information, and by the time they were through, his mood had improved considerably. He launched the page and immediately gave her the number one slot in his top friends. He then got up and allowed Secret a chance to browse Myspace and to learn how to use the features.

Dahlia was at her cousin's house when she saw Jade being featured on the popular entertainment show. She was sitting on her cousin's bed watching the T.V. while she got dressed. They were going to Dudley's, a restaurant and lounge on Oxford Road that had karaoke on a Friday night. Dahlia scowled for the duration of Jade's interview. She hated how much she hated the woman. She only needed to see her image and her blood would start to boil like a pot of soup. *For the discerning and sophisticated woman my ass*, she mused. *I'll never drink that shit.* Her mood got even worse when the top ten countdown came on. Zingo's latest single was number 10. She sucked her teeth and turned the channel. She felt ashamed and embarrassed at what had transpired yesterday. It would be a long time before she got over her stupidity. Her cousin came out of the bathroom clad in her underwear. Absently, Dahlia wondered how Tisha's man could stand to look at her naked. Tisha had a thick, sexy body but she did not believe in shaving. Her pussy was so bushy that hair protruded through either side of her blue and white striped Victoria Secret panties. Dahlia thought it disgusting and unhygienic.

"What's wrong with you?" Tisha asked as she pulled on a pair of skinny jeans with much effort. She was blessed with a pair of wide, childbearing hips and it wasn't easy to find jeans that fit her just right.

"I'm good," Dahlia replied, "just hungry. So hurry up."

"Okay...okay. I'll be ready in five minutes," Tisha said good-naturedly. She knew how moody her cousin could get at times and she wasn't up for it tonight. She wanted them to have a good time.

❧❧❧

After the program, Jade stayed behind and chatted a bit with the show's producer and other members of the production team. Jade could tell that the producer was gay despite his attempts to flirt. She gave them a bottle of the expensive cognac and all the women sampled it immediately to much acclaim. The host of the show, thoroughly taken by Jade, invited her to a party the following night and gave Jade her number, imploring Jade to give her a call so that they could hang out. Jade finally bid them farewell ten minutes later and went out to the parking lot with Mishka in tow.

"So what are you doing tonight?" Mishka asked, looking at Jade steadily. "I'm hanging out with a couple girlfriends...you should join us."

Jade looked at her with an amused expression. Though she knew that Mishka was a lesbian, she didn't feel uncomfortable with her being her stylist. She didn't even care when Mishka saw her naked or in her underwear when she was changing for shoots. She understood that with her kind of beauty and sex appeal, both men and women would find her desirable. But she was strictly dickly. If four years in prison hadn't changed that, nothing would.

"No thanks," Jade replied pleasantly, adding, "Mishka...it will never happen so don't even try."

Mishka laughed. Jade was something else.

"What will never happen?" she asked innocently.

"Feign ignorance if you wish," Jade replied, "but I'm dead serious. I'm not interested in carpet munching."

Mishka continued to laugh as they entered the vehicle. Carpet munching. She had never heard it put quite like that before.

"Oh God...fuck me baby! Right there! Don't stop!" Secret urged as Dunga pummeled her from behind. After spending an hour on Myspace and adding the fifty friend requests that she had received, Dunga had taken her home and had jumped her bones as soon as they had entered her room. Miss G was in bed watching T.V. and they hadn't bothered to disturb her. Secret was bent over in front of the dresser and she maintained eye contact with Dunga as he groped her breasts and fucked her like he wanted to see his dick exit through her mouth. It wasn't far-fetched. It felt as though he was hitting her tonsils with each brutal stroke. But she liked it. It hurt so *good.* When he fucked her this hard and deep, he hit spots that he wouldn't normally have reached at a slower pace. It was time for her period so she was extra horny. Dunga could fuck her to death right now for all she cared.

"Who fucking you? Huh? Who fucking you?" Dunga asked as he slapped her ass cheeks mercilessly. His testicles were noisy as they slapped against her wet skin.

"Oh god!" Secret bellowed. She was about to climax again. Hard. She was sweating so much from her exertions that she could barley see out of her eyes and she couldn't move her hands to wipe her face. She was currently holding on to the dresser for dear life. She needed them both to prevent her from crashing into the mirror.

"God? Mi seh who fucking yuh?" Dunga shouted as he felt his orgasm rushing to the fore.

"You baby! Dunga! Dunga! I'm coming baby! Fuck!" Secret screamed, as tears and sweat rolled down her beautiful, contorted face in a salty mixture. She wondered idly if Miss G could hear them over the alternative mix CD that was playing.

They climaxed simultaneously.

Dunga pulled out and spilled his warm seed all over her back as she shivered and whispered his name over and over again. Secret felt faint. Could it get any better? The scary thing was she was convinced it would.

ઉઉઉ

Weatherburn got home at 9:30 p.m. It had been a long but productive day. He had sent Eddie home as he wasn't sure if he would be going back on the road. And if he eventually decided to, he could drive himself. Maybe take his baby, a grey 2008 Jaguar XK series convertible, for a spin. He hadn't driven it in awhile. He removed his clothing and padded to the study naked. Home alone on a Friday night. His rebellious wife was in Baltimore – his contact at the airport had told him where she had gone, and Jade, though having received his warning several hours ago, had not yet called. He had given her until tomorrow evening to contact him but he had expected her to call him as soon as she got the message. He hoped for her sake that she didn't think he was playing around. He poured a shot of Johnny Walker and downed it in one gulp. He didn't like to be pushed and if Jessica didn't come to her senses soon, she would see a side of her husband she didn't know existed. He would give her one week to have her fun in Baltimore then he expected her to be home. He had no idea why these two women thought they could test him. He was on his way to the bathroom when the telephone rang. There was one on the wall of the hallway leading from the study to the bedroom. He answered the call.

"Hello."

"Hi, Duane," a familiar voice purred. "It's Francine."

Weatherburn was surprised. He was positive she knew that Jessica wasn't here. He hoped she wasn't calling to try and lecture him on Jessica's behalf. He was not trying to hear shit from anyone about the situation.

"What's up?" he asked gruffly.

"Nothing much...was just checking if you're ok..."

Weatherburn walked with the cordless phone to the bathroom. What kind of game was Francine playing? She had not spoken to him since the incident with his wife but now that Jessica was gone she was calling to check up on him? Very strange indeed.

"I'm good...a bit hungry but otherwise ok," he replied, a note of curiosity in his voice.

He heard Francine take a deep breath.

"I have some shredded pork with green peppers, shrimp fried rice and crispy sesame rolls. I also have a nice bottle of Merlot. I can bring you some dinner if you like."

There was a pregnant pause as Weatherburn digested what she had just told him. He didn't know what kind of game she was playing but he would see how far she would take it.

"Sure," he replied in as nonchalant a tone as he could muster.

"I'll be there in fifteen minutes."

Francine was out the door immediately. The stuff was already packed in a bag. She had been confident he would have said yes.

Chapter 36

Dunga went straight home after leaving his mom's house. He knew Dahlia wasn't there as she had called while he had been at the studio to let him know that she was going on the road with Tisha, her cousin. Tisha was a party animal and so was Dahlia, to a certain extent, so he didn't really expect her home until the wee hours of the morning. He had left Secret in bed fast asleep. They had been talking and after a few seconds of not getting a response, he had looked over at her and realized that she had fallen asleep. He didn't know if he had actually fallen in love with Secret yet but he definitely had a soft spot for her and there were few things he enjoyed more than having sex with her. She was a special girl. He hummed the melody for what was to be Secret's first single as he drove into the complex. He parked in one of the two parking slots in front of his apartment and went inside. He was in the kitchen getting some juice when he saw the headlights in front of the apartment. Dahlia was home early. He dashed to the bathroom with a speed that even Usain Bolt would envy. He locked the door behind him and ripped off his clothes before jumping in the shower.

❧❧❧

"I love this part!" Jade exclaimed as they watched Uma Thurman and Vivica Fox battle it out in the kitchen of Vivica's suburban home. She was in Theresa's comfortable and very girlie pink and green themed living room. They were watching *Kill Bill Vol. 1*, one of Jade's favourite movies, on DVD. Theresa had called and invited her over while she was on her way home from the television studio. They were having barbecue chicken wings, peppered shrimp and rolls, along with a bottle of La Roseda that Jade had bought over. There was a case of it in the trunk of the SUV that was assigned for Jade's use.

"Yeah," Theresa agreed. She was so happy that she had met Jade. She used to have girlie nights like this with her best friend all the time and when she had migrated, she had sorely missed the female camaraderie. Jade could be on the quiet side sometimes but it was a comfortable silence. She was just someone who was easygoing and comfortable in her own skin. But then again, when you had her looks how difficult could that be? Theresa knew it wasn't as simple as that though. There were many beautiful women all over the world who had low self-esteem despite their good looks.

There was only one chicken wing left. They looked at each other and burst out laughing as they both reached for it at the same time. Jade laughed triumphantly as she came up with it. She teased Theresa mercilessly as she made loud, exaggerated noises of enjoyment and affected an expression of pure bliss. Theresa rolled her eyes in mock disgust.

∞∞∞

"Baby?" Dahlia called out as she placed her keys on the cute key holder on the wall beside the refrigerator. She had bought it at a flea market in Boston a few years ago when she had gone to spend a week with a friend of hers who had relocated there from New York. Her bad mood had persisted and after arguing with a waitress at Dudley's about the length of time it was taking for her to receive her order, she had dropped home Tisha and come straight home. She knew Tisha was pissed but what to do. It just wasn't her night. Best to come home. She had been pleasantly surprised to see Dunga's vehicle when she arrived home. She placed the juice Dunga had been drinking into the refrigerator and made her way to the bedroom. She could hear the shower running. Smiling, she stripped down and tried to open the door. She was surprised to find it locked.

"Baby? Hun?" she called out as she knocked on the door.

Dunga could hear her knocking. He opened the shower curtain and stepped out and opened the door.

"Why you all locked up...hmmm?" Dahlia purred as she hugged his wet body and kissed him.

"I don't want to be kidnapped while I'm taking a shower," he joked. "Suppose someone broke in while I was in the bathroom?"

Dahlia rolled her eyes.

"Then you would shoot them between the eyes with that," she said, pointing to his licensed firearm on the floor on top of his clothes.

"You got that right," Dunga agreed laughing. They then went into the shower and Dunga lathered her body. After such a torrid session with Secret he was surprised to see how easily his dick responded to her soft, soapy one-handed caress. Maybe it was the adrenaline from the close call. If he had gotten home two minutes later they would have been engaged in a serious fight right now. He sighed with pleasure as she stroked him gently. The water beat his muscular back like a drum as he turned her around and entered her slowly. Dahlia moaned like a wounded animal. She would take this over hanging out on the road with Tisha any day.

ꕥꕥꕥ

"That was good," Weatherburn said, nodding his head in approval as he poured them some more wine. They were dining on the bedroom patio which had a breathtaking view of Kingston. She had arrived there just as Weatherburn had come out of the shower. He had opened the electronic gate and let her in wearing nothing but a dark blue terry cloth robe with his initials. It had been a birthday gift from his wife. Feeling a bit nervous but excited, Francine had followed him into the kitchen where she had shared the food and brought it up to the bedroom patio where he had suggested they dine.

"Oh yes, splendid," she agreed. The meal had been a memorable one. She had had dinner with Weatherburn on several occasions so she knew how witty and down to earth he could be. Difference was, tonight she was alone with him. And he was in fine form: charming, funny and laid back. She had always been attracted to him. From the first day Jessica had introduced her to him. He was a fine specimen that was aging better than a fine bottle of wine. And he was powerful. An important man in the country. He needed a strong, caring woman behind him, not a whiner like Jessica. A gust of wind caressed them as Weatherburn got up and stood by the balcony. He was facing her. The wind teased her, blowing the front of his loosely tied robe apart, exposing his genitals in the soft light. Francine prided herself as a woman who took advantage of the opportunities which life sometimes presented at the oddest and most unexpected moments. Opportunity was now knocking. She took a sip of her wine and got up to open the door.

Chapter 37

Dunga watched the T.V. with weary eyes. He was exhausted. Sleep would come any minute now. Dahlia was curled up against his body underneath the brown plaid comforter that went so well with the cream-coloured drapes. They had climbed into bed after getting out of the shower. The sex in the shower had been good: wet, slippery and sensual. He was spent. Three intense orgasms in one day could drain a man; even one as virile as he was. He drifted off just as the hero in the action flick rescued the girl, killed the kidnapper and saved the day. A few moments later, Dahlia, feeling sleepy as well, reached for the remote control to turn the T.V. off. She noticed that Dunga had a smile on his face. She wondered what he was dreaming about.

"Mmmm...sweet baby Jesus..." Weatherburn whispered as he teetered on the line of no return. What had felt like a sure climax was receding back to his toes which were curled up like fried shrimp. His dick trembled in confusion. His body quivered in ecstasy. The queen-size matrimonial bed was a mess. Francine had made him whimper and crawl all over it as she licked and sucked every crevice of his forty-five year old frame. She was making love to him with ruthless precision and uninhibited, unbridled lust. Her nimble tongue, dexterous hands and knowledgeable mouth held him captive in a pleasurable zone so intense that he felt like he was having an out of body experience. And he hadn't even been inside her yet. Mercifully, she completed her tantalizing assault on the real estate between his scrotum and anus, and got up to put a condom on his throbbing dick. She used her mouth.

"I've wanted you for a long time...you sexy hunk of a man," she purred as she positioned herself over his dick and sat on it. "Mmmm...so very long..."

She rode him languidly, slowly milking him until he bucked like a bronco beneath her and spilled his seed in the latex condom with a primal roar that resonated throughout the affluent neighbourhood.

"Fuck...Francine...that...was...amazing," Weatherburn breathed. He was an experienced man but his wife's best friend had just rocked his world, leaving him impressed, sated and amazed. He still felt like he was floating.

Francine merely smiled as she removed the condom from his flaccid dick and went to dispose of it in the bathroom. He watched her through half-closed lids. She had an athletic body. Firm, taut buttocks; flat stomach and long, toned legs. She obviously spent a good deal of time at the gym. Jessica was the prettier of the two but with two grown kids and being a few years older, her body couldn't compare. And as he had discovered in the most delightful and hedonistic ways, neither could she sexually. The sex with Jade had been exquisite but for different reasons. He hadn't enjoyed it because of anything special that she had done, it was just *her.* With Francine it was what she did. Her impressive array of sexual skills. He had been putty in her hands. And mouth. Francine returned with a warm rag and cleaned his genitals.

"You need a real woman in your life," she whispered, as she wiped him clean. "One that will appreciate you and treat you like a king."

Weatherburn looked at her with a lazy, satisfied smile. Francine was good for the ego, among other things. She was also one of the coldest, most heartless women he had ever met. She exhibited no guilt at having made a move on her best friend's husband and fucking him senseless in their matrimonial bed. She was a different kind of animal. One which moved in for the kill at the slightest sign of weakness. She finished cleaning him and went back into the bathroom. When she returned ten minutes later after taking a warm shower, Weatherburn was fast asleep. She snuggled up next to him and turned off the lovely bedside lamp that Jessica had purchased in Italy. Weatherburn was a rotten scoundrel but if she played her cards right, and with a little luck, he could be *her* scoundrel.

Howie, the security guard that was on duty at the Weatherburn residence that night – every government minister was allotted one to guard his home – walked back to his station at the front of the house. He had been making his rounds around when the house he had seen the woman who had come to the house half an hour ago having sex with the boss on the patio. His back had been turned and the woman had been on her knees, blowing him vigorously. He had seen the woman many times. She was a good friend of the boss' wife. So good in fact, that she had come over to take care of the boss' needs while the wife was away. Apparently she had done an excellent job, if the loud animal-like sounds he had heard his boss making were anything to go by. Howie shook his head. Mr. Weatherburn was something else. He sat on the chair by the garage and lit a cigarette. It was going to be a long night. Damn he hated the night shift.

ଔଓଔଓଔଓ

Jade and Theresa fell asleep right there on the plush green carpet a few minutes into *American Beauty*, the third movie of the night. Jade dreamt about Chino, her first boyfriend and the reason she had wasted four years of her young life in the penitentiary. In the dream, she ran into Chino at a resort and after convincing him that she still loved him and harboured no hard feelings over what had happened, she seduced him and took him back to her villa where she stabbed him in his heart with an ice pick as she rode his dick. A full bladder woke her up and she opened her eyes to the blue screen watching her. The movie had finished. She looked over at Theresa. She was fast asleep. Jade got up quietly and went to use the bathroom. She thought about the dream as she peed. Too bad it wasn't real. That's exactly what Chino deserved.

She went back out to the living room instead of waking Theresa up so that they could go to sleep on her queen-size bed. The carpet was comfortable anyway and a fitting end to a fun night. She fell back asleep in no time.

Chapter 38

Weatherburn woke up at 8:30 a.m. The domestic helper and the cook did not work on weekends unless so required. He yawned and got out of bed. Francine was not in the bedroom. He went into the bathroom to pee and to take a shower. Eddie would be coming to pick him up at 10. He had a meeting in Bull Bay with a British contractor who was at odds with the residents of the community where he was doing some mining. When he returned to the bedroom, wrapped in a fluffy white towel, Francine was waiting for him with a steaming tray of liver, boiled dumplings, chocolate tea and freshly squeezed orange juice. Weatherburn smiled. She certainly knew how to push the right buttons. They dined on the patio. Weatherburn wondered if he had time to go another round. She was wearing one of his button-ups with nothing underneath. Her breasts jutted and shook provocatively as she gesticulated while speaking. He decided to wait until later. Sex with Francine was a very draining venture and he had a busy day ahead.

ଓଃଓଃଓଃ

Theresa dropped home Jade at 9 a.m. after a quick breakfast of cereal and juice. Jade waved bye to Theresa and murmured a quick greeting to Doreen, her neighbour, who upon seeing Jade, had paused from sweeping her patio. She looked at Jade from head to toe before responding.

"I saw you on *Entertainment Round-Up* last night," she said, adding, "you look better on T.V."

"Thank you bitch," Jade replied with her sweetest smile as she went inside and locked her door, leaving Doreen with her mouth agape in shock. Jade was about to take her clothes off and take a shower when she heard a knocking on the grill. She went out to the patio. It was Doreen, her beefy brown face red with anger.

"How dare you call me a bitch?" she fumed. "You think you're all that! Coming in here with your attitude like yuh better than people!"

Jade was incredulous. What the fuck was this woman's problem?

"Get away from in front of my apartment," Jade replied. "And refrain from speaking to me from this day forward. You are a stupid, miserable woman and I don't have time for foolishness."

Doreen looked like she was going to literally explode with anger.

"Come move mi!" she challenged, lapsing into ghetto mode. "Bright! Yuh mussi t'ink seh mi frighten fi yuh!"

Jade went back inside and returned with a vase filled with water. She opened the grill and threw the water in Doreen's face.

"Hey bloodclaat gal!" Doreen bellowed. "Mi ah go kill yuh rass!"

She rushed towards Jade who sidestepped her and clobbered her in the head with the vase. Doreen tumbled in a heap against the large fern that was in a lovely flower pot by the wall.

"Get up and get the fuck off my patio," Jade said calmly. She really wanted to give her a proper ass whipping but held back. She might really hurt the woman and the last thing she needed was to get entangled with the law over foolishness.

Doreen got up quickly, her face beet red with anger and embarrassment. She ran to her apartment without another word or a backward glance. Jade shook her head and went back inside. Stupid, jealous, lower-class bitch.

ଔଓଔଓଔଓ

Dunga left his home at 10:30 to go on the road. Dahlia left out at the same time to go by her store. Dunga swung by his mom's house to pick up Secret. He chatted with his mom for a bit then they left and headed to the home of a disc jockey that played at Bembe, a popular weekly party that was held every Thursday night on Constant Spring road. Dunga introduced him to Secret and gave him a copy of her promotional mix CD. They made several more stops like this throughout the course of the day, including a few radio stations. Jimmy was doing the same thing as well with a street team of twenty attractive girls that had been organized to give away copies of the promotional CD all over Kingston. Five hundred CDs had been burnt and packaged to give away. Jimmy had also organized ten guys to put up the poster of Secret all over Kingston. It was an illegal practice and though Dunga planned to do more formal advertising, guerilla marketing on the streets was also very important. Dunga took Secret up to his Sports Bar and Lounge to have a late lunch. The cook, Mama Chin, a tiny woman of Chinese ancestry whose booming voice belied her small frame, was very good. The lounge offered a take-out service which was very popular with the corporate lunch crowd during the week.

Secret was digging into her sweet and sour pork and shrimp fried rice when she heard the sound of her own voice filtering through the speakers in the lounge. The radio was on Flex FM and that was the first station they had visited today. The disc jockey was playing one of her songs, *Lust.* Secret screamed and everyone in the lounge turned to look at her. She was too excited to be embarrassed. Her song was playing on the radio!

"Oh baby," she said to Dunga, as she fought back tears. "It's really happening..."

Dunga grinned. "Yep...this is just the beginning babes...just the beginning."

Dunga had paid this particular disc jockey forty thousand dollars to play the song today. Most disc jockeys will play a song if they like it or if they think it's a quality joint but this particular one was young, greedy and hype. His daily afternoon show was popular with listeners however, so Dunga paid him to get the song played today. Soon, when the single became a hit, Dunga would never again pay a dime to get any of Secret's music played anywhere.

Secret listened in rapture to the sexy ballad inspired by the man sitting across from her. No matter how big she eventually became, she would never forget this moment.

ᴄᴓᴙᴄᴓᴙᴄᴓᴙ

Weatherburn looked at his Rolex watch, the last extravagant purchase he had made for himself eight months ago to celebrate his party's victory at the polls. It was 5:30. The meeting with the contractor and the residents had been a volatile one. It had taken a threat by him to walk out of the meeting to get everyone to settle down. The residents were accusing the contractor of causing a health hazard in the area with the excessive dust and several of them had come to the meeting armed with receipts from visits to the doctor where they had taken their children to get treatment. Weatherburn promised to do something about the situation in the coming week. The residents had a case. The dust was really terrible. He had instructed the contractor to submit a report to his office on Monday as to what steps he planned to take in order to rectify the situation. After the meeting, he went to one of his colleague's rum estate in St. Thomas to have lunch and to do a bit of bird shooting.

He noticed the billboard featuring Jade when they got to the Harbour View roundabout. He hadn't seen it when they passed earlier. God she was beautiful. The devil in a white swimsuit. He sighed. He was giving Jade until 7 p.m. to get in touch with him. If he didn't hear from her by then, he would instruct Snake, his clean-up man, to pay her another visit. He took out his phone and dialed Francine's number. She had asked him to call when he was on his way home so that she could get ready to come over. A repeat of last night was music to his ears. He wondered what she would be bringing for dinner.

ঔঌঔঌঔঌ

Jade woke up groggy after sleeping for most of the day. She had missed two calls. Both from Mr. Hassan. She stretched, then got up and returned his call. He commended her on the good job she had done on the program last night and that the main reason he had called was to invite her to dinner. His partner, Lavi Cohen, had arrived in the island yesterday and he wanted Jade to meet him. Jade readily agreed. She called Nathan to pick her up in an hour and rushed to take a shower. Dinner was at 7 at a posh Japanese eatery in Manor Park. After showering, she browsed the closet and selected a brown and ivory stripe dress by BCBG and Gucci stilettos. Nathan arrived exactly at six-thirty but had to wait ten minutes for Jade to finish applying her make-up. Nathan whistled when she came into the vehicle.

"You look and smell like a million pounds Jade," he quipped.

Jade laughed and slapped him playfully on the back.

They got to the restaurant in twenty minutes and the maitre d', an elegant Japanese lady in a blue kimono, led her to her party's table. The two men stood when she arrived at the table. Mr. Hassan introduced his partner and they sat. Jade appraised Lavi Cohen discreetly. He was everything Mr. Hassan was not. He was very attractive and suave. Reminded Jade of that popular soccer coach, Jose Mourinho; only taller. They sipped osumashi, a soup, while they decided what to order. Jade settled on yakitori, sushi rice and satsumaimo cakes. Mr. Hassan told Jade that the response to the ad campaign was tremendous. Orders were pouring in and the feedback from the few people lucky enough to have gotten samples was very positive. The official launch was going to be next week Saturday and it was going to be a lavish, exclusive invitation only affair. One of Europe's hottest club DJs, DJ Dulce, will be providing the music. Jade couldn't wait. It would be the hottest ticket in town. She pretended not to notice that Lavi Cohen couldn't take his piercing blue eyes off her as she dug into the scrumptious exotic food. He would be staying here for eight days. If his game was tight and he was willing to be discreet, who knows what could happen. She was looking for a man after all. And Lavi Cohen had an impressive resume. As usual, dinner with Mr. Hassan was an event. She was having a ball.

ଔଓଔଓଔଓ

Weatherburn sighed in contentment. He was lying in bed with Francine watching the fight between Mike Tyson and James "Buster" Douglas on ESPN classic boxing. His heartbeat was just now returning to normal. After a delicious dinner of lobster with lime butter sauce and red wine, Francine had cuffed him to the bed and transformed his body into a carnal buffet. She had come armed with a full arsenal: padded handcuffs, vibrating penis ring, whip cream, chocolate syrup, strawberries and grapes. At one point he had been certain that he was going through cardiac arrest. He wondered what Jessica was doing now. Probably fucking her young lover. He was convinced that she had one. He hoped she was getting it as good as he was. He doubted it. He thought of Jade as

Mike Tyson landed a crushing blow to Buster Douglas' stomach, causing the Madison Square Garden crowd to jump out of their seats. She still hadn't called. She was forcing his hand. He was feeling too comfortable to get up to call Snake. He would call him in the morning.

ଔଔଔ

"Hi baby," Dahlia said when Dunga came on the line. She was on her way home from the store and decided to give him a call as she hadn't spoken to him since they left the house this morning. She wanted to know what he was doing tonight. There was a party at Murphey Place that she was thinking of attending. If he didn't want to go she would go with Shawna, her friend who handled her business account at a commercial bank in Half-Way-Tree. She would rather go with him though.

"What's up D," Dunga replied. He was still on the road with Secret. They were now heading to a studio on Red Hills road so that he could introduce Secret to Jah Blood, the roots reggae producer who owned the small studio that was responsible for some of the best roots reggae music that had come out of Jamaica in the past six years. Dunga, being the most versatile producer in Jamaica, had forged a good relationship with the humble Rastafarian over the years.

"I'm heading home now," she said as she slowed down, wary of hitting a man of unsound mind who was walking in the middle of the street wearing only a filthy orange sweater. He was well-endowed. *What a waste*, Dahlia mused. "What are you doing tonight? I want to go to a party at Murphey Place."

Dunga had heard about it. It would be a good one but he was in work mode today. He wasn't feeling the party vibe.

"I've been doing some promotions all day and I'm still at it," Dunga told her. "When I'm through I'm just going to get some rest."

"Ok baby," Dahlia responded. "I'll just go with one of my friends. Love you and see you later."

"Ok, have fun," Dunga told her and hung up.

They arrived at the studio and Jah Blood, who had just finished a session with a reggae band from Sweden, greeted Dunga heartily. He led Dunga and Secret around to his office as he joked that Dunga was taking away his business. Foreign reggae acts, when they came to Jamaica to record, usually came to him. He knew about Dunga's work with Ras Che. Dunga shook his head and laughed. Nothing missed Jah Blood.

ℭℭℭ

Jade, Lavi Cohen and Mr. Hassan went by the office after dinner. Cohen, who had arrived in Monetgo Bay and had spent the night at a new resort a friend of his had recently opened, had yet to see the office as he had only gotten to Kingston a couple of hours ago. Jade, who also had not yet been at the office, readily agreed with Cohen's suggestion that they go there to have a look. Jade noticed the tinted black Audi Q7 that had pulled out behind them when they left the restaurant, entering the parking lot behind them. Cohen saw her questioning look. He explained that they were his bodyguards. After an attempted kidnapping in Brussels several years ago, he never went anywhere without at least two bodyguards. Jade was impressed. Whereas Phillip Hassan was perhaps merely rich, Lavi Cohen was obviously a very wealthy man.

The office was located in the heart of New Kingston in the E. Jasper Wellington building. It occupied the entire fifth floor. It consisted of Mr. Hassan's office, a conference room equipped with laptops and video communication equipment, a lobby and reception area, a small office for Mr. Hassan's personal assistant and an office which housed the accountant and his junior clerk. There was also a kitchenette, two bathrooms and a small lounge with two leather couches and a 72 inch plasma screen on the wall. A framed poster of Jade, one of the stills taken from the commercial, adorned the wall in the reception area along with a picture of a bottle of La Roseda, and pictures of the company's overseas offices and the other products they offered. Expensive artwork with Judaic themes also sprinkled the walls throughout the office. The office was decorated in dark shades of blue and yellow, the company colours. The actual warehouse, where the stock and the company fleet of four delivery trucks were kept, was located at a secure industrial complex in downtown, Kingston. Jade was suitably impressed with the posh digs. They spent fifteen minutes there before departing.

"What are your plans for tonight?" Cohen asked Jade after they had dropped Mr. Hassan off at his apartment.

"I'm supposed to be going to a party with a friend," she responded. She had told Theresa about the party that the host of *Entertainment Round-Up* had invited her to and she had agreed to accompany her.

Jade was still trying to figure out which fragrance he was wearing. It was subtle but very masculine and alluring. She wondered where he got his sense of style. Middle-aged white men rarely dressed so well; even one as exotic looking and handsome as he was. Cohen was nattily attired in black Prada loafers, skinny black jeans and a fitted black shirt with a black blazer. An exquisite diamond encrusted Vacheron Constantin watch adorned his slender wrist. He looked like a successful fashion designer as opposed to a wealthy businessman. He was a thin man, tall and wiry. It was impossible to guess his age but Jade figured he was in his mid to late forties.

"I see. I'd like to take you sailing tomorrow morning...say about nine...if you won't be too tired from partying that is," he said.

"I'd love to," Jade responded. She just wouldn't stay out too late so that she could get at least five hours sleep. She loved the sea and it would be nice to spend some time alone with Cohen; to see what he was all about. He took Jade's mobile number and wished her a good night when they arrived at her apartment. They waited until she was safely inside before they drove off.

Jade suddenly remembered that she hadn't called Eddie. She checked the time. It was 10:15 p.m. A bit late but she decided to call him anyway. Eddie answered on the fourth ring.

"Hello, Jade," he said, sounding breathless.

"Ahem," Jade said, clearing her throat. "I hope I'm not disturbing anything..."

Eddie laughed. Actually she was but he had a gut feeling that it was important so he had taken the call.

Jade smiled to herself. She knew he was blushing.

"Not at all," he lied, with a chuckle. "So what's up? Everything ok?"

"Not really," Jade replied and went to tell him about the note she had found by her front door.

Eddie was silent as he digested the information. There was no doubt it was from Weatherburn. And there was only one person that Weatherburn trusted to do his dirty work. Snake, the clean-up man. Eddie sighed. Weatherburn was really upset at her to take it this far.

"Jade you are in danger," Eddie told her seriously. "The man who delivered the note is not someone to play with. His name is Snake and he is a cold-blooded killer. The fact that you haven't contacted Weatherburn since receiving the message means that the next time Snake visits you, he will not be coming there to leave a message."

Jade got his drift. She waited for him to continue.

"I don't think your life is in danger...yet. But he *will* do something drastic to show you that you have no choice."

"Tell me more about him."

"Well...he's in his thirties...tall...skinny and very dark in complexion with the coldest pair of eyes I've ever seen. He drives a white Toyota Corolla. I have no idea where he lives though."

"Thank you very much Eddie. You have been most helpful... as usual. By the way, I need to get an ID. I need a driver's license and a new passport. I don't wish to go through the normal channels. Do you have any contacts where that is concerned?"

"Yeah...I can arrange it for you," Eddie replied. "Will cost you around fifty thousand for both of them. All I need is four passport size photographs and the money, and you can have them in a week."

"You are so resourceful Eddie," Jade said. "Ok, I'll call you when I'm ready."

"Ok, Jade. And be careful. Please."

"I will. Bye Eddie."

Jade hung and went into the bathroom to take a shower. Snake huh? Jade was wary but not scared. She had been the trusted girlfriend of one of the Bronx's most ruthless drug dealers and she did four years in prison. She was no stranger to violence and tough situations. She would find a way to deal with this. There was no way that she was going to allow anyone to use force and intimidation to make her be in a situation that she didn't want to be in. Weatherburn continued to underestimate her. She was a worthy opponent as he would soon discover. She pondered the best course of action as she lathered her body.

ଔଔଔ

Dunga dropped home Secret at 11 p.m. He didn't go inside, merely kissed her goodnight and ensured that she got into the house safely. He then headed home to get some rest. It had been a long and productive day. Two of Secret's songs had been played on three different radio stations several times today. Ras Che, who was now back in France, would call him sometime next week with an update on how things were going regarding Secret's music in France. Dunga expected to hear from him by Friday. Six days was long enough for Ras Che to have given the CD and made the necessary payments to the influential disc jockeys that could break the songs. Jimmy had done a good job as usual with the street teams. All five hundred CDs had been given away to members of the public and posters bearing Secret's likeness were all over the place. He got home, took a quick shower and went straight to bed. Dahlia was already gone. It was not yet midnight so he knew that she hadn't left for the party already. Most likely she had gone over to her friend's house and would head to the party from there. He hoped Dahlia didn't attempt to wake him up for sex when she got home tipsy and horny. He was drop dead tired.

ଔଓଔଓଔଓ

Theresa swung by Jade's apartment to pick her up at 12:30. Jade wasn't ready so she went inside and waited while Jade applied the finishing touches to her make-up. Theresa laughed until she cried when Jade told her about her run-in with the neighbour. She ruined her make-up as a result and Jade had to reapply it for her. They finally left the house at 1:15. They got to the venue fairly quickly. It was packed and it took Theresa a few minutes, and the help of one of the street guys who were outside the venue hustling, to find a suitable parking spot. Theresa gave him the hundred dollar bill he requested for his assistance and to make sure her vehicle was 'safe'.

The two women looked good enough to eat – Theresa was wearing a black, classy, body-skimming turtleneck Donna Karan dress with black knee high boots, while Jade was wearing a red off the shoulder Just Cavalli dress which emphasized her toned, curvy frame and a pair of black Chanel pumps. All eyes were on them as they made their way to the entrance. There were two entrances, and naturally, Jade made her way to the one labeled VIP. One of the guys at the gate who was checking for armbands recognized Jade. He worked at the television studio and was part of the promotional team that had put on the party. With a broad smile, he quickly allowed Jade and Theresa to enter. She thanked him and he pointed out Gypsy, the host of *Entertainment Round-Up*, who was talking to three men a few meters away. Jade was about to walk over there to say hi when Gypsy, seeing an expression of wonder on one of the guys' faces with whom she was having a conversation, turned around and saw her. She excused herself and came over to Jade excitedly. An onlooker would have assumed that she and Jade were very good friends. Jade introduced her to Theresa and the annoyingly bubbly Gypsy walked with them over to a section of the venue that was not too crowded. A photographer who worked for an entertainment website came over and snapped a photo of the three women. On a whim, Jade had put a bottle of La Roseda in Theresa's car when they were leaving her apartment. She asked Gypsy if she could send someone trustworthy to retrieve something from their ride. Gypsy, anxious to please, left and came back with the guy that was helping to man the VIP entrance. Theresa gave him the keys and told him where the car was parked.

He returned in five minutes and Gypsy went to the bar for ice and cups – no glasses were available – and Jade opened the bottle and poured a round for everyone. Two brave young women, who recognized Jade and Gypsy, came over to say hi and to ask for a taste of the not yet available cognac. Jade filled their outstretched cups and the girls thanked her heartily and went back into the thick of the crowd. During the course of the night, no less than six photographers came over to take Jade's picture. The party was good, and despite Gypsy's annoying tendency to say something to her every chance she got, Jade had a great time. They left the party at 3 a.m., and while the two women were walking to the car, Jade saw a familiar face standing beside a SUV conversing loudly with a group of four women. It was Dahlia.

Chapter 39

"Bitch!" Dahlia said as Jade walked by.

Jade looked at her like she was a pool of muddy water and gave her the finger as she kept on walking.

"A weh yuh know har from?" Jade heard one of the women ask Dahlia loudly. "Nuh she did deh pon de T.V. de other night ah promote dis new drink?"

Dahlia, hating how she felt every time she saw Jade, decided that enough was enough. It was time to get this bitch out of her system. Ignoring her friend's questions, she walked out into the road.

"Bitch! Come here and talk shit now! See if I don't slap the shit outta you!" Dahlia shouted in her Brooklyn accent as she walked towards Jade.

Theresa turned around to look at Dahlia who was storming towards them.

She recognized the girl from the movie theatre when they had gone to see *Wanted*. Jade was supposed to have told her what the vibe between her and the girl was about but being typical private Jade, she never did. They got to the car and Jade quickly removed her earrings and placed them in the car along with her Chanel clutch purse. She then went out into the road to meet Dahlia who had almost reached them.

"Jade! No!" Theresa said. "Let's just leave!"

Jade ignored her and walked up to Dahlia who had slowed down a bit in surprise when she saw that Jade was coming towards her. She looked behind her to see if her friends had followed. They were standing a little distance away in the middle of the road where they could see everything. When she turned back around Jade grabbed her by her weave and pulled her over to the side of the road.

"Ow! You fucking bitch!" Dahlia screamed in pain as Jade, holding a fistful of her hair slapped her in the face repeatedly before pushing her hard to the ground. Dahlia rushed to get up but Jade administered a vicious kick to Dahlia's stomach which took the wind out of her sails and expelled the gum that she been chewing.

"Next time you see me...act like you don't," Jade warned as she walked off, leaving Dahlia moaning and holding her stomach.

"Bumboclaat!" she heard one of Dahlia's friends exclaim. "De pretty gal can fight doah!"

Theresa looked at Jade in awe as she calmly went inside the car and sat down.

Shaking her head in disbelief, Theresa hopped in and laughed as they drove out. Jade was something else. She had never met anyone like her.

ଔଔଔ

Dahlia, upset with Shawna and the three other friends they had met up with at the party for not coming to her aid during the fight with Jade, left the venue alone though she was supposed to have given them a ride home. She was so angry and embarrassed that she couldn't stop crying. She was also in a lot of pain. She had a massive headache and her jaws ached. Her stomach was also hurting so badly she was seriously wondering if she had a fractured rib. Everything had happened so fast. One minute she was heading towards the girl then the next minute the girl was heading towards her and then all hell had broken loose.

She had never been so badly beaten in a fight, not even the ass whipping she had received from Bertha, the class bully back in 9th grade at high school, came even close. She groaned as she got home and exited the vehicle. What would Dunga say? There was no way she could hide this from him. Her face felt puffy and swollen and she could barely stand up straight. She went in as quietly as she could but was unable to suppress the scream that escaped her lips when she tried to take off her top.

Dunga jumped out of his sleep and turned on the bedside lamp. He looked at her in shock.

"What happened to you Dahlia?" Dunga asked as he flung the comforter aside and got up. Her face was red and swollen and she was doubled over in pain.

Dahlia hollered in response.

"Baby who did this to you?" Dunga demanded. Whoever was responsible was a dead man.

When Dahlia finally calmed down enough to tell him what happened, Dunga sucked his teeth in disgust. He couldn't believe Dahlia had picked a fight with the mystery woman on the street. What the fuck was wrong with her? Fighting in the street like a little commoner? And to add insult to injury; got a royal ass-whipping. He was pissed at her actions but he didn't even bother to curse. Muttering a few expletives, he cleaned her face and checked her ribs. He didn't think there was a fracture. The pain would probably ease up considerably in the morning. He undressed her and put her to bed. Dunga sighed as he tried to go back to sleep. The mystery woman, Jade, from what he recalled her saying her name was on the T.V. program last night, had kicked Dahlia's ass like a man. Who would have thought such a pretty, sophisticated looking young woman could throw down like that? There was way more to her than met the eye. He was having that weird feeling again. It was like it would never go away.

Chapter 40

Lavi Cohen called Jade at precisely 9 a.m. to let her know that he had arrived to pick her up. Five minutes later, she exited the apartment and climbed into the SUV. Cohen was sitting in the back sipping a latte. He was wearing a black knee length Prada swim trunk, a black Prada tank top and Prada flip flops. Oversized dark Prada sunglasses hid his hypnotizing eyes, and most of his face. Jade wondered if he had shares in Prada. One of the bodyguards was the driver, while the other rode shotgun.

"Good morning, Jade," Cohen said as they headed out.

"Hi Lavi," Jade replied.

"You're looking exceptionally gorgeous as always," Cohen commented. Jade couldn't see his eyes but she knew they were roaming all over her body. She was wearing a two piece Burberry swim suit with a pair of denim shorts and flip flops. She looked at him through her Chanel lenses.

"Thank you, Lavi," she replied.

"Are you hungry?" he asked.

"Famished," Jade responded truthfully.

"Good. Breakfast is being prepared on the yacht. You'll be well fed in about half an hour."

They were silent for the rest of the journey. Coldplay's 2000 debut album, *Parachutes,* filtered softly through the Audi Q7's state of the art sound system. They passed two billboards featuring Jade on the way to Morgan's Harbour but Cohen didn't comment. They arrived at the harbour and made their way onto *Chelsea,* Cohen's mid-size blue and white yacht named after his favourite British soccer club. The bodyguards did not come onboard. Cohen told her that a chef and a maid were below deck but would remain out of sight unless summoned.

He led her to the deck and they set sail immediately. It was a beautiful Sunday morning; sunny with a nice breeze. A young woman in a French maid outfit - when Jade saw her she had to try hard to suppress a laugh – served them breakfast which consisted of crabmeat quiche - a luscious egg pie with crabmeat, red pepper and Swiss cheese with a hint of white wine. It was absolutely delicious. After breakfast, Jade removed her shorts and accepted Cohen's offer to rub some sunscreen on her. His hands were soft, yet strong.

Jade asked him a lot of questions as she tried to get into the mind of the attractive, wealthy businessman. He was born in Lebanon but had lived in Britain for over twenty years though he had homes in other countries. He had been rich since the age of twenty-five - he didn't say how - and was now a very wealthy man who, in addition to being the majority shareholder of the very successful Hassan & Cohen LLC, owned a company in South Africa that was the sixth largest exporter of non-conflict diamonds. He was also a silent partner in a chain of clothing boutiques in Europe and he owned a vineyard in Italy that produced white wine. He had been married twice. According to him the first had been a mistake on his part; the second a mistake on hers. The last marriage had been twelve years ago. After sailing about fifty miles out to sea, they then headed over to lime cay. However, the beach was too packed so they stayed onboard.

"You are a special beauty Jade," Cohen said as they munched on grapes and looked at the people on the beach. "But that's not why I want you. I'm used to exceptionally beautiful women of all races. Show me a beautiful woman and I'll show you a man who is tired of fucking her."

Jade chuckled.

"What I like about you is your aura...your vibe...there's something about you that rubs me the right way...quickens my pulse...penetrates my soul. Yet I know nothing about you. Incredible."

Jade looked at him but didn't respond.

"I am a man of the moment Jade, I don't wait for anything. If you are interested you'll have to act now. "

Jade watched a young woman, whose humongous breasts were threatening to vacate her swimsuit top, frolic in the water with two guys. Lavi Cohen was a man that was forthright and to the point. She could appreciate that. She was similar in that respect. Jade looked over at him. Should be interesting making love to a man from another race. She laughed inwardly as she thought of Chino. He hated white people with a passion. Cohen wasn't exactly white though. He was middle-eastern. Not that Chino would have given a fuck about the distinction.

"I'm interested," she replied.

"Good. Another thing...I want you now but I'm a fickle person where women are concerned so that feeling could change at any time and when that happens, whatever we have will be over. Just like that."

"I'm not looking for a conventional relationship Lavi. I have no problem with that whatsoever," Jade told him. "So that goes for you too."

Cohen laughed. This young woman was of a different species. Her sophisticated and calculated approach to life belied her young years. He knew, but was not offended by the fact that he wouldn't have stood a chance with her if he wasn't a man of substantial means. That was fine. An ordinary man couldn't handle a woman of Jade's caliber. She would be a fun and interesting companion. She was wrong about one thing though. What went for the goose in this case did not go for the gander. She could only walk away if he wanted her to. He turned the yacht around and headed back out to sea. He wanted to make love to her in the middle of the ocean.

Chapter 41

Weatherburn called Snake at midday. Francine, after making him breakfast, had left for home, telling him to call if he needed her. Snake picked up immediately.

"Yes chief," he said.

"The little bird has not responded," Weatherburn said, getting right to the point. "Clip a wing, but don't kill it."

"Ok," Snake replied in his raspy whisper. He had been the recipient of a cut across his throat many years ago. Lucky for him, he had survived but his voice had been almost inaudible ever since. The man, who had attacked him and left him for dead, was found in a gully in Duhaney Park a month later with his head lying next to his body.

Weatherburn then hung up and went into the closet to find something to wear. He was a special invited guest to the car show that was being held at the National Arena. Eddie was outside waiting to take him there. He hummed a Frank Sinatra tune as he got dressed. Soon Jade would be back where she belonged. After Snake's next visit, she would surely understand that he was not playing around with her. He didn't want to hurt her but a man had to do what a man had to do. There was no doubt that she would be contacting him soon. He hoped Snake got in touch with her today.

Jade felt as though she was soaring above the clouds as opposed to lying on her back thousands of feet beneath them. She was nude with the exception of her dark Chanel sunglasses which were protecting her pretty brown eyes from the brilliant sunshine. Her legs were on Cohen's shoulders and he was doing delightful tricks with his tongue and lips. The swell of the waves gently rocked the yacht from side to side as Jade moaned softly in approval. Cohen's tongue was deeply embedded in her wetness. He flicked it back and forth continuously until Jade began to writhe beneath his mouth. Her moans got progressively louder as she became more and more aroused. He began to lick her turgid clit in a firm upward motion and Jade gripped the sides of the lounge chair as she felt her climax steadily approaching.

"Right. Fucking. There. Don't. Stop." Jade breathed through clenched teeth.

He stopped.

Jade looked at him in confusion as her clit throbbed in frustration.

"Get up," Cohen instructed.

Frowning, Jade complied.

He led her to the side of the yacht and spread her legs. Jade bent over slightly and held on to the edge as Cohen knelt behind her and resumed his oral assault. He spread her ass cheeks as wide as possible as he buried his face between her legs. Jade howled with pleasure.

"Oh shit...I'm gonna drench your face Lavi!" she shouted as he licked her from behind mercilessly. She heard a sound and looked skywards. A helicopter was passing by. It was an army helicopter. Jade could clearly see one of the soldiers sitting by the open door. He was watching them through binoculars. She couldn't hold it anymore. She climaxed all over Cohen's face as the helicopter passed over their heads.

"Oh Lavi...ohhh...ohhhh...mmmm..." Jade groaned as she experienced back to back orgasms. She could feel her juices trickling down her thighs.

Cohen then turned her around and kissed her deeply, letting her taste herself. He then removed his trunks and uncoiled his anxious, circumcised member. His pale dick was long and sinewy, just like the owner. She gripped it with both hands and stroked it gently. Cohen groaned and leaned against the edge of the boat. She knew what he wanted.

"Not yet Lavi...that's a treat you'll have to earn," she said as she led him by his dick over to the lounge chair. Jade could tell by his expression that he was surprised at her words. And disappointed. Too bad. She had only sucked one dick in her entire life but she was very experienced at giving fellatio. Oral sex had been a big part of her relationship with Chino. The next dick she blessed with her oral skills would have to be a special one.

Jade climbed on to the chair and got on her hands and knees.

She turned her head around and looked at him.

"Fuck me Lavi," she said softly.

The sensual look on her beautiful face and the sight of her fleshy, glistening mound from behind threatened to drive him berserk. Cohen quickly retrieved a condom and rolled it onto his throbbing dick. He then got behind her and entered her with a hard, firm thrust.

Jade wailed like a banshee.

"Lavi...I feel it in my brain!" Jade cried as he buried his shaft to the hilt. Jade used one hand to spread her ass cheeks to give him more leverage. His dick seemed to go on forever. "Go easy Lavi...fuck...easy Lavi..."

Cohen was amazed at how tight she was. He knew he wouldn't last long even if his life had depended on it. Her pussy was choking the living daylights out of his dick. He fucked her as slowly as he could, moving his waistline in a circular motion as he went deep into her depths.

"You're so fucking tight," Cohen whispered in disbelief as he increased his tempo.

"Lavi! Oh God!" Jade cried out as he really began to sock it to her. Jade reached behind her to restrain him but Cohen was having none of that. He swatted her hand away like a fly. His movements were a blur as he fucked her at a torrid pace.

"Oh shit! I'm coming! Fuck! Fuck! Ahhh!" Cohen groaned as he filled the polyurethane condom with his juices.

Breathing like he had just ran a 400m race; Cohen sat down on the chair and tried to catch his breath. Jade was still in the same position. She was unable to move just yet. Cohen looked at her exposed pussy, which was pulsating before his very eyes. He was convinced that it had been constructed entirely of honey and sugar.

Chapter 42

Dunga heard when the motorbike pulled up in front of the apartment. It sounded like a lawnmower. Then a horn began blowing insistently. He grabbed his wallet and went outside. The food he ordered from Meals to Go had arrived. Dahlia was in no shape to cook today. He paid the delivery guy and gave him a two hundred dollar tip. The man thanked him heartily. Dunga then took the food into the kitchen and shared out some for himself and Dahlia. She had slept late and when she finally crawled out of bed at 1 p.m., she had taken a shower and snuggled up on the couch where she had been watching a movie for the past hour. She was feeling better physically but mentally she was out of it. Her phone had been ringing incessantly all morning but she wasn't taking any calls. Based on the number of calls, and the fact that some of the people calling had not called her in a long time, she knew that it was because they had heard about the fight last night. Apparently her friends had told everyone about it. Fucking bitches. Dahlia was so embarrassed that she did not plan on leaving the house until it was time to go to the airport on Tuesday evening to catch her flight back to New York.

She absently accepted the small plate of rice and peas, ox tail and potato salad that Dunga handed to her. She had no appetite but she hadn't eaten all day so she sat up and tried to eat. She knew that Dunga was mad at her and she didn't blame him. She was mad at herself. Her decision making over the last couple of days left a lot to be desired. Usually Samantha would have been here with them but Dunga didn't go to pick her up because he didn't want her to see her mother in this state. Her right jaw, which had had received the majority of Jade's ferocious slaps, was still swollen and there was a lump on her left forehead where she had hit her head when Jade had pushed her to the ground. Her stomach felt stiff and sore but at least nothing was fractured or broken and it didn't hurt as much as it did last night. Dunga had been really sweet about the whole thing despite his anger and disappointment. He hadn't cursed her out and had been making sure that she was ok. She loved him so much. It scared her everytime she thought about how close she had come to ruining everything. If she had fucked Zingo and Dunga had found out; that would have been it. She doubted she could have hid it from him anyway. The guilt would have probably been too heavy a burden to bear. Thank God it hadn't happened.

ଓ଼ଃଓ଼ଃଓ଼

"Hi Francine," Jessica said. "What's up girl?

Jessica was in North Carolina. Her cousin had driven her down to visit Penelope, her daughter. They were having McDonald's at a mall about three miles from the college Penelope attended.

"Hi Jess," Francine replied. She was at home relaxing and reading the newspaper. "How you doing?"

"No too bad, I'm in North Carolina...came down to spend the day with Penny," Jessica told her.

"Ok, let me say hi to her."

"Hi Auntie Fran," Penelope said when she came on the line. She loved her mother's best friend. She was young, hip and cool and she could talk to her about anything.

"Hello darling, how is everything?" Francine asked. Penelope was such a sweet girl. They had always been close.

"I'm good, just trying to help mom deal with her stress," Penelope said without elaborating. There was no doubt that her mother had confided in Francine about what was happening between her and her husband.

"Yeah, it's a rather dicey situation but I'm sure everything will work out...they love each other and things will be ok eventually," Francine told her.

"Yeah, I hope so...I'm really disappointed in dad though," Penelope related.

They conversed for a bit longer then Penelope handed the phone back to her mother.

"So when are you coming home dear?" Francine asked when Jessica came back on the line.

"Fran...at this point I honestly don't know," she replied.

"Well take your time to figure things out in your head Jess...no sense rushing back into an uncomfortable situation," Francine advised.

"Yeah...guess you're right," Jessica agreed.

After a few more minutes, they ended the conversation after promising to catch up during the week.

ଓଃ෴ଓଃ෴ଓଃ෴

Secret spent the day alternating between chatting with Miss G and doing some writing. Dunga had told her that she should keep at it because he wanted to release her debut album this year. He wanted it to be the best reggae album of the year and that could only happen if she took the time to write the best songs she possibly could. He figured that they could put together an excellent album in eight months and release it in December. By then, if everything went according to plan, Secret would be noted as one of the best new reggae artists around and anticipation would be great for her debut album featuring nothing but new songs. He planned to keep guest appearances on the album to a minimum but Ras Che would definitely be featured on it. These were exciting times for Secret but other than Dunga, she had no one to share it with. She and her mom were not on speaking terms and she didn't have any close girlfriends. She didn't get along with other females very well - they just didn't seem to like her very much for whatever reason- and most of the males she knew only befriended her with one objective in mind. Orane, who had introduced her to Dunga, was the exception - or so she had thought. When he realized that Dunga was moving full speed ahead with her, he had called a few times to invite her out but each time she had been busy working at the studio. Based on some comments he had made, especially the last time he called two days ago, he thought she was indebted to him. She missed her dad now more than ever. If he was still alive things would have been different. Thinking about him made her feel sad. Yet inspired. Without even thinking about it, the words for a song flowed like they had been already stored in the pen. She knew what she would name it: *Daddy*.

ଔଓଔଓଔଓ

"What's up Jade," Theresa said. She had just finished cooking and decided to call Jade to invite her over for dinner.

"Hi hun," Jade replied. "I'm in Portland having dinner at a resort."

After their intense sexual episode, Cohen had spontaneously set sail to a mariner in Portland and had called a businessman he knew to send someone to meet them there. The guy, an entrepreneur from Germany, whom Cohen had known for a number of years, and who owned the hotel Cohen had stayed at in Montego Bay when he had arrived in the island on Friday, sent the general manager for the small exclusive resort he also owned in Port Antonio, Portland, to meet his wealthy friend. The guy, an unsmiling, lanky fellow with a British accent, who probably thought that this task was beneath him, picked them up in a white Mercedes sedan and took them to the resort, which was a few miles from the mariner. Though the cook on the yacht had prepared more food, Cohen had felt like having something different.

"Is that right...with who?" Theresa asked, surprised that Jade hadn't mentioned that she was going out of town. Then again, maybe she shouldn't be.

"Talk to you later hun," Jade replied. "I'll call you when I get in."

"Ok, later then," Theresa said and terminated the call, feeling a bit peeved. Sometimes Jade's secretive nature really got on her nerves.

The resort was located on a plush forty acre spread off the Port Antonio main road. There was no sign at the entrance to the property, located at the end of a dead-end two mile private road. There was an eight foot wrought iron gate manned by electronic security. The resort consisted of twelve luxurious villas – each done in a different theme – and they dined on the patio of the only unoccupied villa. This one had a medieval theme and they were served by a young woman who was appropriately attired in a purple servant bodice made of burnet and kersey. Jade found the whole thing rather amusing and a bit over the top. They had French onion soup, filet mignon, lobster salad and wan kati, a popular Thai dessert which consisted of jelly with a coconut cream topping.

"This place is so exclusive they don't even advertise – at least not through the regular channels," Cohen told her as they ate. "It costs four thousand US dollars a night to stay here."

"Ok," Jade commented nonchalantly. She wasn't overly impressed. Chino had taken her to the Turks and Caicos Islands one weekend and they had stayed at a two thousand dollar a night villa. And that was over four years ago.

Cohen looked at her thoughtfully. Not much moved her apparently. He wondered what was going on in that beautiful head of hers. He knew absolutely nothing about her – not that he had asked – except that she was twenty-two years old, beautiful, intelligent, free-spirited, sexy and possessed what he was sure was the tightest, most delectable legal age vagina in the world. He usually never cared about what went on in a woman's head outside of anything business related but Jade intrigued him.

"I have a small problem," Jade said, slicing into his thoughts.

"What might that be?" Cohen asked.

She took a sip of her red wine.

"Somebody wants to kill me," Jade calmly stated.

Chapter 43

"ho is trying to kill you?" Cohen asked with an amused expression. Surely she couldn't be serious.

"A man who goes by the name of Snake," Jade replied. "He was hired by an ex-lover of mine."

Cohen looked at her steadily as he digested this unexpected bit of information. She was looking him dead in the eyes. She wasn't lying. There were a million questions he could and probably should ask but he was positive that not only wouldn't she tell him everything, she didn't expect him to care about the intricacies of the matter, only to assist in eliminating the problem. He was no stranger to violence. Back when he was just spreading his wings as a young entrepreneur, and had opened two sewing factories in Mexico, providing cheap labour for three clothing companies, he had successfully dealt with the problem he had with a ruthless Mexican gang that had tried to extort him.

"Do you know where he can be found?" Cohen asked.

"No, but he knows where to find me. I think he will attack me at my home," Jade replied. She congratulated herself on being so perceptive. She had just *known* that a man like Cohen could easily deal with a matter like this without asking a bunch of stupid questions and making a big deal out of it. It would just be dealt with. Quickly and efficiently.

"I see. If that is indeed the case then the problem can be resolved quite easily," Cohen assured her.

"Ok, good."

And that was the end of the conversation. After dinner, they walked the grounds together and he showed her the basics in golf at the mini golf course. Then they went back to the villa and Cohen gave Jade a resounding fuck in the unusually designed queen-size bed with the dragon headboard. She almost felt like Valeria Messalina, the infamous Roman Empress, as she looked up at the two tier chandelier with 12 burning candles, while Cohen plunged into her like he was mining for diamonds. He lasted a little longer this time, but not long enough for her to climax from penetration. Maybe the third time would be the charm. It had been good though. He was rough but she liked it. At least she *felt* like she had just gotten fucked. She declined his offer for them to spend the night at the resort and he summoned the general manager to take them back to the yacht. Jade checked the time as they set sail back to Kingston. It was 7:30 p.m. It had been a very interesting day.

Secret was getting worried now. Her period still hadn't come. It was now three days late. She looked at her pretty face in the mirror above the face basin, her forehead creased with worry. She had just taken a shower. Dunga had called to invite her to hang out at Rollers, a popular karaoke spot on Sunday nights. She wondered what would happen if she was indeed pregnant. What would happen to her fetal career? How would Dunga respond? She decided to give it three more days maximum. If it didn't come by Wednesday, she would not only take a pregnancy test, but would go to the doctor as well. She sighed and went into the bedroom to get dressed. Dunga would be picking her up at 8:30.

***

The Audi Q7 drove by Jade's house and made a U-turn at the end of the dead-end street. There was no sign of the white Toyota Corolla that Eddie had told her Snake drove. Only two vehicles were parked on the street: a grey Honda Accord and a red Subaru Imprezza. Neither of them was tinted and they both appeared to be empty. They then entered the yard and stopped in front of Jade's apartment. One of the bodyguards, a short, bulky man who had an uncanny resemblance to Mike Tyson, exited the vehicle and checked along the side of the apartment. No one was lurking there. He then stood by the door and waited for Jade.

"All seems to be well," Cohen said to Jade. "He will have to try and get you going in or coming out and when he does, one of my men will be there to take him out of his misery."

"Thank you, Lavi," Jade responded. "I had a really good time today."

"Yes, it was fun," Cohen agreed. He then kissed her long and hard. "Call me immediately if you hear anything outside or if you suddenly feel uncomfortable."

"I will. Bye, Lavi."

Jade then nodded her thanks to the Mike Tyson look-alike and went inside the apartment, locking the door behind her.

She turned on the loving room light and threw her Dooney & Bourke tote bag on the sofa. She hurriedly made her way to the bathroom. She had needed to pee on the drive back into Kingston from Morgan's Harbour but had decided to hold it until she got home. She turned on the bathroom light and went into the bathroom. A scream died in her throat as a man, coming from behind the bathroom door, held a sharp, thin blade at her neck.

"Scream and yuh dead," a raspy, croak said matter-of-factly in her right ear.

Jade was paralyzed with shock and fear. She wasn't even sure if she was breathing. She had no doubt as to the identity of the owner of that terrible voice. How the fuck had he gotten into her home? The shock proved to be too much for her full bladder and it emptied itself of the half bottle of champagne she had consumed on the yacht on the way back to Morgan's Harbour.

It amused him.

"Yuh scared eeh gal? Yuh should be. This ah yuh last chance. The next time yuh see mi...mi ah go 'ave mi way wid yuh before cutting yuh up inna some tiny pieces," he promised as he used an almost skeletal finger to lightly caress her right cheekbone. He moved the hand downward and slipped her right breast out of the confines of her swimsuit top. He caressed it; rubbing the nipple between his thumb and index finger. Jade trembled in revulsion and anger. His hand was cold and rough. Felt like an icy piece of sandpaper. She wanted to puke but dared not move. The cold steel resting underneath her chin was a sobering reminder that death was a mere body movement away.

"Contact de big man by midday tomorrow or else..." he warned.

Snake then instructed Jade to lie on the floor and put her hands behind her. He then tied them and placed a piece of electric tape over her mouth. Jade was scared to death but figured the worst was over. Then he was gone. She waited a few moments before struggling with the piece of electrical cord that he had used to tie her hands. She got it off after a few moments. Obviously he had only tied them tight enough to give himself time to make good his escape without any interference. Jade then ripped the tape from her mouth in one go. She squealed. It hurt like hell. She checked the mirror to see if her lips were still there. Her reflection scared her. Her face was a picture of absolute terror. She went into the kitchen and grabbed a knife then frantically rummaged through her tote bag for her mobile to call Cohen. Her hands were shaking so badly it took her several attempts to scroll to his name in her phonebook.

"He was here...inside my house...held a knife to my throat..."Jade whispered as soon as Cohen came on the line.

"I'll be right over," Cohen replied and hung up.

He got there in fifteen minutes.

Jade let him in and the two bodyguards went to look around the apartment.

Cohen sat with her on the couch and hugged her as she cried. He didn't speak until she composed herself. She was about to tell him what happened when the Mike Tyson look-alike called for them to come into the bedroom. Half of the grill covering the window had been removed as well as one side of the window. By now all Jade could feel was anger. She was angry at the violation of her home, the threat on her life, being made to feel such wretched *fear*, the *humiliation* of peeing on herself, and the *feeling* of that bastard's hand on her body. She had thrown up twice since she had made the call to Cohen. And to think she had done nothing to deserve this. She was not going to sit around and wait for Snake to come back. She discussed with Cohen what she wanted to be done. She then went back with him to his hotel. He was staying in the Presidential Suite at The Castello, Kingtson's latest and most luxurious hotel. After a warm shower, a couple glasses of La Roseda, and Cohen's agreement to her plan, Jade began to feel better. She was in good enough spirits to go on the balcony and give Theresa a call. She didn't mention the incident.

Secret received a thunderous applause after singing Anita Baker's *No One in the World*. A few people recognized her face from the posters that had been put up all over Kingston. There were several on the light posts and on the wall in front of this very venue. She took a few pictures of the let-me-get-one-with-her-before-she-becomes-a-star variety with a few guys and a couple girls. When she rejoined Dunga at the table, a rotund potbellied guy with a bald head and draped in a Burberry shirt which showcased his prominent stomach, came over and introduced himself. He was a producer from

Britain and he loved Secret's look and sound. He and Dunga talked business for a few minutes and exchanged business cards. Dunga had never heard of him but was familiar with the names of two of the people that the producer had said he worked with. The guy then wished them a good night and a few minutes later, he could be heard massacring a Barry White classic. Secret was happy that she had come out with Dunga. Lots of jokes listening to people who were so terrible that they should not even sing in the privacy of their bathrooms. Took her mind off the pregnancy concerns. At least for a few hours.

Jade was curled up with Cohen in the queen-size bed watching an old Robert Deniro gangster movie. The movie was good but she was unable to focus. Her mind was all over the place. What a day today had been. Cohen would be sending someone to repair her window in the morning and to install an alarm in the apartment. She was supposed to go shopping with Mishka tomorrow but she planned to call and cancel. She was not in the mood. There were more important things to take care of. She was looking forward to the coming day. The late Tupac Shakur had once said that revenge was the sweetest joy next to getting pussy. Jade didn't know about that but she knew without a doubt that she would thoroughly enjoy what was going to happen. She fell asleep with unpleasant thoughts on her mind.

Cohen looked at Jade's sleeping form. She was smiling. He admired her. She was a tough cookie. He could understand how a lesser man could be driven to such bastardly acts to try and coerce her to be with him. She didn't explain the reasons behind her ex's actions but he knew. Jade was a special woman. Unlike any he had ever met, and he had met a lot, all across the globe. So much had happened since he met her less than forty eight hours ago. Never a dull moment with Jade. He hadn't realized how fond he had become of her until she had called him after she was attacked. His heart had felt too heavy for his chest. He was going back to Europe in a week's time. He wondered how long he'd be able to stay away from her.

Chapter 44

Miriam, one of the Weatherburns' two domestic workers, frowned as she got ready to put the sheets in the washing machine. It smelled of sex and was covered with stains. The sheets had obviously been placed in the washroom over the weekend. She knew that her employers were not getting along and that Mrs. Weatherburn had gone to the United States to visit the children. Mrs. Weatherburn could be a very miserable woman at times but deep down she was a good person. Miriam had been working for her for ten years and during that time, she had gotten a lot of assistance from Mrs. Weatherburn. When she didn't have the money to pay for her daughter's surgery after she was involved in an accident when a bus she was travelling in collided with a trailer, Mrs. Weatherburn had graciously paid for the medical expenses. When Hurricane Dean had practically left her homeless last year, Mrs. Weatherburn had gotten her husband to use his influence and get her assistance. And the list goes on. She did not deserve this. Her husband had obviously taken someone here and had sex with them in the very bed that he shared with his wife. *No wonder the country is in such a sorry state*, Miriam thought with disgust. Our so-called leaders have no morals and principles. She shook her head and placed the offensive sheet set into the machine. She then went into the kitchen to gossip with Edna, the cook, about her discovery.

~~~

Timex swaggered towards the customs area. He was feeling exuberant. The show in Canada had gone well. The sell out crowd had lapped up his electric performance, singing his impressive catalogue of hits word for word. He had come back to Jamaica thirty thousand Canadian dollars richer. The show had netted him twenty, and he had found the time to do a couple 'specials' –dub plates of his original songs – for a few of Canada's top sound systems, netting him another ten. The promoter had rolled out the red carpet for him. He had stayed in a five star hotel and was given the VIP treatment everywhere he went. And none of it had cost him a dime except for the clothes that he had purchased for his boys; and the bottle of Notorious, the new Ralph Lauren scent for women, and the Louie Vuitton bag that he had purchased for Jade. He hoped she liked her gifts. There was always the risk that she wouldn't accept them – Jade was as feisty as they come – but he hoped she did. If not, he could always give them to one of his baby mothers. He chatted amiably with the customs officer for a few minutes and then made his way
~~~

outside. Breeda and six other members of his crew were out there waiting for him. He greeted a few fans and tipped the porter fifty Canadian dollars which would have the porter telling his peers all week "dat is why mi affi rate Timex because 'im nuh figet weh 'im ah come from". He then greeted his boys and climbed into the passenger seat of his Range Rover. Breeda then drove off and the other members of the entourage followed on six powerful CBR motorcycles. Timex accepted the marijuana joint that Breeda handed to him and lit it. He took a deep drag and exhaled. It was good to be home.

ଔଓଔଓଔଓ

Jade woke up at 11:30. She stretched and got out of bed. Cohen was on the balcony in his robe. Remnants of his breakfast lay on a tray while he was busy talking on his mobile and typing on his state of the art laptop. Jade didn't disturb him. She went straight into the bathroom to take a shower. He was still hard at work when she came out of the bathroom twenty minutes later. She combed her hair and slipped on one of his white, crisply laundered Gucci button downs. She then called room service and ordered roasted corned beef brisket, chicken fajitas and garlic bread. He looked around at her, still conducting his business on the phone. She smiled and blew him a kiss. He returned her smile and then frowned as he turned his attention back to the computer. Apparently the person with whom he was speaking was telling him something he did not want to hear. Her food arrived in half an hour much to Jade's annoyance but she tipped the waiter nonetheless. After she ate, she called Eddie.

"Hi Eddie," she said when he came on the line. "How are you?"

"Hello, Jade," Eddie replied. He was in front of the National Land Cooperative, where Weatherburn had a meeting. He was standing by the vehicle enjoying a cigarette. "I'm good...but how are *you* doing?"

"Everything is just great," Jade told him. "What time are you getting off work tonight?"

Eddie thought for a moment. "Well the boss has a meeting at 4 this evening...which will probably be over by 5:30. Once I take him home that should be it for the night."

"Well I had wanted you to collect the money to deal with that thing for me but I won't be available at that time...guess you can collect it tomorrow or some other time," Jade lied.

"Oh...ok sorry about that. Hopefully I can pick it up tomorrow. Remember that you have to take the four pictures," Eddie replied.

"Ok, thanks for the reminder. Bye Eddie, talk to you soon."

Jade hung up feeling satisfied. She had gotten the information that she needed without Eddie knowing that anything was amiss. She trusted Eddie but he didn't need to know what was going on. She then called Mr. Hassan to see how the preparations for the launch were going. He was pleased to hear from her and related that everything was going fine. He had hired a firm to deal with the planning and they seemed to have everything under control. He informed Jade that they would be having a meeting at the office on Wednesday evening at five and reminded her to submit the names of anyone she wanted to invite to the launch by tomorrow evening. They then said their goodbyes and Jade turned on the T.V. She surfed through the channels and stopped on a local music channel when something caught her eye. It was a Timex video. She then remembered that he was supposed to return from Canada today. She would give him a call later in the week. She watched him as he stood in front of a group of about twenty men and deliver his violent lyrics with a deadly flow. He was really talented. And he had swagger. She watched until the song was over.

ଓଃଓଃଓଃ

"Yes baby! I missed you ...fuck me...oh yes!" Leah squealed as Timex fucked her like he had just gotten released from prison after doing a ten year bid. Leah was supposed to be in her Spanish lecture at the University of the Caribbean, where she was a second year business student majoring in business administration with a minor in international relations, instead, she was in Timex's bed, having a ball. Timex had called her while she was in her quantitative thinking lecture. She had excused herself and immediately left for his apartment. His boys were there as usual but she had long ceased to be embarrassed by them overhearing her having sex.

Timex had her long, milky legs tucked behind her ears and he was watching his extremely dark shaft disappear inside her over and over again. He loved the sight of it. Leah didn't have much in the ass department thanks to her Syrian ancestry but she more than made up for it with her pretty face, beautiful skin, generous breasts and a very fleshy mound that was always devoid of hair. He loved having sex with her. Leah took dick like a porn star. Any position, any time, no matter how rough he gave it to her, she didn't back down. His little freaky, nymphomaniac uptown princess.

"Yuh sure yuh miss mi?" Timex growled as he flipped her over like a pancake without removing his dick. He then pulled her to her knees and grabbed a fistful of her hair. He began to give her hard, measured strokes.

"Yes baby! Of course baby! Fuck! Timex! Good God!" Leah hollered at the top of her lungs. She was going to come. He was hitting that spot. "Don't stop! Don't stop! Don't stop!"

Leah came all over his unsheathed shaft, bathing it with her warm, sticky essence. Timex pulled out at the last moment and Leah turned around quickly and wrapped her lips around his throbbing dick. She swallowed every hot drop as Jamaica's most popular entertainer trembled like it was the middle of winter.

Fifteen minutes later, after Timex had sent Leah back to school and was chilling in the living room with the fellows, Breeda got a call. He frowned slightly and muttered tersely that he would pass on the message. He hung up and looked at Timex.

"Dat was Jimmy...de youth weh work fi Dunga," he said. "Him seh Dunga want fi meet wid yuh at 'im studio tonight if yuh can mek it."

Timex was surprised. There was no love lost between himself and Dunga. A long time ago, when he was just a shotta and had yet to even set foot in a studio, Dahlia, Dunga's baby's mother, had been his girl. Then she met Dunga and had moved on though he had fucked her once when she and Dunga had been going through some problems early in their relationship. He didn't think Dunga knew about that but the two men did not like each other. Their paths have never crossed directly, only by association. Dunga's good friend Bowler, leader of the Black Talon Crew had killed one of Timex's cousins five years ago during an altercation outside of a night club. Dunga had also disrespected Zingo, his label mate and good friend. Dunga used to be the promoter for a now defunct major show held every Christmas and had never booked Timex to perform there. It had been a glaring omission to everyone. Dunga was the hottest producer and Timex was the hottest deejay yet they had never worked together. Now Dunga wanted to meet with him. He would go. It had to be about business. Couldn't be anything else. Besides, he wasn't afraid of Dunga. He wasn't punk ass Ratty from Wicker Lane. He ran the streets. He was all about his money and if Dunga wanted to talk dollars, then it made sense to him.

"Call back de youth and tell 'im we'll be there at 8 p.m. Don't call him now though...wait a few hours," Timex told Breeda. He didn't want to seem too eager.

ঔঔঔ

"Yes?" Miriam enquired. She had been in the living room finishing up her dusting when the buzzer for the main gate sounded.

"Good afternoon," a voice said. "I have a delivery for Mr. Weatherburn. It's a household item so we were told to deliver it here."

"Ok," Miriam said and opened the gate. She wasn't concerned about any security issues. Prento, a new young security guard who Miriam suspected was sleeping with Edna, the cook, was on duty today. He would thoroughly check the van to ensure that everything was on the up and up.

The vehicle, a non-descript panel van, pulled up in front of the house. Two men dressed in white overalls alighted from the vehicle as Prento approached them.

"What's up?" one of the men greeted the guard. "Delivery for the minister. A sculpture he ordered."

Prento nodded at the man, trying to place his accent. Sounded British. He looked at the delivery note and handed it back to him. Miriam would sign it after they had taken the delivery inside the house.

"Anybody ever tell yuh seh yuh look like Mike Tyson de boxer?" Prento asked with a smile.

The man laughed.

"I hear that all the time mate," he responded with a chuckle as he handed the delivery note to the other guy. He continued to chat with Prento as the other two men went inside the house with the delivery. Miriam had been by the door waiting. The guy steered the conversation to cars and Prento walked him over to the garage where Weatherburn's 2008 Jaguar XK series convertible was parked. The fourth man, who had remained hidden inside the back of the van, quietly crept out and entered the house.

"He had said to put it in one of the guest bedrooms," one of the men said to Miriam as they held the sculpture, which was a depiction of a nude pregnant woman, waiting for her direction.

Miriam didn't like the piece. It looked obscene. Rich people didn't have a clue what to do with their money. She led the two men to the guest bedroom. The fourth man walked stealthily behind them and went upstairs where he would hide until he was certain that the house was empty. He was positive that the staff, with the exception of the security guard, would leave by 5 p.m. which was less than an hour away.

Miriam escorted the two men back outside and their co-worker, who was still standing by the car with Prento, told him bye and they headed out. Mission accomplished.

ଔଔଔ

Jimmy picked up Secret at 5:30 p.m. She wasn't needed at the studio before 8 but he had been taking care of some business close by so he had called ahead and told her to get ready.

"Hi Jimmy," she said chirpily. She was in high spirits. Her period had finally come. She could never have imagined ever being so happy to see blood. It had been a close call. She would definitely go and see her doctor this week and make him recommend the right contraceptive for her.

"What's up pretty girl," Jimmy responded.

"I'm good...do you know what the meeting at the studio tonight is about?" she asked. Dunga had called to let her know that she had an important meeting at the studio but he didn't tell her any details.

"Nope," Jimmy replied, though he knew that Secret wouldn't believe him.

Secret smiled but didn't press. Jimmy was Dunga's right hand man. He knew everything. She would find out soon enough. She looked at her likeness on a wall at the stoplight at Trenton Crescent. They were definitely creating awareness. People who she hadn't heard from in ages had been calling her since yesterday. They realized that she was definitely on the rise and they wanted a piece of the action. Everybody loves a winner. It amused Secret. She knew that she wouldn't change when she became a successful singer. No entourages or fake friends to bring her down and lead her in the wrong direction. Matter of fact, it might be a good idea to change her number. Dunga had made fun of her cheap Nokia phone saying that it was not a good look for her. He had promised to get her a phone that according to him was becoming of a budding superstar. When he did she was going to take the opportunity to change her number. Get rid of the vultures before they started to descend.

"You need me for the rest of the night boss?" Eddie enquired as he followed Weatherburn inside the house. He was carrying his boss' files and attaché case. Weatherburn went straight into the study and made himself a quick drink. Eddie placed the stuff on Weatherburn's desk and patiently waited for a response. Weatherburn downed the shot of whiskey in one gulp.

"You may go," he told Eddie without looking at him. He was preoccupied with his thoughts. He still hadn't heard from Jade. He found it incredible that after what happened to her last night she still hadn't called him. She really despised him that much? That no matter what he did she wouldn't comply? He wasn't having it. He had invested too much. Yearned for her too much. He had to have her back. He was not going to take no for an answer. He was going to break her down to the very last atom. By any means necessary. All is fair in love and war. He stretched and wondered what to do with the rest of his night. The boys would be playing poker at the usual spot tonight. Maybe he would go over there and win some of their money. Or maybe he should call over Francine. He would relax for a bit then take a shower. He would decide what to do later. It was still early. He headed upstairs to the master bedroom. He was about to undress when he heard the sound of running water in the bathroom. Frowning, he went in there to turn it off.

He gasped as someone grabbed him from behind and held a blade at his throat.

"Do not struggle mate. I don't wish to kill you but I will if I have to," the British accented voice told him matter-of-factly.

Weatherburn tried to remain calm but his efforts were futile. His heart was pounding so loudly that he was sure the intruder could hear it. How the fuck did this man get inside his house? If he made it out of this alive god help the security guard who was on duty.

"I'm a very powerful man," Weatherburn responded, as he tried his best to remain still. Dying from a slashed throat was a very nasty way to go. The only thing worse that he could think of was being burnt to death. "I can give you anything you want. Just remove the knife and don't hurt me."

The man emitted a mirthless chuckle and applied a bit more pressure on the knife, giving Weatherburn a small cut. He gasped loudly when he felt the cut but did not struggle.

"You only think you are powerful," the man said scornfully. "Listen to me carefully. I know fifty ways to kill a man. Forty-five of them include excruciating pain for hours, sometimes days, prior to death. Hopefully, with your cooperation, I won't have to resort to choosing one of these techniques to use on you. You have a man in your employment. Snake. I need his address."

"Snake?" Weatherburn whispered in surprise. Snake must have messed with someone very important for this to be happening. But he had only given Snake one job recently. Surely this couldn't have anything to do Jade?

"Yes asshole. Snake. The man your cowardly ass sent to terrorize a young lady last night," the man replied.

Oh God! Weatherburn cried inwardly. Jade. Who was this woman really? How could she have pulled this off? Turning the tables on him like this and in such dramatic fashion? He rued the day he met that beautiful devil.

After Weatherburn had written down the address for Snake's main home - he was a man who stayed all over the place – and had called to ensure that he would be there at 10 p.m. as he would be sending Eddie over with a package for him, the man further instructed Weatherburn to strip naked and to sit on the floor. Flushed with humiliation and dread, Weatherburn did as he was told. He prayed that somehow he was dreaming and would soon awaken from this nightmare. This could not really be happening to him. The man sat on a chair across from him. He had a Ruger GP100 in his hand. A silencer was attached to it.

The man hummed an unfamiliar tune as he sat there in silence for a few minutes. Weatherburn thought it best not to speak. He was still in disbelief that Jade was the reason that he was going through this. The Minister of Mining, Energy and Environment; prominent businessman; board member of three important non-profit organizations and upstanding member of society was sitting on his bedroom floor naked and humiliated at the mercy of a stranger. Look how far he had fallen. And all because of that bitch. He touched his neck. It was still bleeding but not heavily.

The man's phone beeped and he answered it quickly.

"Ok," he said and hung up.

He gestured for Weatherburn to get up.

"Buzz the security guard and tell him that he's to open the gate as you have visitors."

Covering his private parts with his hands, Weatherburn waddled over to the intercom by the bed and instructed the guard on duty to open the gate. He then returned to his spot on the floor without having to be told. The man smiled his approval. The man's phone beeped again.

"We're in the bedroom upstairs," he said and hung up.

Weatherburn felt sick to his stomach. The stress and humiliation he was enduring was threatening to get the better of him. Now others were here to share in his humiliation.

Two men and a woman entered the bedroom.

"Hello Duane," Jade said sweetly as she stood over his pathetic figure on the floor. "Good to see you."

She then spat in his face.

ଔଔଔ

Timex arrived at the studio for his meeting with Dunga a few minutes late. It was a deliberate slight. He came there with an entourage of twelve men in assorted vehicles and motorbikes taking up nearly all of the available space in the parking lot. Dunga for his part let Timex wait for five minutes before he went out to the chill room to greet him. He told Secret to stay in his office until he summoned her. Timex was sprawled out comfortably on one of the sofas. He was flanked by Breeda and another guy whom Dunga knew for a fact was wanted by the police in connection with several murders in Kingston and Spanish Town. Dunga was not impressed. He walked over to Timex and offered his hand.

Timex looked at it for a few seconds before he shook it.

"Thanks for coming," Dunga said to him.

Timex nodded.

"Let's talk in private," Dunga said to him and gestured for him to follow. Timex made a big show of fixing his shirt. He wanted Dunga to see that he was armed. There was a desert eagle in his waist. Dunga pretended not to notice.

"You guys make yourself at home," Dunga said, gesturing to the trolley filled with alcohol of all kinds. The two men looked at him stonily but helped themselves to a drink of Hennessy. Jimmy stayed out there to keep an eye on them.

Dunga took Timex around to the recording area.

Timex stood by the door and waited for Dunga to speak.

"I have an idea for a collaboration," Dunga began. "Listen to this hook and check out the beat."

Timex loved it. He tried valiantly to remain cool but his genuine love for music prevented him from masking the fact that he was feeling what he just heard.

"That's my new artist. Her name is Secret. If you do a love song with her...singing instead of deejaying..." Dunga trailed off to let him finish it mentally.

Timex was intrigued by the idea. He whispered the melody to himself and a verse came to him. He grabbed a notebook and pen that was on the mixing board and scrawled some words onto the page. Dunga smiled and buzzed the intercom in his office. Secret came into the room a few seconds later.

She was surprised to see Timex. She loved his talent though she wished he would do more uplifting songs as opposed to those of a violent nature. The ghetto youths looked up to him a great deal and it would be nice if he could set a better example for them.

Dunga introduced them and explained to Secret what he had in mind. She listened to the hook and the beat and punched him on the shoulder. This was a brilliant idea. She remembered the evening when she had showed it to him and he had sent her in the booth to record it. Now it was going to lead to a collaboration that though it would raise a few eyebrows on paper, was odd enough to work. Think Mariah Carey teaming up with rapper Ol' Dirty Bastard. Dunga was a musical genius.

Timex appraised Secret. She was hot. And talented. She had a wicked sound. He had seen posters of her around town. He was sure Dunga was fucking her. It was written all over her face when she looked at him. It was an excellent idea Dunga had though. Jamaica's biggest gangster deejay singing a love song for the ladies. Brilliant. How the fuck he had never thought of that? It would show his versatility and most importantly, it would definitely be a hit. He would do it as long as they could agree on the business side of things.

"The idea wicked still," Timex said grudgingly. "Mi ah go do some writing and we can link up back here and put in some work Thursday night. Call me tomorrow mek wi chat 'bout de business side yeah."

He gave Dunga a number that only his closest associates had and Dunga escorted him back out to the chill room.

"Alright so we'll talk," Dunga said to Timex and they shook hands in parting.

Breeda was surprised to see how at ease the two men were. He knew how much they disliked each other. He shook his head as they headed out to the vehicles. Music was indeed a powerful force.

Jade felt good as she rode in silence with the three men that were accompanying her to deal with Snake. Weatherburn would not be the same after tonight. He had been rattled and humiliated to the core. Just like she had been. An eye for an eye the good book said. Now it was Snake's turn. She couldn't wait to get there. Her adrenaline was pumping. They were in a tinted forest green Mitsubishi Pajero that was identical to the one that Eddie drove to transport his boss so as not to arouse Snake's suspicion when they pulled up in front of his gate. The guy that Cohen had put in charge of the operation had thought of every detail. They got to the neighbourhood where Snake resided in half an hour. It wasn't exactly a ghetto but the area had seen better days. Snake lived alone in a one bedroom house beside an open lot where the youngsters in the community played football and cricket. A white Toyota Corolla was parked in the yard. It was the right place. They pulled up in front of his gate and blew the horn twice. The house was in total darkness. *Creepy fucker*, Jade mused as they watched him open the door and come towards the vehicle. He went around to the driver's side.

The Mike Tyson look-alike lowered the window.

Snake froze as he stared down the barrel of a desert eagle.

The back door opened quickly and two men exited. They grabbed him and took him back inside the house. The driver nodded at Jade. She put on a pair of leather gloves and slipped on a set of brass knuckles on her right hand. She then went inside the house.

The men wasted no time in securing Snake to a chair. He still had not spoken. He couldn't believe Weatherburn had set him up like this. He had gotten careless of late. You can't trust anyone, especially in his business and you definitely cannot trust a politician. He smiled tightly when Jade entered the room. He should have killed that bitch when he had the chance. One of the men taped his mouth shut.

Jade looked around the shabby room. It was filthy and the smell of a freshly deceased rodent, perhaps a rat, was fresh in the air. She stopped in front of him.

"This is for breaking into my house," she said and crushed his nose with a vicious punch from the brass knuckles.

Snake screamed into the tape on his mouth.

"This is for threatening my life," she continued and punched him again, this time in the left eye.

"Untie his right hand," she instructed to one of the men.

He did and Jade held the skinny, trembling hand firmly.

"This is for touching me," she whispered as she pushed his index finger back until they heard the bone crack. She repeated the maneuver with his thumb.

She noted with satisfaction that he had lost control of his sphincter. The air stank of his waste.

Jade gave him one last look then nodded at the men. She could hear the thuds from the silencer as she went through the door. It was over. Her revenge was complete. Her life could go back to normal now. She hopped in the SUV and a few seconds later the men emerged from the house. They drove off leaving the place in flames.

ଓଃଓଃଓଃ

Half an hour after his tormentors had left, Weatherburn finally managed to get up from off the floor. He went into the bathroom and fell to his knees in front of the toilet bowl. He vomited everything he had consumed that day. He then took a long shower and crawled into bed. He could hear his cell phone vibrating on the bedside table. It was probably the boys calling to see if he would be coming to play poker or it could be an important call from one of his colleagues. He didn't check. He was not in any condition to have a conversation with anyone right now. He was drained mentally and physically. The overwhelming feeling of embarrassment and shame had broken his spirit. To know that Jade had not only orchestrated this symphony of humiliation and utter degradation, but had also actively taken part, coming into his home to contemptuously spit in his face, had broken his heart. After all he had done for her. Yes he was wrong to try and force her to be with him but she should have at least spoken to him about it instead of reacting in such a brutal fashion. Weatherburn pulled the covers over his head and tried to stop the tears from falling. He couldn't. It was going to be a very long night.

❧❧❧

Dahlia had stayed home for most of the day. She still wasn't taking calls or responding to any text messages. She had left the house briefly in the afternoon to pick up Samantha from school so that she could spend some time with her. The swelling on her face had receded significantly and with tons of make-up and a pair of over-sized Prada shades, she had ventured out without feeling too self-conscious. Her mom had quizzed her as to what was wrong with her as Dahlia had been very quiet and subdued, but had given up after Dahlia snapped at her. She had left there after a couple hours and told her mom that she would call her when she got back to New York. She had wanted to tell Dunga's mom goodbye but she didn't feel like going around there or even calling. She packed the things she would be taking back to New York, then took a shower and went to bed. She had only spoken to Dunga once all day when he called to check up on her just as she was leaving to go on the road. She had asked him if he was going to be able to take her to the airport. He had said yes. She couldn't wait to leave. A month away from Jamaica should do the trick. Or maybe longer. She would do some serious shopping when she got there. That would help to cheer her up.

"How do you feel now?" Cohen asked as he nibbled on her ear. They were standing on the balcony of his suite, sipping champagne. Jade was wearing a sheer, white night dress. She was naked underneath. She could feel Cohen's erection poking a hole in her back.

"Mmmm...I'm feeling great. Everything went according to plan. Thanks again Lavi. I really appreciate it," Jade responded. Her window at home had been repaired earlier that day but she had decided to stay at the hotel with Cohen. He was pleased that she did.

Cohen slipped a finger between her legs and stroked her protruding clit. Jade moaned. She took a sip of the ice cold champagne and leaned over on the rails of the balcony. She spread her legs slightly and poked her ass out.

"Fuck me Lavi," she said softly.

He fetched a condom and quickly rolled it on.

Jade groaned when he entered her.

"Mmm...yeah...give it to me Lavi...fuck me like you're never going to see me again..." Jade breathed. All the violence and excitement of the past few hours had made her feel powerful and horny. She was dripping wet.

Cohen's dick swelled even more at her words. He grunted as he increased his tempo, fucking her deep and hard.

"Harder! Harder!" Jade cried. It was going to be an intense orgasm. She could tell. Her knees felt like jelly and her clit was throbbing almost painfully.

The glass of champagne slipped from her fingers and smashed below as she climaxed. Her screams could be heard ten stories down.

The man sitting in the dark on the adjoining balcony, a motivational speaker from Tennessee who was in Jamaica for a seminar, ejaculated the same time Cohen did. He had thoroughly enjoyed the unexpected show.

Chapter 45

“Sir?” Miriam called out as she stood outside of Waetherburn’s bedroom door. Earlier this morning she had barged into the bedroom to clean it thinking that he had already left for the day. He hadn’t seen her though. He had been curled up in a fetal position underneath the comforter fast asleep. It was now almost midday and he was still in bed. “Mr. Weatherburn?”

“Come,” he answered gruffly. He had just gotten up a few minutes ago. He had awakened at six and had immediately called his personal assistant to let her know that he wasn’t feeling well and would not be coming in. She was to reschedule all of his appointments until Wednesday and was not to call him about anything unless it was an emergency. Then he had gone back to sleep. He was sitting up in bed checking his email on his Blackberry. He didn’t respond to any of the messages. His stomach was empty but he didn’t have an appetite. He needed to eat though.

Miriam entered the room cautiously. She was afraid of her boss. She wasn't used to dealing with him directly and she had heard how miserable he could be most of the time.

"Would you like something to eat sir?" she queried timidly. She averted her eyes, irrationally thinking that he would see her guilt. She planned on telling Mrs. Weatherburn about her discovery whenever she called or when she got back; whichever came first.

"Get me some chicken soup and a tuna sandwich with pickles. Bring a can of Red Bull as well."

"Yes sir," Miriam replied and hurried out to prepare the food. Weatherburn turned the T.V on. It had been a rough night. He had taken forever to fall asleep and when he did, he had only slept sporadically. He couldn't remember the last time he was home like this on a Tuesday morning. It was on a local channel and to rub salt in his still very open wound; was a drink commercial with Jade. He quickly changed the channel.

Dunga and Dahlia were mostly silent on the ride to the airport. Neither commented when they passed the billboard featuring Jade at the Harbour View roundabout though Dahlia's face had visibly reddened. He pulled up in front of the departure lounge behind a black Lexus RX350. Dahlia absently thought that the vehicle looked familiar. It was. It was Zingo's truck. He had just disembarked the vehicle and was standing there joking with his entourage. She sighed and averted her eyes as she exited the vehicle. Just what she needed. To be on the same flight with that asshole. She swore she would slap him in his face if he said anything at all to her. Dunga removed her two suitcases and a porter, having recognized Dunga, raced over to put them on his trolley.

"Have a safe flight and call when you get home," Dunga said as he hugged her.

"Ok, bye baby," she replied and gave him a peck on the lips.

She then walked briskly into the departure lounge.

Dunga ignored the stares from Zingo and his boys and hopped into his vehicle. He didn't even look at them because if he caught Zingo even looking at him the wrong way there would be a problem and he didn't need to be at the airport creating a scene. He turned his music up and headed back towards the city. Dahlia was gone. He had a feeling he and Secret were going to get a lot closer in the coming days.

***

Jade decided to pay Theresa a surprise visit at the salon. When she had told Cohen that she was going on the road, he had given her an envelope. She had nonchalantly accepted it and told him that she would call him later. She looked in the envelope when she got inside the SUV: five thousand US dollars. She had instructed Nathan to take her home where she had quickly changed her clothes. He then took her to a foreign exchange trader where she changed half of the money that Cohen had given her. That netted her a hundred and seventy two thousand Jamaican dollars. She then went to the mall where she purchased a 36 inch flat screen T.V. and a DVD player along with ten movies. She also purchased a six disc CD player set with surround sound and twelve of the latest hip hop and R&B releases. She had then gone back home and Nathan had set up everything for her and made sure that all was in working order.

"Bye Nate, and thanks," she said when they arrived at Theresa's salon. "I'll call if I need you."

"Ok Jade," Nathan replied.

Jade then went inside. Theresa was pleasantly surprised. And busy. The salon was full as usual. Jade didn't mind though. She chatted with Theresa while she worked. She took up the newspaper to browse through it and a story about arsonists burning down a house on Wigan Avenue last night was on page two. The charred remains of an unidentified man were found. Jade smiled. Snake and his smelly house had made the news.

Weatherburn did a lot of soul searching during the course of the day. He suddenly missed his wife. Jessica, for all her faults, had a knack of making him feel better about himself and life in general when he was down. And to be honest, though she was spoilt and liked to try and impress people with her lifestyle too much, she had been a good wife and had done a good job raising the kids. He decided to give her a call and apologize for the way he had been treating her. He felt ashamed at the lies he told the children about their mother. He would have to find a way to fix that without admitting to deliberately lying.

Jessica was at her cousin's apartment reading a novel when her husband called. She was surprised to see his name on the caller ID. She steeled herself for an argument and answered the call.

"Hi Jess," Weatherburn said. "Baby I'm so sorry about everything. I don't know how I could have been so unfeeling and arrogant. I'm so very sorry. I miss you baby."

Jessica's mouth became a wide O. She was shocked. This was the last thing she expected to hear. She was so surprised that she couldn't find the words to respond immediately.

"Please accept my apology Jess...come home baby. Come home tomorrow," he continued, pouring on the charm.

Jessica exhaled.

"I miss you too Duane...and it means a lot to me that you have at least taken the first step to make things right," she replied. "But its not going to go away just like that....we'll need to have a long talk about everything that happened. You really hurt me. Deeply. Okay?"

"Yes baby, I totally understand that. Just come home and let's have that long talk...and other long things..."

Jessica laughed.

"Don't think its going to be that easy...you're still in the doghouse but I'll call the airline and see if I can get a flight for tomorrow," she told him.

"Ok darling. I love you so much. And, again, I'm sorry. If I could turn back the hands of time I would."

"I'm sure you'll think of lots of ways to make it up to me."

"Call me as soon as you get through with the airline. Later baby."

Weatherburn felt a lot better after he hung up the phone. That was the right thing to have done. He then dialed his son's number. He would tell Peter that it had turned out to be a big lie that his mom was having an affair. That someone had planned the whole thing to create problems in his marriage. He was sure Peter would believe him. After all, a politician who could not lie convincingly when he had to needed to find a new line of work.

ଔଊଔଊଔଊ

Secret went to the pharmacy to purchase two packs of the contraceptive that her doctor had recommended. She had just left his office which was on the same complex as the pharmacy. The matronly woman looked at Secret sternly as she rang up the purchase on the register.

"Birth control pills do not prevent HIV and STDs you know young lady," she commented as Secret handed her a thousand dollar bill.

Secret did not respond. The woman was rude and out of line. Miffed that Secret had ignored her comment, she muttered something that sounded like 'stupid young bitch' and shoved Secret's change and the bag with her purchase aggressively on the counter. Secret pretended not to hear and collected her stuff and left without a word. She hated unnecessary confrontations. Some taxis were parked at the entrance of the complex and she hopped in the back of one and told the man where she was going. The taxi driver, whose head had been buried in a newspaper, nodded and put up the windows and turned on the AC as he headed out. He turned on some really loud music and Secret didn't like the way he was driving. Taxi men, as a rule, were certified road hogs, but this man was taking it to another level. By the time he ran the second red light she was downright scared for her life.

"Driver! You need to slow down!" Secret protested, shouting to be heard above the extremely loud music.

The driver did not appear to hear her. Secret's heart skipped two beats as the man dangerously overtook a line of traffic and nipped back in line just before a large bus came around the corner.

"Jesus Christ! Are you mad? Stop the vehicle and let me out now!" Secret shouted, close to tears. She slapped the man on his back when he didn't respond.

Secret then noticed that he was not going in the direction that she had given him. She was now terrified. She pleaded with the man to stop the car and let her out. He continued to ignore her. Secret realized that her life was in danger. He was probably taking her somewhere to rape and kill her. She panicked and grabbed his throat from behind squeezing as hard as she could with her tiny hands as she screamed that she was going to make him crash.

"Hey gal! Yuh mad!" the man finally said as the car swerved dangerously in the middle of the road.

"Stop the fucking car!" Secret screamed as she squeezed even tighter and dug her nails into his neck.

A policeman who was pulling out of a gas station saw the car swerving erratically in the road. He quickly switched on the siren and gave chase.

"Alright! Alright!" the man shouted as he narrowly missed running into a light pole. He pulled over to the side of the road and stopped the car.

Secret hurriedly opened the door and hopped out of the car. She ran in the opposite direction and flagged down the police car as it approached. The man drove off in a hurry without even closing the back door.

"Jump in!" the police man shouted. Secret climbed into the car and he tried to give chase but the taxi had disappeared. Cursing, the policeman pulled over at the side of the road.

"Yuh ok miss?" he asked.

Secret nodded through her sobs.

"Tell me what happened."

Secret told him and the cop shook his head. He didn't know what this country was coming to. In broad daylight a young woman couldn't even take a random cab and get to her destination safely without having to worry about being raped or murdered. Secret declined to go the police station to give an official report. It didn't make any sense as she didn't have any details. She couldn't identify the man if she saw him again and she didn't know his license plate number. All she wanted to do was go home. The cop offered her a ride and she accepted. Miss G was there when she got home and Secret rushed in her arms and the tears came roaring back. Startled and gravely concerned, Miss G hugged Secret until she calmed down enough to speak. Miss G could not believe it. Poor girl. Good thing she hadn't passively sat there and waited for something to happen. Her actions had probably saved her life. Miss G prayed and told God thanks for sparing Secret's life.

Chapter 46

Timex smiled as he read the lyrics he had just written. After a good lunch of roast breadfruit, cornmeal dumplings and stew chicken, he had settled down with a spliff and a drink of Hennessy and red bull. This was definitely something the ladies would love yet it was hard-core enough not to alienate his core fan base. Definitely not your typical love song. It had been easy for him to write the three verses. He just thought about Jade and how much he wanted her and the words had just flowed. He took a drag of the potent weed. Jade had yet to call him but he was confident that she would. He should have gone to New York today for a show but the promoter wasn't talking his kind of dollars. His label mate, Zingo, would be performing on it though. Timex heard his cell phone ringing. The ringtone was a freestyle he had recorded just to have as his own custom ringtone. He checked the caller ID. It was Leah. He ignored it. He didn't like to be disturbed when he was working. There was only one person he'd welcome hearing from now.

ଓଃଃଓଃଃଓଃ

"What!" Dunga exclaimed. Secret had just called to tell him about what had happened to her. She was in bed relaxing. After a long chat with Miss G and two slices of potato pudding that Miss G had baked earlier that morning, she was feeling a little better. "Why you didn't tell me you needed to go on the road?"

Secret didn't respond. She really should have told him but she had remembered him saying that he had to go to the airport and she didn't want to bother him. How could she have known a simple trip to the doctor would have turned into a near death experience?

"Even if I couldn't take you I would have sent Jimmy or somebody to take you wherever you needed to go," Dunga continued, trying not to be angry with her but he was very disturbed about what had transpired. Just the thought of something happening to Secret gave him a migraine.

"I should have called you baby...I'm sorry," Secret replied, as her tears returned. The last thing she needed was Dunga to be upset with her.

"Its ok babes...I'm sorry for getting mad but the mere thought of something happening to you is enough to drive me crazy," Dunga told her.

"I love you Dunga...so much," Secret said between sobs.

"Don't cry baby...everything is ok now. You're safe. Just ensure that you call either me or Jimmy whenever you need anything."

They chatted for awhile longer and Secret came off the phone smiling. Dunga had told her they would be spending the night together.

ଔଔଔ

Jade used her iPhone to email the office the list of people that she was personally inviting to the official launch of La Roseda. It was a short list. She had Theresa, Timex and Gypsy, the host of *Entertainment Round-Up*, on the list. She was still at the salon. Theresa was on her last client. Jade's mind ran on Zachary, the guy she had met a few nights ago by the hotel pool. She went into Theresa's office for some privacy and gave him a call.

"Hello," his deep baritone boomed in the phone. He was sitting at his desk checking the close of the major stock markets around the world. A 27 inch flat screen T.V. was on a business program on FNBC. The reporter was interviewing the C.E.O. of the largest investment bank in the United States.

"Hi, trying to reach Zachary," Jade purred.

Zachary sat up in his chair and reached for the remote to quickly turn the volume down on the T.V. He would recognize that voice anywhere. But he needed to be sure.

"This is he," he replied, maintaining a professional tone just in case he was wrong.

"Hi Zach, it's Jade," Jade said. Not bothering to remind him where and when they had met. She was positive he hadn't forgotten her.

"Hi pretty lady. It's a pleasure...and a relief to hear from you."

Jade laughed at his honesty.

"How are you?" she asked.

"It has been a very challenging day but somehow it feels so much better now," he replied.

"It's good to know my call brightened your day," Jade told him.

"So when will you be gracing me with your presence?" he queried.

"I don't know...store my number and give me a call on Sunday. I won't be available before then."

"Well, there is a soccer match on Sunday at the National Stadium. Jamaica will be playing Argentina in an international friendly. It begins at 6 p.m. I'd love for you to accompany me."

Jade thought for a moment. She would be tired after the launch and after-party on Saturday night but 6 p.m. was a good time. She would be ok by then.

"Sure, no problem. Call me on Sunday and I'll tell you where to pick me up."

Zachary was all smiles when he got off the phone. She had finally called. And he had a date. Sunday couldn't roll around fast enough. The security guard in the lobby buzzed him to say that a Ms. Assad was here to see him. He told the guard to send her up. His sister Leah needed his help with her economics course. He had told her to swing by the office this evening so that they could spend an hour and a half or two to address her problems. *If she studied more and hung out with that thug Timex less maybe she wouldn't be having any problems*, Zachary mused. Sometimes he was tempted to tell their dad about it just so that it would end but he couldn't do that to Leah. The old man would kill her.

Weatherburn was in high spirits as he had his dinner on the bedroom patio. Miriam had cooked oxtail and beans with rice and peas and steamed veggies. She had acted a bit peculiar when she had brought him the food. She had seemed very nervous this morning but just now she had this rather contemptuous look on her face. He didn't like her. He was going to have Jessica get rid of her and find another helper. But then again Jessica would be back and he wouldn't have to deal the help personally as was usually the case so the grumpy, weird bitch could stay for all he cared. Jessica had called him back an hour ago. She had managed to get on a flight tomorrow. She was supposed to be arriving in Kingston at 6:50 p.m. He didn't tell her that he had taken the day off from work. The calls to Peter and Penelope, his children, had gone well; especially the one to Peter. Penelope was still upset with him but happy that they were going to work things out. Francine crossed his mind. He wouldn't mind continuing to see her but that was playing a little too close to home. Perhaps it was best to put that on pause for now. But having gotten a taste of what she had to offer he knew he'd be back. Eventually.

"Hi baby," Dahlia said when Dunga came on the line. She had headed straight to her store from the airport. Sheree, her friend and manager for the store, had picked her up. After satisfying herself that everything was fine at the store, she had stopped at the Green Acres mall and purchased a Coach bag and a pair of sexy Marc Jacobs boots. Shopping always put a smile on her face no matter what. She had then called a couple of her friends to let them know that she was back. They would be coming over later to chill and have a few drinks. After taking a shower and getting something to eat, she then called Dunga.

"What's up babes?" Dunga said. "How was the flight?"

"It was ok," Dahlia said. "And everything was fine at the store. I stopped there before coming home."

"Ok, good. I'm at the studio working on some tracks," Dunga told her. Actually he had finished working and was in the process of locking up to leave when Dahlia called. He had promised Secret that he would be there to see her by 7.

"I won't keep you then," Dahlia replied. "I'll talk to you tomorrow. I love you."

"Love you too boo."

Dunga then headed out to his mom's house. Though Secret had told him that she was menstruating, he would still spend the night with her. He wanted to make sure that she was fine mentally. He needed to have her focused and stress free. What had happened today would be a very traumatic experience for any woman, especially one as innocent and sweet as Secret.

Miriam was so outraged by what Edna, the cook, had told her this evening that she just could not focus on the T.V. Prento, the security guard, had confided to Edna that his colleague who worked the night shift had witnessed Mr. Weatherburn having sex on the bedroom balcony with Francine Meadows, his wife's best friend on Friday night. She had also spent Saturday night at the house with Mr. Weatherburn. Miriam had been shell-shocked. Mr. Weatherburn was such an evil, unconscionable man. How could he sleep with his wife's best friend? And in their marital bed at that? She raised her hands to the heavens. She was glad she given up on men. After her husband Bernie had run off the farm work program in Canada, and had not contacted her in over four years, she had sworn off men. Jesus was the only man she needed now. And by God she would tell Mrs. Weatherburn what her husband had done. She wouldn't be able to live with herself if she didn't.

Chapter 47

Wednesday rolled around and proved to be a busy day for Jade. She hit the road at 10:30 a.m. with Mishka to do some shopping. She had to get something to wear to the upcoming launch on Saturday as well as a presentation next week Tuesday to the chairman of the Jamaica Football League. Hassan & Cohen LLC in a bid to become good corporate citizens and to help cement further brand awareness was donating USD$50,000 to the cash-strapped league. They were also going to sign on as the major sponsor for the league when the new season started in October. Their first stop was at an upscale shoe boutique in Manor Park. The cheapest shoe in there went for fifteen thousand dollars. Jade purchased four pairs. They then went to the boutique that Weatherburn had taken her to when she had just arrived in Jamaica. The owner, Chante, remembered Jade immediately.

"Hi there!" she greeted Jade warmly, giving her a peck on both cheeks. "I've been seeing you all over the place...billboards, commercials, T.V..."

"Hello," Jade replied with a pleasant enough smile though inwardly she was cringing. Knowing that Chante was into women made all the difference in that otherwise harmless greeting.

"You have perfect timing," Chante said, as she took Jade by the hand and led her to the new arrivals section of the store. "We got some stuff in from Europe just yesterday."

Mishka followed wearing an amused expression. Chante was flirting heavily with Jade but she was barking up the wrong tree. She should look her way. Mishka could easily see Chante sitting on her face with that delectable little butt of hers. She resolved to put a word in before they left the store. She got her chance when Jade went into the dressing room with seven dresses.

"You're hot," Mishka whispered in her ear as they stood by the rack filled with European couture. "How would you like to hang out with me tonight..."

Chante appraised Mishka from head to toe. She had been so caught up with Jade that she hadn't realized just how cute the little petite girl with the sexy British accent was.

"I like her too but she's not into women," Mishka continued.

Chante laughed. This girl was something else.

"Yeah...we could hang out later," she said. She had a date later that evening but nothing that couldn't be cancelled. This girl was way cuter.

They exchanged numbers just as Jade came out wearing one of the Dolce & Gabbana dresses. She looked stunning.

"I think this will be fabulous to wear to the launch," Jade said to Mishka. Posing and turning around so that they could see it from all angles.

The two women looked at her with lust-filled eyes. Chante licked her lips, unaware that she was doing so. Mishka nodded in agreement.

"Wow...damn Jade, you're going to turn every head that night," she commented.

"Please...they'll turn regardless," Jade boasted with a smile. She then went back into the changing room.

After they finished shopping and had a late lunch, Jade rushed home to get ready for the meeting at the office. It was already 3:30 p.m. and the meeting was at 5.

ꕥ ꕥ ꕥ

Dunga was feeling horny. Cuddling with Secret last night and being unable to make love to her had been a bit frustrating. But he was happy that he did it. She was fine now, the incident firmly behind her. Though she said she couldn't identify the taxi driver – she only knew that it was a white station wagon – Dunga decided to send Jimmy down to the complex to have a look and chat with some of the other drivers. They might get lucky. With Dahlia away and Secret out of commission for at least the next six days, he would have to look in the black book and call up someone to satisfy his carnal hunger. He had stayed with Secret until midday then he had made his way to his sports bar to see what was happening there. After that he had gone up to Belvedere Heights to have a look at a new apartment complex that was being built. Only twelve were being constructed - six three bedrooms and six two bedrooms. He was interested in one of the three bedrooms. It was a very good area and with the real estate boom that the country had been experiencing in recent times, it would be a solid investment. He decided to call Crystal, an athlete who represented the country in the long jump event. She was based in the United States but had called him three weeks ago to let him know that she was in Jamaica recuperating from a hamstring injury. He hadn't had a chance to visit her yet. Today was as good a day as any. It always amazed him that she was able to clear those hurdles when she was racing with that ass of hers. Her face wasn't anything to write home about but her body was a voluptuous, well-oiled machine. She was pleasantly surprised to hear from him and yes, she was home alone. Dunga stopped at a mini-mart and purchased some condoms then made his way up to Calabar Mews where she stayed with her older brother when she was in Jamaica.

❧❧❧

Weatherburn was in a good mood as he headed to the airport. Today had been a good day. He had cancelled his 6:30 appointment with a freelance writer who wrote environmental articles for a major newspaper so that he could meet his wife at the airport.

"Boss, you heard the news about Snake?" Eddie asked as they headed up the Palisadoes road. Eddie had been shocked to see it in yesterday's Star.

"Yes, I saw it on the news last night," Weatherburn replied tartly. He still found it hard to comprehend how Jade could be such a vicious person. She had actually had the man killed.

Weatherburn sighed and pushed away the unwelcome thoughts. The last thing he needed now was to think about his humiliating and frightening experience at the hands of Jade. Damn Eddie for bringing up Snake.

Eddie had glanced in the rearview mirror to look at his boss when he hadn't elaborated on Snake's death. He found it strange, seeing as Snake had done many deeds for him on and off for a number of years. But he dropped the subject. He didn't like the expression that was on Weatherburn's face. They were silent for the rest of the journey.

Being a government minister, Weatherburn was able to go inside the airport to meet his wife. He had one of the workers page his wife on the intercom and tell her to report to the VIP lounge.

Jessica had just cleared customs when she heard her name on the intercom. She walked into the VIP lounge and her husband was there waiting. She smiled and hugged him. He had definitely started out on the right foot.

Jade was feeling very happy as she relaxed in the backseat with Cohen. They had just left the meeting at the office and were heading up to Gordon Town to have dinner at Wild Boar, home of some of the best jerk pork in the world. The meeting had gone extremely well. A short term marketing plan for the next six months had been drawn up and Jade had been offered the job of Special Projects Manager. She would be provided with a laptop and other equipment which would enable her to work from home. The job would entail liaising with promoters of big events to secure advertising as either a major or minor sponsor; to identify and get involved with charities that would enhance the image of the company; to organize promotional events and to help the marketing team come up with new and cutting edge advertising concepts for La Roseda. Mr. Hassan was convinced that along with being the face of the drink, Jade was the perfect person to handle these tasks. Jade thanked him for the vote of confidence and had accepted the job which in addition to her fee for being the face of La Roseda, would net her a monthly salary of five hundred pounds or the Jamaican equivalent. Her performance would be reviewed in three months. Things were definitely falling into place. With a steady income supplemented with great benefits and wealthy admirers, her plan to become financially comfortable within a year's time was very much feasible. Once she saved her money and invested wisely, she would never be broke again.

ഗ്ദ്ദ

"Oh god," Jessica murmured. "This is so good!"

Weatherburn smiled. His wife loved pork so much she would eat the pig's grunt if she could. They had headed straight from the airport to Wild Boar to have dinner. The food here was expensive – the jerk pork was twice the cost anywhere else – but then again, it was twice as good too. The place had a sizeable crowd as always, despite the prices and the long drive from Kingston city. It took at least an hour to get there from Kingston and the road was very small and winding.

"I'm so happy you're home," Weatherburn said as he took a sip of his ice cold beer. He waved to an acquaintance a few tables away.

"Yeah...it's good to be back," Jessica agreed. Her husband had been very attentive and loving from the moment she stepped off the plane. Naturally that was expected as he was trying to right his wrongs but it still felt good nevertheless. It had been awhile since he had been so attentive and sweet to her.

"Does Francine know you're back?" Weatherburn asked nonchalantly. He had not spoken to her since she left his home on Sunday morning.

"No, I haven't spoken to Fran yet," Jessica replied. "I plan to swing by her home and surprise her tomorrow."

Weatherburn decided it would probably be best if he called Francine early tomorrow and give her a heads up. He had no idea how good of an actress she was. Besides, he needed to let her know that they could not see each other for awhile. He changed the subject and was in the middle of telling Jessica a joke when he felt the energy in the room change. He followed the wide-eyed gaze of the man facing him at the adjoining table. His appetite immediately disappeared. Jade had just entered the restaurant.

Chapter 48

Jade soaked in the stares as she made her way to the far corner of the restaurant where there was an unoccupied table for two. Apparently it had just been vacated as one of the waitresses, a plump light-skinned woman who beared more than a passing resemblance to the animal whose flesh they were about to enjoy, was still in the process of clearing the table. She saw Weatherburn with his mouth agape and his eyes bulging in shock like she was the last person he had expected to see. She looked right through him. Cohen seemed oblivious to all the attention. They sat down and the same waitress that had just cleared the table took their order. Jade was almost expecting the woman to grunt. They ordered a pound of the scrumptious jerk pork along with dinner rolls and bammy. The weather was very cool up there on the hill, and a chilly breeze embraced Jade, making her nipples harden. Good thing she had worn a blazer to the meeting.

"That woman is stunning," Jessica commented.

"Y-Y-Yeah," Weatherburn stammered.

"Are you ok babe?" Jessica asked, concerned. Her husband looked suddenly ill.

Weatherburn took a long swig of his beer before responding. He couldn't stand to be so close to Jade. He had to leave soon. Thankfully Jessica was almost finished eating.

"I'm not feeling too hot babe," he replied. "Suddenly feeling nauseous."

"Ok, let's go home...you really don't look well."

Jessica beckoned to a waitress and quickly paid the bill. She hoped it wasn't food poisoning. He had only had a small portion of the pork but maybe his system was rejecting it. If he didn't feel better by the time they got into the city, she was going to take him straight to Dr. Wilmot, her husband's physician for the past nine years. Jessica held on to him as they walked out to the parking lot where Eddie was waiting. They hopped in and headed out. Jessica put the windows down so that Weatherburn could get some fresh air. Thankfully, he felt better by the time they got to Papine Square, and by the time they got home, he was good as new.

Jade had noticed when Weatherburn left. She *knew* that it was because of her. She didn't mention him to Cohen. No need to get into that. Water under the bridge as far as she was concerned. The woman that Weatherburn had been sitting with was probably his wife. She was attractive but was chugging around a few extra pounds in unflattering places. The food arrived and Jade dug into it with gusto. The swine was divine. Cohen underestimated the peppery sauce and Jade laughed as his eyes watered as he valiantly tried to hold in the cough. He had to drink a tall glass of water before he could breathe normally again. Jade wondered idly if Weatherburn's wife knew what kind of bastard she was married to. Maybe, just maybe, what she had done to him would make him a better man. His wife should send her a thank you card. Jade chuckled at the thought.

ᴄᴚᴐᴄᴚᴐᴄᴚᴐ

"Oh baby...mmmm...right there...mmm" Jessica moaned as her husband licked and sucked her folds enthusiastically. It had been a long time since he had gone down on her. The last time was at least two years ago. Good thing she had shaved this morning. She had forgotten how good he was with his tongue. He had just started and already she was threatening to flood his mouth with her juices.

"I'm so sorry baby...I love you...I missed you..." Weatherburn murmured as he latched on to her protruding clit and sucked it insistently.

"Oh God! Duane!" Jessica said in a hoarse whisper as her husband wrestled her first orgasm of the night from her trembling body. "Mmmm...mmm...Jesus..."

He then positioned her on her hands and knees and slid into her easily. He caressed her ample breasts as he fucked his wife slowly, as though savouring every stroke. Jessica was in heaven. She was going to climax again. She could feel it building up. There was no sex like make-up sex she mused as she moaned loudly. Her husband was hitting spots tonight that she thought he forgot existed. And to think he wasn't feeling well not so long ago. She whimpered as she climaxed again, backing her plump ass against him as she bathed him with her juices. She felt as though she could fuck all night. Apparently so did her husband. He was showing no sign of letting up any time soon.

ꕥꕥꕥ

Secret was in Dunga's office browsing the internet. They had just finished recording the song she had written yesterday. Dunga loved it and had said it was definitely a keeper for her album but he didn't think it was going to be a single. She was on Myspace checking her messages, comments, and friend requests. She was pleased to see that the two songs they had uploaded had both been played over five thousand times by visitors to her page. She also had eighteen hundred friends already from all over the world and her friend request box was full. She was getting a lot of love on Myspace. A few people from France had also sent her comments saying that they heard her music on the radio over there. Dunga would be pleased to hear that. He was in the mixing room putting the finishing touches on a track he had produced for a reggae artist out of Guyana. The guy was talented but Secret found his accent annoying. After talking with him for a few minutes about music, she was ready to scream. She needed to have a lap top at home so that she could go online and interact with the fans whenever she had the time. She would ask Dunga to get her one tomorrow when they went on the road to buy gifts for Miss G. Friday was her birthday.

ꕥꕥꕥ

Jade was in an introspective mood as she relaxed on the balcony of Cohen's Presidential Suite. Her life was going well.

Way beyond her wildest dreams. She couldn't have imagined that things would have turned out this good so soon. She sipped her chilled glass of La Roseda. She was thankful to God for all the blessings he had bestowed upon her since her arrival in Jamaica. She glanced behind her at Cohen. He was in bed reading a novel, Junot Diaz's *The Brief and Wondrous Life of Oscar Wao*. He sensed her eyes and smiled at her. She smiled back and turned away. She knew that Lavi Cohen was going to play a major role in her development over the course of the next few months. She knew that despite his declaration that he tired of women easily, he would not be walking away from her anytime soon. Problem was, despite her declaration that she would walk any time she saw fit; she didn't think he would allow her to. Cohen had an ego that was bigger than the island of Jamaica. He was a nice guy and he treated her well but beneath that polished, sophisticated exterior was a steeliness and ruthlessness that lurked just below the surface. She knew that one didn't acquire Cohen's level of wealth without breaking a few arms along the way. He was a man who would play dirty if he had to. A dangerous enemy to have. She was enjoying herself now but she didn't think that she would ever fall in love with him. Care for him yes, but that do-anything-for-you-want-to-spend-the-rest-of-my-life-with-you-kind-of-love? No, she didn't see that ever happening. What was going to happen when he wanted; *demanded* more than she would give? She wondered if she had jumped out of the frying pan into the fire. Well it was too late now to ponder such things. Wherever this road took her she would have to complete the journey and deal with whatever problems might arise from this strange union. She finished her drink and went inside. She slipped off her robe and climbed into bed. She plucked the book from his hands and threw it behind her. She pulled his dick out through the slit in his boxers. She manipulated it like a master clay potter and when it was turgid, she dressed it in a purple durex condom. She then straddled him and impaled herself on his shaft. She wasn't in the mood for foreplay. She just wanted to ride his lengthy pole until she came and then go to sleep.

Chapter 49

Weatherburn woke up late the following morning. After a long and intense round with Jessica last night, he had slept like a log. It was now 7 a.m. and he had a very important meeting at 8:30 which would be attended by the Prime Minister. He could not afford to be late. He jumped out of bed and raced to the bathroom where he took a quick shower and got dressed in a charcoal grey suit. He kissed his sleeping wife on the cheek and popped into the study to retrieve his attaché case. Miriam had his breakfast waiting in the study along the morning paper but he had no time to eat. He grabbed the paper to read on the way to the meeting and headed out the door. A few seconds later, he was cursing at Eddie to step on it.

"Mrs. Weatherburn!" Miriam gasped in surprise when she entered the bedroom and saw her boss going into the bathroom. She was naked. Miriam averted her eyes. "Sorry ma'am. I didn't know seh dat yuh did come back."

"Its fine Miriam," Jessica replied and continued on into the bathroom. She paused before closing the door and told Miriam to bring her some breakfast as she was starving. She looked at herself in the full-length mirror. She was surprised to see a huge hickey on her left breast. When was the last time she had gotten one of those? She smiled as she climbed into the shower. Last night had been really good. Spectacular even. She lathered herself as her stomach protested its empty state. It was so good to be home. After breakfast she would go and pay Francine a visit. Share the good news that her life was back on track and that she was happier than ever. When she exited the shower, clad in a pink terry cloth robe, her breakfast was on the patio waiting. There was fresh fruit, an omelet, a slice of wheat bread, black coffee and grapefruit juice. Jessica made quick work of the food and Miriam returned upstairs thirty minutes later to retrieve the dirty dishes.

Miriam was feeling nervous. She wanted to tell her employer what she knew but she was afraid. She was not one of those people who enjoyed being the bearer of bad news. And this was bad. Really bad. But as a Christian woman, she felt that she had to do the right thing. She would be an accomplice in the Lord's eyes if she didn't come clean. Secrets like this were a burden that she wasn't willing to bear. Lord knows she had enough.

"Are you okay Miriam?" Jessica asked. Miriam had a very strange expression on her worn, wrinkled face.

Miriam released a heavy sigh and looked at Jessica mournfully.

"I have something to tell yuh Mrs. Weatherburn," Miriam said. "I have to sit down for this if yuh don't mind."

Her curiosity peaked, Jessica gestured to the chair across from her and Miriam sat.

Miriam's hands were fastened together tightly in her lap as she thought of the best way to begin. She opened her mouth several times but the words couldn't come out.

"What is it Miriam? Out with it man!" Jessica snapped, suddenly tired of the suspense.

"Yuh husband soil yuh marital bed Mrs. Weatherburn!" she blurted. "Him carry another woman in dere while yuh was away!"

Time stood still for Jessica as she tried to wrap her brain around the words that Miriam had uttered.

"You think she'll like this?" Secret asked Dunga, as she held up a black and gold ribbon shepherdess church hat. It had an all black crown and black and gold mixed brim with black and gold sequin and beaded band.

"Damn...this is a very snazzy hat," Dunga said with a laugh. It was hot as far church hats went anyway. He liked the two gold and pearl buttons on it as well. "She might think it's too fussy but I think she'll wear it. It's really nice."

"I love it! I'm going to get it," Secret said. Then she looked at the price tag and her eyes bulged. She looked at Dunga in surprise.

Dunga laughed.

"This is a very expensive store hun...so even a church hat is going to cost a lot."

The hat was going for $8500 and it was on sale. Secret had only carried $6000 to spend. Dunga took the hat and placed it with the stuff that he had picked out for his mother: two pairs of shoes – one for church and one for casual wear, three church dresses and a pretty pearl necklace. He then headed to the cashier. Secret protested that she wanted to pay for her gift herself so Dunga should loan her the additional $2500 until she got home and could pay him back. Dunga waved her suggestion aside but Secret was adamant. To shut her up, Dunga agreed. They stopped by a small gift shop and picked out two birthday cards. They then headed for the studio. Secret would wrap the gifts there and get them out of the way as the rest of the day was going to be busy. Dunga had booked four sessions and Secret was taking part in three of them, including the recording of the duet with Timex, who was supposed to be there at 6 p.m. She couldn't wait. She was looking forward to see how that would turn out.

Jessica suddenly got up with a start and grabbed the front of Miriam's dress with both hands, knocking the tray with the dishes down onto the terrazzo floor.

"What the fuck did you just say?" Jessica asked in a hoarse whisper.

Miriam was speechless. She didn't know how she had expected her boss to respond but she hadn't anticipated this. Her mouth was a wide O.

"Answer me!" Jessica shouted, showering Miriam with spittle as she shook her like a rag doll.

Miriam wondered what the hell she had gotten herself into. Mrs. Weatherburn looked like she wanted to kill her. In a trembling voice she told her boss everything. Jessica released her in shock when she learnt the identity of the woman. She fell back on her chair as though Miriam had given her a hard punch to the stomach. She had a vacant look in her eyes and her breathing sounded loud and laboured. Apart from her heaving bosom, she was very still. Sobbing and frightened, Miriam ran away from the scene. It was too much for her.

Jessica wasn't sure how long she sat there after Miriam's shocking revelation. It could have been seconds. Or minutes. Or even an hour. She felt like she was having an out of body experience. Things like this happened to other people. Not her. She wondered how long they had been having an affair. She wondered how Francine could be her best friend, confidant, 'aunt' to her kids, and fuck her husband behind her back. In her own house. In her own *bed.* She wondered how a man whom she had given the best years of her life and stuck with through thick and thin, could be so unconscionable and cruel. He didn't even have enough respect for her to do his dirty deeds away from his home and his wife. If someone had stabbed her in the heart with a blunt instrument it could not have hurt any more than the pain she was feeling now. Every part of her body ached. Her palms and feet were sweating yet she felt so cold inside. She glanced at the broken dishes on the floor. A perfect depiction of her life at this very moment. The various emotions surging through her body were threatening to push her over edge: Shock. Anger. Disbelief. Pain. Acceptance. Action. She got up from the chair and went into the bedroom to get dressed.

Everything now seemed crystal clear like she was viewing the world in high definition. She now knew what she had to do. Nothing could ever be the same. There was no coming back from this. Life was playing a cruel joke and it was up to her to deliver the punch line. She slipped on a pair of jeans and a red sweater. She was so cold her body was shivering. She didn't recognize the eyes that stared back at her through the bathroom mirror as she brushed her hair in a bun and washed her face. They seemed haunted and hopeless. She dried her face and quickly turned away. She then strode purposefully over to the night table and opened the drawer. She removed the .38 revolver – her husband's licensed firearm – and checked to ensure that it was loaded. God bless the day he had insisted that she learnt how to use it. She then stuck it inside the waist of her jeans and exited the room. She saw no one as she hopped into her husband's Jaguar convertible. Her car was still over by Francine's house. She reversed and veered a little too much to the left, and hit a huge flower pot which broke the left taillight. She didn't miss a beat. Without a backward glance she opened the gate and exited the premises.

❧❧❧

Cohen was not in the hotel suite when Jade woke up. She didn't see his white Prada running shoes so she assumed he was down by the gym. She took a shower and then buzzed room service to order some food. She didn't officially start her new job until next Monday so she was pretty much free today. She checked the time. It was close to midday. She decided to give Timex a call. He had been back since Monday and she knew that he was anxiously awaiting her call. She decided to take him out of his misery.

Chapter 50

Jessica got to Francine's home in thirty minutes. The lunch time traffic had added an extra fifteen minutes to the journey. Jessica pulled up behind Francine's car and got out. She noted that her car was park faced out. That was not how she had left it. Francine must have taken it for a little spin so that the battery wouldn't die. How sweet. Such a considerate friend. Jessica wondered if she did it before or after she had drained her husband's semen from his body. She made her way to the patio. She rang the door-bell. Twice.

"I'm coming!" she heard Francine shout from upstairs in an annoyed tone.

Well sorry for disturbing you my friend but I just wanted to have a chat with you regarding how you have been stabbing me in the back while my husband stabbed you between your slutty legs.

Jessica rang the doorbell again for good measure.

"Jesus!" she heard Francine exclaim in disgust. Jessica could hear the patter of her feet as she hurried down the stairs. No doubt armed with some choice words for whoever had dared to show up at her house unannounced.

Francine opened the door and the angry expression on her face became one of surprise. Her greeting died in her throat the same time her smile passed away when she looked into Jessica's eyes. She *knew.*

"J-J-Jess..." she managed to stammer before Jessica's right hand connected with her jaw painfully and sent her crashing into the coffee table inside her living room.

Jessica walked in calmly and closed the door behind her. She supposed her hand was throbbing as it had hit Francine squarely on the left side of her jawbone but if it was, she couldn't feel it. Francine was propped up on the floor holding her jaw in pain. Her eyes were wide and wild like she had just taken a dose of three ecstasy pills.

"How long have you been fucking my husband?" Jessica asked conversationally as she knelt down on the floor beside Francine.

Francine began sobbing.

Jessica punched her in the same spot.

The scream Francine unleashed was not human.

Jessica repeated the question.

Francine could not speak. Her jaw was broken. In more than one place.

Jessica sighed and stood.

She looked down on Francine dispassionately. It was just as well. She didn't want to hear anything from this bitch's mouth anyway. She pulled the firearm and Francine shook her head in terror as Jessica leveled the gun at her face. The front of Francine's denim shorts changed colour as her final thoughts travelled through the contours of her mind at the speed of light. The question was apparent in her pain-filled, teary eyes: *Are you really going to kill me Jessica?"*

The .38 revolver replied loudly, blowing her face to smithereens.

Jessica walked out of the apartment without treating her messy handiwork to another glance. She placed the gun on the passenger seat and headed out of the apartment complex as the few neighbours who were home scrambled to peek through their windows and two, a man who had recently lost his job at a pharmaceutical company for fraud and a stay-at-home mom, frantically dialed 119. Jessica didn't have an opinion or a feeling about what she had just done. She was in a dark place where she could feel nothing and nothing mattered. Absolutely nothing. She headed to the mammoth grey building which housed the Ministry of Mining, Energy and Environment.

***

Cohen still hadn't gotten back by the time Jade finished her food. She had ordered a ham and cheese pasta. She sipped the last of her fruit punch and went into her overnight bag to find a pair of shorts and a top. After her food digested she planned to go and work out for an hour or so. She hadn't done any form of exercise apart from sex in the last couple of days. She couldn't afford to get sloppy. Timex had been happy to hear from her though he admirably managed to keep his excitement at an acceptable macho level. He told Jade about her gifts and invited her to accompany him to a studio this evening. He was going to record a new song that he was very excited about. He claimed that she was the inspiration. She had agreed to go with him and he would pick her up at Theresa's salon. Jade didn't want him to know where she lived. At least not yet. She was actually looking forward to hanging out with him at the studio. She had never been to one and it would be nice to watch him in his element and to hear the lyrics to the song that she had inspired.

"Good afternoon Mrs. Weatherburn," the security guard in the lobby said respectfully when the Minister's wife walked in. He was very surprised at her appearance. He had never seen her looking so *casual*.

She smiled tightly at him as she walked by. He was caught off guard as she stepped briskly to the elevator and went in. Despite the fact that she was the Minister's wife, protocol dictated that she stop by the desk and allow the guard to buzz upstairs to the Minister's personal assistant or secretary. Mrs. Weatherburn knew that and usually cooperated. Something was definitely off about her today other than her dress code. He got the impression that she didn't really *see* him though she had appeared to look at him. It was as though she was in another world.

Jessica stepped out of the elevator when she got to the 10th floor. She stood by the main door to her husband's office suite and watched as the secretary with an astonished look on her bespectacled face, buzzed the door open. Jessica walked in and headed straight to her husband's closed office door.

"Mrs. Weatherburn! Can you please..." the secretary protested, trailing off as Jessica ignored her and opened her boss' door. He was going to have her head for this.

Weatherburn looked up in shock as his door flew open without even a knock. His wife? What the hell was Jessica doing here?

"Hi honey," he greeted her with a wary smile as he got up from around his desk. He nodded at his personal assistant who had been standing next to him as they looked over some graphical data, and she took up the file and made her way out of the office. She said hi but Jessica didn't even look at her. "What a pleasant surprise."

Jessica removed her wedding band with some effort and threw it at Weatherburn, hitting him in the face as he approached her.

"Jess! What the hell is wrong with you?" he cried out. He rubbed the spot and watched as his wife quickly went over to the door. She locked it and turned around to face him.

"Stop right there," she said in a low, commanding tone.

Weatherburn was bewildered but he did stop. Instinctively he knew that something was *very* wrong.

"Jessica...honey...what the hell is going on?" he asked in a conciliatory tone. He leaned against the edge of his desk, facing her. "Talk to me sweetheart. Tell your husband what has gotten into you. Tell him why you have removed your wedding ring."

"Sure, Duane," she replied as she looked at him coldly. "Right after you tell me why you have been fucking my best friend."

Weatherburn gasped audibly like she had given him a well-placed kick to the testicles. He tried to recover from the initial shock. *How the hell had she found out? Sweet Jesus!*

"J-J-Jessica! What kind of stunt are you trying to pull?" he demanded, going on the offensive. "Barging into my office with crazy accusations! Have you lost your goddamn mind?"

Jessica pulled out the gun.

Weatherburn froze. He looked at her face and knew that the game was finished. Playtime was over. He had to tread carefully. Jessica meant business. He tried a different tack.

He started to cry.

"Jess...I messed up...it was only one time...I swear...it didn't mean anything...oh God Jess...she caught me in a vulnerable moment and seduced me..."

"In *our* bed?" Jessica mused sarcastically. "I wonder how that happened."

Weatherburn wiped his forehead and loosened his tie. He was sweating profusely.

"Jess...she came by one day when I was home missing you...and ...one thing led to another...oh baby...I can call her right now and she'll admit that she was the one who forced herself on to me..." Weatherburn babbled, tears flowing freely. This one had been a serious gut check. He hadn't seen it coming. Not by a long shot. He wanted to know how she found out but he couldn't very well just ask now could he? Not when she was holding a gun, *his* gun, at him. Eddie was out front and he was armed but no one could help him now. He just had to find a way to get close enough to Jessica and disarm her.

"The only way you'll get through to Francine is if you have the number for hell," Jessica announced matter-of-factly.

No...it couldn't be. Had she really killed Francine? Lord have mercy! Jessica what have you done?

Weatherburn's eyes became saucers. His mouth was open and there were a million things he wanted to say but in the end nothing came out. He gaped foolishly as he wondered how his entire world could become undone in mere hours.

ꕥꕥꕥ

"How could you do this to me? My best friend Duane? In *our* bed Duane? You are a wicked man Duane Weatherburn and a despicable human being," Jessica continued. "You are a pathological liar and you don't deserve the air you breathe."

Weatherburn didn't like the sound of that. There was a note of finality in her tone.

His survival instinct kicked in and he found his voice.

"Jessica...think about what you're saying...what's done cannot be undone but it doesn't have to get any worse... put the gun down and lets find a way to deal with all of this Jess.." he pleaded as he walked slowly around to his desk. He discreetly pressed the panic button located just above the right hand drawer.

Jessica looked at the man that had been an integral part of her life for twenty years. She should be hurting. She should be filled with hate and disgust. She should be afraid. Afraid of the consequences of what had already been done and what she was about to do. But she felt none of these things. She felt *nothing.* She liked this dark place. Emotions were nonexistent here. Logic had no meaning.

ꕥꕥꕥ

Eddie was surprised to see the light for the panic button flashing. There were three lights in the suite connected to the button and they were all flashing insistently. His boss was in danger. But from who? His *wife?* Baffled but spurred into action, Eddie pulled his firearm as the secretary, the personal assistant and a young lady who was sitting in the reception area – a bit early for her 1:15 appointment with the Minister – looked on with the kind of look onlookers had when something exciting yet dangerous was taking place.

He tried the door. It was locked. When he heard the sound of gunfire he threw all of his weight against the door. It didn't budge. Adrenaline pumping, he moved back several steps and rushed to the door, kicking it with all his might. This time it budged but didn't open.

❧❧❧

Jessica looked at her husband slumped on the floor, his body partially hidden by the desk. Blood flowed freely from the wound on his neck. He was not moving. She assumed he was dead. She felt no remorse. She heard the banging on the door. Someone was trying to get in. Probably Eddie. She sighed. She had arrived at the end of the road. It was actually a welcome sight. No more pain. No more disappointments. No more betrayals. No more lies. Just darkness. Where *nothing* matters. A brief illumination occurred when she thought of her two children. Then it was extinguished as she placed the gun to her head and pulled the trigger.

❧❧❧

Another shot was fired. Eddie doubled his efforts. Two more kicks and the door swung open. Eddie rushed in with his gun held high.

"Jesus Christ!" he exclaimed at the unbelievably tragic scene that greeted him.

Chapter 51

Eddie couldn't believe what he was seeing. He lowered his gun and placed it in his waist. He would no longer need it. The contents of Mrs. Weatherburn's head were grotesquely scattered across the beige carpet. The revolver lay next to her lifeless hand. Eddie stepped around her body, careful not to disturb the crime scene and went to check on his boss. Weatherburn was on the floor by his desk. He was suffering from a gunshot wound to the neck and had lost an alarming amount of blood but he was still alive.

"Call a fucking ambulance!" Eddie yelled. Heather, the personal assistant, was standing by the door with her hands covering her mouth. Her eyes looked like they were going to pop out of her head. Silent tears streamed down her face. Eddie's words galvanized her into action. She rushed back out and got on the phone. The police were already on the way as the secretary had called them while Eddie was attempting to break down the door. The police, the entire unit from the Half-Way-Tree station it seemed, converged on the scene in five minutes. The lead detective, a burly no-nonsense fifteen year veteran, took charge of the crime scene. The ambulance arrived a few minutes after that and Weatherburn was rushed to the emergency wing of St. Theresa's University Hospital, Kingston's finest private hospital.

ଓଃଓଃଓଃ

Despite the best efforts of the Ministry's public relations department, the press got wind of the dramatic shooting of the prominent government minister and within three hours, one of the nation's top reporters, with a stroke of luck and the go ahead from his boss to promise money in exchange for information from the Weatherburns' cook and home security guard, had pieced together most of the details of the sordid love triangle. It was as juicy as the plot of a steamy novel. The whole city, and indeed most of Jamaica, was abuzz with the news of what had transpired.

Theresa, listening to the radio while she did a client's hair, listened in disbelief when the regular programming was interrupted to give the public the breaking news. The reporter didn't know all the details but the Minister of Mining, Energy and Environment had been shot and had been admitted to a prominent hospital in critical condition. It is alleged that he was shot by his wife.

She was sorry to hear as Weatherburn was a good friend of the family and a mentor to her brother. She hoped he survived the shooting. The reporter didn't have all the details but would be updating the public periodically as new information became available. Theresa sighed. Prominent politician and businessman shot by his wife? This was going to be a huge scandal. She wondered if Jade had heard about it.

ଔଓଔଓଔଓ

Bradley Saunders, Weatherburn's nemesis, was in 7th heaven. He was ecstatic to hear about what had happened to Weatherburn. He had just gotten back to the office after interviewing a lawyer who was suing the Jamaica Public Hospital for gross negligence on the behalf of the family of a nine year old boy who was now in a vegetative state after a brief stay at the hospital, when he heard everyone in the newsroom hotly discussing what had happened. His only regret was that he was not the one to break the story. He hoped Weatherburn survived the shooting. All the humiliation, shame and public scrutiny from this would certainly spell the end of his political career. He would be forced to resign. Saunders was so pumped about this development that he left work early and joined a colleague for drinks at a popular watering hole for Kingston's media personalities.

ଔଓଔଓଔଓ

The Prime Minister was not in a good mood. After returning from a contentious CARICOM meeting in Grenada, his chief aide had given him the disturbing news about the Weatherburn situation. It was bad. A prominent member of his cabinet had been shot by his wife after she had killed his mistress – her best friend by the way – and then committed suicide by putting a bullet in her head. Jesus Christ. What had he done to deserve this? He was planning to call a snap election later this year but with a juicy scandal like this tarnishing his government, it would be best to wait until things blew over. Jamaicans tended to forget things easily. It would pass in time. His immediate concern was right now. He hoped Weatherburn had the dignity to succumb to his wounds. He would be a lot more helpful dead.

~~~

Jade, after spending most of the day with Cohen, had gone home at 3:30 p.m. to get ready for her date with Timex. Her muscles were popping from her intense 90 minute workout at the hotel gym. Cohen had been impressed by her stamina. The other patrons had been mesmerized by her sweaty, tights-clad, perfectly proportioned body at work on the various equipments. It was now 5 p.m. and Nathan, her driver, was taking her over to Theresa's salon where Timex was supposed to pick her at 5:30.

"Jade, yuh heard about the politician whose wife shot him and then killed herself?" Nathan asked, as they waited at the stoplight on Trafalgar Road.

"Nope," Jade replied. "When did that happen?"

"Just today," Nathan replied. "She killed his mistress – who was her best friend – then went to her husband's office and tried to kill him. He's now in hospital battling for his life."

"Damn," Jade commented. It sounded like something out of a novel.

"Yeah!" Nathan continued excitedly. "It's the only thing people are talking about. The man is the Minister of Mining and Energy. And I think the environment too. He was doing a good job...I really hope he makes it."
~~~

That rang a bell. Wasn't that Weatherburn's portfolio?

"What's his name?" Jade asked, suddenly actively interested.

"Umm...Weatherburn, Duane Weatherburn," Nathan replied as the light turned green and he turned down onto Knutsford Boulevard.

Wow! Jade mused in surprise. *His wife was no joke.*

She was just happy that she had cut ties with him. With a crazy wife like that who knows if she could have gotten caught up in some shit. The wife reminded Jade of that astronaut that had driven across state wearing a diaper so she wouldn't have to make any restroom stops on her way to confront and harm the woman her lover was two-timing her with. Jade shook her head. Some women were just downright crazy. It wasn't a big deal to her what had happened to Weatherburn. She was indifferent as to whether he lived or died.

They arrived at Theresa's salon and Jade told Nathan that she would call him if he was needed. She then went inside. There were only three people there: Theresa, a client whose hair was finished and Nerissa, one of the nail technicians. They were in deep conversation about the Weatherburn situation.

"Hi girl," Theresa said. She hugged Jade and introduced her to the customer.

"You heard about what happened to Duane?" she asked.

"Yeah, my driver just told me about it," Jade responded nonchalantly.

She sat down and took up a copy of Celebrity Hair magazine.

Theresa was incredulous.

"Jade?" she said, taken aback by her friend's callous attitude. "Let's talk in private."

Jade shrugged okay and they went inside Theresa's office and closed the door.

"Jade...how can you be so insensitive? You know that Duane is a good friend of mine and that he's in the hospital fighting for his life. I know that you guys had some sort of problem or whatever but my God...even for my benefit, you could be a bit more compassionate," Theresa said, as she tried to blink back the tears.

Jade stood with her arms folded and looked at Theresa. This was a pivotal moment in their young, but good friendship. What happened next would either cement or fracture the bond they had forged. Jade sighed. She valued Theresa's friendship so there was only one thing to do. She told Theresa about her short, but dramatic time with Weatherburn.

Secret checked the time. It was 6:05 p.m. Timex should be arriving any minute now. She was in the chill room relaxing with a bottle of cranberry juice. The session she had completed half an hour ago – singing background vocals for an internationally renowned roots reggae singer – had been very taxing. The woman was very difficult to work with but she was a legend and Dunga thought that having Secret doing the background vocals was what the song needed to make it perfect. So she had gritted her teeth and gone through with it. It had not been an easy $10,000 to earn though. Her period was causing her some serious cramps but after her pregnancy scare, she welcomed each pang of pain. It would be over in another couple of days anyway. She heard the buzzer and Jimmy went to the intercom to enquire who it was. He then pressed the buzzer for the gate. Timex had arrived. Dunga came out to greet him. Timex swaggered into the studio accompanied by Jade and Breeda, his right hand man. Surprisingly, that was the extent of his entourage.

Dunga couldn't hide his shock when he saw Jade. His jaw dropped like a sack of potatoes.

"What ah gwaan?" Timex said as he shook Dunga's hand. He hadn't missed the look that came over Dunga's face when he saw Jade. Either she was the prettiest woman he had ever seen or he knew her from somewhere. Or maybe Dunga was surprised that he, Timex, could pull a woman of Jade's caliber. Whatever it was, the look on Dunga's face was priceless. A fucking Kodak moment. Timex's ego soared visibly.

"I'm good...ready to roll?" Dunga replied, trying to recover quickly from his initial shock. Jade was the last person he had expected to see here. Was she dating Timex? How the hell had Timex succeeded where he had failed? His ego was bruised.

"Meet Jade," Timex said, milking the moment. "Jade this is Dunga. Ah him ah go produce de new track."

Jade smiled politely at Dunga and shook his hand. She knew exactly what he was thinking and it amused her to no end. She resisted the urge to laugh. She still didn't know why she had never called him. *Just one of those things I guess*, Jade mused.

"Nice to meet you," Jade purred.

"Same here," Dunga managed. He felt foolish. Her luminous brown eyes seemed to be mocking him.

He released her hand and led them around to the recording area. He tried to clear his head and regain focus. He just couldn't understand the indescribable effect this woman had on him. Secret got up and followed. She had noticed the interaction between Dunga and Jade. She wondered what *that* was about. Why had Dunga seemed so uncomfortable? It was the first time she had ever seen him be anything but confident. Jade was even prettier in person, Secret noted. And she could dress her ass off. She was wearing retro polka dot leggings, with a short black dress and black patent leather Chanel pumps with the matching clutch purse. Jade caught her staring and gave her a knowing look. Secret looked away and went into the recording booth. Jade sat on a chair and settled down to watch the proceedings. She was pleased that she had told Theresa the details about her experience with Weatherburn. Theresa had been mortified to learn of Weatherburn's actions. She had hugged Jade in horror when she heard about the incident with Snake. Of course, the story had ended there. Jade didn't tell her about the retaliation. Theresa now understood why there was no love lost between Jade and Weatherburn. Their friendship had survived its first real test and that was all that mattered.

Jade smiled and swayed slightly to the beat when they started recording. Timex did the intro and then delved into the song. His voice was so unique. She listened to the lyrics he claimed she had inspired. He was a very good writer. She was impressed. If she ever decided to fuck him he would have to put this song on repeat. She liked the idea of that. It turned her on. Secret was now singing the hook. She was very good. Had a very powerful and soulful voice that she made all her own. She didn't sound like anyone else. Jade wondered if Dunga was sleeping with her. She was willing to bet a month's pay that he was. Jade rummaged in her purse and took out a small pack of lifesavers. She popped one in her mouth and smiled at Timex. He was watching her through the glass as he sang.

Dunga was feeling a little better now that the process was underway. So far so good. They were killing the song. It was working out exactly the way he had hoped it would. It was a hell of a collaboration. It was going to be a huge hit.

Chapter 52

GOVERNMENT MINISTER SUCUMBS TO HIS INJURIES was the front page headline in one of the island's major newspapers the following morning. Weatherburn had been pronounced dead a few minutes past midnight. The Prime Minister breathed a sigh of relief as he read the paper while having breakfast. With Weatherburn dead, it was now simply a matter of damage control and the master of all things: time. There were quick decisions to be made. The late Minister's portfolio was an important one and a new Minister had to be appointed quickly. But first things first. He would issue a carefully worded statement to the media this morning.

Heather, Weatherburn's personal assistant, was the one who carried out the unenviable task of contacting Weatherburn's children. The daughter, Penelope, fainted at the news and Peter, the son, had to be treated for shock by the campus doctor. Heather then got both of them on the earliest possible flights to Jamaica. The national airline helped out greatly in this regard and also waived the air fares. Penelope was going to arrive first at 3:20 p.m. while Peter was scheduled to arrive an hour later. Eddie would be responsible for picking them up.

❧❧❧

Jade got up at 11:30 a.m. She was feeling a bit sore from her intense workout yesterday. She yawned and went straight into the bathroom. After the studio session last night, Timex had taken her to Tupoi, a gaming lounge which also served really great food. It was an upscale establishment where Kingston's prominent personalities went to try their luck at the wide variety of gaming machines. It was a testament to Timex's celebrity that the manager himself came over to greet him. Jade was recognized as well, aided by the large, framed poster of one of her La Roseda advertisements on the wall in the bar area. Several uptown girls, who lived in a world alien to the one Timex talked about in his music, came over for autographs and to take pictures with the rugged entertainer. They took pictures with Jade as well. They had stayed there for over three hours and Jade had fared much better than Timex at the machines. Her winnings had totaled twenty-two thousand dollars at the end of the night. She had allowed Timex to drop her home but had firmly told him goodnight after thanking him warmly for a great time and for the gifts he brought back for her from Canada. She knew that he had been very disappointed but she gave him brownie points for not whining or insisting. His time would come if he kept up his good behaviour.

She applied some hair remover to her long toned legs and looked at her body critically in the full-length mirror as she waited for the requisite five minutes to pass before washing off the cream and ridding herself of its slightly repulsive odour. It seemed the more expensive and effective the remover, the worse it smelled. She approved of the image that stared back at her. She actually thought she looked better now than before she went to jail four years ago. She was in much better physical shape for one and she had filled out more. Her body had everything going for it: flawless skin, toned legs and arms, a pair of slightly-more-than-a-handful firm mouthwatering breasts that looked like they were light years away from being affected by gravity, a flat stomach that most rail-thin models would envy, an ass that resembled two soccer balls and the kind of general curviness usually found on women with more weight than she had. A body made for sin. A body to die for. *I'm not going to lie…I am one fabulous bitch* Jade mused with a satisfied smile. She then went into the shower.

"Enjoying your lunch mum?" Dunga asked.

"Yes, darling," Miss G replied. Her birthday had been wonderful thus far. Dunga and Secret had gone into her room the minute they figured that she had finished her usual morning devotion to wish her happy birthday and to present her with her gifts. She had loved them all; especially the hat Secret had bought her. She vowed to wear it to church this coming Sunday.

Breakfast had been ordered from Gourmet All Day, a very expensive catering restaurant that only did take-out, and now they were having lunch at a popular seafood joint in Half-Way-Tree. Miss G was having steam fish with crackers while Dunga and Secret had opted for lobster casserole. She thanked God everyday for providing her with such a loving, doting son. He was truly a blessing. She smiled at Secret. She liked the little young girl. Pure and innocent and was clearly in love with Dunga. She had no idea what was going to become of that but she thought that Secret was the right woman for her son.

She took a sip of her guava-pineapple fruit drink. Dunga and Secret were going to cook dinner for her this evening. That should be interesting. Very interesting indeed. Her son was not known for his culinary skills.

ଓଃଓଃଓଃ

Penelope and Peter Weatherburn were both met by the Permanent Secretary of the Ministry along with their Uncle Raymond – their dad's brother who was a high-ranking police officer. Penelope arrived first and was joined by her brother an hour later in the first class lounge where she had been huddled on a couch. She was inconsolable. Peter hugged her tightly and tried to hold back his tears. The pain was indescribable. The reality that they were now orphans under the most heinous and tragic of circumstances was threatening to plunge him into an abyss of hopelessness and despair. But he couldn't crumble. He needed to be strong for his sister. They hadn't been as close in recent times but there was no doubt that he loved her very much. He tried to put a handle on his own pain and bewilderment and they made their way outside where Eddie was waiting. Their uncle walked them out and promised to swing by the house to check up on them later after they had gotten some rest. They were getting into the vehicle when Bradley Saunders, apparently getting wind of their arrival from one of his many sources, snapped pictures and attempted to ask questions about their parents' tragic deaths. Their Uncle Raymond, in a fit of rage and disgust towards the obnoxious reporter whom everyone knew hated Weatherburn's guts, broke Saunders' camera and punched him hard in the mouth, knocking out two of his front teeth. Eddie drove away as Saunders screamed that he was going to sue. The many onlookers had no sympathy for him. Why couldn't he leave the children alone? Weren't they going through enough?

One of the regular hustlers who hung out at the airport on a daily basis and who was an ardent supporter of the political party which Weatherburn had been a member of, threatened to stab Saunders with his knife if he didn't leave "de boss pickney dem alone". A cop on the scene, though smirking with satisfaction at the bloody mouth his superior had given to Saunders, warned the over zealous man to calm down. Saunders quickly and embarrassingly made his way to the parking lot. He would have the last laugh when his lawyer contacted the Jamaica Police Force with his lawsuit.

❧❧❧

Theresa was feeling low all day so she went home a bit early. Jade had called her and not liking how her friend sounded, went over to see her. They drank La Roseda all evening and Jade listened patiently as Theresa talked and talked, dealing with her grief.

"I heard that the kids arrived today," Theresa was saying. "I know them well so I'll give them a call later and maybe go see them if they are up for it. The daughter Penelope is such a sweetheart. You would like her."

Jade nodded agreeably. If Theresa had said that the La Roseda they were drinking was cough syrup, Jade would have agreed. Anything to help her feel better. Though Jade still didn't care about Weatherburn dying, it was sobering when she thought of all the lives that were affected by his tragic passing. She could only imagine how devastated the kids were losing both their parents in such a violent, dramatic fashion. Made her think of her own parents. Though they had totally turned their backs on her at a time when she needed them most, she still loved them. She had not attempted to reach out to them in over two years. She was still angry and hurt at the way they had discarded their only daughter out of their lives as though she were a bad habit. Yeah she had made a mistake – a huge mistake – but did that make it right to treat her like that? Maybe one day she would try again. For a final time.

Jade refilled their glasses and suggested that they watched a Tyler Perry comedy to take off the edge. Theresa agreed and they went into the living room. Jade put the movie on and they relaxed close together on the carpet and settled down to watch *Madea Goes To Jail.* Theresa snuggled up against Jade and Jade, thinking nothing of it, hugged her. To her utter amazement and dismay, Theresa turned and kissed her dead on the lips. Jade's mouth opened in shock and Theresa's tongue, coated with the smooth taste of La Roseda, slipped surreptitiously into her mouth.

Chapter 53

"How could Auntie Fran do this to the family Pete?" Penelope asked tearfully in voice heavy with hurt and anguish.

Peter didn't respond. He just continued to hold his sister close. They were sitting in the family room. The T.V. was on but it was muted. Lil Wayne was soundless as he rapped about being pulled over by a sexy female police officer on the screen. There were so many questions. But who had the answers? Not him. He sighed heavily. Their entire world had been turned upside down. Nothing would ever be the same. Their uncle had already stopped by to see if there was anything they needed. What they needed he couldn't provide. They wanted their lives back. They wanted their parents to be alive. They wanted to be at school. They wanted back their bright future. He had left quickly, feeling helpless in the face of their desolate grief.

"Oh God Pete...I still can't believe it...what are we going to do?" Penelope cried. Her slender frame vibrated with the force of her deep sorrowful sobs.

Peter had no answers. He could only squeeze his sister in reassurance. Whoever had said life was unpredictable had uttered the mother of all understatements.

ଓଃଉଓଃଉଓଃଉ

"Jesus Christ! Timex! Woi!" the girl groaned loudly as Timex, wearing an expression that would impress the invincible hulk, fucked her like she had bootlegged his latest CD before it was released.

"Who ah fuck yuh?" he growled, sweat pouring off his face in huge rain-like droplets. He had been so horny he had thought of nothing but sex all day. After dropping Jade off last night he had gone to a party in the inner-city community where he grew up and had gotten drunk. He had gotten up at midday and had been in the studio all day doing dub plates and working on a track with an artist from his crew that he was trying to put out. As soon as he had finished working, he had taken home one of the groupies who always seemed to know when he was going to be at the studio. She had stood out from the others. She was built like a brick house: wide child-bearing hips, huge breasts, ultra thick thighs and an ass on which one could easily balance a crate of beer. She had been wearing a white Baby Phat sweat suit that hugged her voluptuous body like a second skin. Most of the guys at the studio had been trying to talk to her all evening but she knew why she came there. When Timex had sent Breeda to get her, she had coolly hopped in the front of his Range Rover after exchanging a few words with him, and twenty minutes later, she had been on her knees wrapping her juicy lips around Timex's throbbing shaft. She was still on her knees but now he was filling another orifice.

"Yuh Timex! Bumboclaat! It inna mi womb Timex!" she shouted as Timex, tightly gripping her massive ass cheeks and holding them apart, pounded her into oblivion.

"Mi ah come Timex! Woi! Mi ah come! Mi ah come! Pussyclaat!" she cursed as her juices threatened to wash the latex condom from off his dick. She had been a fan of Timex's ever since his debut single three years ago and she had sworn that one day, she would know what it felt like to have him inside of her. She was not disappointed. She had just *known* he would have fucked the stuffing out of her. She was a sturdily built girl and she liked it rough and hard. Hurt like hell but that was what did it for her. Her orgasm was almost as long as one of his songs. She twitched and whimpered as a series of spasms continued to turn her formidable body into jelly.

Timex uttered a guttural roar and ripped the condom off as he climaxed, spraying the vast landscape of her ass with his hot semen. That had been good. He stood behind her and looked down at his handiwork as he caught his breath. He liked this one. He would definitely be seeing her again.

"So weh yuh name?" he asked as he took up his phone to store her number.

Jade was stunned. Her best friend was kissing her. Deeply. Surprisingly, it wasn't repulsive. Felt kind of good actually. Sensuous. Probing. Erotic. Euphoric. It was also confusing.

And scary. She didn't fuck women. She wasn't attracted to women. So why was her breathing shallow, her nipples at attention like well-trained soldiers and her pussy suddenly moist? Jade broke the kiss.

They stared at each other with their eyes wide and their mouths slightly agape.

"I'm sorry Jade," Theresa said, putting her hands to her face. "I don't know what came over me...I'm not a lesbian...I swear...it just felt so *good* being snuggled up against you...and next thing I know...I'm so sorry Jade..."

Jade didn't respond. Couldn't. For the first time in her adult life she was at a loss for words. She was still grappling with the irrefutable fact that she had been turned on immensely by Theresa's unexpected kiss. She *knew* for a fact that she wasn't into women. Wasn't even curious. Then why?

"I'm so embarrassed...oh God...I hope this doesn't ruin our friendship...say something...please Jade..." Theresa implored, her eyes brimming with tears.

"It's ok," Jade responded. "I know you're not like that. Don't be embarrassed...it's just one of those things you know...just happens."

"Are you sure Jade?" Theresa asked, shocked but relieved that Jade was taking it so lightly.

"Yeah I'm sure," Jade assured her. "It happened and we'll just move past it. Besides it wasn't that bad..."

Theresa's eyes widened and they both burst out laughing.

"You liked my kiss!" Theresa teased, so happy that they could laugh about it.

"Maybe..." Jade responded, teasing her back.

"I love you girl," Theresa said, adding quickly, "no homo!"

Jade laughed heartily.

"I love you too...now lets stop this mushy shit before I puke and watch this movie," Jade joked as she reached for the remote to restart the movie.

Theresa laughed and slapped her playfully on the arm. They then settled down in a comfortable silence and watched the movie. They laughed sporadically at Madea's antics onscreen but truth be told, neither of them was concentrating on the movie.

⁂

"Yeah, everything is good," Dunga said to Dahlia. It was the only the second time that they were having a conversation since she had gone back to New York. Dunga hadn't noticed until she mentioned it.

"So you can't give me a call babes? We have only spoken twice since I came back up and I had to call both times," Dahlia complained.

"I'm sorry about that...just been caught up with work and stuff," Dunga replied.

Dahlia wondered what the *stuff* was but didn't go there as she didn't want to start an argument.

"I cooked dinner for Miss G today," Dunga bragged, though he had done very little in the kitchen except to play around while Secret did most of the work. Secret had only allowed him to knead the flour. She had cooked everything: the deep fried chicken with her 'secret' recipe, the white rice, the potato salad and the fried plantain. Miss G had enjoyed her meal tremendously. It had been a long time since he saw his mother so happy on her birthday and he knew that Secret being around had something to do with that. Miss G loved her to death and the two of them got along beautifully. More complications.

"Ha!" Dahlia snorted. She knew Dunga could barely boil water and besides, he *loved* his mother's cooking. Why would he just get up and try to cook for her? "Yeah right...why would you even attempt to be cooking for your mother?"

"It was part of her birthday present," Dunga explained.

"Oh shit!" Dahlia exclaimed. She had completely forgotten. She felt bad. She knew that she wasn't one of Miss G's favourite people and this just made it worse. "Damn Dunga! You could have reminded me!"

"How was I supposed to know you had forgotten?" Dunga retorted.

Dahlia looked at the time. It was 8:30 p.m. Miss G usually went to bed early if she wasn't at church in the evenings. She would give her a call now. Hopefully she was still up.

"I'm going to try and call her," Dahlia said. "I'll call you back."

"Ok, later," Dunga replied. He hung up and resumed listening to the demo that an upcoming deejay had given Jimmy to bring to him. The two songs he had listened to so far were okay. The guy had talent. Dunga liked his flow. Maybe, just maybe, he could do something with him.

Dahlia called Miss G's home. The phone rang out and went to voicemail. She decided to try again. An unfamiliar voice picked up on the third ring.

"Hello?"

"Good night, let me speak to Miss G please?" Dahlia said.

"She has gone to bed. Would you like to leave a message?" Secret asked. Miss G had told her to feel free to answer the phone when she was home.

"Tell her Dahlia called to wish her happy birthday and will call her back tomorrow. Who is this by the way? One of Miss G's relatives?"

"I'll relay the message and no I'm not related to Miss G," Secret replied. *How rude*, Secret mused. "Have a good night."

"Well who are you then?" Dahlia pressed rudely. She was curious. As far as she knew Miss G wasn't in the habit of having people stay over and this person was obviously spending the night. If she wasn't a relative then who the hell was she? The voice sounded kind of young too.

"Have a good night ma'am," Secret said and hung up the phone. This Dahlia person was very rude. She would ask Miss G about her tomorrow. Secret picked up her notepad and resumed writing.

Dahlia could not believe the person had hung up on her. She called back but the phone just rang out to voicemail. She then called back Dunga.

"Dunga who is that woman at Miss G's house?" she began, unable to contain herself. "I asked her who she was and she hung up the phone on me. She's very out of order."

Dunga shook his head. Seems as though his mother had already gone to bed and Secret had answered the phone. Secret didn't have any reason to hang up the phone on Dahlia so he knew that it must have been a situation where Dahlia was being nosy and obnoxious for that to happen.

"You called for Miss G and didn't get her. All you had to do was leave a message. Why are you questioning who is in the woman's home? That doesn't have anything to do with you," Dunga replied.

"So why you can't tell me Dunga? What's the big deal?" Dahlia persisted.

"Look...I have some work to do so if you don't have anything sensible to talk about I'll ring you back tomorrow. If you need to know my mother's business ask her yourself."

"Geez...you don't have to be like that Dunga. I was just curious. Anyways bye. Don't let me keep you from your important *work*," Dahlia said, her voice dripping with sarcasm.

"Whatever, later."

Dunga terminated the call and turned back up the music. That should be the end of that. Dahlia wouldn't dare ask Miss G anything.

Jade called Cohen at 9:30. The movie had ended a few minutes ago and she was ready to go. Cohen was at Diamonds, Kingston's premier gentleman's club, having drinks with a business acquaintance. Beautiful women from all over the world danced there. A couple of Russians, several Brazilians, a Nigerian and one from Slovenia were in the mix. Needless to say, the club was a big hit with those who could afford it; and those who could get in. Not everyone was welcome, even if you were willing to pay the ridiculously high entry fee. Cohen told her that he would pick her up in another hour after he left the club. She couldn't wait. She needed to be fucked tonight. Really hard. So hard that the confusing demons that have been plaguing her since Theresa's kiss got exorcised. Or at the very least be silenced and pushed back deep into the recesses of her mind.

Chapter 54

Miriam had been very shaken by what had transpired with the Weatherburns. She had prayed nonstop for their poor souls. What a tragedy! Sweet Jesus son of Mary! She had fainted when she heard the news. If she could only turn back the hands of time. What if she hadn't said anything? They would have been alive now. Maybe she should have allowed things to take their natural course. The good book said what was in the dark must come to light but why did she have to be that light? The violent deaths of the three people were a heavy burden on her poor heart. She had barely eaten since yesterday. The security guard had told her that the children were home. She wondered if they were up yet. She was about to go up the stairs when she looked up and saw Peter standing at the top of the stairs. He was looking down at her. His eyes were red and puffy. They were also ice cold. She felt startled and uneasy.

"Maas Pete...mi so sorry about yuh parents. Lord 'ave mercy! What a tragedy!" she exclaimed.

"Why you couldn't just keep your fucking mouth shut? Eeh?" Peter responded, looking at her with utter disgust and contempt. "If it wasn't for you and your big mouth none of this would have happened. If you had just minded your damn business..."

He trailed off as tears came flowing in a sudden torrent.

Miriam was shocked out of her wits. She held on to the banister for support as her sturdy legs suddenly felt like twigs, unable to support her two hundred and twenty pound frame. The kids hated and blamed her! *Oh God! Why art thou testing me like this?* She cried out inwardly.

"Get out and don't come back!" Peter shouted, as he composed himself. "You don't work here anymore."

Miriam flinched as though he had physically struck her and fled to the helper's quarters to get her things. She felt sick to her stomach. Things were not supposed to be this way. She quickly changed back into the clothes she had worn to work and grabbed her handbag. She didn't answer the cook who asked her where she was going. She stumbled outside into the bright sunlight and tearfully made her way out to the gate.

ఌఌఌ

Miss G frowned as Secret told her about Dahlia's telephone call last night. Dahlia was so out of order. How dare she question a guest in *her* home? Miss G hoped she really called back today so that she could give her a piece of her mind. She loved her grandchild to death but she didn't know how a disgusting wretch like Dahlia had produced such a sweet, well-behaved child. *Damn butu.* She didn't tell Secret who Dahlia was but she felt the need to tell her something else.

"I don't normally interfere in my son's personal life, but Secret, I have to tell you that I hope you stick around. You are the perfect woman for Dunga," Miss G told her.

Secret beamed.

"Awww...that's so sweet of you to say Mis G," she grinned as she hugged Miss G tightly. It was nice to be endorsed by the mother of the man you loved – even if he wasn't fully yours. Yet.

"Lawd Secret...yuh going to squeeze out mi life?" she joked.

Secret laughed and released her. Miss G then went back into the kitchen to finish doing the dishes and Secret resumed watching The Tyra Banks show. Today's topic was women who wanted to be porn stars.

Jade yawned and picked up her phone to look at the time. It was 10 a.m. She needed to get up. Theresa had told her to come by to get her hair and nails done today as Saturday was a very busy day. It was also the day of the launch and most likely she wouldn't have any time to go to the salon. She was supposed to be meeting Mr. Hassan at the office at midday to go over a few details relating to the launch. She stretched and moaned softly as she got out of bed. She was sore. Cohen had indeed followed her instructions last night. He had fucked her like a man possessed. Jade was certain he had been on ecstasy. His energy had been unbelievable. He had extracted four gut wrenching orgasms from her and after the second round; she had had to tell him no more. She looked over at him as she touched herself. Yep, she was very tender down there. He was dead to the world. Cohen was a morning person. Always up early tending to his many business interests across the world via the telephone and internet. Yet here he was sprawled out on his back butt-naked. He looked almost comatose. He definitely had been on something and Jade was convinced it was ecstasy. She then went into the bathroom to take a shower. Though she had thoroughly enjoyed the sex last night, it had failed to accomplish what she wanted. The pungent memory of Theresa's kiss still lingered like the scent of an expensive perfume that stayed in the room long after the wearer had gone. Jade sighed as she gently lathered her body. There was only one thing to do.

❧❧❧

Dunga finally heard from Ras Che. He was at his sports bar checking on things when he received the call. Everything had gone according to plan. He had paid the money to three influential disc jocks and two of Secret's songs were receiving heavy rotation. By the time she came to France to do the show with him, people would be familiar with her music. He asked Dunga to email him a marketing poster of Secret so that people could know what she looked like. Dunga told him he would do that as soon as he got to his office at the studio. Things were definitely going well for Secret so far. She had appointments at the French, German and Dutch embassies next week to secure visas and work permits so that she could do the three shows with Ras Che; and she was scheduled to appear on a popular cable show next week Thursday. The single with Timex would also be officially released shortly. That was going to create an incredible buzz in the streets for Secret. A video would have to be shot soon. He would probably use the same video director that he was using to shoot the video for Secret's first single which was scheduled for Monday. He was very excited about Secret's progress. His first female artist was destined to become a star.

ଓଃଓଃଓଃ

The family attorney, a tall light-skinned man who always looked as if he was bored with life, came by the house to see Peter and Penelope. They met with him in the study.

"I'm sorry about your loss," he began, as he extracted some paperwork from his worn, archaic attaché case. Peter wondered absently where his father had found this strange unkempt lawyer. His grey suit, which had seen better years, was rumpled and looked as though he had slept in it last night.

They mumbled their thanks.

"There is no will," he continued, "so everything goes to you the children."

They were both stoic as they waited for him to continue.

Not getting a response or reaction, he moved on.

"The inheritance is substantial. This house; an apartment in Kingston and one in Montego Bay; a business complex in Montego Bay in which he is the majority shareholder; shares and stock in several businesses – I've attached the details to this document for your perusal – a small but profitable trucking company with a fleet of four trucks and a trailer; three non-commercial vehicles and six bank accounts and investments totaling sixty thousand pounds, forty thousand US dollars and twelve million Jamaican dollars."

The air conditioner hummed loudly in the silence. Peter and Penelope looked at each other. They had known that their father was very comfortable financially as the family had always been able to do whatever it wanted without any worries but it turned out that he was much wealthier than they had imagined. There was a lot of money and assets to divide between the two of them.

"Give me a call after you guys have digested everything," he said after a few moments. "I'm on a yearly retainer so whatever legal advice or action you need, just simply give me a call."

He handed them both a copy of the document and rose.

"Take care of yourselves and I'll see you at the funeral."

Peter thanked him and showed him out.

Penelope was still seated in the study when he returned. She looked up from the document.

"Oh God Pete...I'd give all of this up to have mommy and daddy back. All the money in the world can't replace them," she said mournfully.

Peter nodded and rubbed her shoulder. He agreed but life goes on. They were now young millionaires. Decisions had to be made but he would deal with everything after the funeral.

"C'mon...lets go get some lunch," he suggested.

She agreed and got up wearily. She didn't have any appetite but she had to eat. She had already lost some weight since the news and she couldn't afford to lose much more. They went into the kitchen to tell the cook what to prepare.

"Hi hun," Theresa said as she hugged Jade in greeting. Jade had just arrived at the salon for her appointment. She was half an hour late but Theresa didn't mention it. The salon was packed as usual. Jade, seemingly oblivious to all the envious stares and dirty looks she was getting from most of the women present, waved hi to a woman that Theresa had introduced her to a few days ago. Jade wondered idly if all she did was come to the salon.

"Let's get started right away," Theresa said. Jade put her pocketbook inside Theresa's office and then sat in the chair to get her hair washed. She almost moaned as Theresa massaged her scalp. It was never like that before. The kiss. That fucking kiss had changed everything. Her senses were much more heightened where Theresa was concerned. She was now keenly aware of the way Theresa smelled, her touch...everything. Jade wondered if it was the same for Theresa. It had to be. There was no way she could be the only one affected like this. Jade sighed contentedly as the warm water washed the suds away. Theresa had better be ready to finish what she started. She was tired of wondering how it would feel. She wanted to *know*.

Chapter 55

Saturday was a blur for Jade. She met up with her boss midday at the office for a two hour meeting. She then met with the ten models that had been chosen to be hostesses to ensure that they fully understood their duties for the night. The airport was next, where she had to go to meet and greet the guest celebrity DJ, and two of Mr. Hassan's special guests, a Grammy award winning composer from New York and a noted fashion designer from Italy. It was 6 p.m. before she got the chance to run home to get ready for the launch which was scheduled to begin promptly at 8:30. She needed to be there early. The hard part would be to do her make-up. Tonight she was going all out. She used black eyeliner faded with light grey to create a nice gradient. She then used a brown pencil to shape her brows to top off the smoky eyes effect. She then applied Mac's new red lip gloss. The process took her close to an hour but she was pleased with the result. She looked absolutely stunning. Her outfit was already picked out: a short, black Dolce & Gabbana dress, black leggings and fire-engine red Chanel pumps with the matching clutch purse. Nathan, the driver, was outside waiting to take her to the venue when she exited the house at 7:45. He shook his head in admiration as she walked towards the vehicle. It was impossible to get used to Jade's beauty.

There was a sizeable crowd there when Jade arrived at 8:10 and lots more people were streaming in, dispelling the notion that Jamaicans were never on time. She found Mr. Hassan standing close to the buffet table. He was having a word with the manager of the company he had hired to decorate the venue for the launch. Jade was positive that he wasn't complaining about anything. The decorations were lovely. The venue had a European fashion event feel sans the run-way. Three large flat screens silently played montages of La Roseda commercials and advertising campaigns. A club remix of Kanye West's *Flashing Lights* filtered through the surround sound courtesy of DJ Dolce. The menu was exotic and scrumptious: crab cakes; roasted fingerling potatoes; asparagus with orange butter; spice rubbed roasted pork loin; rice salad with olives and red peppers; bacon stuffed mushrooms; rib roast beef with horseradish cream sauce; eggplant with stewed tomato, fresh basil and grated hard cheeses; and bittersweet chocolate cake with vanilla oranges and whipped cream.

"Hello Jade," Mr. Hassan said when she walked up to him. "I was just commending Ms. Walters on the splendid job that she and her staff has done."

"Yes, the décor is truly magnificent," Jade concurred.

Mr. Hassan checked his watch.

"We begin in a few minutes," he said.

Jade looked at the program which was designed like a bottle of La Roseda. Mr. Hassan would greet the guests and give a ten minute presentation after which Jade would take over.

Theresa spotted Jade and came over to say hi. They chatted until it was time to begin. Jade then went and stood close to the podium while Mr. Hassan got the proceedings underway. She spotted Cohen walking in with a group of people that included a rail thin brunette who looked like a model. Jade wondered idly how her thin body managed to lug around her fake gigantic breasts. Her features and complexion suggested that she was European. Cohen, as usual, was dressed in full black.

When she had taken over from Mr. Hassan and was at the podium telling the gathering more about the product, Timex walked in. He was alone. Jade had instructed him to leave the entourage behind tonight. He looked like what he was: a successful entertainer from the streets. Black fitted Japanese denim, white Gucci trainers, white shirt and white blazer along with the usual assortment of shiny diamond encrusted platinum jewellery. A pair of oversized Gucci sunglasses hid most of his face.

Five minutes later, Jade made presentations of six limited edition bottles of La Roseda to the owners of some of the country's most successful clubs and entertainment spots. Then it was party time. Most of the large crowd descended on the buffet table while others headed to the dance floor with glasses of La Roseda in hand as DJ Dolce showed why she was the hottest DJ in Europe. Jade was in demand as she circled the party, mingling with the guests. In a room full of attractive and well-dressed women, she was undoubtedly the star of the night. Every straight man in the room had mentally fucked her at least four times. She was feeling great. The launch had gone extremely well. She couldn't wait to see the write-up and pictures in the entertainment section of the newspapers tomorrow. Gypsy, the host of *Entertainment Round-up*, spotted her talking with Timex and came over. Jade was amused as Gypsy flirted with him. To Timex's annoyance, Jade excused herself and went over to speak with a man whom Mr. Hassan had told her was the Minister of Tourism.

It was 1 a.m. before people finally started to leave. Jade, having consumed several glasses of La Roseda over the course of the night, was feeling quite randy. She wondered who she should spend the night with. Cohen was out; she didn't want to see him tonight. Should she sample some of Timex's thug passion? Or should she go home with Theresa and partake in the unfamiliar but undoubtedly pleasurable experience that was waiting in the wings? She sipped her final glass of La Roseda as she decided what to do.

Chapter 56

The look in Theresa's eyes when she came over to tell Jade goodbye was the clincher. They were glazed with lust. Jade had already told Timex that she was going to be busy so she would give him a call tomorrow. Cohen was chatting by the poolside with the same group of people that he had arrived with to the launch. The brunette was sitting next to him, apparently paying rapt attention to whatever he was saying.

"I'm coming home with you," Jade said softly.

Theresa seemed to sway imperceptibly.

"Okay," she replied, her voice suddenly a hoarse whisper.

"Wait here," Jade instructed and went over to bid Mr. Hassan goodbye and to give DJ Dolce a hug, promising to hang out with her before she went back to Europe on Tuesday.

She went back over to Theresa and they walked silently to Theresa's car. They got in and Theresa headed out. She turned on the radio and appropriately, perhaps prophetically, Nina Simone's sexy song *Do I Move You* was playing. The sexual tension in the car was so thick it threatened to fog the windows. Theresa had beads of perspiration on her upper lip despite the air conditioning. Jade watched her out of the corner of her eye. Yes. Theresa was definitely excited. And so was she. Jade wanted to reach over and rub Theresa's exposed thigh. Her cute, short, green Isaac Mizrahi dress was exposing a tantalizing amount of thigh. Jade was afraid to though. She didn't want to start a fire. She sighed and looked out the window. Her panties were so drenched it was uncomfortable. She couldn't wait for Theresa to take them off. She still couldn't fathom why she was horny for a woman. Life was so unpredictable. Never say never.

Cohen left the venue a few minutes after Jade. He was proud of her. She had done very well at the launch. She had presence and personality. Being beautiful and intelligent didn't hurt either. Hassan had done well in choosing her to be the face of La Roseda in the Caribbean. Perhaps he should use her image worldwide. She certainly looked better than the model they used in Europe. He would be going to Belgium on Monday before going to his main residence in London on Wednesday. There was a business opportunity that he wanted to explore. He deliberately ignored her for the entire night to prove a point to himself. He was getting too attached to her. She invaded his thoughts way too frequently. He didn't do attachments. At least not the emotional kind. To her credit, she hadn't paid him any mind either. Jade gave as good as she got. He loved that about her. He looked over at the woman seated next to him in the back seat. She was one of the Russian strippers from Diamonds. He nodded at her and she unzipped his Prada slacks and freed his semi-erect member. She pleasured him with her wide knowledgeable mouth as the driver headed to the hotel.

ଓଃଓଃଓଃ

Jade waited impatiently as Theresa nervously tried to open the door. She emitted an embarrassed chuckle as she bent to pick up the house key for the second time. She finally got it right and they went inside. Jade locked the door behind them. Theresa turned on the nightlight next to the sofa, bathing the room in a soft glow. Jade threw her clutch purse onto the sofa. They stared each other down.

"Come over here and finish what you started." Jade's look was intense. Demanding. Sure.

Theresa emitted a soft, almost feline moan. She walked slowly over to Jade.

Her knees buckled as Jade bent her head and claimed her trembling lips.

The kiss deepened quickly and they caressed each other passionately as their tongues danced a frenzied tango. Still kissing, they knocked into things as they blindly made their way to the bedroom. Theresa didn't realize or didn't care that her favourite vase –a birthday gift five years ago from her former best friend – had fallen and was now an expensive jigsaw puzzle on the floor.

When they finally got inside the bedroom, Jade breathlessly broke the kiss.

"Let's slow it down," she breathed. She wanted her first time with a woman to be extra special. Memorable in every way. Passionate, yes, but not rushed. It was to be savoured, like an exquisite five course meal at an expensive restaurant. As far as she was concerned, this was her first time. That sexual assault when she had been incarcerated did not count.

Theresa unsteadily made her way over to the bedside lamp and turned it on.

"Music," Jade demanded.

Theresa turned on the stereo. The sultry poetic sound of Floetry's latest album filled the room.

She watched with bated breath as Jade slowly undressed. Her pulse quickened at the sight of Jade's sculpted, curvy nude body. A perfect body. A body that could be on the cover of any men's magazine. It was obvious that she was soaking wet. Her plump, hairless mound was practically dripping, like a leaky faucet.

Jade climbed onto the bed seductively and laid there with her legs spread invitingly. The fleshy gates of heaven.

Theresa groaned loudly and removed her clothing. She almost came as she watched Jade slip a finger inside her wetness and taste herself.

Theresa joined Jade on the bed and climbed on top of her. She kissed her deeply but slowly. Jade caressed Theresa's back and ass as Theresa kissed her like she wouldn't get the chance to do it again. They kissed until their lips were slightly swollen. Theresa then took Jade's left breast in her mouth and sucked and nibbled on it until Jade cried out in ecstasy. She paid equal attention to the right before blazing a wet trail along Jade's flat, smooth stomach down to her pulsing mound. She licked the inside of Jade's thighs and nibbled around the outskirts of her pussy until Jade begged her to stop teasing.

"Taste it Theresa...taste my sweet fat pussy...oh God...now...lick it..." Jade implored.

Theresa obliged. Tasted her first pussy.

Jade wailed when Theresa's nimble tongue invaded her dripping wetness.

"Fuck! Mmmmm! Ohhhh!" Jade moaned as Theresa licked her fleshy folds and tongue-fucked her deeply.

Theresa explored Jade's depths with her tongue and lips like a curious but eager and fearless explorer.

Jade's first orgasm of the night was so sudden and intense that she almost blacked out.

"Fuck! Fuck! Fuck!" Jade shouted as she climaxed in Theresa's mouth.

Theresa didn't let up. Neither did Jade's orgasm. She came until she was certain that there was no more fluid left in her body. She was wrong.

Theresa started licking her clit in a firm, upward motion and Jade saw stars. She heard a weird frightening sound in the room above the music and it took her a few moments to realize that it was coming from her. Theresa licked Jade until her pussy exploded once more against her ardent tongue. This one rocked Jade like a tsunami. The sounds she was emitting could not be coming from a human being. Theresa finally rose and crawled up to lay beside Jade's shivering frame. She played with her own nipples as she watched Jade recover from her oral assault. They were hard like bullets. She couldn't wait for Jade to suck and caress them. It was still surreal that they were actually making love but it felt so *right*. She licked her lips. Jade's pussy had tasted so *good*. It was a full ten minutes before Jade could find the strength to rise and conduct an assault of her own.

Theresa's eyes were tiny slits of lust and anticipation as Jade climbed on top of her. She looked high. She *felt* high. From somewhere above the clouds she felt Jade's warm lips against her neck. She felt them move to her shoulder and collarbone before claiming her right nipple.

"Mmmm...Jade...oh Jade...that feels so good..."Theresa groaned as Jade sucked her nipple with the hunger of a newborn. Jade took turns sucking, licking and caressing each breast before gently biting and nibbling her way down to Theresa's lower body.

"Jade...ohhhh...Jesus Christ!" Theresa blasphemed as she arched her pelvis trying to make contact with Jade's teasing mouth, which was hovering tantalizingly over her sarcoid mound. Her fleshy lips unfolded like hibiscus flowers awakening from their slumber as Jade's hot breath tickled her unusually huge clit unbearably. It was her turn to beg.

"Fucking hell...suck it Jade...suck that big clit like a dick...suck it rass Jade...oh fuck...please Jade...put it in your mouth Jade...please...ohhh..."

Jade was amazed at the size of Theresa's protruding clitoris. It looked like a small, stubby penis. It was the biggest one Jade had ever seen. It sported a cute little silver knob. *Damn! She could fuck me with this!* Jade mused inwardly. She rubbed her lips against it before covering it with her hot mouth.

Theresa went berserk. She writhed beneath Jade and howled as she gripped a fistful of Jade's hair.

"Jade! Jade! Jade! Jade!" she cried out like a broken record as Jade sucked on her clit mercilessly. Her body stiffened like a corpse as she flooded Jade's mouth with her sweet, sticky nectar. And just when she thought it couldn't get any more intense Jade proved her wrong.

Jade grabbed both of Theresa's legs and thrust them backwards until her feet were tucked behind her ears and attacked Theresa's obscenely spread orifice with a tongue that moved like it was battery operated. Theresa lost her mind. She started to cry as four back to back orgasms mere milliseconds apart transformed her body into a quivering mass of jelly.

Jade then got on top of her and held Theresa's left leg straight up in the air as she rubbed her throbbing pussy against Theresa's rock hard clit. Theresa became delirious. She thought she was climaxing again but everything was a blur. It wasn't until Jade climaxed and plopped down next to her in utter exhaustion that Jade realized that Theresa was unconscious.

They had a good laugh about that when she revived in less than a minute.

"Jesus Christ Jade! That was out of this world," Theresa said, her voice tinged with wonder and contentment. "I had never in my wildest dreams thought that sex could be so fucking amazing. And with a *woman* at that. My body still feels like its floating in mid-air."

Jade chuckled.

"Yeah it was indescribable...damn...so *different*...so fucking erotic..."

They fell silent; each preoccupied with their own thoughts.

Floetry was singing about a relationship gone bad.

Theresa snuggled up against Jade and fell asleep almost instantly. Jade watched the rise and fall of her bosom as she slept. She had a smile on her face.

They had done it.

Tasted each other's essence.

Fucked each other senseless.

The dynamics of their relationship had changed forever.

You don't go back to being just friends after such a mind blowing experience.

Best friends.

Now lovers.

Jade fervently hoped that what had happened would not make their friendship awkward and complicated. Only time could tell how things would pan out.

She yawned and reached over to turn off the bedside lamp.

Theresa stirred but didn't awaken.

Jade then closed her eyes and tried to go to sleep.

Oh what a night.

Chapter 57

Zachary picked up Jade at her home at 5 p.m. to attend the football game. Kick-off time was at 6 but it was a big game and Zachary wanted to ensure they were there early. He smiled when Jade entered the vehicle. He had been on pins and needles all week, eagerly anticipating his date with Jade.

"Hi Jade, you look ravishing as always," he said as he expertly turned the convertible around and exited the premises.

"Thanks Zach," she replied with a smile. It was a cool, beautiful evening. The sun was just getting ready to hide behind the clouds and there was a nice, light breeze blowing of which Zachary was taking full advantage by driving with the top down. They received a lot of stares in traffic. He knew they were staring mainly because of Jade. The car was hot but the chick inside it was hotter. Heads twisted and turned frequently as they drove to the stadium.

There was a lot of traffic on the road and it was obvious that most of the vehicles were also going to the game. People were waving flags through their windows and many of them were dressed in the Jamaica team colours of black, yellow and green. Jade was being patriotic as well. She was wearing a yellow and green Christian Audigier sweat top with the matching green shorts and white Gucci trainers. No reason why she couldn't represent for the Reggae Boyz, as the team was affectionately called, and still look fly. Zachary was representing as well in a close-fitting yellow polo shirt which accentuated his nice build.

They got to the national stadium in thirty minutes, and Zachary, courtesy of a VIP sticker on his windshield, was allowed to drive into the main area away from the lot designated for public parking. He parked next to a black Mitsubishi Pajero and exchanged greetings with the two guys standing next to it.

"The driver for one of my dad's colleagues," he explained as he ushered Jade through the VIP entrance.

That reminded Jade about Eddie. She should give him a call to see how he was taking his boss' death. She also needed to give him the money to get the passport and driver's license for her.

Jade said hi to several of the men that were coming through the same gate. They were businessmen and politicians that had attended the La Roseda launch. Three of them had invited her to the game but she had demurred. Turned out Zachary knew them - they were his dad's colleagues – and Jade pretended not hear when one of them crudely whispered 'yuh lucky nuh rass Zach' to Zachary as they made their way down the tunnel leading to the Royal Box which naturally had the best seats in the entire stadium.

An usher took the passes from Zachary and led them to their seats.

"That's the Prime Minister," Zachary whispered nodding to the bespectacled man in the front row chatting with the woman next to him.

Jade's mobile rang and she answered it.

"Ah dah punk deh why yuh nuh come ah de game wid me?" the voice said.

It was Timex.

"What?" Jade responded in an irritated tone.

"Look to yuh left," Timex said.

Jade looked over and saw him sitting in the lower grandstand a few feet away.

She gave him a quick wave and terminated the call. He called her back but she didn't answer. What the hell was his problem? He was supposed to be a gangster yet he was acting like a jealous schoolboy. She planned to talk to him sternly about his behaviour.

"I didn't know that you knew Timex," Zachary commented. "He's the guy that I was telling you that my sister is dating."

"I met him over the weekend at a launch," Jade told him.

"Oh," Zachary responded.

Jade turned her attention to the crowd.

It was a turbulent sea of yellow and green waves. The massive stadium was packed to capacity and the place was electric. One would think it was a world cup game as opposed to an international friendly. It was a big one though. Argentina was ranked number one in the world – having dethroned arch rivals Brazil – and some of the top footballers in the world would be on show. Everyone was anxious to see how the Reggae Boyz –currently ranked 80th – would fare against the mighty Argentines.

The crowd cheered boisterously as the teams walked out onto the well-manicured field. Jade couldn't help but get caught up in the excitement though she didn't know much about football. She was sure Zachary would take pleasure in explaining whatever she didn't understand. The announcer then asked the crowd to stand for the singing of the national anthem. Everyone stood and Jade turned around and caught the man standing directly behind her staring lustfully at her ass. He quickly averted his eyes and his female companion killed Jade a million times with her squinty eyes. Jade smirked and turned back around. Women could be so stupid. She couldn't wait for the game to begin.

Theresa was at home reading a romance novel that she had bought over a week ago. She had just had dinner and was relaxing with the book and a chilled glass of La Roseda. She still had shivers when she thought about her experience with Jade last night. It had been the singularly most pleasurable experience of her entire life. She could still taste Jade's succulent pussy. She could still feel the intensity; pleasure so suffocating and exhilarating that she had literally lost consciousness.

She had slept late - they both had - and had gotten up at 11:30 and taken a shower. By the time Jade had crawled out of bed at 1 p.m., she finished whipping up a lunch of stewed chicken and boiled green bananas. They had eaten and spent a few hours lounging on the patio browsing through fashion magazines and chatting about any and everything. Jade had left at 3:30 p.m. to go home and get ready for a date. The vibe had been comfortable and it seemed as though the experience had brought them closer. She was happy for that as she had been a bit worried how things would have been between them after the act. She sipped her drink and turned to chapter ten. The book wasn't as good as the author's previous one but it was ok to pass the time with until the movie she wanted to see came on at 8.

Dahlia had just gotten back home after attending a birthday party for one of her friend's kids. The little girl, 3 going on 30, was a real character. The party had a Dora theme and had been attended by fifteen of her friends and a few parents. She changed into shorts and a T-shirt and went on the computer. She thought about Dunga as she waited for the PC to boot. It was rather slow. She made a mental note to call her friend who worked at Computers and Gadgets to come and have a look at it. Maybe it had a virus. She didn't like the way things were going. He had not called her in almost a week. Not even once. And the only real conversation they had the second time she called had resulted in an argument. She checked her Facebook account, answered a couple messages, poked and hugged back a few friends, then signed into Myspace. She replied to the only message she had, added the two rappers that had sent her friend requests, denied one from a weirdo who only had a picture of his dick and then checked out Dunga's page.

She listened to the songs on his playlist. Secret. Admittedly, the bitch could really sing. The songs were hot. Dahlia then checked out his top friends. She was there but way down at the bottom of his top 24. Everyone else was either entertainers or producers. Secret was in his top row, number 1. A deep frown creased Dahlia's face. The girl was hot. She looked really sweet and sexy. Dahlia's heartbeat accelerated as she clicked on Secret's profile. There was no way under the sun that Dunga could convince her that he wasn't fucking Secret. She drummed her fingers on the desk as the waited impatiently for the page to load. The girl was smoking hot. They spent a lot of time together. He was acting distant and neglectful. Shhhhiiiittt! They had to be fucking. Dunga was number one in her friend's list. *Bitch.* Dahlia clicked on her pictures. She didn't have a lot. Just eight from two different photo shoots. No pictures of her with Dunga. Dahlia went back to the home page and read Secret's bio. She then scrolled through the entire page, taking in every detail, looking for something, anything. She then saw that Secret had a voice intro welcoming people to her page. She clicked on it and turned up the volume on her speakers. When she heard the voice her face became the colour of blood. She fumed as she listened to the voice message over and over again. It was the same person who had answered the phone at Miss G's house. Secret was staying with Dunga's mother? Hell fucking no.

ଓ୪୬ଓ୪୬ଓ୪୬

"GOAL! GOAL!" the crowd shouted as one of the forwards, after dismissing two defenders, rifled a powerful left foot shot towards goal.

It was a false alarm.

The shot went agonizingly close but in the end, went just wide of the far post.

The crowd groaned in disappointment but applauded the efforts of Clifton "Ronaldo" Richards, who played his club football in Belgium. He was proving to be a handful for the Argentine defense; he had come dangerously close to scoring on several occasions.

Jade was having a great time. The match was very exciting. Jamaica was playing extremely well. Despite the trickery and skillfulness of world class superstars Lionel Messi and Carlos Tevez, the game was still scoreless and against the mighty Argentina, a draw would be a victory for Jamaica. They had thirty minutes left to secure the draw or even better, score and pull off what would be a phenomenal upset.

❧❧❧

Dunga was at the game with Secret and Jimmy when his mobile rang. It was Dahlia. He didn't answer the call. It didn't make any sense. It was too loud to have a conversation. He was sitting in the lower grandstand, close to the royal box. Timex and some of his goons were sitting four rows down. He had seen Jade and noted that she had come to the game with someone else. That gave him some measure of satisfaction. He knew Timex and there was no way that Jade could be his girl and come to a match that he was also attending with somebody else. Timex had simply been posing with Jade at the studio; trying to impress him. Dunga had laughed out loud and Secret had asked him what was so funny. He had kissed her and told her it was something he remembered. His phone vibrated again and again. She called six times and left three voice messages. Dunga wondered what was up now. There was always some drama where Dahlia was concerned.

Well, he would find out soon enough. The game would be over in a few minutes.

ଓଓଓ

Dahlia paced the living room like a raging bull. She was furious. Why the fuck Dunga wasn't answering his phone? He was probably fucking that bitch and ignoring her calls. She was so mad that she couldn't see straight. Her head throbbed painfully. She had a massive headache. It seemed as though she would be going back to Jamaica a lot sooner than she had anticipated. If that bitch thought she was going to sit by idly and let her take her man of seven years she had another thing coming. She picked up the phone and called Amoy, one of her best friends. She needed to vent.

ଓଓଓ

The match ended in disappointment for the Jamaican fans. A free-kick just outside the eighteen yard box by star midfielder Juan Riquelme had given Argentina a one goal lead in the final minute. The Reggae Boyz had nothing to be ashamed of though, they had played well against the best team in the world. The crowd gave them a well-deserved standing ovation when the referee blew the final whistle.

"So...you want to hang out some more or am I pushing my luck?" Zachary asked as they left immediately, trying to get a head start on the crowd.

Jade smiled. She liked Zachary. He was just...*different*. Yeah he wanted to fuck her brains out just like everybody else but he was a gentleman about his. Very classy guy. She remembered when she had almost slept with him the first night they met. If only he had known how close he had come to getting some.

"What do you have in mind?" Jade asked as they made their way to the parking lot.

"Hmmm...a bite to eat...a couple of drinks..." he replied.

They got into the car and he immediately hit the switch and put the top down.

"Ok," Jade agreed.

Zachary stopped briefly to chat with a guy he knew. They were old schoolmates and they had seen each other yesterday so Zachary knew that it was because he wanted to look at Jade why he flagged him down. They then headed out to Zachary's favourite watering hole, a classy bistro and bar off Barbican Road.

They sat at the cute, circular bar instead of taking a table. The two bartenders knew Zachary well and they were very excited to meet 'the La Roseda angel' as the one with the bald head referred to her and Jade graciously signed a poster of her that one of them had and took a picture with him.

They ordered barbecue wings and Jade drank La Roseda while Zachary had Remy Martin. The place wasn't packed which suited Jade just fine. After that massive crowd at the stadium, she could appreciate vibing at a nice laid back spot with just a few people around. Erykah Badu's hit song *On and On* filtered through the speakers at the perfect volume – loud enough to hear it clearly but low enough to have a conversation without having to shout. The wings were delicious.

"I love this place Zach," Jade told him. "The atmosphere is just wicked. Almost feels like one of those nice hole-in-the-wall bars you can find in East Manhattan."

"Yeah! Exactly!" Zachary agreed excitedly and the conversation turned to bars in New York. Jade knew some of the ones he mentioned but the newer ones had come about while she was incarcerated.

She smiled at Zachary as he told her a joke. It was kind of lame but he told it with such animation that she laughed anyway. He had this boyish charm that she really dug. A hot nerd. That's what he was. Maybe, just maybe, tonight would be his lucky night.

Chapter 58

Dunga checked his voicemail as he headed to his sports bar. Jimmy was driving and Secret was in the backseat. They were going there to hang out for a bit and have a few drinks. He listened to the first message:

Dunga I need to talk to you.

Then the second:

Dunga why the fuck you're not answering your phone?

And the third:

It's like that huh? Ok, I know what the fuck I have to do. Don't worry yourself. You motherfucker!

Dunga was perplexed. And annoyed. Who the hell was Dahlia talking to like that? And what the hell was she upset about? Dunga sighed and placed the phone back in the case. He wasn't even going to feed into her madness. He was not going to call her and find out why she was tripping. Let her do whatever it was that she *knew* she had to do. Dahlia didn't feel good if she wasn't bitching about something. Dunga sucked his teeth. Whatever.

ଓଃଓଃଓଃ

Timex was silent as he nursed his drink of Hennessy and red bull.

He took a toke of the huge marijuana joint that he was smoking.

He was alone in his bedroom.

The door was closed.

Breeda and a couple of the boys were out front playing videogames.

He was pissed.

Jade had embarrassed him in front of his friends.

And in front of Dunga.

When he was getting up to exit the stadium, he had seen Dunga a few seats up, getting ready to leave as well. They had nodded to each other but he had seen the smirk on Dunga's face. He had been so mad that he didn't even acknowledge Secret's wave.

How dare Jade show up at the match with somebody else knowing that he would be there? Yeah she wasn't his girl – yet – but she knows how he feels about her, she should have a little more respect. His boys hadn't said anything but he knew what they were thinking. And to add insult to injury, the guy she went with was the son of the politician who was the Member of Parliament in charge of the area where he grew up.

A little uptown punk.

Leah's brother.

Such a small world.

He was fucking the sister and the brother was fucking the girl he wanted.

The girl he had spent his hard earned money on.

Buying her gifts.

Taking her out.

She was playing him like a fucking chump.

Maybe he had been too nice.

Maybe he needed to show Jade that his gangster image wasn't an image.

Maybe then she would act right.

ଔ৯ଔ৯ଔ৯

"Your place is really nice," Jade commented as she looked around Zachary's spacious apartment. It was very masculine – dark hues; big comfy chairs; a large couch; an exquisite home theatre system; 56 inch flat screen T.V. mounted on the wall; expensive artwork and a massive antique book shelf with everything from *The Nicomachean Ethics* by Aristotle to Aleksandr Solzhenitsyn's three-volume *Gulag Archipelago* to *Native Son* by Richard Wright.

"Thank you," Zachary said as he poured them drinks.

He handed Jade a glass of white wine.

"No La Roseda?" Jade teased.

Zachary laughed as he showed her the rest of the apartment.

He led her to the bedroom.

Jade nodded in approval as she looked around. Mirrored ceiling; retro-inspired round bed that was literally center-stage in the room; barely-there clear tables which housed the bedside lamps without competing with the bed for attention and a shaggy, rust area rug along with orange, brown and red pillows completed the groovy look.

Jade stood by the glass door which led out to a small balcony. The view was lovely. They were in an exclusive section of Red Hills. A little too far from the city and the road leading up there was way too narrow and winding for Jade's liking but it was a breathtaking view. She hadn't come here to fuck Zachary. But she was open to it. Her primary reason was to see where he lived and just chill at his home for a bit. If it happened, no problem. She was very attracted to him and she was unattached emotionally to anyone. She could do whatever she wanted, whenever she felt like it. She had spent four years of her young life behind bars, having to follow rules and do what she was told. She sipped her wine. There was nothing like freedom. *Real* freedom.

Zachary came behind her and stood close.

She could feel his warm breath on her nape.

Smelled his Tom Ford for men cologne.

She rubbed her ass seductively against his crotch.

She expected the fleshy apparatus between his legs to roar its approval.

It didn't.

That was a first.

Jade turned around and kissed him hard.

He responded passionately, his eager tongue darting in her mouth, seeking exquisite pleasures.

He found them.

He groaned in her mouth as he kissed her deeply, the same way he had dreamt of doing so many times since the night he first laid eyes on her.

She removed his shirt and moaned in approval.

He was so muscular and firm.

She caressed him. Feeling his strength.

She lowered her mouth to his chest and bit his nipples gently.

Zachary made unintelligible sounds. When Jade had told him that she wanted to see his home, he had been pleasantly surprised. While it wasn't a certainty that had meant that she would sleep with him, it had definitely increased the odds of it happening. And it was.

Her mouth felt so good.

Hot and sweet.

Made the hairs on the back of his neck stand on end.

Jade pulled the button on his fitted denim and unzipped it.

She pulled it to his knees.

His green Polo boxers followed.

Jade reached for his dick.

Her hand froze.

Chapter 59

Jade gasped. Zachary was rock hard. All three and a half inches of his dick.

She looked up at him with her eyes like saucers and her mouth a silent O. To say that she was stunned would be the understatement of the century. So much for big hands and big feet equaling a well-hung man. *Theresa's clit is bigger than this shit* Jade mused in wonder.

Zachary shrugged with a what-the-fuck-can-I-do-about-it smile. "Yeah...as you can see and feel...I'm not very well-endowed."

Jade didn't know what to say. She looked back down at it as she rubbed it with her fingers. Unbelievable. This sexy hunk of a man. Wielding a dick that was about as lethal as cotton candy. There was no justice in the world.

"I've stopped being embarrassed about it for several years now," Zachary continued. "Girls usually pretend its ok because of who I am...and I'm extremely good at oral sex so that kind of helps too."

Jade still didn't know what to say.

Or do.

What now?

She wasn't horny anymore. All the moisture from her pussy had evaporated. She was as arid as the Sahara. Just as well because there was no way she would have allowed Zachary to penetrate her. It was impossible for him to satisfy her with *that*.

She released it and sat on the edge of the bed.

He was still hard.

"Do you have a girlfriend Zach?" she asked.

Zachary chuckled. "Yeah...she's in Cuba studying medicine." He sat down beside her.

"Our sex life is actually good," he continued. "We are both freaky so we have a lot of fun in bed...despite my shortcomings."

Jade was amazed at how comfortable he was with his size – or lack thereof. Zachary was a really cool guy. Too bad they couldn't be more than friends.

"Can't believe I'm still hard," he chuckled. "I wanted to fuck you so bad."

Jade smiled.

"I'm going to have to take care of this...its getting uncomfortable."

He got up to go into the bathroom.

"Do it in front of me," Jade said, looking around at him. "I want to watch you..."

Zachary laughed. He retrieved a bottle of lube from a drawer and squeezed some in his right palm. He then stood in front of Jade in a wide-legged stance and massaged his dick slowly, moisturizing it, getting it ready for some serious friction.

For the next five minutes, Jade watched as the sexy, well-built man stroked his miniature dick, imagining that he was stroking her. The look on his face was priceless when he climaxed, spilling his hot juice all over his hands and his expensive rug.

Jade sighed.

Such a waste.

"Mmmm...mmm...love...sucking... your...big... black...dick..." Leah moaned as she devoured Timex's rigid shaft. He was lying on his back with his legs spread. Leah was naked between them, sucking his dick like it was the sweetest tasting candy bar in the whole world. She sucked him languidly, savouring the feel of his throbbing length and bulging veins in her hot mouth. Timex watched the long-haired beauty through half-open eyes as she worked her magic. She was gorgeous and rich. And she was totally captivated by him. If he told her jump, her head would hit the roof. His ego had needed a boost. Jade had delivered a hard blow to his swagger. So he had called Leah to come over. To remind him that he was the man. Timex. The object of lust for many women worldwide. The most popular entertainer in Jamaica. The gangster deejay that could get any girl he wanted. Leah elicited a loud groan from him as she stroked his dick while she moved her mouth further down south. He raised his pelvis off the bed slightly as she licked his testicles and the bit of real estate between his scrotum and anus, raising his level of ecstasy. Jade faded to the background of his consciousness.

At least for now.

Zachary dropped off Jade at her home at 11:45 p.m. After his brief masturbation show, they had relaxed and watched the first half of a Lakers and Spurs game before Jade told him she was ready to go. She removed her clothing and went into the bathroom to take a shower. It had been a very interesting evening to say the least. Cohen was leaving Jamaica on Tuesday but he would be going to Montego Bay tomorrow. Tonight was the only time left to spend with him. She knew that he was waiting for her to call. She would page him in a little while. So that he could finish up what Zachary had started.

Timex called her just as she got off the phone with Cohen.

He had felt much better after having sex with Leah. His ego, among other things, had been stroked just right. However, the euphoria soon wore off and his mind kept reverting to the incident at the match. He really felt disrespected and embarrassed and he needed to address it.

"Yo Jade," Timex began, "weh yuh deh?"

"Don't yo me," Jade replied tartly. "I didn't appreciate your behaviour earlier. Acting like a jealous school kid...thought you were a gangster."

Timex bristled at her words.

"Careful how yuh ah chat to me enuh Jade," he growled.

Jade continued as though she hadn't heard him. "I'm my own big woman. I do as I please. And if I wanted to go to the game with someone else...then that's my prerogative. I don't expect you to act like a little bitch about it."

Timex saw red.

"Hey yankee gal...mi nuh know weh yuh use to ah foreign but man ah bad man! Mi wi – "

Jade hung up the phone. She was surprised at Timex's behaviour. She had thought he was a cool guy – yeah very rough around the edges but cool nonetheless. Imagine if she had made the mistake of sleeping with him. He would have lost his mind. Jade shuddered at the thought of all the drama she would have had to deal with. Oh well, so much for that. She deleted his number from her phone.

ଔଔଔ

Timex had had enough. He was going to teach this yankee gal a lesson. Show her that he was not the type of man that she should take lightly. He got dressed and went out front. Only Breeda was out there. He was talking on the phone while looking at music videos on the large, flat screen T.V.

"Come on yo," Timex commanded and headed outside.

He got behind the wheel much to Breeda's disappointment. He loved to drive the Range Rover. Felt like a king. He adjusted the desert eagle in his waist so that he could recline comfortably. He looked over at his long time friend. Timex had been upset since earlier at the game. The minute he had seen the girl there with that punk his whole vibe had changed.

"So wah gwaan? Weh we ah go?" Breeda asked.

Timex scowled and took awhile before responding. "Wi ah go teach somebody a lesson. De yankee gal dis de program."

Breeda nodded. He was down for whatever. He didn't like the bitch anyway. She thought her shit could make pizza. Timex was flooring the luxurious SUV. They got to Jade's home in fifteen minutes.

ଔଔଔ

Jade heard the vehicle pull up and assumed it was Cohen. She grabbed her pocketbook and headed outside. She frowned as she glanced at the vehicle before closing the door.

"What the fuck are you doing here?" Jade asked angrily as she stood by the door. How dare he show up at her home unannounced?

Timex put the vehicle in park and hopped out. He strode purposefully over to Jade and grabbed the front of her Juicy Couture top, crushing it in a tight fist. Breeda also came out of the vehicle. He came around and leaned against the vehicle to get a front row seat of the action.

Jade was shocked that Timex had dared to put his hands on her. Had he lost his fucking mind?

"Are you crazy nigga?" Jade asked with an incredulous look on her face. "Do you think I'm one of your little stupid groupies? If you know what's good for you unhand me, apologize and I just might make it slide."

Timex couldn't believe that she was still talking shit.

"Hey gal! Yuh t'ink seh mi ah play wid yuh?" he growled menacingly.

Jade was about to respond when four sets of headlights came into the yard.

Cohen had arrived to pick her up.

Chapter 60

"I missed you so much...missed you being inside me...mmmm...oh baby..." Secret murmured as she moved in sync with Dunga, who was buried deeply inside her. Her legs and arms held him in a tight embrace as she moved her waistline like a seasoned exotic dancer.

Dunga groaned as she whispered sweet and nasty nothings in his ear. He had missed her too. Making love to Secret was pure bliss. A pleasurable journey that was as intense as it was emotional. He was in love with her. He had recently admitted it himself. No use pretending that she was just a nice girl that he simply cared about. He was ready to give her his heart.

Secret could feel him throbbing in her depths. He was close. She urged him on. She loved the feel of his hot semen when it flooded her insides. Her period had finished two days ago and she was now on the pill. She could now fully enjoy his incredible loving without fear of getting pregnant.

"Mmmm...I feel it baby...I know you want to come...come for me baby...wet up your pussy...oh Dunga...I feel like I'm coming again...I'm coming too baby...shit...wet me up baby...oh God..."

Dunga claimed her mouth in a bruising kiss as they experienced their first simultaneous orgasm. Their bodies twitched like they were in an electric chair as Dunga's river of juices flowed into Secret's hot sticky lake.

"I love you baby," Dunga said as his body trembled uncontrollably.

Secret who was still in the throes of her orgasm, swore her heart stopped when Dunga uttered those words.

"Oh baby...I love you too...so much...you are my world," Secret told him, feeling as though she was going to burst with happiness. There were few things in the world as satisfying as being loved in return by the one you love.

She started to cry.

Dunga was still inside her. His erection was fading though not enough for him to slip out as yet.

He looked at Secret lovingly. She just came out of nowhere and ambushed his heart.

The cute little half-Indian virgin with the big voice.

Where was all of this going to leave Dahlia?

The answer was obvious. And he didn't feel too bad about it. Kind of relieved actually. Obviously he wasn't happy with her or it wouldn't have been so easy for him to fall for another woman. Especially in such a short space of time.

They had been together for seven years. That was a long time. But he never saw himself marrying her and that in itself was telling. If a man was with a woman that long and couldn't see himself making her his wife, then something was wrong.

He would simply have to tell her that it was over. She was not getting custody of Samantha though. He didn't want his daughter living and going to school in America. He wasn't in love with Dahlia anymore but he still cared about her. He wasn't looking forward to delivering the bad news but it had to be done.

And the sooner the better.

ଔଔଔ

The lead vehicle stopped and the two men alighted quickly when they realized that Jade was in trouble.

"A weh de bloodclaat dis?" Timex muttered as he watched the two men walk over to them. Each was holding a handgun equipped with a silencer. Breeda started to reach for his desert eagle but froze when a bullet whizzed past his left ear and embedded itself in the trunk of the mango tree a few meters away.

Timex released Jade slowly and faced the men. He didn't like this one bit. Who the fuck were these people?

"That was just a warning," the short, stocky man who resembled Mike Tyson said to Breeda as he walked over to him. He searched him and removed the gun from his waist.

The other man stood off at an angle where he could have a clear view of both Timex and Breeda.

Jade, now smiling wickedly, searched Timex and removed his firearm. It was also a desert eagle.

Timex scowled.

Jade smiled.

She hit him with it in his face, opening up a deep gash over his right eye.

"I gave you a chance to apologize and walk away," Jade said to him as Timex looked at her with a dazed expression, as though he couldn't believe what was happening. The blood trickling down his face was real though. "You should have taken it."

"What do you want us to do with them?" the Mike Tyson look-alike asked Jade. "Did any of them harm you?"

Timex exploded. His life was being spoken of as though it wasn't important. Like he was *nobody*. A bug to be squashed if Jade said the word. "Weh de fuck yuh mean 'do wid dem'? Eeh pussyhole English bwoy! Yuh know who mi is? Yuh better gi wi back wi bloodclaat gun dem and left yah so. Cause trust me...dah gal yah ah go dead by ah mawnin'!"

The man moved so quickly that the words had barely come out of Timex's mouth before he screamed and held his leg in agony. His left leg was broken, courtesy of an expert kick to the shin.

The lights came on in the other apartment and Jade's neighbour, whom she hadn't seen since they had the argument, looked through the window to try and see what was happening.

She could see the vehicles and hear the voices but she couldn't see anyone as they were standing on Jade's patio. She would have to come outside and she didn't think that would be wise. She wondered if she should call the police.

"Listen to me carefully. I'm going to allow you and your friend to go seeing as you haven't harmed Jade. Lucky for you we came just in time because if you had laid a finger on her..."

He allowed his words to linger as he looked from Timex to Breeda then back to Timex.

Jade beckoned to the other guy and gave him Timex's gun. She then locked her door and grill, and made her way to the vehicle that Cohen was in. He had stayed put, allowing his bodyguards to deal with whatever was happening.

He smiled at Jade. "Good night drama queen."

Jade laughed. "I'm not and you know it."

"Never a dull moment with you Jade...never a dull moment. The boys are happy that you're around. Without you their stay in Jamaica would have been rather uneventful."

Jade chuckled.

They watched as the bodyguards said something else to Timex and Breeda then hopped into their vehicle. The two vehicles then exited the premises and made their way to Cohen's hotel suite.

ꕥꕥꕥ

Timex tried valiantly not to scream as Breeda helped him get on the back seat. He failed. The pain was excruciating. They were both shocked and humiliated at what had just taken place. No one could know about this. If word of this got out on the streets, Timex's street credibility would take a serious hit. Breeda sighed as he rushed to the nearest hospital. The man had told them in parting that it could end right here or they could retaliate and die painful, unpleasant deaths. As if death could ever be pleasant. He cringed as he heard the moans escaping Timex's lips. Anything Timex wanted to do he'd be with it but it might be wise to just chill and take their losses. Even if they harmed Jade, they didn't know who those people were and one couldn't fight an unknown enemy. First things first though, Timex needed to get his leg taken care of. They would decide how to proceed later.

ꕥꕥꕥ

Jade snuggled up comfortably against Cohen. She was completely satiated. He had performed cunnilingus on her for at least twenty minutes before he had fucked her for another thirty minutes. Cohen had fucked her like he was never going to see her again. Maybe he wasn't. She had climaxed at least six times. He was good in bed, equally adept with his tongue and dick. He was cool and generous as well but Jade couldn't help thinking that there was something almost creepy about him. Not creepy enough to gross her out but *something* was off. It wasn't important though, he served his purposes well and it wasn't like they'd be getting married or anything like that. It had been a very eventful and interesting day. She soon fell into a dreamless sleep.

Chapter 61

Dahlia arrived in Jamaica at 10:40 a.m. After searching for over an hour online last night, she had finally found an early flight. The ticket had been expensive but even if it had been twice the amount she paid, she still would have booked the flight. She had barely slept last night. Heavy make-up and over-sized Burberry sunglasses hid her tiredness and the luggage underneath her eyes. After clearing customs, she headed outside to catch a cab. No one knew she was coming. She decided on a tinted, gray Nissan Sentra – the driver was clean and polite – and gave him directions to her home. Whatever happened today, she knew that Dunga was going to be downright furious. She didn't give a fuck. He would have to kill her today but it was not going down like that. She was not going to sit idly by and let someone take away seven years of her life. He hadn't even called her back though she had left three voice messages and called him six times.

It was a beautiful, sunny Monday morning.

A stark contrast to what she had left behind in New York. But Dahlia didn't even notice.

Her mind was too preoccupied.

ꕥꕥꕥ

Leah came to look for Timex at the hospital. She had brought him breakfast – scrambled egg platter and tea from a fast food restaurant. The bone had been shattered in three places. It had required surgical treatment. The orthopedic surgeon had used small-diameter inter-locking nails to result in improved limb function when healed as well as a shorter healing time. He was checking out in the afternoon.

He hated hospitals.

He hated Jade even more for putting him in one.

Fucking bitch.

He wanted her. Still.

He hated the fact that he still desired her.

Would forget everything that happened if she called him right now and wanted to see him.

He wanted to kill her.

He wanted her to want him.

He was going to leave her alone though.

Breeda had come to see him an hour ago and he was right. They didn't know the people that she had in her corner so if they did something to her they'd be sitting targets. The official story was that he had been involved in an accident. There was no way they could allow the truth to be known. Timex sucked his teeth. His hospital bill was going to be a pretty penny. The surgery had been very expensive. He sucked his teeth again. He was very frustrated that he wouldn't be able to get back at Jade. He had imagined killing her in so many different ways since last night. He had imagined fucking her in so many different ways since he first saw her. Leah was talking to him but he was in so much pain and feeling so much anger that he couldn't hear a word she was saying.

"This is for you," Cohen said as he slid into his black corduroy blazer. He was getting ready to leave. He was about to head over to the helipad by the golf academy just down the road from the hotel. A helicopter was waiting to take him to Montego Bay where he would spend the night at his friend's hotel, and conduct some business before heading to Belgium through a connecting flight in London tomorrow morning.

Jade was sitting on the bed. She opened the box. It was a diamond necklace. It was absolutely beautiful.

"Thank you Lavi," she said. "This is gorgeous."

He took it from her and they stood in front of the mirror as he slipped the flawless eight carat diamond necklace around her neck. It looked like it belonged there. A beautiful necklace on a beautiful woman.

He had gotten it this morning - just in time, having ordered the general manager at his company in South Africa to deal with it and send it by courier since last week Wednesday.

She turned and kissed him deeply.

Cohen looked at her silently for awhile.

They kissed again.

He then buzzed the bellhop to get his bags and they made their way downstairs.

The two Audi Q7s were waiting by the lobby door and they hopped in. Five minutes later they were at the helipad. He told Jade that they would speak soon and exited the vehicle. His two bodyguards went into the helicopter as well.

"Home Miss?" the driver asked.

"Yeah," Jade replied. She checked the time. It was 12:30. She would go home for a bit then have Nathan pick her up at 3. She needed to get some work suits and to also pop by the office to choose the lap top and whatever accessories she would need for her work station at home. She was excited about her new role as special projects manager. She already had some ideas bubbling in her head. She would put them down on paper later this evening.

ఆఇఆఇఆఇ

Dahlia had been very busy since her arrival. After making a few preparations, she had driven over to Miss G's home. She was there now, parked out front. After a few minutes, she took a deep breath and exited the vehicle. She knocked on the front door loudly. She didn't get an answer. She tried the handle. The door was open. She went in. Both Miss G and Secret entered the living room at the same time to see who was at the door. Miss G had been looking for something in her closet and Secret had just gotten out of the shower when they had heard the loud, insistent knocking.

Miss G was shocked out of her wits. "Dahlia? What are you doing here? Yuh supposed to be in New York!"

Dahlia didn't respond. She only had eyes for Secret. She looked at the young, pretty, innocent-looking girl who was trying to take her man. She wasn't so innocent after all now was she? Taking Dunga's big dick and loving it. Fucking a man that belonged to somebody else.

"Bitch!" Dahlia screamed and rushed towards Secret.

Secret backed up a little in shock as the enraged woman rushed towards her. So this was Dahlia. The mother of Dunga's child. She had come here to fight her. Had found out that Dunga was seeing her.

Dahlia leaped on top of her a second later. They toppled to the floor. Secret hit her head against the wall. She became angry. Very angry. This girl had no class. Invading her man's mother's home to fight a guest. Dirty bitch.

"Fucking whore!" Dhalia shrieked as she tried to get a hold of Secret's hair.

"Dahlia! Lawd Jesus!" Miss G screamed in disbelief. This couldn't be happening. Not in her home. She rushed over and grabbed Dahlia. She flung her off of Secret.

Secret scrambled to her feet instantly as did Dahlia. They rushed towards each other but Miss G got between them and inadvertently got poked in the eye by Dahlia. She received a busted lip as well, courtesy of a wild punch thrown by Dahlia.

Miss G cried out in pain and rushed to the bathroom. Dahlia realized what had happened but she had to stay focused. Do what she came here to do. Kick Secret's ass.

It was an accident. Nothing she could do about that now. Casualties of war.

Seeing Miss G get poked in the eye and punched gave Secret extra strength. She ducked under Dahlia's wild punches and grabbed both of her legs, toppling her to the floor. She then slapped Dahlia in the face repeatedly. Dahlia screamed and raising her knees, pushed Secret away.

Miss G came back out holding a hand over her right eye.

"Mi just call Dunga!" she bellowed to Dahlia. "Yuh just wait until him reach here!"

That slowed Dahlia's roll. When Dunga saw that she had injured his mother, he would probably beat her within an inch of her life.

"This aint over! Yuh hear gal? Yuh better watch yuh back!" she said in parting to Secret.

"Fuck you!" Secret shouted and threw a vase filled with flowers and water at Dahlia. It hit her in the back as she ran through the door. She cried out in pain but did not turn back. Crying and rubbing her back, she hopped into her SUV and quickly headed out. The last thing she needed was for Dunga to catch her here. She headed over to her cousin's house. She would be hiding out there until it was time to go back to the airport in a couple of hours.

Dunga was stunned as he broke several traffic laws hurrying to get to his mother's home. He had been at the studio working when he received her frantic call. Dahlia was in Jamaica. At his mother's home fighting Secret. Injured his mother in the process. So that's what her calls had been about. That's what she had meant when she said that 'she knew what she had to do'. Dahlia was a master at making a bad situation worse. By her actions today, she had ceased being the victim. She was no longer the wounded party. She was now the villain; the wrongdoer and God help her when he got a hold of her. Out of order. Damn disrespectful. Invading his mother's home and hurting her. He wondered if Secret was okay. He narrowly avoided a collision with a slow-moving garbage truck as he turned onto Barbican Road. He was almost there.

ଓଃଓଃଓଃ

"Hi Jade," Eddie said. He was home; having been given a week's leave by the Permanent Secretary while they re-grouped from the Weatherburn mess. He would be reassigned when he returned to work.

"How are you Eddie? Sorry to hear about your boss," Jade said appropriately.

Eddie released a heavy sigh. "Thanks, Jade. It was a really bad experience, having to discover the bodies in the state that they were in...the whole tragic and embarrassing situation...it was really fucked up."

"I can imagine. If you are up for it I'd like to arrange for you to pick up the money tomorrow to deal with the passport and driver's license."

"No problem but I don't have a vehicle Jade...they didn't allow me to drive home the Pajero."

"Ok, just give me a time and your address and I'll send my driver to drop it off."

Eddie gave her the information and thanked her for calling.

There was a knock on Jade's door when she got off the phone. Curious and a bit wary, she looked out the window.

Mrs. Allen-Whyte.

The landlady.

She went outside to her.

"Good afternoon, young lady," Mrs. Allen-Whyte said, her beady eyes staring disapprovingly at Jade above the spectacles balancing on the bridge of her nose.

"Hi,"Jade replied. "How can I help you?"

"Well...it has come to my attention that there was a commotion at your apartment last night."

Jade knitted her brows. "Commotion?"

"Yes, screams were heard and there were some vehicles in the yard. The type that drug dealers drive."

"I see...well I have no idea what you are talking about. There was no commotion here last night and I have no idea what kind of cars drug dealers drive. Did you hear a commotion Mrs. Allen-Whyte?"

"Please just keep it down late at night," she responded tartly, ignoring Jade's question. "We have to be considerate to other people."

With that she turned and made her way back to her apartment.

Jade shook her head in disbelief. That cunt next door must have heard when Timex screamed last night and told Mrs. Allen-Whyte that she had been making a commotion. Stupid, nosy bitch. Apparently she wanted another beat-down.

☙❧☙❧☙❧

Dunga shook his head in disbelief as he looked at his mother's eye and swollen upper lip. Fortunately, the eye seemed to be ok though Dunga was going to send her to the optician to be certain. It was very red. Dahlia had clearly lost her mind. She had to have known that there was no coming back from pulling a stunt like this.

"You okay baby?" he asked Secret as he checked out her face. She only had a slight scratch on her left cheek. There were no other visible marks.

"I'm fine boo...slight headache but I'm good," Secret replied with a smile.

Dahlia had pulled her hair really hard. Her head was throbbing.

"I'm sorry you had to go through that," Dunga told her.

"Don't worry about it baby...I don't mind fighting for the one I love. Besides I kicked her ass."

Dunga laughed. He gave her a quick peck on the lips.

He then called Jimmy to come and take his mother to see the optician.

He then left the house, dialing Dahlia's mobile number as he made his way to the car. She didn't pick up. He checked the time. It was now 2:30. Time for Samantha to be picked up from school. Her grandmother had an appointment today and had asked Dunga to arrange for her to be picked up. Shit. He hopped in the car and dialed Dahlia's number again. It rang out once again to voicemail.

Dunga arrived at the expensive preparatory school in fifteen minutes. He didn't see Samantha by the mango tree where she usually sat on the benches and waited with Kimmy, a half-Korean girl who was her best friend. He parked and went to her classroom. Miss Harper, Samantha's form teacher, was in the classroom putting some things inside a box.

"Hi Mr. Gilbert," she greeted, addressing him by his surname.

"How are you doing Miss Harper," Dunga responded. "Have you seen Samantha?"

Miss Foster looked at him surprised. "Her mother came by to pick her up at lunchtime. Said she had a family emergency. She didn't mention it you?"

Dunga's heart skipped a beat.

"No she didn't. Thanks, I have to rush."

He rushed back out to his car and quickly headed to his apartment. Dahlia obviously had a death wish. She was playing a very dangerous game. She knew what he was capable of. Why was she pushing him like this? What did she hope to accomplish by all of this? She had no right to drag Samantha into this. It was as though she had gone stark mad after somehow finding out about him and Secret. It was not a good time of the evening to be hurrying to his apartment. The traffic leading to Constant Spring road between the hours of 2 – 5 was ridiculous. He sighed in frustration.

❧❧❧

"I said to stop crying!" Dahlia shouted at Samantha as they made their way to the departure lounge. People stared at the woman roughing up the sweet little girl. Samantha had been crying ever since her mother had picked her up from school unexpectedly and told her that she was taking her to New York. 'I want my daddy!' she had screamed. It had taken two slaps by Dahlia to calm her down and get her into the car. She had left her at her cousin's house before going over to Miss G's home where all hell had broken loose.

Samantha continued to sob. Why was her mother being so mean? She hated her so much. She didn't want to go anywhere. What about school? It wasn't holiday time yet. She wanted to call her daddy but her mother wouldn't let her and had slapped her the last time she had asked. Her mother pulled her by the hand roughly and they sat in a chair next to a swarthy man in an ill-fitting black suit who was surfing the internet on his Mac notebook.

"If I have to tell you to the stop the damn crying one more time I'm going to take you into the bathroom and give you a proper beating," Dahlia snarled in a loud whisper.

Samantha miserably tried to control her sobbing. Her mother was so evil. She hadn't done anything. She wanted her daddy.

ઉઙઙઉઙ

Dahlia wasn't at the apartment. Neither was her SUV. Dunga called Dahlia's mother. She answered after the third ring. She told him yes, Dahlia had come by the house to pick up a few things for Samantha but no, she had no idea where she was right now. No, she hadn't known that Dahlia was coming to Jamaica today.

"Wha' happen Dunga?" she asked. "Everyt'ing alright?"

Dunga told her he had to go and terminated the call. He then called Tisha, Dahlia's cousin.

"Tisha, where is Dahlia?"

"Hmm...I don't know," she replied, but had hesitated despite being briefed by Dahlia that Dunga would call and she should tell him that she had not seen or heard from her.

"Tisha," Dunga said irritably, "don't fuck with me right now. Where is Dahlia?"

"Dunga I –"

"If you ever let me waste time and come over to the store you're not going to like it trust me," Dunga promised.

Tisha gulped. She knew Dunga was not to be played with. Why did her cousin have to get mixed up in this shit? Cho bloodclaat!

"Sh-sh-she gone back to New York," Tisha confessed.

"Samantha is with her?"

"Y-y-yes," Tisha stammered.

Dunga hung up without saying goodbye.

Dahlia had clearly lost her fucking mind. She was obviously unable to think straight. She had plucked Samantha out of school and spirited her out of the country without his knowledge and permission.

Hell hath no fury like a woman scorned.

Truer words have never been spoken.

He called his friend at the travel agency on Waterloo Road to get him on the first available flight to New York.

He was going for his daughter.

Chapter 62

Jade purchased four Escada work suits from a boutique on Dumfries Road that specialized in upscale work attire for professional women. She then went over to the office. Mr. Hassan wasn't there but had left instructions with his personal assistant. Jade examined the laptops – a Sony Vaio, a Mac and a Toshiba. She chose the Mac.

She then selected a web cam, printer and a small computer desk. She also received a Blackberry that was hooked up to the company's network. She could receive company faxes and emails on it. Everything was loaded into the SUV and a freelance IT guy who was contracted to the company came with them to Jade's home to teach her how to properly use the Mac. After he left an hour later, Jade immediately started working. She listed her promotional ideas and formulated an implementation plan for each item. She was so excited. She was going to do a hell of a job.

The travel agent called back Dunga two hours later. The best he could do was a 10 p.m. flight which connected at Miami. Dunga hated connecting flights but he would be travelling with just his hand luggage so it wouldn't be too bad and besides, he just *had* to get to New York tonight. The agent emailed his e-ticket and he printed it when he got back to the studio. He made a few calls and cancelled all of his sessions and meetings for the rest of the day plus the next two days.

"Dahlia ah real mad woman to rassclaat," Jimmy commented as the two of them sat in the chill room having a drink. Jimmy had just gotten back from taking Miss G to see the optician. She was ok. Thankfully the eye had not been damaged.

Dunga emitted a mirthless chuckle.

He sipped his Hennessy.

"All she accomplished was making leaving her ass much easier," Dunga responded. "Once I go and get Sam, that's it man. I never want to see her again. And I'm sure neither will Sam."

He knew his daughter well. Her relationship with her mother had never been a very loving one as it had been clear from she was a baby that there was no one to her like her daddy. That had always been a difficult pill for Dahlia to swallow and with Dahlia acting so recklessly, he could only imagine how she was treating Samantha. Most likely she hated her mother right now. She was probably crying for her daddy. The thought of Dahlia mistreating his princess instilled a deadly anger inside of him.

The single that Timex and Secret had done together blared from the speakers. The radio was on Trends FM, Jamaica's hottest new radio station that had locked down the coveted 18 – 34 demographic. Dunga had gotten five thousand copies pressed to go into distribution in two days. The major disc jockeys had received their copies before midday today. Already, the song was receiving significant airplay. Dunga heard that Timex had been in a motor vehicle accident last night. He had tried calling him to see if he was okay and to let him know that the song was already on the radio but he hadn't gotten through. Timex's phone had rung straight to voicemail. He had left a brief message telling Timex to give him a shout.

Dunga rubbed Tupac's head. He growled appreciatively. He was sitting up on his haunches looking at Dunga as he spoke like he was a part of the conversation.

Dunga gave Jimmy a list of things that had to be dealt with tomorrow and then he made his way home to put a few necessities in a small travelling bag. He then called a good friend of his in New York to let him know what time to pick him up. He then went over to Miss G's house. He would spend some time with his mother and Secret before Jimmy came by to take him to the airport in a few hours.

Samantha toyed with her pizza. She didn't want it. She wasn't hungry. But her mom was forcing her to eat. She was tired. So tired. She just wanted to sleep. She wanted to go back home to Jamaica. She wanted to be in her nice bed with the Dora sheet set. She wanted her daddy. She didn't know what was going on but she didn't like it. Why did her mom take her to New York? Why wasn't she allowed to call her daddy?

"I said to eat your food!" Dahlia screamed at her.

Samantha cringed. Her mother had been screaming at her all evening. Slapped her hard a few times too.

"I don't want anymore mommy," Samantha pleaded.

Dahlia looked at her daughter angrily.

She was mad at the way she was treating her.

Mad at her actions today.

Mad at Dunga.

Mad at that bitch Secret.

Mad at Jimmy – he knew what was going on.

Mad at Miss G.

Mad at the world.

Scared.

She was scared too.

What the fuck was going to happen now?

She felt like she was going crazy. She had slipped into an abyss during the past twenty four hours. Stress and anger were the only things she had found down there. They had grabbed her and wouldn't let go. They consumed her.

She told Samantha to go to bed.

Samantha scampered away quickly. Happy to get out of her mother's sight.

Dahlia could only imagine how scary she was looking. Clothes crushed and dirty. Face a hot mess of tears and runny mascara. Eyes red and puffy. Hair disheveled.

She sighed and took another swig of vodka.

Grey Goose.

Straight from the bottle.

Trying to dull the pain.

Failing.

But still trying.

ଓଃଓଃଓଃ

"What!" Theresa couldn't believe what she was hearing. Drama followed Jade like a shadow. Never a dull moment with her best friend. "He's crazy!"

"Damn right that negro is crazy," Jade concurred. "Coming over here uninvited; threatening me and shit."

"So that's how he broke his leg...I heard on the radio that he was involved in a traffic accident last night."

Jade scoffed at that. "Guess they put that out there to protect his street credibility. Timex is a straight up punk. Pussy whipped before getting the pussy. Some gangster."

Theresa chuckled. "Well I'm just happy that your friend turned up when he did. Things could have gotten sticky for you."

They chatted for awhile longer and Theresa laughed until her head hurt when Jade told her about her evening with Zachary.

After coming off the phone with Theresa, Jade looked up the number for Pizza Palace. Her stomach had started growling, reminding her that she hadn't eaten since this morning.

ଓଃଉଓଃଉଓଃଉ

"What's good my nigga?" Roscoe, Dunga's friend greeted him. He could have called any number of persons to come and get him but he didn't want anyone who had close ties in Jamaica to know his business. Roscoe was a budding rapper who Dunga had met a year ago at a studio in Flatbush. They had been cool ever since.

"I'm good man...just popping in real quick to get something sorted out," Dunga replied as he hopped in the pearl white Chevy Tahoe.

"This my new shit," Roscoe said as he put on a CD with six new songs that he had recently recorded. "DJ Moo played the first track on his radio show last night."

Dunga bopped his head to the music as they lit up the Van Wyck Expressway. Roscoe was definitely improving. His flow had gotten tighter and his lyrics more profound. Had stepped up his vocabulary as well. Seems like he had taken Dunga's advice and started reading some books.

They got to Canarsie and Dunga directed Roscoe to the block where Dahlia lived.

"I'll be back in a few minutes."

Dunga stepped out into the balmy spring night and checked his pocket to see if the key was there. It was. He looked up and down the block. No one was on the street. This was a relatively safe area. No drugs were sold on this block. At least not on the street.

He climbed the steps to Dahlia's two bedroom apartment and quietly let himself in.

He closed the door and shook his head in disgust as he stood there looking at Dahlia. She was sitting at the table with her head down. Dead to the world. An almost empty bottle of Grey Goose vodka was on the table next to her head. The living room smelled like a distillery.This was a blessing in disguise. At least there wouldn't be an ugly confrontation. After the stunt she had pulled today, God knows it wouldn't have been pretty. Dunga took out his phone and videoed her for a few minutes. With the phone still recording, he made his way to the spare bedroom.

"Shssssh...I've come for you baby," he whispered.

Samantha smiled sleepily. Daddy had come for her in her dream.

He lifted her up and retrieved her little bag. He took a last look at Dahlia and left the apartment.

He sat in the back seat with his still sleeping daughter and told Roscoe to take him to the New York Marriot hotel by the Brooklyn Bridge. It was now 3 in the morning. He was tired. And so was Samantha, who had yet to wake up since he lifted her out of the bed. Dahlia knocked out in a drunken stupor was a blessing in more ways than one. He could use the video as evidence that she was an unfit mother in a custody hearing if it came down to that. The child could have left the house without her knowing or if there was a break-in anything could have happened to Samantha. He kissed his daughter on her forehead. Supervised visits. That's the only way she would be seeing her daughter from this day forward.

Chapter 63

"Daddy!" Samantha jumped off the bed into his arms. She had just woken up. Dunga had been standing next to the bed checking messages on his phone.

"It wasn't a dream!" she said gleefully.

Dunga laughed. She was his heart. His little princess.

She looked around. "Where are we daddy?"

"At a hotel baby. Are you hungry?"

She nodded vigorously.

Dunga smiled. "Go and take a quick shower. I'm taking you to Ihop for breakfast."

"Yeah! Pancakes!" Samantha exclaimed as she ran off into the bathroom.

Dunga smiled as he rummaged through her bag and selected an outfit for her. His little princess was a true American. Her favourite breakfast in the world was pancakes and scrambled eggs with lots of cheese.

He looked at the time. It was 8:45. He had gotten up half an hour ago. His phone was roaming and he had missed several calls; one from Secret, one from Miss G and another from a number he didn't recognize. Dahlia hadn't called. That meant her drunken ass still wasn't up yet.

Samantha made quick work of her shower and hurried back in the room, almost tripping over the large towel that she had wrapped herself in.

She chatted nonstop as Dunga helped her to get dressed. She told him everything that happened since her mother had picked her up from school. Dunga's jawline tensed angrily when Samantha related how her mother had slapped and roughed her up.

"Don't worry about it sugar," Dunga told her. "Everything is ok now. Daddy won't let that happen again. Ok?"

Samantha smiled and kissed him. "I love you daddy."

Dunga's heart melted. "I love you too baby. So much."

☙❧☙❧☙❧

Dahlia finally opened her eyes at 9:30. She groaned as she tried to focus. Her head felt like it was split in two. Her mouth tasted like she had been eating jackfruit all night.

She felt like shit.

Looked even worse.

She got up from around the table with considerable effort.

Felt like a hundred years old.

She went into the bathroom and urinated for what seemed like an eternity.

Her head was still pounding.

The off-beat rhythm penetrating her skull mercilessly.

Samantha.

She was probably hungry.

Needed to go check on her.

She wiped and flushed the toilet.

Forgot to wash her hands.

Made her way to the guest bedroom.

The bed was empty.

She wasn't in the mood for games.

That little girl had better stop playing.

"Samantha? Samantha!" Her head was pounding relentlessly and her daughter wanted to play hide and seek. She looked under the bed and in the closet. Nothing. She went into her bedroom, looked everywhere. No sign of her.

"Samantha!" Dahlia was now screaming at the top of her lungs. She ripped away the shower curtain. Nothing. Kitchen was empty too.

"Oh God! What the fuck is this on me now? Jesus Christ!" She was getting scared. Had Samantha run away? But where could she have gone? She didn't know her way around. She had been living in Jamaica since she was two years old.

Dahlia searched the entire apartment again though she knew Samantha wasn't there. She held her head and sat on the floor in front of the bathroom. She tried to think. She couldn't call the cops. She would be in trouble. She had been intoxicated. Too intoxicated to keep an eye on her child. She would be arrested. They would take Samantha from her.

"Oh God! Why me?" She had to call Dunga. Wait. Dunga. He had a key to the apartment. Could he have been here last night? Kind of far fetched but not impossible. She prayed he had her. She had no idea what she would do if Samantha had run away and something bad had happened to her. She scrambled to her feet and looked around for her mobile. She found it in her pocketbook.

❧❧❧

Dunga and Samantha were taking a stroll in downtown Brooklyn when his mobile rang. Dahlia. *Your drunk ass finally realized that daughter is missing huh?* He mused coldly. He thought of letting her go through the entire day in mental anguish but in the end he answered the call.

"Yes?"

"Dunga! Don't fuck with me! Do you have Samantha?" Her voice was frantic, hoarse.

"Yes, I have my daughter." His voice was cold, controlled.

"Thank God!" She almost peed herself in relief. Then she flipped. "You fucking bastard! Making me wake up and not seeing her! Had me thinking the worse! You motherfucker!"

Dunga hung up in disgust. He needed to tell her a few things but he didn't want to talk in front of Samantha. His phone beeped incessantly. He ignored it. He would call her later tonight. When he was back in Jamaica. He couldn't wait to get back. He was going to pack up all of her stuff and send everything to her mother's. It was over. The curtains had come down on this act.

Seven years.

Seven was his lucky number.

It still was.

A new beginning.

Change was good.

As long as it was for the best.

Chapter 64

"Everything good?" Jimmy asked as Dunga, carrying a sleeping Samantha, entered the back of the vehicle.

"Yeah...just tired as hell," Dunga responded. It was 12:30 a.m. All that travelling in such a short space of time coupled with all the emotional drama had his eyes looking like he had smoked a large quantity of potent marijuana.

Dunga filled him in on what had taken place in New York as they headed to his apartment.

Jimmy shook his head in disbelief. Dahlia had always been a drama queen but she had really taken things to another level this time.

They got to the apartment and Jimmy helped him take everything inside.

"Alright, see you later," Dunga told him.

Jimmy left in Dunga's Yukon Denali. The CRV that he usually drove was parked at the studio.

Dunga put Samantha to bed and despite his fatigue, immediately started packing up Dahlia's clothes. He didn't stop until he had filled two large suitcases and four jumbo trash bags. By the time he finally went to bed it was 4:25 a.m. He fell asleep the moment his head touched the pillow.

ఌఌఌ

Jade was up early on Tuesday morning. She wanted to speak with the general manager of The Royal Marriot, an upscale all-inclusive resort in Ocho Rios. She had an idea to put on a big, one-night only jazz and R& B show on the first Sunday in June, which was a little over a month away. She had checked out several venues online and the sheer beauty of the resort had won her over. They would have it on the beach – the best stretch of white-sand beach on the North coast – and party with the stars, under the stars. Hopefully the general manager would agree to collaborate with her on this project. She didn't have a lot of time. She called his office at 9 a.m. His secretary informed her that he was in a meeting and wouldn't be free until 10. Jade left a message, advising the secretary that it was very important that he returned her call. Getting the venue would be the easy part – she was positive that she could get the hotel on board. The hard part would be getting the acts that she wanted to perform. The event would be billed:

The Royal Marriot, the Caribbean's most sophisticated resort, in association with La Roseda, the world's most sophisticated cognac for the diva in you, presents: The Ultimate Divas in Concert.

She wanted to get Diana Ross, Toni Braxton and Mariah Carey. That would be an irresistible line-up. It would be difficult to get them but not impossible. She sent Cohen an email telling him about the project. He knew important people around the world. If any one could make it happen, it would be him. She would need three good local acts to open the show. She would discuss that with Theresa; take some suggestions from her as she didn't know much about the local talent. The girl that Timex had done the song with came to mind. She had the look and the sound for a show like this. She was a possibility. Jade was so excited. It was an ambitious project but if she pulled it off, it would be a fabulous accomplishment.

CSEDCSEDCSED

Timex was in a sour mood. At least twelve weeks with a fucking cast on his leg. Shows would have to be cancelled; money would be lost. Good thing his bank account was healthy and he owned a couple of businesses. At least some money would be coming in while he waited for the leg to heal. He couldn't be out there promoting his new single which had taken off like a rocket. Despite being released just yesterday, it was already the most requested song on radio. Breeda had been fielding his many calls. So many people wanted to interview him about the single. His duet with Secret had taken everybody by surprise. He and Dunga finally working together had also raised everyone's eyebrows. When he first heard it on the radio yesterday, he had barked for Breeda to turn it off. The pain he was feeling in his leg had intensified when he heard the song. Knowing that it had been inspired by Jade had somehow intensified the pain in his leg.

He wasn't in the mood to talk to the media or anyone else for that matter. Everyone in his inner circle was staying away from him, except for Leah, Breeda and his road manager.

Breeda had hired a full time helper for the next three months. The domestic helper, a timid young woman from the country, who had gotten the job because she was the cousin of Breeda's brother's girlfriend, had the task of cooking for Timex, changing his bed linen and pretty much be on call to get him whatever he needed. The apartment had come with a small helper's quarters so she stayed there as well. Leah didn't like her. The girl, Doreen, looked like a typical country girl: natural hair, large breasts, wide-childbearing hips, thick thighs and strong legs. She was very shy and quiet but Leah didn't trust her. As they say, still waters run deep. She was sure Timex would be fucking her soon. Breeda had already started.

"What is all of this? What is going on Dunga? Dahlia called me dis mawnin very hysterical," Marjorie, Dahlia's mother said, when Dunga, making three trips to the vehicle, placed Dahlia's things inside one of the bedrooms.

"Your daughter is a crazy woman and I don't deal with crazy people. I don't run an asylum." Dunga was all business as he packed up everything there that belonged to Samantha. She would no longer be staying with *this* grandmother.

"Lawd 'ave mercy! Dunga yuh caa just bruck up wid Dahlia just like dat because she mek one mistake."

"I don't know or care what she told you but I know what *I* need to do."

She trailed behind Dunga as he took Samantha's stuff to the car.

"So yuh just going to take away Samantha from here because yuh an' Dahlia inna problems? Dat not fair Dunga! After everyt'ing weh mi do fi di likkle girl?"

Dunga placed the bags on the back seat next to Samantha and turned to face her.

"I gave you a lot of money every month to facilitate your granddaughter staying here most of the time. So don't act like it was a favour you did out of the goodness of your heart."

Marjorie seethed silently. She was going to miss the fifteen thousand dollars that Dunga gave her every month. Samantha's expenses rarely went over five thousand and the extra money used to come in very handy. Though Dahlia sent money to her monthly as well, Rex, the man she was seeing who was twenty years her junior, was unemployed and always needed money.

"Hi grandma," Samantha said with a wave.

"Hi chile. Yuh not telling yuh daddy that yuh want to stay with your grandma. Eeh?

Samantha smiled but did not respond. She was happy to be going to stay with her other grandmother. She didn't like the big, ugly man who came here all the time. He and grandma would go into her room and stay there for a long time, during which grandma would make all sorts of scary noises.

"Leave her alone," Dunga said. "Your grandchild is not a pawn. Take care of yourself, whenever Samantha wants to see you I'll arrange it."

Marjorie would never go to Miss G's home to visit Samantha. Marjorie hated Miss G. Said Miss G acted like she was better than her.

With that Dunga drove off, leaving Marjorie to ponder what had really happened between him and her daughter to cause such swift and decisive action on his part.

The general manager for The Royal Marriot had returned Jade's call. The conversation had gone well. She would be going down to Ocho Rios tomorrow to meet with him and to have a first hand look at the proposed venue. She had emailed Mr. Hassan the proposal and he had given her the greenlight to go ahead. She just needed to move quickly and provide a budget to the accounts department by Friday. Jade had advised the secretary to book her and her driver a room at Sunset Sands Resort. Though it was located just a mile from The Royal Marriot, the difference in the quality of the hotels was as glaring as the difference between a Mercedes and a Suzuki Swift. She only had one reason for staying at Sunset Sands.

Maxine worked there.

That's where her gift shop was located.

At least that's what she had claimed.

Her so-called friend that had played her for a fool.

Befriended her and lied to her.

Left her hanging when she arrived in Jamaica.

She just wanted to know why.

"Hi grandma!" Samantha gushed as she jumped into Miss G's arms. She hadn't seen her in over three weeks.

"Hello my baby!" Miss G said as she playfully kissed Samantha all over her face. She loved her granddaughter to death and was happy that she would be staying with her and not that loose woman who didn't act her age. When the decision had been made that Samantha would live and go to school in Jamaica as opposed to America, Dahlia had quickly chosen her mother for Samantha to stay with. She had been disappointed but didn't want to cause a fuss so she had settled for Samantha spending the occasional weekend.

Dunga removed Samantha's bags from the vehicle and took them inside.

Secret was inside the living room watching T.V. Dunga placed the bags inside Samantha's room and came back and hugged and kissed her.

"You ok baby?" Secret asked, her big brown eyes filled with love and concern. She had been so worried about his trip to New York last night. She knew that when it came to domestic squabbles, Uncle Sam always favoured the woman. And with Dahlia being the evil, vindictive bitch that she was, Secret had feared that Dunga would have gotten in trouble.

"It is now." He smiled and let her go. "There's someone I want you to meet."

Samantha had been watching her daddy and the pretty woman from her vantage point in Miss G's arms.

"Come here baby," Dunga said and Miss G put her down so she could go over to her father.

"Sweetheart, this is Secret, she's a very good friend of mine. Secret, meet my princess Samantha."

Secret stooped down and smiled.

"Hi pretty girl," she said. "It's so nice to finally meet you."

"Hi, what kind of name is Secret?" Samantha asked.

The adults laughed.

"Well I'm a singer and that's my name," Secret replied sweetly.

"You're a singer? Your songs play on the radio? You have videos?"

Secret chuckled. This little girl was something else. "Yes my songs are on the radio and I will be shooting my first video soon."

Samantha nodded in approval. "Well I want to come to your video shoot."

"You'll have to ask your dad about that one sweetie," Secret replied, looking at Dunga.

"Can I daddy? Please?" Samantha begged.

"If it's not during your school time or past your bedtime you can go," Dunga promised.

Samantha gave him a look that said she knew that she was being outsmarted.

"You're pretty," Samantha told her. "I want to hear your songs."

Secret smiled. Samantha was a handful but at least she seemed to like her.

"Sure, come on." Secret took her by hand led her to her room.

Miss G shook her head and laughed. Samantha was much happier and more her precocious self when she was around this side of the family. She was much more reserved when around her cantankerous mother and other grandmother. They could hear Secret's melodic voice bumping from the CD player in her room.

"So what happened in New York?" she asked her son.

They went into her bedroom to talk.

Later that evening, after a delicious dinner and a couple of drinks, Dunga went for a walk. He called Dahlia as he headed down the quiet street. She answered on the second ring. She was crying.

"Dunga...I can't believe you moved out my clothes...I'm sorry for the incident at your moms...I wasn't thinking straight...I was angry baby...don't do this...you can't leave me...seven years... I lo–"

"Its over," Dunga interjected bluntly. "You can't make me happy anymore. You're a bad mother. You don't think. You're unstable. You don't have a good heart. Yo–"

"Fuck you!" Dahlia screamed, cutting him off in mid-sentence. "I used to be good enough for you now all of a sudden

I'm the worst thing that ever happened to you! Fuck you! And fuck that bitch! I'm going to press charges against you for kidnapping my child. You motherfucker! I hate you!"

"I have a video of you sitting at the table, drunk and dead to the world," Dunga told her calmly. "No judge in their right mind would grant you custody. The only way you'll ever see Samantha again is by supervised visits. You're unfit to be a mother. I don't even think you really love her. And if you can't love that sweet little girl then there is no love in your heart. When you come back to Jamaica do not come anywhere near my apartment or any of my businesses. You may call me and we arrange for you to spend some time with Samantha – supervised of course – as I said earlier. Throughout this entire ordeal, I have yet to deal with you like you deserve to be dealt with even though you have attacked and disrespected my mother in her own home, and mistreated our child. Behave your fucking self and leave me alone. Or you're going to be really sorry. You know how I get down. Don't push me any harder."

Dahlia didn't even hear the click. All she could hear was a cachophany of voices.

Its over! You're a bad mother! You don't make me happy anymore! You don't love your daughter! You attacked my mother! You're unstable! Its over! Its over! Its over!

Dahlia threw the phone into the wall but the voices wouldn't stop. They were relentless. She released a gut-wrenching continuous scream that made her neighbour, a fifty year old widow who was getting ready to have a snack, drop her glass of milk in fright. She called 911.

Chapter 65

The two patrolmen, an Italian-American who had followed in his dad's footsteps and became a cop, and an African-American rookie who had only been on the force for two weeks, could hear the chilling screams as they quickly exited their vehicle.

"Jesus Christ! Sounds like somebody is being raped or beaten!" The Italian-American commented as they headed up the stairs to the apartment with their guns drawn. The African-American, his heart pounding so loudly it was almost drowning out the hair-raising screams coming from the apartment, glimpsed the worried face of the woman next door at Apartment 2C, peeking out of her living room window. He wondered what the hell was going on in the apartment. It was his first time responding to a call. His palms were sweaty as he gripped the handgun tightly. He prayed his training wouldn't let him down.

"Mmmmm...that feels good baby...damn..." Dunga was in bed lying on his stomach as Secret gave him a massage. He could feel all the stress and tension seeping out of his pores. Her hands were magical. He could have fallen asleep like this if it wasn't for his turgid erection piercing a hole in the mattress. "You missed your calling baby...mmmm..."

"Are you trying to say that I'm a better masseuse than singer?" She ran her tongue along the middle of his back.

"N-n-no baby...mmmm...you do everything well..."

She nibbled on his ear lobe as she kneaded his shoulders. "Everything?"

"*Everything*...especially this..."

Dunga turned over and his raging manhood pointed tremblingly at the ceiling.

"You mean this?" She lowered her head and took him inside her mouth.

"Oh shit...ohhh....yessss...baby..."

Secret's head bobbed as she increased her tempo and pursed her lips, sucking him in like a hoover. She tasted a bit of pre-cum and went for the prize. She massaged his tingling scrotum and concentrated on the bulbous head, driving Dunga crazy as she tried to push her tongue in the slit.

"Oh. My. Fucking. God." Dunga's body tightened as she coaxed his hot semen to the surface. He ejaculated with a torrent. Secret swallowed every drop. They both moaned as she licked his trembling shaft clean.

ᴕᴕᴕ

"Police! Open up! Police!" the Italian-American shouted as he gestured for his partner to cover him. There was no response.

The screams continued unabated. The voice was getting hoarse. He wondered if the person was going to scream until her vocal cords were completely destroyed.

He tried the door.

It was locked.

He had to get in.

He stepped back and pumped three shots into the lock.

He then rammed the door with his shoulder.

It gave way.

"Police! Freeze!" he shouted, adrenaline pumping like he was on acid, as he entered the room and assumed a shooting stance. His partner was to his left.

He beckoned to his partner to check the rest of the apartment. He holstered his firearm and went over to the young woman who was stooped down by the wall in the passage screaming her ass off as she held her hands to her ears.

"Miss...Miss...what's wrong Ma'am?" he asked as he got down on one knee in front of her.

She reeked of alcohol.

And sweat.

Her breath was fetid.

Her screams were deafening this close.

He tried to shake her out of it.

Her eyes were vacant as she looked at him.

She finally stopped screaming.

"Make them stop!" she begged, holding on to his shirt.

"Make who stop?" The officer was confused.

His partner returned to the living room; relieved that there wasn't going to be a confrontation. "Empty."

"Make them shut up...please. I can't take it anymore!"

"Call an ambulance," the Italian-American said to his partner.

The woman was obviously going through a nervous breakdown or something. Either way there was nothing he could do for her. By the time the ambulance arrived ten minutes later, she had begun screaming again.

Chapter 66

Jade, having departed Kingston at 7:15 a.m., arrived in Ocho Rios at 9:30. Nathan had told her about Faith's Pen, the popular rest stop, and they had stopped there for breakfast. Jade had feasted on ackee and salt fish with roast breadfruit while Nathan had consumed an enormous breakfast of callaloo, stew chicken, boiled dumplings and boiled green bananas. By the time she arrived at The Royal Marriot, she was a few minutes early for her 10 a.m. meeting with the general manager.

The secretary, who was polite but rather frosty, told her to have a seat. Jade leafed through a Time magazine article about Barack Obama until it was time for the meeting. She could feel the secretary's eyes on her the entire time. She pretended not to notice.

"Mr. Brodber will see you now," the secretary announced at precisely 10 a.m. "Third door on the right."

Jade murmured her thanks and headed to Mr. Brodber's office. She knocked once and went in.

He stood up to greet her, unable to hide the look of astonishment that had taken over his bearded face. Clearly he hadn't expected her to be this young and beautiful.

"A pleasure to me-me-meet you Miss Jones," he managed, his hand outstretched. He had huge hands, reminded Jade of Zachary's. She wondered if he suffered the same fate down below.

"Good morning Mr. Brodber, thank you."

She shook his hand firmly and quickly before sitting down.

They then got down to business, Jade tactfully steering the conversation back to the matter at hand whenever he tried to get personal. They then took a walk out to the beach to look at the venue. Jade was blown away. The pictures on the resort's website did not do the beach justice. It was beautiful. The water was sky blue and the sand was whiter than granulated sugar. Breathtaking. This was the spot for her show. No doubt about that. The ambiance alone would be worth half the price of admission. They discussed the best place to set up the stage and bars. Brodber had a hard time staying focused on business. He had seen a billboard with her in the town center but he hadn't realized it was the same person whom he had spoken to on the phone and besides, she was even more breathtaking in person. She looked like a super sexy business executive in her beige Escada pants suit but he knew what she looked like in a bikini. It was fucking with his head. Big time.

They then went back to the office to finalize the details of the joint venture. Jade got the better of the negotiations. Her company would control the gate while the Resort would control the bar. La Roseda would be complimentary but all other beverages would be for sale. They would both be billed as the promoters of the event. The venue would be rented to Hassan & Cohen LLC at a much lower price than the going rate.

Jade promised to get back to him by Friday with a confirmation of the acts that would be performing so that they could get the promotions underway. Time was of the essence. She declined his invitation for lunch citing another appointment. He walked her out, apparently milking every drop of her visit. She shook his hand goodbye and entered the the back of the Audi Q7. Nathan pulled off and Jade observed Brodber still standing there looking at the departing vehicle.

She didn't like him.

But it didn't matter.

Nothing was going to stand in her way of getting this show done.

She told Nathan to take her to the Sunset Sands Resort.

Time to pay her old friend Maxine a visit.

❧❧❧

Dahlia was silent on the ride home. The ambulance had taken her to Kings County Hospital where they had treated her for severe trauma and kept her overnight for observation. Her friend, Amoy, had come to pick her up.

"You hungry D?" Amoy looked over at her. She had never seen her friend looking like this. Dahlia wouldn't even go to the neighbourhood grocery store without make-up and getting all dressed up. She looked a hot mess. Amoy still didn't know the whole story except that Dahlia had freaked out last night, screaming so badly her neighbours had called the cops. She got that information from her friend who worked there as a receptionist. Dahlia wasn't saying much. Matter of fact Dahlia wasn't saying anything at all. She had given Amoy's number to the nurse when she had asked for a next of kin.

Dahlia shook her head. She hadn't eaten in twenty four hours except for whatever fluids she had gotten through an intravenous drip.

Amoy was worried about her. She looked sick. She looked like she had aged ten years since she last saw her three days ago. Good thing she was off from work today. She would spend some time with Dahlia; make her some soup or something. And try to find out what the hell was going on.

"Yes, how can I help you?" the security guard at the gate asked politely.

"Going by the gift shop," Jade announced after rolling down the back window.

The man's eyes brightened in recognition. "Jesus Christ! It's you! Can yuh sign something for me?"

With that he hurried back inside the security post and retrieved a poster of Jade advertising La Roseda.

Jade smiled and graciously signed it, making it out to Wilbert, as instructed by the guard. Jade thought it was a rather old-fashioned name for such a young man. He thanked her profusely and gave her directions to the gift shop. A hundred and twenty meters and one left turn later, Nathan parked in one of the empty slots in front of the gift shop. Jade exited the vehicle and made her way up the stairs. There were a few shoppers in the store, most of them caucasion tourists. Jade stood by the door momentarily, looking around.

A young lady, dressed in a yellow polo shirt which read *Sunset Sands Gift Shop* above the left breast, and tight blue jeans, came over and asked if she needed any assistance. Jade told her that she was here to see Maxine, the owner.

A look of consternation came over the young lady's face. "The owner is Miss Chung...a Maxine works here but she's just a *clerk* like me. Sure you're at the right place?"

Jade described the Maxine she was looking for.

It was obvious that the girl didn't like Maxine very much.

"That sounds like the Maxine that works here but she's *not* the owner. She just went out for lunch." The girl looked beyond Jade through the glass door. "Oh here she is, looks like she forgot something."

Jade turned her head as Maxine came through the door.

Their eyes met.

Maxine's widened in recognition and shock.

Jade smiled.

Maxine wanted to disappear.

ᘓᘒᘓᘒᘓᘒ

"Dunga left me. For some singer bitch that he's producing. Last few days were very stressful. I feel like I'm going crazy. He took my daughter. Said I can't see her without *supervision*. I keep hearing voices in my head. Taunting me. It was so bad last night I couldn't stop screaming."

Amoy had to strain to hear what Dahlia was saying. Her voice was gone. She could barely speak. So that's what this was all about. That was fucked up, especially the part about Samantha. Could Dunga do that? Hell no. That shit could not be legal.

"He can't tell you that you can't see your daughter just because y'all not together no more! Fuck that!" Amoy said.

Dahlia was silent. Amoy didn't know the full story and it hurt too much to talk. Her head was pounding. She had some of the soup Amoy prepared but she still felt sick to her stomach. She had absolutely no appetite. No energy. No nothing. She was hurting mentally and physically. Life was fucked up. One minute you're on top of the world, happy, having everything that you want and in the blink of an eye, it was gone, like it had all been an illusion.

It was painful.

Intolerably so.

She needed to get rid of the pain.

But how?

ଓଃଓଃଓଃ

"Hello Maxine," Jade said sweetly though her eyes were as cold as the Arctic Circle – before global warming.

"Hello Jade," she answered slowly and reluctantly. She had been halfway to the hotel canteen when she realized she had left her purse at the shop. Jade had been the last person on earth that she had expected to see. Stacey, her co-worker, was hovering, being nosy. The last thing she needed was to have them all up in her business. She told Jade to give her a second and she brusquely passed Stacey and went around the back through a door that said *Employees Only* to retrieve her purse.

The girl, Stacey, whom Jade had been speaking to, had not moved. She was very curious about the pretty woman who looked very familiar though she couldn't quite place where she saw her before; and her conncetion with Maxine, who had looked like she had seen a ghost when she saw her visitor. Why did the woman think that Maxine was the owner of the store? It wouldn't surprise Stacey if Maxine had told her so. Maxine invented lying. If one was to look up the meaning of liar in the dictionary, a picture of Maxine would be displayed there. No other meaning necessary. Ever since she had started working there three months ago, she had caused so many problems and everyone knew that the only reason she hadn't been fired yet was because she was the niece of Mrs. Chung's husband.

"So you guys are friends?" Stacey enquired.

Jade didn't get a chance to respond.

Maxine returned and took Jade by the arm.

"Let's talk while I have lunch." Jade nodded and followed her out of the store.

They walked silently towards the staff canteen which was a floor down. Guests were not allowed there but the security guard at the entrance didn't say anything to Jade.

She looked at Maxine critically as she ordered her lunch. Jade was hungry but she didn't want to eat here. Maxine looked the same but something was different. Her demeanour. She didn't portray the same level of confidence and poise as she did at the immigration detention center.

Maxine got her food and they went over to a corner table as far away from other people as possible.

She toyed with her food as Jade looked at her. She had a hard time meeting Jade's eyes.

"Just tell me why."

Maxine sighed and glanced at her before looking back down on her curry goat and white rice.

"Almost everything I told you was a lie Jade. My family is not rich. I was at the center because I went to America on a school and work program and ran away. They caught up with me after 6 months and deported me. I never went to jail. As you can see the store exists but I'm just an ordinary employee there. My uncle's wife owns the store and he begged her to give me a job when I returned home."

Jade was stoic.

And silent.

Maxine continued. "It was messed up building up your hopes like that knowing that I couldn't do anything to help you when you came to Jamaica. I really shouldn't have taken it that far but one lie led to another and before I knew it I was offering to help you and stuff."

"Your diction...your knowledge...you're so well-spoken..."

"I read a lot...that's all I do with my spare time and I learned how to speak so well over the years by practice. I've always had this vision of who I wanted to be and how I wanted others to perceive me...so I had to act and sound the part."

She looked up at Jade. "I'm really sorry."

Jade didn't respond.

She was ready to go.

Maxine was a con-artist.

A compulsive liar.

And God knows whatever else.

Jade rose and looked at her with disdain. "And I'm sorry for you. That's a really sick way to live your life. Get help."

Maxine watched Jade walk away until she was out of sight.

She didn't look back.

Not even once.

Later that night, Jade was home relaxing - she had changed her mind about staying overnight in Ocho Rios - with a glass of La Roseda and watching *Queens of Comedy* on DVD, when Cohen called. He sounded tired. He was in Kortrijik, a city in Belgium. He told her he had gotten her email and that it was a marvelous idea. He would do everything in his power to get the acts she wanted. He had already sent two emails out to people who could get him in touch with the direct handlers of Mariah Carey and Toni Braxton; and he would make some calls regarding Diana Ross tomorrow. He told her that he would get back to her on it by Thursday evening. He brushed aside her concerns that Mr. Hassan might not approve the budget if it proved to be too expensive to get all three. He told her that money was no object and they would make a great deal of money from the show as he was sure that it would be the first time that those three superstars would perform on the same show. He asserted that even if they didn't break even, the publicity from such an event would further help to cement La Roseda as the premium drink for women. He praised her for her skilful negotiating with the general manager at the resort. Jade felt very good after their conversation. Cohen had her back. He genuinely respected her abilities and wanted her to do well. So did Mr. Hassan to be fair. It went against conventional wisdom to mix business with pleasure but so far Jade had no complaints. She laughed as Mo'Nique launched into her diatribe about skinny women.

Chapter 67

Secret told Jimmy to take her straight to the studio after her appointment at the French embassy. She had gotten the visa. One down two to go. Tomorrow she had appointments at the Dutch and Italian embassies. She was itching to get inside the booth. There were two songs bubbling in her head that she wanted to get out. They were inspired by the whole drama with Dahlia as well as the fact that she was now the queen of Dunga's heart. The single with Timex was heating up the streets. She had heard it at least five times since this morning: twice in vehicles passing by and several times on the radio. Dunga wanted to shoot the video as soon as possible but Timex had yet to return his calls. Dunga wanted to incorporate Timex's broken leg in the video. The concept would center on his girl dropping everything and staying home to take care of her man. That would be the perfect visual representation of the song. Dunga had decided that if Timex didn't return his call by Thursday evening, he would shoot a video over the weekend protraying Timex as having passed away and his girl was reminiscing by looking at pictures of Timex and excerpts from his performances. Either way, he was shooting the video this weekend. The director was ready to go and the casting for the extras would be on Thursday. Dunga was having a session with a group that had just recently won a national singing competition so Secret went into his office and logged into Myspace until the recording booth was free.

❧❧❧

"Dad is not getting a state funeral," Peter told Penelope as they had lunch at The Patio. He had dragged Penelope out of the house. She had not left the house since they arrived in Jamaica. A couple of her old girlfriends that she went to high school with had tried several times, unsuccessfully, to get her to leave the house and try to have some fun.

The Permanent Secretary in the Ministry of Mining, Energy and Environment, had called Peter to personally advise him. Usually, a prominent politician such as Weatherburn would have been given a State funeral, but due to the circumstances surrounding his death, the government had decided against it. Peter had simply said ok and hung up the phone. It didn't matter to him one way or another. He had told his uncle, who was dealing with everything that he wanted the funeral to be held as soon as possible so that they could begin to get some closure. His parents would be buried beside each other at the family plot in Smokeyvale.

"I didn't expect them to," Penelope said sadly. "The government is embarrassed by the whole thing...I bet that the Prime Minister won't even come to the funeral."

"Yeah you're probably right. I don't give a shit though. I just want this over with. I told Uncle Raymond that next week Saturday would be a good date."

Penelope nodded in agreement. They needed to begin to heal and that could not happen until their parents were buried. Several of their relatives, from both sides of the family, and some that they hadn't seen in years, would be coming down to Jamaica from various locations abroad for the funeral. Penelope was not looking forward to that.

☙❧☙❧☙❧

It was raining cats and dogs, and a few pigs, in New York City. Dahlia was home alone; if you didn't count the many voices that had been conversing with ever since she had woken up from a restless, nightmare-riddled sleep. Her eyes were bloodshot red. Her body was extremely weak. Her head still pounded. Her voice was still cracked. It hurt to talk. She was in bad shape. Mentally and physically. She still wasn't answering her phone. She had missed countless calls. Her mother. Tisha, her cousin in Jamaica. Her friends. The girl who managed her store. She hadn't spoken to anyone since Amoy left her home yesterday. Said she would come back this evening after work. Whatever. It didn't matter to her either way. With considerable effort, she sat up in bed and looked out the window. It was like looking inside her soul. Gray, cold and bleak. The voices in her head were telling her bad things.

Fuck this shit! You have nothing to live for! You're a loser! Might as well call it a day! Aren't you tired of the pain? Do something about it! Coward! You can't do anything right!

She wanted them to stop. Would do anything to make them stop. She was tired of hearing the bad things they kept on saying to her, about her. She was tired of the recurring migraine. She was tired of being tired. She had no energy. The life had been sucked out of her. Might as well listen to the voices and do something about it. She summoned all of her strength and made her way unsteadily to the bathroom.

"Oh my God!" Theresa exclaimed. "That's a wicked line-up Jade. Brilliant!"

Theresa had dropped by Jade's home after she left the salon. Knowing Jade would rather die than cook, she had bought them dinner: oxtail and beans, fried chicken and rice and peas. They were in the living room on the couch, glancing at the T.V. as they talked and ate. It was on the history channel; they were doing a special on the Aztec civilization.

"Yeah...hopefully it will go down just as I plan."

Jade sipped her fruit punch and glanced out the window. It was drizzling. By the time she got up and took both of their plates to the kitchen, the rain had come down heavily. Theresa was not in the living room when Jade returned after doing the dishes.

She could hear the shower running. Jade poured two glasses of La Roseda and reclaimed her spot on the couch. She turned the volume up the T.V. The rain was falling so hard she could hardly hear anything. Theresa didn't stay long in the bathroom. She returned clad in a towel and smelling of one of Jade's many perfumes.

"I bought something today," she announced, wearing a cheeky smile.

"Ok...what?"

Her eyes were devilish as she took up the glass and had a sip.

She didn't answer. Still smiling, she went over to a plain black shopping bag and extracted a strap-on.

Jade erupted in laughter.

"You freak!"

Theresa laughed and dropping the towel, she tried it on.

Jade stopped laughing as she looked at Theresa's slightly wet body adorned with the strap-on. It was thick, black and veiny. Almost looked real. It was about eight and a half inches long.

Jade's breathing became shallow.

This would bring a whole different dimension to their lovemaking.

She wondered if their second time could be just as intense as the first.

Only one way to find out.

"Put a condom on it and take it off. I'm going to fuck you with it until you speak in tongues."

Theresa's kness wobbled as she quickly did as Jade instructed.

Jade rose and shrugged off her T-shirt.

Her red g-string followed.

The rain continued to fall ferociously.

Theresa walked over to Jade and handed her the strap-on.

It was sheathed with a red durex condom.

Theresa was willing to bet that the weather outside was no competition for what was happening between her legs.

She was so wet that her juices were trickling down her thighs.

Jade liked the feel of the strap-on.

It was resting right on her protruding clit.

She could just imagine how the friction would feel when she started to fuck Theresa.

She stopped imagining.

She started doing.

Theresa started moaning.

Then groaning.

Then screaming.

Then climaxing.

Again. And again. And again.

ઉઝઉઝઉઝ

"Lord Jesus Christ! Fuck! Dahlia!" Amoy was in panic mode. Dahlia was on the bathroom floor unconscious. Beside her lay a bottle of sleeping pills. It was empty.

Amoy checked Dahlia's pulse as she quickly dialed 911. Her breathing was erratic but at least she was alive. When Amoy had left Dahlia last night, she had taken a spare key. Good thing she had, as Dahlia had not answered her phone all day and she would not have been able to get inside the house. The ambulance arrived in six minutes and for the second time in seventy two hours; Dahlia was being rushed to the hospital.

Amoy thought about the situation as she drove to the hospital. Dahlia could not continue like this.

She would die.

Amoy sighed.

Love.

Love was bullshit.

Love made people crazy. She had recently read on the website of a major Jamaican newspaper about the wife who had committed suicide after killing her husband and her best friend after she discovered that they were having an affair. Last month a man in the Bronx had killed his two children and his wife after she told him she was getting a divorce. Now Dahlia was trying to kill herself because her man had left her for another woman. Yeah seven years was a long time to be with somebody and for them to just up and leave you like that, it had to hurt. But life goes on. Dahlia has to get herself together before it's too late. She arrived at the hospital and parked inside the parking lot. An ambulance, sirens screaming, pulled up at the emergency entrance and two medics quickly rushed a young black male inside. His white sweater was now crimson. He had clearly lost a lot of blood. Probably a gun shot victim. Amoy sighed and looked away as she made her way towards the main entrance. Seeing the young man had taken her back to three years ago when her little brother had been shot by a guy who wanted his chain and sneakers. He had died during surgery. She prayed that once they pumped the pills out of Dahlia's stomach she would be ok.

ઌઌઌ

Theresa grimaced as she undressed. She was sore. Jade had put a hurting on her with that big, black strap-on. She could have never imagined that a dildo could have given her so much pleasure. Strapped around Jade's tiny waist, the dildo had felt like a real dick. Jade had fucked her so *good*. She must have been a man in her former life. Theresa chuckled at the thought. It was now 1 a.m. She set her alarm to wake her at 6 a.m. An important client, the head of a successful remittance service, would be coming in at 7:15. She went under the covers nude and was soon in slumber land. She dreamt that she was on a deserted island with Jade and Gerald, her ex boyfriend.

Chapter 68

The weekend was upon Jade and it was a busy one. Cohen had indeed come through for her. He had called her on Friday morning to give her the good news. It had come at a gigantic cost but he told her not to worry about that. Just put together a fabulous production. She had immediately called the general manager at the resort to let him know that it was a go. He quickly emailed her the logo for the hotel to put on the flyer. Jade had then met with the grapic designer for the company and they designed the flyer together, using pictures of Diana Ross, Toni Braxton and Mariah Carey that they got off the internet. Theresa had given her some suggestions regarding which local acts she could use to open the show and she had spent most of Friday getting in touch with the different managers and working out a deal. The flyers, designed like a bottle of La Roseda, were hot. It would be very expensive to print but this was a high profile event, no expense could be spared. Jade organized for billboards to be put up at strategic points in Kington, Montego Bay and Ocho Rios over the course of the weekend. She was now at an advertising agency trying to put together a quick commercial. She needed it to start airing on Monday.

ଔଔଔ

Dunga was pleased the way the shoot was going. They had started on time and things were flowing smoothly. Timex had not returned his call so he had decided to go ahead and shoot the video without him. He watched as the make-up artist touched up Secret for the next scene. Secret winked at him. She was having fun. Her first video shoot. Dunga had spared no expense. He wanted it to be a high quality video that could be aired anywhere. The director was the best in Jamaica, having worked alongside one of the most celebrated video directors in America. Secret had gotten her Dutch and Italian visas. She would be leaving for France this coming Friday. The first show was on Monday so she would only have two days to rehearse with Ras Che and his band. Dunga had told her that he wasn't sure if he would be accompanying her but he was. He had gone to pick up the last of the three visas today. It would be a great trip. He was definitely looking forward to it.

ଔଔଔ

Dahlia was released from the hospital on Saturday afternoon. They had kept her for three days for treatment and observation. Amoy looked at her as they drove to Dahlia's home.

"D...you have to get it together. You have so much to live for...you have a successful business, a child, people that love you....you're still an attractive woman...why would you want to kill yourself?"

Dahlia didn't respond right away. Irrationally, she was a bit upset at Amoy for saving her life. She had felt so peaceful when she was losing consciousness. Nothing had mattered at that time. She had just felt serene and peaceful. The voices had ceased, the pain had seeped away. Now the pain was back. And she was sure the voices would be returning soon as well. Why did Amoy have to interfere? It was her life. And she was tired of living it.

"I'm lost Amoy...too lost to find myself. I'm just tired. Tired of living." Her voice was still hoarse but Amoy could hear the note of finality in her tone.

Amoy lost it.

"Dahlia what the fuck is wrong with you? Relationships end everyday! You think you're the first woman to lose her man? You need to wake the fuck up and get it together! I'm your friend and I love you but I can't just sit here and condone this bullshit. You're being selfish and immature. Your daughter is going to be a motherless child just because you can't get over losing your man. Does that make any sense to you?"

Dahlia seethed but she didn't respond. What could she say? Amoy was right. But Amoy didn't understand how she was *feeling*, the things that were going on in her head. She didn't understand it her damn self. She was in a fog that just refused to dissapate. It was draining her energy, her substance, her essence, her zest for life.

They arrived at Dahlia's apartment and Amoy placed the vehicle in park.

She turned around and looked at Dahlia.

"Look D...I've done all I can. Took off time from work, tried to make sure that you're ok but I can't continue on this crazy emotional roller coaster. I can't help you if you don't want it. If you're determined to kill yourself there's nothing me or anyone else can do. I love you and if you need me I'm just a phone call away."

Dahlia looked at Amoy and started crying. She felt bad for putting her friend through all of this.

"I need help Amoy. I can't do this by myself!" she sobbed.

Amoy reached over and hugged her.

"Don't worry D...we'll do this together. I'll call a psychiatrist and set up an appointment. Whatever it takes to get you back to normal."

"Th-th-thanks and I'm sorry," Dahlia sniffed. "I just feel so *stressed*...so torn apart inside..."

"It's ok D...I understand that its not easy. You want me to stay with you?"

Dahlia nodded.

They then exited the vehicle and went inside the apartment. Amoy sighed in relief. Finally they were getting somewhere. Maybe, just maybe, Dahlia would eventually be alright.

❧❧❧

The following week began with a bang for Secret. Her duet with Timex was number one on the local dancehall charts and her single, *Lust*, was number one on the roots reggae charts. And last, but not least, her collaboration with Ras Che was number three on the French reggae charts. She screamed when Dunga called her with the news. It was really happening. After all the hard work and disappointments of situations not working out because she had refused to sleep with producers to get ahead, she was now on her way to becoming a star. Nothing happened before its time, and now was definitely her time. She owed everything to Dunga. Her career and her happiness all rested in his capable hands. She loved him so much. It was real. She was only nineteen years old and already had found the love of her life. It just didn't get much better than that.

ＣＳＥＯＣＳＥＯＣＳＥＯ

Dunga had expected Secret to make a splash - she was too talented not to - but things were moving at a faster pace than even he had anticipated. And this was only the beginning. He was already receiving calls for interviews and from promoters who wanted to add Secret to the line-up of their upcoming shows. He was taking it slow though. He didn't want her performing on too many local shows. He wanted her to have that aura of exclusivity. He would only allow her to appear on the biggest show of the summer. The work on her album was going well; they had already completed six tracks. He didn't want a lengthy album. Something short, sweet and full of substance. Ten tracks with two bonus tracks should do the trick. He would do a remix of *Lust* with his rapper friend from New York and another more established big name rapper. He would decide who when the time was right. He would make that be one of the bonus tracks as well as release it as a single in the US. He was very excited about Secret's project. A Grammy nomination was not a far-fetched scenario. He wouldn't say that to her though. If it happened it happened.

All they could do was put out the best album possible. The rest would take care of itself.

ᏣᏕᏍᏣᏕᏍᏣᏕᏍ

On Tuesday evening, Jade had been at home doing some work and watching the local channels to ensure that the commercials she had paid for were running during the programs they were supposed to, when she received a call from the marketing manager of a popular local cable network. They wanted to know if Jade would be interested in hosting a weekly half hour show that dealt with fashion and entertainment. She was open to discussing it with them and a meeting was set for Friday at 10 a.m. As long as it wouldn't interfere with her work for Hassan and Cohen LLC, it would be a good opportunity to further cement her name in the eyes of the public. One of the commercials for her jazz and R&B show came on the T.V. during the first break in the 7 O' clock news. The venue was being set up to accommodate 3000 people and she was only printing 2500 tickets to go on sale. The remainder of the patrons would be media personal and certain VIPs who would receive complimentary passes. The tickets would go on sale in two weeks and none would be sold at the venue on the day of the event. Her mobile rang. She checked the caller ID. It was Zachary. Smiling, she answered the call. She hadn't spoken to him since the day she had gone to his apartment.

ᏣᏕᏍᏣᏕᏍᏣᏕᏍ

"Yo it bad!" Jimmy said giving Dunga an enthusiastic pound. They had just finished watching the world premiere of the video for Secret's duet with Timex. The director had done an excellent job of bringing Dunga's concept to life.

He was there along with Secret, Jimmy, Dunga and one of the studio engimeers that worked with Dunga from time to time. Jimmy popped a bottle of champagne and they toasted to Secret's impending success. Dunga's mobile rang. It was Timex. He didn't answer the call. Timex called back three more times during the next forty-five minutes. Dunga finally answered.

"Hello?"

"Yo Dunga! Weh yuh a deal wid? Mi just see the blood-claat video fi mi tune wid Secret. How yuh fi shoot video widout mi?"

Dunga smiled to himself. Timex must be deranged. Look how many times he had called him and he never returned his call?

"Pussyhole!" Dunga responded disrespectfully. He was tired of Timex's attitude. "Look how many times I called you. Eh? Left like two messages and you didn't buzz me back. You think I have time to waste? I'm a businessman so I did what I had to do you get me? Matter of fact, don't call back mi bumboclaat phone yeah? When its time for you to get your royalty checks, I'll have them delivered to your barbershop."

Dunga hung up in disgust. Timex could kiss his ass. He would never work with him again.

ଓଃଓଃଓଃ

Timex was stunned. He couldn't believe Dunga had talked to him like that. And hang up the phone on him. First Jade, now Dunga? Seems like everyone thought he was a punk or something. Dunga didn't know who he was messing with. Shooting a video for *his* song without him? Fuck that. He wasn't having it.

"Yo Breeda!" he shouted.

Breeda came back into the room. He had seen the video as well but had gone out to the living room when Timex called Dunga.

"De bwoy Dunga ah dis the program. Ah come deal wid mi like mi ah some likkle punk. Line up the squad and go 'round 'im studio an' page him. Buss some shot over dat bloodclaat."

Breeda nodded and went to his bidding.

Three of the guys were already at the house chilling. He figured the four of them would be enough so they headed out on two motor bikes. They were all armed to the teeth.

❧❧❧

"How the delivery bwoy nuh reach yet man?" Jimmy grumbled. He had ordered food for all of them forty-five minutes ago and the girl who had taken the order had told him 30 minutes. He was sorry he hadn't picked it up himself. He would have been back with the food already. Another ten minutes passed before he heard the buzzer.

He went to see who it was. The food had arrived. He took $5000 from the petty cash and opened the gate. He went outside just as the bearer rode in.

Two powerful CBR motorbikes entered the complex as he walked down the steps towards the bearer.

Jimmy was caught in no man's land. The man on the back of the first bike opened fire immediately. He released a barrage of shots from his assault rifle.

The bearer's body did a curious dance as several bullets ripped through his frame, toppling him from off of his delivery bike. Jimmy was shot in the right shoulder as he crouched and ran quickly to the opposite side of the building. Grimacing in pain, he pulled his gun and crouched low, wishing they would try and come around. They didn't, but they sprayed the area with bullets.

"Go into my office!" Dunga told Secret in an urgent whisper as he pulled a submachine gun from its hiding place in a compartment in the bottom of the sofa. He cautiously made his way to the door. He could hear the roar of the motorbikes as they rode out of the premises. He hurried out and fired parting shots but he was too late. They had already gone through the gate.

"Fuck!" he muttered as he shook his head in dismay. The innocent bearer had been cut down. He hoped he was still alive. He looked around. Where the hell was Jimmy? He crouched to check the man's pulse. He was breathing, but barely. Had to get to him to a hospital quickly. "Jimmy? Jimmy!"

Jimmy came around the corner with his gun in his hand.

"Timex?"

Dunga nodded. "Yeah I'm sure it was his goons. Nobody else would be stupid enough to pull a stunt like this. How's your shoulder?"

"Bullet went right through it. Hurt like shit but nothing big."

"Alright I'm gonna take you and this guy to the hospital real quick."

Dunga then lifted the bearer and placed him on the back seat of his Yukon Denali. Jimmy hopped in and Dunga ran inside to tell Secret that he would be back soon. He told her to keep the doors locked and then he jumped into his vehicle and headed to a private hospital on Mayfield Drive. The bearer would die if he took him to a public hospital. He might still die, but the odds for his survival were better at a private hospital. Dunga dialed Bowler's number as he drove. Bowler answered on the second ring.

He was incredulous when Dunga told him what had just transpired.

"Dah deejay bwoy deh look like him have a death wish," he said angrily. "Mi ah go round up some of the crew and meet yuh down ah de hospital. We ah go strike back immediately."

Dunga hung up and dangerously ran a red light at the intersection of Old Hope Road and Lady Musgrave Drive. Jimmy would be ok but he really didn't want the bearer to die. Poor guy was just in the wrong place at the wrong time.

Bowler and six guys from the Black Talon Crew were waiting outside by his vehicle when he came out of the hospital. Jimmy was getting treated and the bearer was headed to surgery. He paid for everything upfront with his credit card which had a $500,000 limit.

"Jimmy getting treated...we'll come back for him," Dunga said. "Let's ride."

They piled into their vehicles, four in all, and headed to the apartment complex where Timex resided. Dunga was really pissed but grateful that Jimmy had only suffered a flesh wound. *Stupid ignorant punk* Dunga thought derisively. He glanced around at his back seat. He would have to get it detailed later at Bowler's car wash. The bearer's blood had redecorated his plush, tan leather seats. They got to the complex in fifteen minutes. The security guard at the gate, recognizing Dunga, allowed the vehicles in with no problem. Three men stayed outside while the other five, led by Dunga and Bowler, made their way towards Timex's apartment. His black Range Rover, three motorbikes and a Ford F150 were parked out front. One of the men slashed all four tyres on the Range Rover while another punctured all three motor bikes. Guns drawn, the others stood back as Bowler, armed with a 12 gauge shot-gun, blasted away the lock on the front door. They then rushed in.

"Bumboclaat!" one of Timex's goons shouted as Dunga and Bowler came in to the living room with guns blazing. Dunga shot him in the shoulder and the gun he was about to raise clattered to the floor, going off as it did so. The bullet lodged in the wall just below a framed gold plaque for one of Timex's most popular songs. The other two guys in the room had been sitting on the carpet in front of the gigantic flat screen T.V. playing *Midnight Club: Los Angeles*. Bowler shot the one who tried to reach for his gun in both legs. They didn't plan on killing anyone – if they didn't have to. The other one dropped the game controls and held his hands in the air.

"Mi nuh have nuh gun pon mi," he declared seconds before Dunga removed all of his front teeth with the butt of his rifle.

Timex, Breeda and two other men were in his spacious bedroom chatting and drinking when they heard the barrage of gunfire in the living room. Breeda kicked the bedroom door shut and they all pulled their guns as two of them removed Timex from the bed and placed him on the ground gently, mindful of his broken leg despite the urgency of the situation.

The men were upset with themselves. They had been caught slipping. They just hadn't expected Dunga to retaliate so quickly. Now what?

ᴕᴕᴕ

Everyone got out of the line of fire as Bowler aimed at the closed bedroom door and pumped four rounds from the 12 gauge shotgun into it, blasting it to pieces, the empty shell casings falling on the head of one of the guys sprawled out on the floor in pain.

The guys inside the room were shook. That was some serious fire power. Plus they were outnumbered and out flanked. Breeda looked over at Timex. He nodded grimly.

"Yo! Hold yuh fire! We ah put de gun dem down. Hold yuh fire!" Breeda announced.

"Put them on the floor and everybody walk out of the room with your fucking hands high!" Dunga shouted back.

"Alright. But Timex can't walk enuh," Breeda replied.

"Tell that pussy to crawl then but everybody come out of the fucking room now!" Dunga responded.

The men did as they were told and came out of the room, holding their hands in the air. Timex was still in the room.

"Hey pussyhole! If yuh nuh crawl outta the room in ten seconds you are a dead bloodclaat man!" Dunga promised.

Timex crawled out of the room in humiliation. He had never felt so embarrassed and angry in his entire life. His nemesis had him, Jamaica's most popular entertainer, crawling on the fucking floor like a little bitch.

Dunga walked over to him and stooped down.

"Listen to me, and listen keenly. You might think you're a gangster or a bully but you're way out of your league fucking with me. This ends tonight as far as I'm concerned. You test me again and your fans will be flooding your Myspace page with tributes. You understand me?"

Timex glared at Dunga but he nodded his head.

Dunga rose and turned to walk away.

Then he turned around abruptly and shot Breeda in his right shoulder.

"Bloodclaat!" Breeda screamed.

"That's for Jimmy," Dunga informed him.

He turned and walked away, while Bowler and the others kept an eye on them as they backed out of the room.

"Oh baby!" Secret gushed when Dunga returned to the studio two hours later. She practically jumped on him. "Is everything ok now?"

Dunga kissed her. "All is well boo."

"I was so worried but I didn't want to call...knew you were handling your business an–"

"Shsssh...its ok baby," Dunga said as he placed a solitary finger on her lips.

He was touched by her concern. He could see the stark relief in her eyes that he was okay. He could *feel* her love.

She looked beyond him. She saw Jimmy's bandaged arm in a sling.

"Jimmy! You're hurt!"

Jimmy smiled. "Just a little scratch princess."

They went into the chill room and sat down. Dunga suddenly realized that they still hadn't eaten. Those idiots had come by at the same time the bearer had brought the food. His stomach was growling fiercely.

"We still haven't eaten," Dunga commented.

Jimmy laughed. "I just ate a bullet."

Everyone snickered, happy that they could laugh about it now.

"Let's go get some food."

They locked up the studio and hopped into Dunga's Denali. All the blood had been cleaned off the back seat. Dunga drove out and headed to a fast food joint in Half-Way-Tree.

Word of the showdown between Dunga and Timex reached the streets quickly. It was the hottest topic in every ghetto and even in the uptown areas. Dunga's legend grew. He had the type of street credibility that any dancehall artist would kill for. First he had demolished Ratty, the don from Wicker Lane, and now Timex, Jamaica's most popular gangster entertainer, had been tamed in no certain terms. What the streets respected about Dunga was the fact that he didn't push war and conflict, but if you crossed him, you were dealt with swiftly and decisively. His new nickname, which caught on like wildfire, was Mr. Untouchable.

Chapter 69

"Baby! You are so evil!" Secret exclaimed as she hit Dunga on the head with a pillow. They were in her room at Miss G's, packing her stuff as she would be leaving in the morning, when Dunga told her that he would be going with her. She was ecstatic.

Dunga grinned and pulled her down onto him. Secret made him feel like a teenager. Young and free. It was a wonderful feeling being in love. True love. That wholesome, love-you-unconditionally-give-you-butterflies-sex-is-so-good-it-makes-you-want-to-cry kind of love.

"I love you Garfield Amari Gilbert," Secret said. "And I'm so happy that you're coming on the trip."

Dunga frowned playfully at her use of his government name.

"Wouldn't miss it for the world baby...your first major performance in front of a foreign audience? Gotta be there to witness the birth of reggae's biggest star."

Secret grinned. She knew she was talented but having Dunga, who had been in the business so long and was so successful, believe in her so much, made her really believe that she could take over the game. The new young queen of reggae. The sky was the limit as her style and sound was not confined to reggae. She could see herself doing a straight R&B album in the near future.

CSSOCSSOCSSO

"That is fantastic Jade!" Theresa said, as they enjoyed a late dinner at the Village Grill, a trendy roof-top restaurant on one of Kinston's tallest buildings. The food was expensive but great.

They were having pan fried snapper with oriental sauce, grilled chicken drumsticks, vegetable roll with lettuce and lemon grass sorbet. Naturally, a bottle of chilled La Roseda accompanied the meal.

Jade was telling Theresa about her new gig with the popular cable station. She had met with them earlier that day and had accepted the job. It paid well, the exposure and experience would be great and it wouldn't interfere with her job at Hassan & Cohen LLC.

"Yeah I'm excited about it. We begin shooting in three weeks."

"Girl...your life is so exciting damn!"

Jade laughed. Yeah, she definitely had a lot going on. Modeling, event planning and now her very own cable show. She would be a household name very soon. She was truly blessed and highly favoured. And she deserved it. Not so long ago she had been languishing in prison, not knowing what the future had in store for her. Now her future was so bright it hurt her eyes. The only thing that kept gnawing at her was Chino. She wanted, no *needed* to pay him back for what he had done to her.

She would not allow him to get away scotch-free.

He had to pay.

And one day, when the time was right, and the opportunity presented itself, he would.

Epilogue

Secret had been fantastic in her stage debut in Europe. Even Dunga had been awed by her riveting performances. A star had indeed been born on that first show in France. By the third performance in Holland, Secret was receiving more attention than Ras Che, the headliner. Dunga proposed to her on the night before they were to return to Jamaica. They were dining at Oud Sluis, rated as Holland's best restaurant, when Dunga popped the question. Secret had been so shocked that it took her nearly a minute before she could actually speak to utter an emphatic yes. She had cried when he slipped the beautiful engagement ring on her finger. It was the happiest moment of her young life so far. Only the actual wedding day could eclipse that moment. Mrs. Jaunelle Gilbert. Definitely had a nice ring to it.

Dahlia was getting better. She had been seeing a noted psychiatrist three times weekly for the past three and a half weeks and it was paying off. She was no longer suicidal and believed in herself; and the gift of life again. God bless Amoy. If it wasn't for her she would have foolishly ended her life. She heard about Dunga's engagement. The knowledge of it had almost made her relapse but Amoy and the angelic Dr. Swanson, her psychiatrist, helped her to deal with it effectively. It had hurt though. Worse than any other pain she had felt in her life. And that included childbirth. She had been with Dunga for seven years, and had given him a child, and he had never mentioned marriage. He had been with this girl for less than two months and had put a ring on her finger. But she would survive. And she would find happiness again. One day.

ꕥꕥꕥ

With their parents having been buried over two weeks ago, Peter and Penelope, especially Peter, were well on the road to closure. They had decided to sell off everything, except the family house and the two apartments. Peter had decided to drop out of college. He wasn't sure what he was going to do with the rest of his life but he would have some fun until he decided. He had enough money to last him a lifetime. He wasn't in any rush.

Penelope decided to take the rest of the semester off but planned to complete her studies. She just needed some time to get her strength back, mentally and physically. Her parents' death and the circumstances surrounding it had left her deeply scarred. But time was the master healer. She would come to terms with everything eventually.

ꕥꕥꕥ

After his humiliation at the hands of Dunga and his cronies, Timex took a break from the Jamaican scene. He went to England on an extended vacation. He was still extremely popular but his street credibility had taken a beating. Somehow the streets had also found out the truth about how his leg was broken. He wasn't unduly worried about keeping his fans though. As long as he continued to put out hot, gangster music, they would still love him. He would work on building back his street cred. Even if he had to manufacture a beef with another high-profile artist, he would repair his broken gangster image in time. In the meantime, he was enjoying England. They worshipped him there and he basked in their affection. He changed a new groupie every other day.

Jade's big jazz and R&B show had been a smash. The tickets had sold out two weeks before the event and the three divas: Toni Braxton, Mariah Carey and Diana Ross, had brought the house down. The local acts had done well for themselves too. It had been a fabulous show. Breathtaking in so many ways. From the ambiance to the performances, it had been a night that no one who attended would soon forget. They didn't make a profit, or break even, as the expenses of obtaining the three superstars, ensured that there was no way they could have made a profit. But they would recoup from the sale of the DVD. Besides, one couldn't put a dollar value on the intangible benefits for the La Roseda brand from putting on a show of this caliber. It had been a world class production.

The first episode of her fashion and entertainment cable show was the highest viewed program in the station's ten year history. They had a hit on their hands but Jade declined to sign a long term contract. She wanted to wait and weigh her options.

She had received her new passport and driver's license from Eddie. It had taken longer than Eddie had expected. She would be going to the bank to open a US currency account and a Jamaican account on Monday morning. She had a nice chunk of change with which to open the accounts. Cohen had given her $10,000 US dollars when he came to Jamaica for the show – a bonus for the excellent job she had been doing for the company.

Life was splendid.

Every day was a blessing.

Twenty-two years old, glamourous, fabulous and on her way to becoming rich and famous.

The world was hers to conquer.

Forrest Gump was right.

Life was indeed like a box of chocolates.

You never knew what you were going to get.